In the
Deep
Midwinter

Also by Robert Clark
River of the West
James Beard: A Biography

In the
Deep
Midwinter

ROBERT CLARK

PICADOR USA
New York

Picador® is a U.S. registered trademark and is used by St. Martin's Press under license from Pan Books Limited.

Book design by Patrice Sheridan

LIBRARY OF CONGRESS CATALOGING-IN-PUBLICATION DATA

Clark, Robert.
    In the deep midwinter / Robert Clark.—1st ed.
        p.   cm.
    ISBN 0-312-15149-7
    I. Title
    PS3552.L2878I5   1997
    813'.54—dc20   96-30530
                                         CIP

First Picador USA Edition: January 1997

10   9   8   7   6   5   4   3   2   1

For my mother, Elizabeth,
and my daughter, Tessa

In the
Deep
Midwinter

I

N o v e m b e r

PERHAPS THE WORLD WAS A WOUND, AND NOW THE COLD
lay over it, coagulating its waters like blood under air, forming a
crust. Soon the snow would shroud it in a bandage, and then,
months thereafter, the scar would emerge, and all the earth anew.
But now the wheels keened on the rails, as though every motion
were unbearable, as though the sounds themselves might shatter
in the cold. The moon was a shard of mirror hung in the sky and
it let down gray light on the fields, where the withered cornstalks
lay among the furrows like battle dead. The train labored on, an
icebreaker pressing through the night, its windows amber as oil,
the crossing whistle a moan.

The porter, white-haired with desiccated brown skin, dropped
into view like a bird descending. "Another, sir?"

"No, not now, thank you."

"Next stop Little Falls," the porter said, as though in reply, and
slipped away down the car. Richard was not going to Little Falls,

Richard sat up in the club car by the window, ice cubes rocking in his beaker of Scotch, the air scented with steam heat and
tobacco, the cold stealing through the glass, penetrating his left
shoulder like the blunt pinch of a hypodermic. He faced backward and watched the semaphores blink past, red and, faintly in
the distance, yellow.

but to Finlay, a town on the North Dakota-Manitoba border. He was going to fetch his brother's body home.

THE TRAIN STOOD FOR A MOMENT HISSING AT THE PLATFORM IN Finlay, and then pulled away with a lurch. Frost effloresced from blisters in the asphalt, and the dawn light was stark and blue. A man in an Eisenhower jacket and dull brown oxfords loped toward Richard.

"Mr. MacEwan?" The man didn't wait for a reply. He shambled onward with his introduction. "I'm the sheriff, Jim Ratcliff. I'm awfully sorry to meet you—not to meet you, I mean, but under the circumstances, to make your acquaintance at this particular time. And of course the whole county feels terrible about your brother's accident, and offers our condolences—if there's anything we can do." Ratcliff stopped, apparently relieved to have said his piece.

Richard took the hand Ratcliff seemed to have forgotten he'd extended. "Well, we very much appreciate your help. I know my brother loved hunting around here," Richard said. He had sat up all night and could think of nothing more.

Ratcliff led him to a gray car that smoked and idled throatily by the ticket office. Richard clutched his small gladstone bag and hunched his shoulders against the cold. They got in and drove through Finlay, the heater roaring. The main street was brick with a Sears catalog outlet, a Ben Franklin five-and-dime, a Rexall Drugs, and taverns and cafés hung with Grain Belt and Schmidt beer signs. In the distance there were a few dozen white houses, copses of pine, grain elevators, and a hulking silver water tower.

Ratcliff pulled in behind a building of sallow brick. "I only need to keep you a little while. For some questions and formalities, you understand, and then we can get you over to . . . " he hesitated " . . . to the funeral home and you can make the arrangements and be on your way home."

Inside the sheriff motioned Richard to a chair covered in forest-green vinyl. The fluorescent light poured down on them like mother-of-pearl. Ratcliff seized a sheath of paper, interleaved it with carbon paper, and threaded it into a typewriter on a rickety stand. He lit a cigarette.

"First, I need some information about your brother. Full name?"

"James Wright MacEwan."

" 'Mc' or 'Mac'?"

"Mac."

"And his date and place of birth?"

"March 12, 1904, St. Paul, Minnesota," Richard said crisply. He was infallible on people's birthdays and anniversaries.

"Names of parents?"

"Douglas Wright MacEwan and Anna Davis MacEwan."

"Wife? Children?"

"Divorced, no children."

"And his address?"

"Two-thirty-eight Portland Avenue, St. Paul 2, Minnesota."

"His occupation and place of employment?"

"Stockbroker, Lewis, French and Company, St. Paul."

Ratcliff finished typing, looked up at Richard, and ground out his half-smoked cigarette in a beanbag ashtray.

"We need a general physical description. Height and weight—just roughly?"

"Five-ten, maybe one hundred seventy-five pounds."

"Hair?"

"Brown."

"And eyes?" Richard halted. Ratcliff reached for his cigarettes and lit one while he waited for Richard to reply.

Richard could not remember or even say if he had ever known. He felt slightly embarrassed. "I'm not sure—brown, I think."

"That's good enough. Now we need a little information about you and we're done." Ratcliff looked at Richard earnestly, and put his cigarette down. He moved his hands to the typewriter.

"Your full name?"

"Richard Douglas MacEwan."

"And your date and place of birth?"

"St. Paul, February 11, 1899."

"Address?"

"Six-fifty-five Furness Avenue, St. Paul 5."

"And your occupation and place of employment?"

"Attorney, Miles, MacEwan, and Booth, First National Bank Building, St. Paul 1."

Ratcliff took his cigarette, inhaled, and ground it out. The ashtray rustled beneath his fist. "Well, that's all I need to bother you with." He pulled the papers out of the typewriter and the carriage-ratchet purred. "Now, if you just sign and date at the bottom to attest everything's accurate."

The sheriff handed Richard a pen, and Richard signed himself "R. D. MacEwan, November 9, 1949, Finlay, North Dakota."

THE MORTUARY WAS TWO BLOCKS AWAY, AND RICHARD TOLD Ratcliff he would enjoy walking. There were patches of brown grass among the cracks in the frost-heaved sidewalk and clots of leaves frozen in the gutter. The naked elms threw a tangle of skeletal shadows onto the street. The mortuary was in an old house with a porch and a turret.

A fat man in a dark brown suit showed him in and they sat at a desk. The room had narrow windows and heavy curtains of oxblood velvet. The carpet was thick as moss. The man breathed heavily and asked him questions and filled out papers much as Ratcliff had done. James's body would be put on the train and shipped to the Husch Brothers Funeral Home in St. Paul. The coffin would be plain pewter-colored metal. Richard drew his checkbook from his coat.

"That won't be necessary, sir. Everything will be handled through Husch Brothers," the man said.

Richard pushed back his chair and rose. "Well, I appreciate that. But before I go I'd like to see my brother."

A ragged exhalation of breath sawed the stillness as the man pulled himself up. "With all respect, sir, I'm not sure that would be wise. Your brother's body sustained great trauma. The remains are just as we received them from the sheriff's department. There's been no opportunity for any restoration or preparation of the remains. Naturally, no change of clothing was available—"

Richard interrupted. "Well, I appreciate your concern, but I'd like to see him just the same. I've dealt with this kind of thing before. I was an ambulance man in the war, the 1917 war, of course."

The man nodded. "Very well, then."

He led him through what once must have been the dining room of the house and into a large room floored in sea-foam-green linoleum and lit by fluorescent tubes. In the back there was a heavy door with a chrome handle and a latch. A compressor motor hummed and ticked. The man told Richard to wait. He crossed the room as though on tiny feet and opened the cooler and withdrew a gurney, which he pulled to the center of the room, next to a welled porcelain steel table with a drain in one end.

"I'll leave unless you prefer—" the man said.

"No, that will be fine. I won't be long," Richard said, and the man was gone.

Richard touched James's arm through the sheet that covered it. The flesh was cold but yielding. With the tips of his fingers he picked up the edge of the cloth and pulled it back. James's head was turned slightly away from him. His face was unshaven, stubbled with two days of beard, his skin white with mauve patches, veined darker here and there like marble. His mouth was slightly ajar, as if about to speak. One eye was closed; the other, the one closest to Richard, half open. The iris was brown. He looked as if he had just awoken and was now caught in that moment forever, like a butterfly pinned to a specimen board.

Richard lifted the sheet down to James's waist. He hadn't seen his brother's body naked since he was a teenager. Now James's flesh was coarse, the muscles of his chest and abdomen slack, the skin grainy, seeded with spots and moles, shrubbed with the taut-curled salt-and-pepper body hair of a middle-aged man. The wound was on the far side of James's chest, a little below the right nipple. It was round verging on oval, a little larger than a quarter-dollar, black around the edges where the flesh was burned. It gaped slightly, like lips expressing a sigh.

Richard had seen men far worse off in France, their bodies and faces harrowed by shrapnel. He felt the urge to touch James's wound and to weep. Then, just as quickly, he was revolted at the impulse; not by its morbidness, but by its pointlessness and by the sense that he wanted something for himself from it, like a pilgrim at a shrine stroking the soapstone robe of a medieval saint. This was no longer the brother he knew; it was no longer his brother at all. Then Richard saw how it must have happened: the edge of the field and the bolted stalks of goldenrod and milkweed; the gun laid against the fence, the tangle of James's limbs threading themselves through two parted strands of barbed wire; the gun tipping and falling; the bolus of shot cleaving his rib, rending his heart; and only after he had ceased to be, the roar of the shot soaring like a flock of birds among the poplars.

JAMES WAS BURIED IN THE BROWN EARTH, THE GROUND INCISED with a portal in the sleeping autumn grass. Richard's wife, Sarah, stood beside him in gloves, veil, and pearls, and Richard read the verses the priest had assigned him: "We cry, Abba, Father," they said, and continued with a promise that "neither death, nor life, nor angels, nor principalities, nor powers, nor things present, nor things to come, nor height, nor depth, nor any other creature, shall be able to separate us from the love of God, which is in Christ Jesus our Lord." Sarah held his hand while he read the words, less a declaration of belief than a charm, a spell. The priest spoke while they sifted dirt into the grave: of how the earth and sea shall give up the dead; of how the dead are blessed, "for they rest from their labors." Then they were done, and they went out for drinks, as James himself would have been the first to propose.

At the club, Richard stood near the fireplace and graciously accepted the pro forma condolences, the forked-tongued encomia, and the unmeant offers to help of nearly one hundred people. It was not that people had disliked James, but rather that what they liked about him did not lend itself to public utterance: the profits reaped for his brokerage clients, the beauty of his face, the fluency of his conversation and the patient dexterousness of his lovemaking, bestowed on dozens of women; the benison his participation laid on the drinking, hunting, and whoring bouts of his male companions; his unimpeachable discretion, good humor, and incapacity to find fault with any word, thought, or deed of a friend. He was not so much a character in his own right as an exceedingly pleasing mirror upon which others could regard their reflections. They liked what they saw. James had been a man of parts; whether he was a good man was beside the point.

Sarah glided up beside him, her fox stole swinging. "I think everyone would understand if we made an exit now. You've certainly done your duty by James." She unclasped her purse and riffled through it, the contents clacking like stones on the beach.

Richard said, "Well, dear, if you wouldn't mind too much, perhaps I should stay just a little longer." Sarah pulled a cigarette from its pack, looked at him, and brightened. "I suppose it is the thing to do under the circumstances. Once-in-a-lifetime occasion for Jimmy, so to speak." She eyed Richard with amused expectance, then feigned injury. "Aren't you going to light my cigarette?" Richard took the lighter from her hand. She tilted her face into the flame. It burnished her like a Pre-Raphaelite Guinevere. She drank in the smoke, turned, and over her shoulder said, "Back in ten minutes, and then we depart, yes?"

He stood alone, although only a moment ago it had seemed there was no end to the stream of people pressing themselves upon him. Behind him, the fire wheezed and spit like a grumbling radiator. Out of the crowd, Henry Finch hove into view. His cheeks were florid and a stray hank of hair had tumbled down his forehead. In his right hand he clutched a sweating tumbler of Scotch, in his left, a knotted-up cocktail napkin. Henry was James's best friend, or imagined himself to be. He had been hunting with James in Finlay. He lurched into speech.

"I don't want to say any of the usual crap. I suppose I'm presumptuous as hell to mention it, but I feel like he was my brother too. I can't know what you're going through, but this is hell. Christ," he sputtered, as though mired in his words. His eyes grew large, and Richard could see Henry was about to cry. He began to speak again with an intake of breath and the words sounded as if he'd swallowed them and now he was burping them up. "You need to know there was nothing . . . untoward. There hadn't been any drinking. None of us was even there when it happened. We were down in the next field. The dogs had flushed out some birds. We just heard it. We thought Jimmy'd bagged something." Henry tilted his head and his mouth rounded, his eyes narrowed, and his forehead wrinkled. He sighed a great watery "Jesus, oh Jesus" and collapsed on Richard's shoulder, weeping.

Henry shook in his lamentation like a repentant boy who had been caught in an enormous mischief or lie. Richard usually found Henry distasteful, the kind of self-immolating eternal adolescent that James surrounded himself with. But now Richard thought to pat Henry's back or stroke his hair. He withdrew from the impulse as suddenly as it had struck him, but raised his arms and held the sobbing man for a moment. Henry's neck smelled of cologne and there was a wisp of dried shaving soap in his ear. Richard whispered to him, "There's nothing and no one to blame. It was an accident. It's as though he died in the war."

Henry slowly pulled free from Richard, like a man picking himself up off the ground after a fall. "You can't know how much it means to me to hear that from you." He tugged on his tie and took a sip from his glass. "You're a hell of a guy, Richard." He sighed and his mouth formed a half-smile and he backed away. "We should have a drink sometime," he said. "Definitely," Richard replied.

In a minute, Sarah had returned. He fetched their hats and her coat, and slipped it onto her arms, which she held out expectantly behind her. She adjusted her hat and lowered the veil. Her skin was like crushed silk. He left her in the club foyer and went to get the car.

The boulevard was hemmed by two rows of elms and there

were streetlamps glowing nacreous in the dusk. Down the block and across the street to his right he could see a light in the second story of the white-columned house he and James had grown up in. It had been sold ten years before, after their mother's death. Between him and the house was a triangular park with a statue of Nathan Hale at its apex. Hale had his hands tied behind him, poised for execution, and when they were boys, James had liked to insert objects into Hale's grip for comic effect: baseball bats, hockey sticks, snow shovels. Richard had always laughed at such displays, even as he knew they were wrong and feared detection. But James had feared no such thing from this or any other mischief: He could not fathom the notion that he might get caught, and, perhaps as a result, he never was. Nor did he weigh the virtue or wickedness of his actions; he seemed to be the author of his own creation, and he inevitably found it good.

Richard brought the car into the driveway of the club, jumped out, and opened the door for Sarah. She slid in with a rustle. They drove away and the face of the radio, switched on but silent, glowed between them. Sarah spoke lazily. "Henry Finch seemed rather at a loose end."

"He's terribly distraught about Jimmy," said Richard. "Feels he's lost a brother. Crazy as it sounds, I think Jimmy was sort of his anchor."

"I don't see how Henry would know, being half in the bag most of the time." Sarah paused. Churches, convents, schools, and their flagpoles bobbed by in the dark like lighted ships at anchor. "Well, I'm sure you were very good with him," she continued.

"I tried," Richard said. "Did you see Anna?"

"Only for a second. She was with her new beau. They seemed rather lost in each other, or at least he was—couldn't be attentive enough."

"She's your daughter. Poor fellow's probably totally bewitched."

"You're very sweet. But don't you think it's a bit soon for her to be getting so involved? She's scarcely been divorced six months. And she's the mother of an eighteen-month-old child."

"She's also nearly thirty years old. But I could talk to her, see which way the breeze is blowing, point out the realities. I don't suppose she'd resent it."

Richard pulled up to the house, got out, and went around and opened Sarah's door. The light on the car ceiling went on and Sarah swung her legs out. Her shadow fell into the street and her face was hidden in the dark, behind the veil. She looked up at Richard. "Do I forget to tell you how sweet you are? How very lucky I am? How good you are? Do I say the words enough?"

THE FIRST TIME CHARLES NORDEN TOOK ANNA MacEWAN OUT on a date, she was wearing a red sweater and it seemed to Charles that Anna's face drew color from the sweater like a well. It was not that she was embarrassed or ill, but that she was tapping a reserve of warmth and optimism and radiating them in his direction. When he spoke, she nodded eagerly, and then sometimes she rounded her lips as if ruminating carefully on what he said, as if cradling his words in her hands. He thought she must like him, and he thought he must like her.

Charles had taken her to the best restaurant he could find, and when the waiter came and asked them what they'd like to drink, Charles cupped his hand over hers as though to beg leave for his interruption of what she might be about to say. He told the waiter they'd like two martinis, very cold, very dry. The waiter nodded and laid menus down on the table and Charles looked at Anna and said, "I thought it might be fun—sort of elegant, something to toast our first evening with—if you don't mind."

"I don't mind at all," Anna said smiling, and he saw her press herself backward into the upholstery while she curled her shoulders forward and seemed to sigh all at once, one of those impossibly dexterous gestures women struck, apparently without conscious effort or practice, insouciantly feline. Charles had come to believe such poses were somehow designed as much to warn as to tantalize, to exhibit an inner feminine essence that was both incomprehensible and ultimately untouchable, and that must forever remain so. But Anna seemed to be saying something else, or so Charles imagined: I would give you this, utterly and unreservedly, if you were kind.

Charles straightened himself and took up the menu. He scanned it for a moment and looked at Anna. She held the menu closed, her red nails spanned the cover, and she looked at him with expectation, brightly, as though the world were all before them. "Any idea what you're going to have?" he asked.

"I don't know," she said. "What are *you* having?"

"The New York steak, I suppose."

"I should have guessed that—you look the type. Red-blooded." Anna laughed, and then the laugh trailed off weakly. Maybe she was thinking she'd been a little forward. Charles jumped in.

"Well, I don't know about that. But let me try to guess what you're going to order," he said and took a quick sip of his martini. "It's only fair." He looked at the menu again, running his finger up and down the entries, shaking his head. "Here we are. I'll bet you'll have the creamed chicken—the creamed chicken in the pastry shell. With the 'bouquet garni,' whatever that is."

Anna had leaned forward toward him, and he saw that her menu was still closed. She said, "You're absolutely right. That's what I'm going to have."

"But you haven't looked." He felt a little embarrassed now, a little silly.

"It doesn't matter," she said. "It's what I *would* have chosen if I had looked. And now it's sort of my destiny, don't you think?" She laughed, and Charles saw that it was a gentle laugh, a merry acceptance of happenstance—that even if his prediction wasn't true to start with, it was true enough now; that she was willing to let whatever he said be true for her. Charles laughed too, and the waiter came and took their order.

As the waiter walked away, Anna whispered, "He looks like Thomas Dewey, or maybe like Ronald Colman, but all rigid and starched and sallow." She tilted her head to one side and leaned her chin in her hand, grinning.

"It's just the mustache," Charles said. "And besides, I voted for Dewey."

Anna's mouth broadened into a circle, and Charles could not tell if her alarm was real or feigned. "You *didn't*!"

"Well, I didn't really like him, really believe in him, you know," Charles said. Feeling discomposed, he went on. "I liked Eisenhower, but he didn't get into it, did he?"

Anna was now smiling placidly. "Eisenhower," she said. "Eisenhower and steak. I could have guessed."

Charles sensed there was nothing to be lost in sparring gently with her. "And you? Truman, I suppose?"

Anna grinned and patted her hand firmly on the tablecloth as though it were a bridge table on which she was laying down a large no-trump bid. "Henry Wallace," she said, pausing triumphantly between the first and last names. And then she emptied what was left of her martini.

"So you're a bit of a radical?"

"No. I just thought Wallace would be more likely to do what Roosevelt would have done if he were alive and that Truman wouldn't."

"An idealist, then." Charles meant it to be a compliment, but Anna sighed and shook her head. "I don't know if it's that," she said. "Idealism, I mean. Or at least I've hardly led an *ideal* life, have I?"

"In what respect?" Charles was puzzled at this turn in the conversation.

"Oh, being divorced, for example."

"It happens to the best of us. It's happening to me. Right now."

Anna seemed relieved at his response. "Yes. I'd heard that. I'm sorry."

"There's nothing to be sorry about. It's not like anyone died."

Anna looked a little apologetic and said, "No, of course not. But I suppose it can feel that way. It did to me, a little."

This was a subject Charles would have preferred to postpone to another time. But he sensed that Anna was raising it with some deliberateness. He took a swallow of breath and began. "It felt like suffocation at the end, and now, to be frank, it feels like a relief."

"And it'll be final—"

"In a couple of weeks."

"And what were the grounds?" Anna asked.

"Irreconcilable differences."

"And what do you think *really* happened, to make it happen?"

"I'd still say irreconcilable differences. That's about as precise as I can be. Maybe it will be clearer later."

"Not if you're like me," Anna said. "At the end, when it was going on, I knew all the reasons. They were like this flock of birds, sitting in a tree, and I could see every one of them and name them out loud: all the things Jack did and didn't do, the slights and omissions and oversights, all the things he should have known to do without my saying. And the things I did and the things I withheld and took back and pretended didn't exist to punish him, to keep him away. And then, after the divorce was final and he was gone, it was like the whole flock flew all at once up into the air, like a big blurry cloud, and scattered this way and that and was gone and I really couldn't put my finger on any single part of it anymore. Now, sometimes I think of it all, of Jack and me, and I wonder, Who *were* those people?" Anna stopped, and then she said, as though it were an exhalation, "And now it's just the bare, empty tree, the branches."

Charles felt he should offer something consoling or profound—that what he said would be a kind of test—but all he could think to say was "You still have your child."

Anna smiled and looked up at him. "Dougie. Yes, I do. But it's almost as if he'd been with me all my life, before Jack and me, before anything."

"You must love him very much—to feel that way."

"I guess I do. He's like my faith, what I believe in to make the world seem decent and good. What about you? What do you think about children? Did you want them?" She said it softly, kindly, but the remark made Charles nervous. He sensed a great deal hung on the answer, and he wanted to please her with what he said. He looked at his hands and then he looked up and into her eyes and said, "I wanted them, but of course I never got the chance. I hope I will someday. And I hope I get to meet your boy—soon."

"I hope you will too—as soon as you like," Anna said, and the words came out of her mouth with her lips scarcely moving, like a prayer or a vow. She smiled at Charles, as though he had just presented her with the solution to a vexing problem, and it was a simpler, easier solution than she ever could have hoped. And Charles saw he had pleased her, and that he hadn't minded at all; that in fact it pleased him to please her. Then the waiter brought their food and they ate and talked and laughed and looked at each other, finishing every bite on their plates yet scarcely aware of a single taste that had crossed their tongues. They drank another martini each, and then another, and they toasted each other, as if they had concluded a transaction to their mutual satisfaction.

Afterward Charles got her coat from the hatcheck girl and slid her into it. Then, in the doorway of the restaurant with the night and the cold curling around their feet, he kissed the side of her head by her ear, not even touching her flesh but just brushing his lips through her hair. Her lips came around to his ear and she whispered, "Thank you for a lovely evening." He thought he could feel and hear her breath for a long time, like warm water sounding and lapping a beach, rocking against the sand, saying, "Come in, come in, come in."

RICHARD PUT THE BRASS KEY INTO JAMES'S DOOR AND TURNED it. The lock snapped loudly, like a breech bolt slammed home, and he pushed the door past the accumulated mail and newspapers. The curtains in the living room were open, and dust spun in pillars of sunlight before the windows. He flicked up the light switch and a train of sconces illuminated the long corridor to his left, to the back of the apartment. James had lived here for fifteen years, ever since his divorce. The landlord was willing to allow six weeks for his things to be cleared out.

Richard put the keys and his hat on the table at the head of the hall. Even with the sconces illuminated, in the middle of a sunny day, the hall seemed dark, as though the walls were blotting up the light; as though the hall were a tunnel and the apartment a cave.

He passed down the hall. To his left was the dining room and beyond it the kitchen. To his right and to the back was James's bedroom and a further bedroom James had used as a study. Today Richard intended only to survey what would need to be done. It would not be difficult to pack up James's things. The apartment was sparely furnished for the most part, bare of the bric-a-brac and miscellaneous impedimenta that crowded his own home. There were ashtrays, a console radio, lamps, two sofas, a stack of magazines, and a wing chair and its hassock, but little more than the minimum of possessions that James's cursory home life necessitated. Such other objects as there were took the form less of belongings or furnishings than collections: James's guns, his school and college trophies and class photographs, his library of nature lore and mariner's tales, his dozens of neckties, his bar tray of bottles and glasses with its jigger and ice bucket huddled against the living room wall. A mummified, half-peeled lemon sat next to a tarnished silver cocktail shaker.

Richard saw the lemon when he returned up the hall and collected his hat from the hall table. He made a mental note to have the contents of the refrigerator and larder dealt with immediately, before they began to putrefy. Sarah could send her cleaning lady, Mrs. Clay, over from the house to do that and to pack up James's clothes. Then Richard could sort through James's papers and personal memorabilia. It could be done after work, in a few evenings.

RICHARD DROVE DOWNTOWN. THE RIVER TWISTED BROAD AND indolent under the bluffs of the city. The sky was gray and gelid. There was nothing pressing at the office. There rarely was. Richard was not a contentious man and he had found the least contentious corner of the legal profession in which to practice: trusts and estates. His clients were the dead, or at least those among the living whose vision was turned in the direction of death, moved to put their lives in order before they ceased at last to live, as though packing slowly and carefully in advance for an ocean cruise of undetermined duration. Otherwise, he dealt with widows and minor children to whom he could offer comfort, support, and sustenance. Occasionally, he had to spar with a discontented beneficiary or legatee, at whom as a last resort he might turn up his palms helplessly, pointing out that he was only the emissary of one who was, alas, beyond reach. When he went to court, which was rarely, he usually worked alone with a judge and a clerk, and their business transpired without dissension or remark, as though tracking the inexorable course of a comet launched long ago in some other time and place.

He left at five o'clock and drove west to Anna's house on the opposite side of the city. The house was less than two years old, and its tidy mock-Tudor architecture served with some success to belie both the house's small size and the raw, scarcely completed block of homes in which it stood. He pushed open the door and called out Anna's name. A radio played in the back of the house and Anna's son, Douglas, sat on the rug shifting blocks of wood. At the sight of Richard, he looked up, smiled, and pointed as though to a faraway landmark, exclaiming, "Grandpa!" He pulled himself heavily off the floor as if his bottom were stuck to it and strode at a purposeful clip toward Richard on queasy, chubby legs. Richard lifted him up. The boy smelled of soap and cream and oranges. He had Anna's enormous, plaintive eyes.

Anna herself appeared, beaming in a red sweater and plaid skirt. She pressed her face to his and said "Daddy" with a sigh of fulfilled pleasure. She drew her arms apart in the expansive gesture of a ballerina. "Sit. Excuse the mess. I'll get you a drink." She pranced off toward the kitchen. "Just a little one, precious," he said, and returned Douglas to the rug. Richard sat down in an angular chair with round tapered legs and nubby gray upholstery. The radio clicked off and Anna returned a moment later with Scotch for him and a martini for herself. A tiny pearl onion floated in it. She sat.

"So?" she chirped expectantly and leaned forward, her chin in her hand, her elbow on her knee, her ankles locked together.

"I just came by to see how you were. I'm sorry we missed you at the funeral. But mother says you were being well looked after."

"Oh, by Charles? Yes, I like him very much. And how are you bearing up?"

Richard told her about James's apartment and the chores to be done there. Anna looked at him with concern, although he was unaware of communicating any distress on his part about the matter. It was Anna's fundamental expression, the nest to which her mien returned between eruptions of ingenuous joy and absorption and dumbfounded anguish and tears. There was compassion in it and, perhaps deeper down, worry, a fretful contemplation of the world's wobbly orbits. Richard looked back at her, at the seamless cascade of brown hair, at the perfectly inscribed line of red lipstick on the upper half of her mouth, and at the pulled-in lower lip below it, just shy of being bitten. And in that and in the eyes, he saw her as she had always been: a timorous, anxious child whose face says merely, "Please, choose me."

Richard was conscious of the need to return to the subject of Charles. He pulled himself upright and adopted a tone of mock conspiracy: "So, you and your friend Charles—is it *serious?*" Anna blushed delightedly. "Daddy!" she laughed, and then composed herself, aware that a matter of some gravity was implicit in the question. "I do like him very much, and I think he's awfully nice. And of course he's got a good job, and a good family from back east." She folded her hands, as though awaiting an evaluation of her reply.

"Yes, I've heard good things about him from lawyers I know in his firm. But . . . ," and Richard drew out the word as though shaking his head, "that doesn't answer my question."

Anna began again. "Well, I think he likes me very much too, and so I suppose that things could develop in that direction—over time, of course."

"He's divorcing, isn't he?"

"It's just a formality at this point—some papers to be signed. And there aren't any children."

"But how do you think he might feel about Douglas?"

"He's very sweet with him. And that's what matters, isn't it?"

"Oh, definitely—that he has a good heart. And is going to be careful with yours."

Anna looked up and her sober tone yielded to one more wistful, almost prayerful. "Maybe it's vanity to say so, Daddy, but I think he adores me."

"That would be wonderful, precious. But remember that your position is still a bit precarious, that it's so easy to make a mistake. Just go easy. Do that for me?"

"Of course," Anna said without hesitation or, as well as Richard could read her, discomfort. He finished his drink. Douglas had been busy around his feet while they were talking, and when Richard stood to leave he noticed his shoes were untied. He sat down again to retie them. "Little fellow doesn't seem to want me to leave," he said shallowly, his breath constricted as he bent to his wingtips.

"He'd like a father around the house," Anna said merrily and without irony.

"Oh, I imagine we all would at times."

SARAH AND RICHARD ATE DINNER IN A RESTAURANT THAT evening, a place called the Madison a few blocks from home. They sat in a red vinyl–upholstered booth. The tablecloth was a rosy pink, and the waiter wore a red vest and black trousers. They ordered drinks, and when the waiter brought them, they eased into conversation as though shuffling the cards for a long session of bridge.

"How was your day, dear?" Richard began.

"Wrote letters this morning. Then I had lunch with Betty Middleton in the River Room at Field's. Ate and then shopped a little. Betty had to stop and pull herself together once or twice—

she's finally getting *the change.*" Sarah leaned over to hiss these last words furtively.

"Getting the what?" Richard asked, genuinely puzzled.

"Change of life—menopause, hot flashes and so on. Sometimes, Richard, you are such a boy—the world's a mystery to you, isn't it?"

"Or at least the female half of it."

"But we girls do *like* you so much," Sarah said, and squeezed Richard's fingers. "Anyway, so at last Betty will wither and blow away like all of us—like I will soon, *sans doute.* Of course there are more grandchildren on the way. That family breeds like rabbits. Or Catholics."

The Middletons were in fact as Episcopalian as the MacEwans. That very afternoon, Betty and Sarah had attended a meeting of the altar guild at St. Botolph's Church, where Richard himself was on the vestry.

Sarah was continuing. "We're going to be absolutely swamped at church with Advent and Christmas coming. Flowers, pine boughs, wreaths, holly, poinsettias—the whole wretched horticultural stew. But the spirit will find a way." She drew a sip from her glass. "Then home and some phone calls for the academy alumnae association. And then, because I wasn't quite sufficiently mortified yet, I talked to Mother."

"And how is the weather in Chicago?"

"She wouldn't know. Off in her own senile milieu, Mother is. About as sensate as a salt lick these days. But mean. And wracked with pain that her doctors can't find. Dicky, promise me that if I ever come to such a sad pass, you will haul me over to the vet and have them put me down. Maybe by intravenous martini."

"Olive or lemon in your hypo?"

"Oh, lemon, of course." Sarah turned up the corners of her mouth to indicate she had concluded. "And you?"

"Office in the morning, checking some wills. Then I went over to James's place to see what needs doing. Shouldn't be too trying. It's surprising how little he actually accumulated in forty-five years. Some photos. Sundry sporting gear. Books from thirty years ago. All his papers and such are stuffed into Papa's rolltop. That will take some time. And of course I've got to get his finances sorted out. See what the government is owed. I don't suppose there will be much in the way of assets. He wanted whatever there was left over to go to the academy. Funny thing—he knew so many people, did so many things. But he didn't really leave a mark, did he?"

Sarah's volubility seemed to have evaporated. "No," she said at last, "that wasn't in his nature. Lived for the day at hand, like a rooster. Not steady. Not thoughtful, like you."

The waiter returned. Richard ordered another round of drinks and both their dinners: filet mignon rare, au gratin potatoes, salad with vinegar and oil for Sarah; New York medium, baked potato, salad with Thousand Island for him. Then Sanka for both of them.

"After that, I went back to the office. Not much doing, but I found ways to occupy myself. I find myself wondering if I'm earning the firm all the hours I should be, but of course no one's ever complained."

"Or ever could find reason to."

"Anyway, I went over to see Anna and Douglas. Both very chipper. Anna seems happy enough."

"And this new beau, this—"

"Charles, Charles Norden, I believe."

"Yes, yes," Sarah said impatiently.

"It sounds as though he's treating her well, is very fond of her. Doesn't seem to mind Douglas being underfoot."

"And Anna?"

"Her state of mind? I think she's fond of him, too." Richard was conscious that he was not being entirely forthcoming.

"You know she's inclined to get carried away."

"She told me she's being cautious, and at her age, I don't think I have the right to press her about the matter."

"But, Richard, you know she has this history, this compulsion to fall head over heels and then live to regret it. There was Carl Farnham, and then Roger Cramer, and that was just when she was at the academy, when she probably shouldn't have been getting that serious about boys at all."

"Seems the most natural thing in the world to me. It didn't do you any harm, as I recall."

"I wasn't high-strung. I always kept my wits about me. I didn't get crushes. Anna has always gotten swept away."

"I think it's rather a fine thing. Sincere, selfless, true love—"

"And extraordinarily dangerous. But you always rather aided and abetted things, didn't you? Let her stay out, commiserated with her."

"I thought they were perfectly fine boys. She got hurt. That's the way it tends to go at that age, and that was all. She didn't get into . . . trouble."

"Perhaps it's a wonder that she didn't."

"She was never that sort of girl."

"Under the right circumstances, every girl is that sort of girl. And now she has a divorce under her belt. Hardly a badge of virtue."

"A mistake." Richard was growing weary, worn down by his own dissembling and Sarah's corrosive view of human affairs. And although it did not accord with his own beliefs or experiences, he was defeated by the sense that she was probably right.

Sarah stopped while the waiter set their dinners before them. She sawed at her steak. "Totally apart from her own inclinations, there's the fact of her being *seen* to be a divorcée. She's a target for any male who's after a fling." She speared a piece of meat on her fork and raised it to her mouth, tines up.

"I don't think Charles is that type. She says he's attentive and kind."

Sarah could not help herself. "Well, wouldn't he just," she said dryly, and as soon as she had finished, realized the conversation was drifting toward rancor. "I'm sorry, darling. I don't want to be unpleasant. But I worry so . . . " She poked languorously at her potatoes.

Richard seized the opportunity. "Of course you do. And you're right to. But there's only so much we can do. And she's promised me to be careful. And perhaps it will prove to be a good match. That would be to everyone's benefit. You have to have faith."

"But faith, darling, without naivete."   ·

"Or despair."

They finished their dinner in silence, without anger and perhaps without enthusiasm, but steadily, tied together head and foot, the two corner pillars of a porch. They stirred their coffee at one rhythm, the cups clanking like a distant buoy at sea. Richard tipped the waiter three dollars on their twelve-dollar check. When they went outside into the night, the first snow of the winter was falling.

TWO NIGHTS LATER, RICHARD LET HIMSELF INTO JAMES'S APARTment. He made himself a drink and tuned the radio to Bing Crosby's show on NBC. He went to the second bedroom, clicked on the lamp, and slid up the cover of the rolltop desk. The top of the desk was inset with red leather and scored with an egg-and-dart pattern in faded gold. He sat down in James's chair and wheeled it forward like a pianist settling in at the keyboard.

Richard expected to find a measure of disorder in James's affairs, the inevitable result of his lack of concern for the morrow. Yet the desk, which he imagined would be the repository for unpaid bills, parking tickets, and long-forgotten receipts, was bare as a putting green. He rose and went out into the hall. Bing Crosby was saying something, his voice a mellow, vulpine drawl, and the audience roared. Richard gathered up the mail by the front door. He put *The Saturday Evening Post* next to his hat on the hall table to take to the office, he consigned *Argosy* to the wastebasket, and he carried the rest back to the desk.

There was a laundry bill, another bill from James's haberdasher, and a third from Northern States Power. Richard pushed these off to his left; he would take these to the office along with any others he found and write checks for them. There were three letters, two that appeared to be social invitations and a third from the Drake Hotel in Chicago. He shunted those to his right. He sipped his drink. From the hall, Bing Crosby's voice echoed, like waves lapping.

In the upper part of the desk there were eight or ten open compartments, most of them empty. Richard sifted through them. One held James's checkbook, another his address book, and a third his calendar. In the fourth there was a savings passbook with a blue cloth cover. Richard flipped through it. The last entry showed a withdrawal of $500, leaving a balance of $5,450. Folded next to it in the same compartment was a statement of James's brokerage account: 100 RCA; 300 General Electric; 100 Packard Motor; 500 International Business Machines; 500 Pennsylvania Railroad. Richard put it with the bills. He would calculate the value of the stock at the office.

The desk had six drawers, three on each side. Richard began at the upper left. There was a box of stationery printed with James's name and address and two smaller boxes, one with business cards, the other with calling cards engraved simply "Mr. James Wright MacEwan." They were ivory-colored and looked to be at least twenty years old. There was a pot of black ink and a small convex blotter, a half-sheet of three-cent stamps, and a bottle of mucilage with a priapic pink rubber tip.

The next drawer down contained three different kinds of bullets and shells, a corroded steel box of fishing flies and a set of needle-nosed pliers, and a half-dozen empty liquor miniatures. In the back of the drawer were a pencil sharpener and a withered carnation boutonniere. The bottom drawer was stuffed with bank statements and canceled checks.

Richard looked at his watch. At the rate he was going he could be home in less than an hour. He went out to the living room and poured himself another drink. Bing Crosby was singing "I'll Be Home for Christmas." Outside the window, a car drove by, its tires sputtering through the snow.

He returned to the desk and opened the top right drawer: pencils, rubber bands, loose pennies and poker chips, a letter opener, a half-smoked pack of Chesterfields, an accumulation of matchbooks, a St. Christopher medal, and a three-pack of prophylactics. The middle drawer appeared to hold nothing but letters, stuffed tightly together. Richard lifted a bundle out. Underneath it lay a large manila envelope with the name of James's firm printed in the upper left-hand corner. It was closed with a thin string wrapped around two cardboard disks. Richard picked it up and opened it. There were pages torn from magazines inside, photos of women, garishly lit, posed separately and in pairs, some tied and bound, some clutching their genitals, some in embraces or licking each other's breasts, all naked save for spike-heeled slippers. Richard gazed at the pictures as though they were autopsy photos, his eyes locked, pulled into them. After a moment, he shoved them back into the envelope, returned it to the drawer, and slammed the drawer shut.

The bottom drawer, deeper than the others, was designed for file folders but contained more envelopes, together with scrapbooks and loose photos. Richard removed everything and laid it on the desk. There were two scrapbooks, swollen with clippings, their pages rigid with glue. Richard paged idly through them. The first was a chronological selection of newspaper sports stories, cut in 1916 and 1917, when James was twelve and thirteen years old. The second contained newspaper cuttings from the First War, chiefly from 1916 on. In the back were maps James had traced in pencil onto onionskin paper and marked with the shifting trench lines of the Western Front.

Richard leaned back and picked up his drink. There was some kind of police drama on the radio, the voices curt, weary, accusatory. He took up one of the manila envelopes and emptied it out onto the desktop. There were perhaps two dozen photographs: His mother, her hair heaped in chiffons on her head; his father, mustached, his stiff detachable collar at his neck like a pair of shears; uncles dandling shotgun breeches on their arms, aunts set out in wicker chairs; James, bonneted in lace, sitting erect in a wicker perambulator; Richard and James together in boys' sailor suits, Richard standing behind James, clasping his shoulders; James smiling wolfishly behind the wheel of his first roadster, two unidentifiable women pressed in the front with him, Henry Finch sprung clownishly from the rumble seat like a jack-in-the-box.

There was another envelope, fat, the paper worn and frayed to the consistency of flannel, with the address of James's prep school in Connecticut printed on it. Inside was a smaller envelope and a book. On the outside of the envelope was a legend in James's reeling, unsteady adolescent handwriting: "Hun shrapnel captured by Dicky, The Somme, June '18." Richard opened it. There was a lump of gray metal inside, so amorphous in shape as to be unrecognizable as descended from any object. Richard remembered sending it; James had accepted on faith that it was what Richard said it was, although Richard himself could no longer be sure.

Richard took up the book. It had a gray-green cover emblazoned with gold lettering and an American flag superimposed on a map of the Arctic. It was called *Finding the North Pole by Cook and Peary, April 21st, 1908—April 6th, 1909*. It had been Richard's book and he had passed it on to James when James had gone to boarding school. Now Richard opened it. In the center was a section of illustrations in sienna ink. Eskimos in kayaks defended themselves with spears against marauding polar bears; a mob of killer whales massacred a hapless family of narwhals; male fur seals squared off in combat for possession of a captured female. A sorrow pressed down on Richard, a grief for the loss of the world as it then was, now sealed behind clear glass, visible but untouchable.

There was a tiny photo inserted among the pages of the book. Richard picked it up between his thumb and index finger and held it up to regard it closely. It showed him and James in a rowboat. Richard was about twelve years old, James about seven. Richard is at the oars. James is perched in the bow, holding the rope. He is smiling. His head has the square, massive solidity of a little boy. His hair rakes his forehead carelessly; Richard's is slicked back. The boat is just offshore of White Bear Lake. There are reeds scattered around them. The water has scarcely a ripple upon it, although it looks warm, as though it were simmering and steaming.

Richard and James are going on a journey. Richard is taking him.

Like a shoal of clouds stealing down a prairie sky, Richard's tears came, overflowing his cheeks, raining on the sepia pages of the book. He put down the photograph, stood, and then lay down on the narrow bed in the corner. He sobbed into the pillow as he had not done since he was a child. He conjured his own ridiculousness, the pathetic sight he must be, but his grief pulled him down like water does a man in heavy clothes. His chest heaved, and he felt he would surely choke or drown on the mucus and tears that seemed to be filling his nose and throat. But he could not compose himself. His heart was like an egg with something aborning inside it, and must break.

After a time, he heard voices in the hall, and he realized the radio was on. It was as though he had emerged from a fever or a delirium. He pulled himself up from the bed and sat for a moment, resting his feet flat on the floor, catching his breath. He thought that when Jacob wrestled the angel, it might have been this way. But now Richard knew two things he had not known before: that he did not truly know James and that because James was gone, he never could. And because he knew those things, he could no longer imagine Jacob's angel and still less the god who had sent him.

LOVE DOES NOT HURRY. DID ANNA KNOW THIS? NO, IT WAITS and watches like a cat, staring at its object, looking away indifferently, losing itself in sleep, in grooming its own flesh. It attends the juxtaposition of signs, the opportune moment, the constellation whose pattern none but it can see. Then, rising with a stretch, it sashays toward the fireplace, presses its head to the hearth, corkscrews its trunk to the floor, and plops down. It is home. It holds the heart fast between its paws like a stunned mouse.

That Sunday, Charles invited Anna to his house. She packed Douglas into a snowsuit with blue mittens clipped to the sleeves and a hood lined with red plush wool. She pulled red rubber boots over his Stride Rites and fastened the black clips. Douglas stood expectantly, stiff as a scarecrow in the snowsuit, the mittens dangling and bobbing like birds on strings. Anna checked her lipstick and her hair. She had brushed it fifty strokes on each side. She tied a scarf around her head, put on her camel-hair coat, picked up Douglas, and went to the car.

The day was bright. The snow glistened and the blue of the sky was as deep as a magnesia bottle. Douglas stood on the car seat and gesticulated at the passing world, naming its objects. "Truck. Bird. Church. Bus. Dog. Bird. Truck."

"Yes, *big* truck," Anna confirmed. "And Charles has a dog. His name is Randy." Douglas sighed in expectation.

They drove across the bridge, over the river and the woods and the floodplain on either side of it. Once there had been nothing but farms here, but now houses had sprung up on the hills. Charles's house had a black mailbox and an orange metal tube for the newspaper. Anna turned into his driveway and drove up a slight incline to the house. It was long and low in the modern style, with a lean-to roof angled upward to the south and a deck overlooking a small pond to the rear.

Charles jogged out to greet them. He wore khaki slacks and a yellow V-neck sweater and there was a Dalmatian at his side. He smiled and the dog leapt up and down by the side of the car. Their exhalations made silver clouds in the cold. Charles pulled Anna's door open. "How *are* you two?" he boomed merrily. Anna's eyes rose to meet his face. Douglas began to climb across her lap, all his attention fixed on the Dalmatian. He would have crawled straight out into midair had not Charles deftly seized his arms and lowered him to the ground. Charles took Anna's hand. "Come inside. It's cold."

The house had an enormous living room with a high sloping ceiling and massive beams to support it. There was a fireplace built of flagstones, a little bar with two stools, and a new phonograph that took long-playing records. The forced-air heating thundered to life, then quieted to a steady whistle. Douglas staggered through the house in pursuit of the dog. "Polka-dot dog, Dougie," Anna called out. Douglas circled the room, squealing "poka dog, poka dog," huffing like a steam train.

Charles brought Anna a cup of coffee. "Douglas seems to find the accommodations satisfactory."

"Oh, I think anyone would," Anna said perkily, and added, more thoughtfully, "You have excellent taste. It's very up-to-date, very modern, very masculine." She smiled, as if to assure him this was not mere opinion, still less a criticism.

"Oh, but then maybe it needs a woman's touch."

"Silly—it's perfect just the way it is." The truth was, Anna found it a little austere, less a home to be inside than a set against which to perform, upon which to strike thoughtful poses and declaim speeches. But she let herself imagine what it would be like to live here. She pictured her hook rugs in the hallway and Douglas stacking blocks on the kitchen floor and Arthur Godfrey's voice on the radio, like a rasping log burning on the fire. She imagined burying her face in the crook of Charles's neck, rubbing her hands up his back, against the wool of his sweater.

"Randy could probably do with some exercise. Why don't we go out and I'll show you the grounds, such as they are. Then we can come in and I'll make us a toddy."

"Sounds like a grand plan." She called to Douglas, "Sweetie, come on—we're going to take Randy for a walk." Charles held the storm door open and the dog loped past, followed by Douglas and Anna. They walked down the slope into the backyard. It overlooked empty cornfields, studded here and there with a house under construction. There was a pond at the bottom. The dog ran off toward its left shore.

Charles pointed at the water. "To think that a month ago there were ducks stopping here. And now it's frozen solid." The sky was bare, save for a row of high-voltage lines in the distance. A few clutches of cattails grew out of the ice at the edge of the pond. They shifted slightly in the wind. A single robin pecked disconsolately at the ice.

Anna asked, "Could you skate on it? I used to love to skate when

I was a girl—it was practically all I did in the winter until I was sixteen or so."

"Oh, you could indeed, with a little shoveling."

"And it's such a beautiful spot—like being in the country, without the drawbacks," Anna said.

"It won't stay this way forever. But I've got five acres, so I'm well set."

"You're here for the long haul, then?"

"Oh, I think so."

"But not as a hermit, I hope."

"Oh no, that wouldn't suit me at all." He began to take her arm, as though prefatory to saying something that was weighing on him, or that demanded to be said. She looked up at him, her eyes a little fearful. There was a soft, crumbling sound, like broken pottery being wrapped in butcher paper, and then there was a scream. Anna looked away from Charles and her breath caught mutely at the top of her throat. Charles exclaimed, "Christ!" and raced toward the opposite side of the pond. The dog gamboled in the snow at the edge, and a little beyond it Douglas flailed in water up to his shoulders, shrieking.

Charles ran into the pond and scooped up the child. He stood there for a moment, holding Douglas like a sheaf of wheat, and water dribbled out of the legs of his snowsuit. Charles sloshed out of the pond. "Let's get him inside," he shouted to Anna. Douglas sobbed, "Mama," again and again. Anna unknit her hands, drew them to her mouth, lowered them, and began to run alongside Charles.

Inside, Charles lay the child on the bed in the guest room. He pulled towels from the closet. "I'll heat him some milk," he said. Anna began to pull Douglas's clothes off. Water and slush spilled from the boots to the floor. Anna tugged at the wet socks shrunk obdurately to the boy's feet. The snowsuit was stained; filthy water wicked up through it as through a cigarette snuffed in the dregs of a glass. Douglas's teeth began to chatter, and he stammered out his wails, calling her name. He was naked now, his skin blotched with crimson, his feet and fingers dark as beets, his tiny sex withdrawn into the taut balloon of his abdomen. Anna buffed and tamped him dry and then held him in her lap, shrouded in towels.

Charles returned with a cup of warm milk and a blanket. Anna swaddled Douglas, returned him to her lap, and tipped the cup to his lips. He drank eagerly. His hands clutched at Anna's body, the fingers tightening and releasing, reaching, easing. Then he was asleep.

Anna laid him in the center of the bed and waved Charles out of the room and followed after. Standing in the hall, she put her index finger to her lips and pulled the door closed. She whispered, "He'll be out for at least an hour and a half; he would've been anyway—naptime."

In the living room, the Dalmatian lay on the floor asleep. Charles looked at Anna imploringly. "I'm so, so sorry. God, I feel like a shit—telling you it was frozen, letting Randy lead him off like that." Anna moved closer and touched his arm. "You mustn't feel bad. There's no harm done. Some wet clothes, some tears. And you were magnificent. Leapt in, shoes and all. You saved him."

She kept looking at him and pressed her fingers a little more deeply into his arm. He looked back, and it seemed as though he was trying to puzzle out a riddle. He rotated the wrist of the arm she was touching and grasped her elbow in his palm. He said, "Thank you," but it sounded like a question. She felt her arm cupped in his grip, and that too seemed to be a question. She felt she wasn't breathing; that fingers were softly drumming on the bottom of her diaphragm; that wings hung over her face, beating hot breath on her, suffocating her, lifting her. Then, a thread at last through the eye of a needle, she was drawn into his arms. His mouth was over her mouth and they breathed against each other's breath, like a standing wave, a boat rocking in harbor. After a time, he lowered his hands to her waist and brought his thumbs forward, hooking her hipbones, inscribing circles on the plain above her mons. She felt something light, a brushing far down in her body but inside, like a burr rolling across the interior of her thigh.

Charles slid his hands up the front of her sweater. He pressed his palms under her breasts tentatively, as though weighing them, as though assaying her, reckoning his choices. She took one of his hands in one of hers and lifted her sweater with the other. She laid his hand on her heart, and then pressed it down onto her breast. They stood that way for a moment and then guided each other to his bed.

A FEW EVENINGS LATER, RICHARD RETURNED TO JAMES'S APART-ment. He put his hat on the hall table. The cleaner, Mrs. Clay, had been in. There were boxes stacked in the hall and sheets draped over the furniture in the living room. He carried his brief-case into the second bedroom and turned on the lamp next to the desk. The shade had been removed and the bulb shone raw and stark. He had come to balance James's checkbook.

He rifled the bottom left drawer and found James's October statement. He unfolded it on the desktop and spread the checks out above it, took down James's checkbook from its slot, and began to tick off the canceled checks. He pulled a legal pad from his brief-case and made a column of numbers. When he had satisfied him-self that they balanced, he got up and made himself a drink.

Richard sat back down in James's chair and then noticed the letters he'd left on the desk the last time he had been there. He took them and opened them idly, rocking in the chair. An invita-tion to a costume ball at the White Bear Yacht Club. An an-nouncement of the appointment of a new vice president at James's brokerage firm. The third was a letter from the Drake Hotel in Chicago:

Sir,
    During a recent audit of our accounts, it has come to our attention that a mistake was made in our bill for your and Mrs. MacEwan's stay with us on September 23 and 24. You were incorrectly charged for a double twin-bedded room rather than a single double-bedded room. In correction of this, we enclose a check in the amount of $5.27 herewith.

We sincerely apologize for this error on our part and trust we may look forward to seeing you and Mrs. MacEwan at the Drake in the near future.

Yours sincerely,
R. H. Tawney
General Manager

Richard found himself a little bemused: another of James's "Mrs. MacEwans" clandestinely bedded in a hotel room. Which one was this? Did she know James was dead? Had it been the sort of affair where she might care? Richard took James's calendar from the niche next to his checkbook and thumbed through it until he found September 23. James's indolent handwriting ambled down the page:

Drake,
Chicago
w/S——

Richard was not comfortable reading James's calendar. In death, especially, his brother was entitled to his privacy. Moreover, there were things he did not want to know about James, and he suspected many of them were recorded here. But perhaps "S" should be notified or contacted; perhaps promises had been made, understandings reached. Perhaps decency as much as curiosity urged a little more investigation. He took James's address book down and flipped through it. James was a creature of acquaintances. There must have been three hundred entries. And that convinced Richard to let the matter of "S" 's identity rest: He was not about to spend hours combing every name in this book.

He sat up in the chair and began to gather his things together. He tapped the edges of the canceled checks on the desk and formed them into neat piles. He slid them into their envelopes. The lamplight was lurid, unforgiving. The shadows of his fingers passed over the desktop, flights of ravens. He felt a sensation between a craving and a pang, between desire and guilt at things left undone. Like a compass needle in the dark, Richard's hand slid into his briefcase and found his own datebook. What had *he* been doing on September 23? Perhaps recalling it would shed some light on James's activities. That seemed shamelessly false, but somehow irresistible, like stealing a glance at a woman through an undetected breach in a dressing room curtain.

He opened the datebook and found September 23. He had gone to court in the morning. That evening he had a vestry meeting at St. Botolph's. Sarah was in Chicago, visiting her mother, or so it said.

NO REMARK HAD PASSED BETWEEN RICHARD AND SARAH THAT night, nor to Richard's mind was there any sane reason why one should. In the morning, on his way up to the office, he stopped in to the First National Bank offices on the ground floor. Henry Finch supervised a warren of automobile loan officers from a glassed-in booth, and Richard saw him at his desk from far away, like a walrus perched on a rock. He tapped on Henry's door. Henry looked up with some surprise.

"Dicky-I'll-be-damned-MacEwan! What brings you down from your aerie? Up for that drink we discussed?"

"Not at this hour, I don't think."

"Killjoy," Henry sputtered in feigned pique. "Well, what can I do for you? I owe you for your kindness—and forbearance—the other evening."

"It was nothing. It was a funeral, a time for mourning. You had every right." He stopped, looked at his shoes, at Henry's brimming wastebasket, and resumed. "I've been sorting through James's affairs and wondered if you might help me out. There are some loose ends."

"Of course. Fire away, counselor."

"I wonder if you knew if James was seeing anyone in particular this autumn, any particular woman he might have been fond of?"

"Jimmy was fond of all women, it goes without saying. And was terribly discreet. But if he was serious about someone, I think I would have met them. We always went out together. And there wasn't anyone this fall, at least to my knowledge."

"Could there have been someone out of town, in another city?"

"A storm in every port?" Henry stopped as though to congratulate himself on his wit. "That would be like him, but he didn't really travel often, did he? Didn't have that kind of job. Not that he suffered for it, old fox that he was."

"Yes, I guess that's true. He didn't mention making any trips to Chicago this fall, did he?"

"No, not to me. What's the mystery, pray tell?"

"No mystery, really. Just a bill from the Drake Hotel that doesn't make sense." The office had a flatulent aroma of cigar smoke and Old Spice and Richard was not bearing up well under Henry's bonhomie. He looked ostentatiously at his watch. "Oh, need to get upstairs. But thank you. And we will have that drink at a more appropriate time."

Once at his desk, Richard worked steadily, if absentmindedly. It was not so much that he was distracted, but that he seemed to have another body, another mind that sat next to him attending to its own business. It rolled the probables and improbables around in its mind. It worked alongside him, an amanuensis to a blind man, recording the thoughts he had forbade himself to think. Its mouth was dry, and there was a ball of dread in its stomach.

THAT THURSDAY WAS THANKSGIVING. ANNA MASHED POTATOES in the kitchen while Sarah fluttered her fingers over the dining room table like a mandarin at an abacus, convinced something was missing: a knife for the cranberry jelly, a ladle for the sauceboat, a trivet, the sharpening steel for the carving knife. There would be only four persons at the table that day: herself, Richard, Anna, and Douglas, who presently napped on a bed upstairs. Perhaps it was this that disconcerted Sarah. She felt rather useless without guests and, worse still, servants to orchestrate. She returned to the kitchen to check on Anna, who had just removed the turkey from the oven. Cooking held no appeal for Sarah, and she approached food in its raw state as she might a barnyard full of muck, repellent smells, and thankless heavy lifting. She hovered over Anna, who was stirring a pan of gravy, beating gyres of flour into the fat, unconsciously hunching her shoulders forward not in effort, but to gain some distance from Sarah.

Sarah inquired, "How are we coming, dear?"

"Oh, ten minutes at most. Why don't you go upstairs and get Douglas ready?"

"Will do," Sarah said, and strode down the rear hall. Bare, clear bulbs hung from the ceiling on twisted black cord, their filaments glowing silver like lightning suspended in a jar. The telephone sat black in its niche, and on either side of it the walls bore scribbled names and numbers, gray inscriptions on paint faded to the color of old newspaper. Sarah opened the closet where the high chair was stored. The closet smelled of Glass Wax and polish and scorched ironing-board covers. The chair had been Anna's but was still perfectly serviceable, a now-chipped and faded pink with a rabbit decaled on the back. She began to lift it out and thought better.

Richard stood in the living room by the fireplace, apparently lost in thought, regarding the surface of his drink like Narcissus at the well. He had *South Pacific* playing on the phonograph.

"Darling, how would you like to fetch the high chair from the hall closet while I go up and wake the son and heir?"

"Of course," Richard said impishly and set down his drink on the mantle. Richard's bouts of whimsy arose rarely and unpredictably, like mushrooms on a rainy lawn, usually on holidays and only in the presence of immediate family. Now he clenched his hands at his diaphragm, pumped up his chest like an overstuffed basso profundo, and joined the voice on the phonograph now reaching the climax of "Some Enchanted Evening." Lifting his arms to the ceiling, his lips thrust out to scrupulously enunciate each syllable, he first implored and then insisted, "Once you have found her, never let her go!" He dropped his arms limply to his sides, and bowed.

"Bravo, bravo," said Sarah. "Now go move some furniture."

Upstairs, she pushed open the door to Anna's old room. Douglas lay on his stomach, his right hand clutching a knot of chenille on the bedspread. She sat down and gently rolled him over. His eyes flickered briefly, revealing nothing but white, and then opened wide. She lowered her head to his and pressed her cheek against him. "Gramma," he cheeped, his breath damp as steam, his skin soft as fur. She could hear his lungs moving in their tiny labors, the rustlings of a fledgling in its nest. He lay quietly, his heartbeats and breaths ebbing and flooding out like water against her body, yielding his body up to her. "Gramma," he said again, a fact, a sigh, a blessing.

"Precious lamb," she said, and sat up. "Now, Master Douglas, what about dinner?" She thrust a finger guardedly into the waistband of his shorts. The diaper was dry. "You are very good to Grandma," she said, and picked him up.

Richard had put the high chair next to the dining room table and Sarah lowered Douglas into it. Anna pushed through the door carrying a bowl of mashed potatoes and behind her Richard bore the turkey on a platter. "I think, ladies and gentlemen, we are ready to proceed. Let me just fetch some wine."

Sarah and Anna sat down, and Anna began to shred some turkey for Douglas and mash it together with potatoes. She sang something to him softly whose melody Sarah could not make out. Richard returned with a bottle and a corkscrew and stood at the head of the table.

"*Mesdames, messieurs, je suis très* pleased to propose you this fine vintage from the ancient vineyards de"—he lifted up the bottle and screwed up his eye at the label—"San Jose, La Californie. *Quel horreur! Sacre merde!*"

"Daddy!" Anna laughed, a little embarrassed.

"Richard!" Sarah said, with mock firmness. "At the table. Please—keep a grip."

"I was temporarily overcome," Richard said sheepishly, and picked up the carving set. He began to slice off additional tranches of meat. They mounted up in neat piles on either side of the turkey, far more than they had any hope of eating. He loaded the plates without inquiry, white meat for Anna, white and dark for Sarah, a leg for himself. They ate mostly in silence, save to compliment Anna's cooking and to encourage Douglas to eat heartily. "We seem so small," Sarah said absently. "So few." Anna appeared to look away.

"But still a dynasty to be reckoned with," said Richard, and stood. He reached around the table to refill Sarah and Anna's glasses. "Now, as is our immemorial custom, I have a few toasts to offer," he said, seizing his glass, pulling himself upright, and hunched his shoulders in preparation. Sarah rolled her eyes; Anna giggled.

Richard began. "Unrecumbent as I am at public speaking, this is clearly a very suspicious occasion, one upon which it behooves us all to raise our cups to the illustrious persons peopling this groaning board as well as their friends, relations, and various impedimenta. To wit: Master Douglas MacEwan, his fantabulous mother, Miss Anna MacEwan, and, not least, the eternally pulchritudinous, girlful Sarah MacEwan. Cheers!"

"And to you, Daddy!" said Anna, and Sarah echoed her, adding, "You are awfully sweet, darling." Richard sat while Anna simultaneously rose to begin clearing the table. "Hold on, precious. Let's relax, talk, enjoy each other's company." Douglas twisted in the high chair as though wanting to extricate himself. Anna said, "I think he's a little restless." Richard responded, "Then perhaps we could adjourn to the living room."

They sat down by the fireplace, Richard and Sarah on one side, Anna and Douglas on the other. Anna set Douglas at her feet. She took a copy of *Life* magazine from the table and held it up. It had a farmer with a champion cow on the cover. "Can Douglas entertain himself with this, Mother? It's likely to get torn."

"Oh, no great loss if it were," Sarah said. "Rather looks like Eleanor Roosevelt on the front, doesn't it?"

Anna said nothing. "Let's not start in, you two," Richard warned.

Sarah directed herself to the floor by Anna's feet and spoke in a schoolmarmish voice. "Douglas, your mother believes that when people die, the good ones—only the very good ones—go to a place called Hyde Park and rest there for eternity with Franklin Roosevelt. He sits on a throne surrounded by his angels and saints—Yalies and Jews, mostly. If the day ever arrives when she's not too busy here among the living, Mrs. Roosevelt will come sit next to him, like the Virgin Mary."

Douglas was oblivious. He pointed to the magazine cover and said, "Moo."

"Exactly, my dear," said Sarah. Anna had averted her face in the manner of someone feigning boredom, and now turned to her mother. "Are we done?" she asked, intending a tone of indifference. But Sarah heard the quaver in her voice, the weight gathering in the corners of her mouth. She pulled back. "I'm sorry, dear. I just can't resist these things. And you know we are a family—we can disagree about some things and still love each other, can't we?"

Richard hurriedly began an anecdote about a will he had heard about at work. The testator wanted to donate his personal library to the reference collection of the university. But the volumes in question consisted largely of Dale Carnegie books and carefully preserved back numbers of men's and "sunbathing" magazines. It was a rather awkward situation. Richard laughed quietly to himself. Anna tittered appreciatively.

Sarah said she was in charge of organizing the decorations at church next week. Could Anna help her? She could bring Douglas. They could have lunch. Anna agreed with as much enthusiasm as she could muster. Then the three of them talked quietly, the content of their conversation of no particular matter, a hum they basked before like a fire. They sat now as they had sat for nearly thirty years, in this very room. There had been others here at other times: friends, pets, strangers, interlopers, and those loved and gone. Now there were four, but the absent and dead might have been sitting among them, nodding, laughing, gainsaying, assenting, their silence woven into the words, speaking low, their voices like the clatter of knitting needles, the turning of windmills.

Douglas sat with the magazine, pushing through the pages with his palm like a shovel grazing the earth, muttering. What did he see there? Who can say? The paper was white, lustrous, and waxy, freckled with letters and halftone dots. The farmer on the cover had a new barn in which hundreds of cows could be tended by one or two people. On another page was a picture of a valley the Soviets had blasted apart with an atomic explosion. They had made its rivers run backward. A few pages farther on a scientist predicted how wars would be fought in the future: planes broad-winged as dragonflies, a half-dozen propellers churning; a rocket, tumescent as a cigar, with fins like a dart; no soldiers anywhere to be seen. At the back of the magazine was a diagram of underground Manhattan, the guts and arteries and capillaries of trains, subways, sewers, pneumatic tubes, and tunnels tangled incomprehensibly.

For Douglas, all these were as shadows of things that were yet to be. They passed over his consciousness like high clouds on a sunny day. There were images and he spoke to them and moved on, but what impression could they make beside the scent of his grandmother's face powder, the tolling of his grandfather's voice, the seethe of his mother's nylon stockings at his ear?

CHARLES CAME TO ANNA LATER THAT NIGHT. HIS DESIRE WAS A boulder he carried before him, staggering and breathless. Anna opened her door to him at nine-thirty, and the cold poured in like light across the threshold. He entered, shrouded in his gray wool coat and green plaid scarf. He unbuttoned his coat, and it hung on either side of him like drapes on a window. Anna pressed herself to him, her body a drawn bow. Charles clutched the small of her back with one hand, her left buttock with the other. She drank up his breath with her mouth. His erection drove against her like a coulter to the earth.

Later, a light went on in the bathroom. Charles's shoes skidded near the bed. Whispers moved down the hall. The front door opened. There were voices, soft in the night like vapors, and the sharp, viscous fragrance of sated lovers. The door closed; the porch light went out. A car door slammed, hollow as a stone dropped in a pond. An engine started and faded away. In the kitchen, the refrigerator compressor shook itself awake for a few minutes; in his crib, Douglas turned, mewled softly, nickered, and was silent. Outside, under a shrub by the house, a raccoon stood in the snow, watching, the mask of her face mottled in shadows, striated black and silver by the light of a gibbous moon.

II

December

SARAH HAD A BOX OF PURPLE CANDLES AND RIBBON AND A heap of spruce boughs at her feet. "Here's what we'll do," she announced to Anna. "You wind the boughs into a wreath about two and a half feet across. Here's the wire. I'll do some bows." Anna said, "Fine." She had done this before. Sarah knew that and was relieved. She and Anna had begun to get along at a certain age— nine, ten?—when Sarah could explain what needed doing, and Anna nodded her head and simply followed instructions. Before that time, their relations had been a leaky dike besieged by the passions of infancy—endless, unpredictable breaches, wariness at the calmest of times—and when Anna reached age sixteen, they returned to that condition again for some years. Even now, Sarah remained wary of Anna's desire, the intermittent fever that bore her away like a mad pony, careening from impulse to accident.

For her part, Anna sought only to be good, and what greater good was there than love? If you were good enough, if you loved enough, love called you, took you in, looked after you, held you while the deluge swept past. Nothing Anna had learned in college disabused her of this. But her mother apparently adhered to some other belief in which the avoidance of disorder was the highest principle. She traveled in the burnished grooves of her certitudes, convinced that all other paths led to disaster. Her theology was pre-Christian, her cosmos ruled by irritable, implacable, occasionally capricious gods.

Anna's hands were sticky with spruce sap, and the bark and needles abraded her fingertips. She had been making Advent and Christmas decorations for twenty years, and still it made her raw. Sarah put down the last of her bows and inspected the wreath. "Fine work, my dear. Let's take it upstairs." They carried the wreath, the candles, and the bows up the stairs from the undercroft into the nave of the church. The custodian was vacuuming at the back. They took the wreath to a small table by the chancel rail. Anna held it up while Sarah threaded a purple ribbon around it, and then Anna laid it down in the center of the table. Sarah handed her a ball of green florist's putty, and Anna put some on the bottom of each candle. Then she stuck the four candles into the perimeter of the wreath, equally spaced at the points of the compass, the bottoms hidden by the foliage. Sarah put a bow at the base of each candle. A candle would be lit this Sunday and another each Sunday thereafter. Then, a larger, white candle would be put in the center of the wreath and lit on Christmas Eve.

"I think that will do very nicely," said Sarah, stepping back. "Now what about lunch?"

"I have to get back and pick up Douglas from the baby-sitter."

"We could pick him up and then have lunch. We never seem to get to talk these days."

"I'd really love to, Mother, but I have so much to do, and then I have a date this evening."

"The new beau?"

"Charles, yes."

"How are things, shall we say, progressing? I understand he's well disposed toward Douglas."

"We like each other very much."

"Well . . . " If Sarah had had a cigarette, she would have drawn on it. "That's good. You should bring him around for drinks."

"I'm sure he'd like that. Actually, I expect he'll be taking me to the club Christmas fete, and you and Daddy will be there."

Sarah's lips tightened slightly. Her hand had been resting on the chancel rail, her fingers arced. Now she drew them to her chin.

"I wonder if that's wise, dear, a public appearance together. He's not divorced yet, technically, is he? People read so much into the smallest things. And they can be so cruel, so uncharitable."

Anna's breath stuck in the top of her throat, and her face bristled. The sensation was unaltered from her earliest memory of it, a wish knocked from its bicycle, sprawled in the street, scrape-kneed and humiliated.

Sarah interpreted Anna's silence to mean that her point had not been absorbed and went on. "The fact remains that you are seen to live in your ex-husband's house, dependent on his largesse—"

"On alimony that Douglas and I are legally entitled to." Anna suddenly felt she might compete with some success on a playing field she had always conceded to her mother. "And yes, I suppose I do depend on a man for my support. As do you. As do all the women you seem to admire. As you taught me—"

Sarah sensed the bull's-eye, could not help but release the bowstring, and regretted it even before the arrow struck. "No one taught you to go out with married men . . ." Her voice trailed off. She and Anna stood silently for a while, as though in a puddle of icy water.

Sarah began to extricate herself. She looked up, expecting to see tears on Anna's face, but there were none. Her lips were a little drawn in, her cheeks were white and glacial, her eyes far away. "*I* understand, precious, of course I do," Sarah said. "But you can't ignore what other people think, the stories they tell, how they color things."

"I really don't care what a lot of old biddies say about me," Anna said petulantly. She strove for a more mature insouciance. "I have nothing to be ashamed of and neither does Charles."

"Of *course* you don't. But sometimes life is simply smoother when one bows to certain conventions, certain realities—silly as they may be."

"I'm not even going to discuss this with you, Mother."

"But you'll keep it in mind, won't you?"

Anna said nothing. The smell of spruce was thick, unctuously sweet like cake frosting, peppery, smoky. The hum of the vacuum cleaner stopped. The custodian ambled up the aisle toward them, dragging the vacuum cleaner behind him.

"That's a lovely wreath, ladies."

"Thank you," Sarah said curtly. She was not in the mood to suffer any fools just now. Anna gazed absently up the chancel to the altar, to the crucifix, where Jesus hung above six candlesticks, not in agony but as though asleep.

"You altar guild gals do such a great job."

"Thank you," Sarah repeated. The custodian began to shamble backward away from them, down the aisle.

"Guess I should get back to work. Don't worry about turning out the lights or anything."

"Yes, thank you," Sarah said. "And Merry Christmas," Anna added, looking up at him.

"So it *is*," the custodian said. "Same to you."

DO WE IMAGINE THE WORLD OR DOES THE WORLD IMAGINE US? Richard had laid out the data that he had discovered in James's apartment, such as they were, and shifted them like Scrabble tiles, attempting to fashion them into words that formed a story. But suppose there was no story? Suppose each datum was unconnected to any other? Suppose any story Richard managed to concoct was wholly artificial, utterly imaginary? But suppose, too, that there was a story that consisted, at least in part, of those same data? Suppose it had existed prior to anything Richard had found in the apartment or any thought that had entered his mind? Suppose it was waiting for Richard to see it, a nebulous gestalt, a ghost clanking its soundless chains, a cold exhalation condensing on his window? Did Richard have the right to ignore it? Did it have the right to insist on being acknowledged?

By the first day of December, Richard had largely persuaded himself that the juxtaposition of James's and Sarah's trips to Chicago was accidental; that "S" could be anyone, and might not even refer to James's paramour at the Drake; and, most crucially, that such behavior on either James's or Sarah's part would be incomprehensible. At present, the only demonstrable wickedness in evidence was his unwarranted suspicion toward his recently deceased brother and his wife of thirty years. It was a sin, and to keep it at bay, he made it a habit to remind himself of its true nature several times an hour, steeling himself against temptation. Still, it crept into his mind. He would feel that someone was watching him, he would look up, and there it would be, the suspicion and the need to follow it, to find out, to bring it to its climax. At those times, it was precisely like the itch of sexual desire, the tug of lust. And he would bend his mind to some other thing and wait for it to loosen.

A week passed in this manner and by its end he was adept at deflecting his suspicion. Preparations for Christmas were massing all around him, and one day—happily befogged in the garlands and polystyrene candy canes hung over the streets, the clacking bells of Salvation Army Santas, the shoppers thronging the pavement like schools of fish, the glassy, attenuated chords of the city hall carillon—he realized it must be gone. But it had only moved, taking up a post adjacent to, rather than inside, his mind. It was now a hound sleeping by his threshold, its chest rising and collapsing slowly as it chased hares in its dreams, and Richard noticed it from the corner of his eye; after some days, he knelt down and scratched its ropy, fretful head. Then, one day not long after that, the hound stood, shook itself, walked a few steps, and looked back at Richard, as if to say, "Are you coming?" And Richard followed.

Richard unlocked the door of James's apartment. The movers were coming tomorrow. Whatever Richard deemed worth keeping would be taken to his and Sarah's house, and the remainder hauled to the St. Vincent de Paul rummage store. The air in the hall was hot and parched. Mrs. Clay had finished boxing up James's things. There were only two boxes Richard wanted to keep, one of framed photographs and another of trophies. He carried them into the second bedroom and set them back on top of the desk. Then he went back into the hall and gathered up James's guns, a deer rifle and a shotgun, and laid them on the desktop and pulled the rolltop down over them. He sat down in James's chair. His hand went to the middle right-hand drawer. The envelope of pornographic pictures lay on top. He placed it gingerly in his lap, and pulled a bundle of letters from the back of the drawer.

The letters went back more than thirty years. There were letters to James at his boarding school, addressed in steel pen by his mother, and letters from Richard himself, sent from France with the censor's franking stamp on the front. Thereafter there were ten or twelve letters per year, the handwriting of James's correspondents increasingly less recognizable, less formal, more backhanded. Sometimes the letters were filleted tidily across the top with a letter opener, sometimes torn open at the side, leaving a ragged laceration, the back flap hanging limply, crusted with glue and violet postmark ink. They smelled of dank, empty rooms, of peeling wallpaper.

The most recent were at the front. They seemed to consist entirely of invitations and social announcements: weddings, births, anniversaries, appointments. There was also a light blue envelope, engraved on the back with the address "655 Furness Ave., St. Paul 5, Minnesota." On the front was James's name in Sarah's handwriting and a postmark of September 26 of the current year. Richard sat bolt upright. The envelope of photographs slid off his lap and skidded under the desk. He quickly thrust the letters back into the drawer, his heart unmoored and battering against his sternum, his hands shaking like a thief's.

IN THE MORNING, THE SKY SHONE THROUGH THE BEDROOM window, bone white. A man entered, followed by two men in overalls. He pointed to the desk.

"Put the desk, the chair, and the boxes on top in the van first. Everything else goes to St. Vincent de Paul. This stuff goes to the address on Furness." One of the men in overalls picked up the two boxes and set them on the floor. "Let's get this first," he said to the other, indicating the desk. It was too heavy. They got a third man, who was toting boxes from the kitchen. The three of them managed to lift it. After ten minutes, the two returned. One noticed a large manila envelope on the floor, a nimbus of lint and dust hooked on its corner. "What do I do with this?" he asked the other. "Put it in one of the boxes," the other replied. He opened the one closest to him and pushed it in among the trophies. "Guess this guy was some kind of champ," he said, and folded the carton shut.

CHARLES TURNED UP UNANNOUNCED ONE AFTERNOON AT Anna's door two weeks before Christmas. "Charles!" Anna exclaimed, and her face bloomed in delight. He smiled tightly, as though barely restraining laughter, as though very pleased with himself.

"I have a little pre-Christmas Christmas present for you and Douglas." He gestured toward the street. "It's in the car. If you would just hold the door open for me, I'll bring it in *toute suite.*"

Charles went back down the walk and opened the trunk of his car. He lifted out a large cardboard box and carried it back up the walk and into the living room, where he put it down. He was a little winded. He pulled the top open and removed some packing material.

"Prepare to enter the atomic age," he said dramatically, and lifted out a gray oblong box which he hefted on top a side table.

"A television set," Anna said, awestruck. "Oh, Charles, Charles, Charles," she repeated, her voice tapering away. She threw her arms around his shoulders. "You're too good. You shouldn't treat me so well." She called out, "Dougie, we have a television!"

"It's the latest model," Charles said. "Ten-inch screen. The sound is tuned in automatically with the picture. It's got a very bright picture. You can watch it in daylight without having to pull the shades."

Douglas scuttled over to them and regarded the television set. He looked puzzled. There was a shiny piece of glass in the front, a dark gray-green color. He put his palm on it. "Oh, Dougie, don't touch," Anna cried. He pulled his hand away, as though the glass were hot.

"Let's fire it up," Charles said jovially. He unraveled the cord and plugged it into the wall. He rotated a knob. There was a sound, like an exhalation or a scarcely audible whoop, and a little white dot appeared in the center of the screen. Bands of light spread outward from it, twisting like kelp on the sea. Then the picture steadied. The glass was full of gray confetti, and the set buzzed and crackled as though it were on fire or the wind was pouring through it.

Charles turned another knob a few more times. The screen cleared, and there, like a photograph, was an image. It had bars on the sides in diminishing tones of gray, and in the center there was a set of rings like a bull's-eye. A shrill, steady tone issued from the set. Douglas covered his left ear with one hand, and reached toward the glass again with his other, his fingers a hair's width from the image. "Don't touch," Anna cautioned again.

"There aren't any programs until about five o'clock, I think. But there it is," Charles said.

"Oh, darling, it's just wonderful. You'll come back tonight?"

"After dinner. But I've got to go back to work for a few hours."

"Don't keep me waiting." She pressed up against his side, stood up on her toes, and kissed him on the cheek. She turned to Douglas and nodded. "Say good-bye to Charles. And thank him." Douglas gazed at the screen silently, his lips a little apart, his own visage dimly reflected on the glass, a cloud on water. Anna shrugged her shoulders and saw Charles out.

Later, close to dinnertime, there were shows to watch, one at number 4 on the knob, and another at number 5. Anna chose number 4. And there, like a movie, but gray and languid, like the play of shadows and moonlight, was Arthur Godfrey. He sat at a desk with a big microphone. Anna had seen his photograph dozens of times and watched him on newsreels. But here, in the glass, he was eerily close and yet at a great remove, as though an inch away but only half-present, like a ghost floating before her. His voice was still deep and warm as it was on the radio, like a milky mug of strong tea, but it seemed farther away than his face.

There was a tap on the door, and it opened. "Anna, precious?" It was Richard. He noticed the lights were out. "Daddy, come in! Look what Charles brought us!" Richard sidled up to Anna and hugged her around the waist. "Good Lord!" he said.

"Isn't it fabulous?" Anna said.

"Oh Lord, yes. Did he buy this for you?"

"For Christmas."

"You know these things cost two hundred fifty dollars or so?" Richard said, his voice a little concerned.

"That much?" Anna paused. "Well, he is a wonderful man. Sometimes I think I'm too lucky. To have met him, I mean. With all the people in the world, and all the ones that are wrong for each other. And here I am with Charles, just by luck or fate. To think we found each other. It's like being struck by lightning."

Richard thought to utter some words of caution at this point, but squelched the urge. He looked at Arthur Godfrey, who was talking to a professorial man in a tweed suit, although everything on the screen looked like tweed to a certain extent. A skein of smoke rose from the cigarette in Godfrey's ashtray. The man was explaining something about solar systems and suns.

"They both look a little . . . pale and wan," Richard commented. Anna said nothing. The man droned on about light-years. Douglas shuffled over to the side of the television set. There was a panel of tiny holes, and orange light glowed inside.

Godfrey had turned away from the man, apparently addressing the studio audience. He glowered, his affability momentarily snuffed out. "If we can't offer our guests a quiet, respectful hearing, we can't continue having an audience here." He turned back to the man.

Richard said, "Seems like they were getting a little restless." He tugged at his hat. "Well, I have to go, you two. Just looked in to see how you two are. Will we see you at church?"

"Oh, I'm sure," Anna said, a little distractedly. He kissed her and knelt to give Douglas a squeeze. "Bye, kids," he said and let himself out.

"Love you, Daddy," Anna called after him. As he was getting in his car, he could see the gray light of the television shifting in shade and intensity through the window, flashing and darkening, as though there were an electrical storm inside the house.

ANNA DID NOT COME TO CHURCH THAT SUNDAY. THE PRIEST read the Gospel: "And there shall be signs in the sun, and in the moon, and in the stars; and upon the earth distress of nations, with perplexity; the sea and the waves roaring; men's hearts failing them for fear . . . " The words slid in and out of Richard's hearing like a fish dancing on a line. Perhaps they were too abstracted, unmoored from their meaning by repetition, by the fifty times they had been uttered on this very Sunday in every year of Richard's life. Or too banal, like the natterings of an old bore; the utterance might be true, but after being beaten and stretched to near transparency by interminable tellings, who cared?

The priest continued to read: "And when these things begin to come to pass, then look up, and lift up your heads; for your redemption draweth nigh." Richard did not look up. His eyes were fixed on the ground, on his black shoes, on the dusky red cloth of the kneeler, the bronze paint on the hot-water pipe running under the pew.

It had been a week since he had pursued his suspicion to James's apartment. Now it pursued him, and it would not relent. It followed him, dogged him, it was behind him every minute, and the only remedy in his power was to look straight ahead and pretend it wasn't there. But he knew that it was there, so the remedy was a lie. And every alternative to the evil that pursued him was another evil: He was not going to confront Sarah; he was not going to interrogate her; he was not going to read the letter she had sent James. Nor was he going to scour James's life, unearth its falsities and betrayals, exhume his brother's month-dead corpse and animate it, set it walking among the living to haunt them all. He had no choice but to bear his affliction without complaint or comment. He was a patient and unostentatious man. Sarah would know nothing.

The priest said, "Glory be to Thee, O Lord." Richard found himself standing. The priest led the congregation in saying the creed. Richard had heard it at least two thousand times. He had been made to commit it to memory when he was twelve. Perhaps when he rowed James in the little boat on White Bear Lake, he had been practicing; his shoulders stretching, the oarlocks yawning. "And of all things visible and invisible." A stroke. A verse. "Light of Light, Very God of Very God." A push, a pull, the keel cleaving the surface of the lake. "And was made man." James in the bow with his fingers lightly trolling the water.

Richard mouthed the words. They formed awkwardly, unwillingly, consonants swallowed, vowels unformed, as though his lips were cold or swollen or his tongue was stuck just behind them like a lozenge of wax. It was not mumbling or muttering or recitation by rote. It was like the speech of the dead, coerced, unconvinced, indiscernible, an empty hum beneath the world.

THE NEXT DAY, SARAH WENT DOWN TO THE BASEMENT TO bring up the Christmas tree ornaments. She clicked on the light at the head of the stair and her feet clunked down the steps. The furnace sighed. Its pipes and ducts spread outward like a banyan tree. Sarah had to squeeze by James's desk to reach the ornaments, which were in a box on a shelf mounted above the sink and the wringer washing machine. A finger of cold from under the door to the backyard touched her ankles.

She lifted down the box. The ornaments rustled inside it like the insides of an electric lightbulb. She set the box down to dust off her hands. She saw a carton on top of the desk. She pulled the flaps asunder and the cardboard squeaked and rasped. Inside, there were trophies and a manila envelope.

Sarah picked up one of the trophies. It was shaped like an

inverted bell or an udder, the metal of an unidentifiable species, tarnished like an ancient mirror with flecks of black and brown. It was engraved "Junior Varsity Lawn Tennis 1919 James Wright MacEwan." Another was shaped like a horn, a long cone supported by miniature gold clubs on either side. There was a third, like a Norseman's helmet with crossed rifles emblazoned on it. There were more, and they were dusty and smelled of the tang of corrosion. These things constituted James's memorial, the residue of his life as a man: monuments to games played as a child. The rest was intangible, amorphous, easily forgotten.

Sarah unwound the thread around the clasp of the envelope and pulled out the contents. She gasped, and then as she took in the details of the photographs—the lolling tongues thrust from pouting lips, the absurdly uprolled eyes, the cheesy baroque contortions of legs and arms, the grimaces and she-wolf snarls, the sheer fakery of it all—she felt she must be suppressing a giggle. She could not hope to penetrate the minds of the women who had posed for these photographs, but she was utterly confident in her belief that no woman would make these faces except under male stage direction. This was not a record of transports of sexual ecstasy, but of women humoring boys, of condescension, of coercion at worst. It was pathetic.

And then, as she clasped the pictures—pinned them between her manicured red thumbnail and the tidy crescent of her fingers—and slid them back into the envelope, she thought that it was rather touching. For when men combed their imaginations, gathering kindling to fuel their desire, this was what they retrieved: tigresses, vixens, witches, damsels, and schoolgirls, a costume party, a circus parade. It was not enough to feel the hunger and to sate it. It had to be dressed up and made to march in a pageant, just as when men played games together they felt the need to exchange boons and toy cups and flagons, as though they were knights or warriors or the gods on Olympus.

Curiously, it was the man among men, James—outwardly the most sophisticated, polished, and unflappable of his set—to whom these things belonged, who had guarded these trophies and surveyed these images, numbering his triumphs, clutching his erection like a spear. This assumed that the photographs in fact were his—that Richard had not hidden his own pornography among his brother's things. But that was unimaginable: Richard might find these photographs arousing, might wish he had some like them, but would be ashamed to act on the feeling. And in that, she thought, Richard, too, was a man among men, yet better than most men.

Sarah and her most intimate friends had spent the last thirty years of their lives trying to comprehend what it was men were about; what and who these most unrevealing creatures—for whom the highest virtues seemed to be egoism and self-denial—were underneath the camouflage; what they saw, and, most puzzling of all to Sarah and her cohorts, what they wanted. Of course, inside the man was a boy. It went without saying. What complicated matters were the urges the trophies and photographs bespoke: the craving for artifice, for fantasy, for mythic narratives to dress up banalities. James had in fact been a boy among boys, but a master at disguising it, a master artificer. That in turn made him a man among men. Men gave him trophies; women lent him their bodies, posed for him and with him in whatever fashions he might wish to imagine.

She lifted the box of ornaments and carried it before her at her waist, like a pregnancy. Richard had bought the tree yesterday and set it up in the living room to the right of the fireplace. Afterward, when she had held him, he smelled of pine and melting snow. She had insisted he kiss her under the mistletoe in the foyer, and he had complied sweetly, good-humoredly, but as though he were somehow absent or afraid.

CHARLES WAS WALKING DOWN ST. PETER STREET DOWNTOWN and he thought he could hear bells in the distance. It was five o'clock in the afternoon, pitch dark, a week before Christmas, and the air was crisp as cellophane. There was a crèche set up in a drugstore window, and it made him think of the manger they had at home when he was a boy and of setting the figures inside it like chess pieces; of pulling back the flaps each day on the Advent calendar, opening another door or gate or pair of shutters, from the first lamb to the shepherd to the baby himself on Christmas Eve.

When Charles was a boy, after church and Sunday school and lunch, his father would work in the yard, cutting the grass or raking leaves or shoveling snow, depending on the season. Charles would help him as best he could, dumping armfuls of leaves into the bushel basket and helping tow the baskets over to the edge of the woods, near the rock pile, where there were supposed to be copperheads. But mostly he just followed his father and asked him questions such as "What are you doing?" and, when his father told him, "Why?" And his father would say he was raking or shoveling and that he was doing it because if he didn't do it they'd be up to their knees in leaves or clippings or weeds or snow—because, therefore, it must be done.

Even after Charles knew what his father would say, he still went on asking. Because the chores were repetitive—undertaken every weekend, every season, every year, seemingly endless and pointless, their value apparent only through faith—so were the questions. And the questions, too, were in truth futile, yielding only another repetition of the naming of things and motions: leaves and snow, raking and shoveling, necessity.

Maybe what Charles was seeking were parables. Maybe he was asking, "Why is the world as it is?" or "Father, how shall I be a good man?" and his father was replying, "I don't know. Watch me labor." In fact, sometimes Charles would be puzzled by something he'd heard at Sunday school. One Sunday in December, when his father was clearing the snow from around the door of the well house, he said, "Daddy, if God was really Jesus' father, what was Joseph? I mean, was he Jesus' father too or was he something else? Was he still Mary's husband?"

His father stopped his shoveling and looked up. He shook his head silently, as if annoyed, and then as if he were genuinely puzzled himself. Water was dripping over the eaves of the well house and running down icicles, plopping in the snow, and there was an explosive chittering of birds in the woods. Then his father said, "I'm not sure. I guess he was Mary's husband, but he was Jesus' step-father, or maybe foster father. Foster father, that's probably closer—like orphans have. Jesus wasn't his son but he raised him like his own son. It's complicated, isn't it?"

Charles said, "But what was Joseph supposed to do, if he was just a foster father—if Jesus' own father wasn't looking after him? If Mary was really married to God, not to him?"

"Same as any father, I guess. Put bread on the table, do what needs to be done. Accept it." Charles's father went back to his shoveling, back to the futility of labor in a world determined to unravel itself every winter, to tilling the barren ground, where all men at all times and in all places bear their lot.

Charles was looking at the crèche in the drugstore window thinking about that day, or the residue of it that lingered in his mind. He saw Joseph, standing just above and to the left of Mary and the cradle, not very much closer to Jesus than the kings and the shepherds. And he remembered how when he was a boy, he would put Joseph in last, feet first into the manger, carefully setting him down a little distance from the other figures, wondering where he belonged and leaving him, for all appearances, lost in his bewildered fatherhood, himself a little orphaned by his orphan son.

THREE NIGHTS BEFORE CHRISTMAS, RICHARD AND SARAH DANCED at the club ball. The band played "Rudolph the Red-Nosed Reindeer" and "Some Enchanted Evening." Richard held Sarah's waist and her bare shoulder. He listened to her amiably. They turned in slow circles. Sarah appraised the dresses and hair of the other women.

Anna and Charles spun by and returned. Anna flung her head back and shook her hair. "Isn't this swell?" she beamed. Richard called to Charles, "Why don't we switch for a dance? All right with you ladies?" They nodded, Anna more eagerly than her mother. Sarah had resigned herself to Anna and Charles's appearing here

55

as a couple. Whether her dancing with Charles would defuse or encourage speculation among the other guests about his and Anna's situation, Sarah could not say.

"You will give him back, Mother?" Anna said.

"Only with great reluctance, I'm sure."

Charles took Sarah's shoulder and arm tentatively, only his fingertips touching her.

Sarah began dutifully, "I'm so pleased Anna has stopped hiding you from us. Richard and I have been dying to get to know you. Anna speaks of you so highly." She imagined she could speak these lines while undergoing oral surgery.

"Well, Anna has told me how much you two mean to her. To judge from what she's said, she has a wonderful family. And a charming and attractive mother."

"I can see we're going to get along very well," Sarah said a little mockingly. They both laughed, and his hands settled a little on her body, and they danced less awkwardly. They talked idly. He spoke about his work. She nodded. He was not dull. He did not drone. He looked at her when he spoke. He was attractive in a bland way. His eyes were gray and serious. They did not seem to conceal anything, but neither did they know anything. They were round, amenable to amazement if pressed. A few tiny lines radiated from their corners. He wore a boutonniere with silly little plastic bells. He was not, Sarah saw, anyone other than what he appeared to be, but who exactly that was he would be the last to know. He was a young man, willing, well-meaning, a little adrift. He made her feel a bit old. She looked at her hand, ungloved and perched on his shoulder. It was faintly spotted, a sleeping fawn.

Three yards away, Anna pressed her head against her father's lapel for a moment and Richard stroked her hair once. She looked up and nudged the two of them toward the edge of the room. "Do you think they're getting along? Do you think she'll approve? Will he pass the test?"

"Oh, I'm sure, precious. Your mother means well, you know. She's very wise about these things—about men and girls."

"I wish she'd admit for once that I might be too."

"That would be contrary to her nature. It doesn't mean she doesn't respect your choices."

"She'd just rather make them for me." Anna laughed. "We're going to be very happy together, you know. All of us." And they danced back out to the center of the floor.

ON CHRISTMAS EVE, MRS. CLAY—SARAH'S CLEANER, WHO HAD packed and boxed James's shirts, pants, ties, handkerchiefs, sweaters, socks, and underwear—tended Douglas while the MacEwans were at church. Late in the evening Douglas awoke and cried, and Mrs. Clay climbed the stairs slowly in her heavy black shoes to quiet him. She picked him up, held him, dandled him on her knee. She sang "Sweet Little Jesus Boy" to him and when he was still, she laid him down again and tidied his blankets. She climbed slowly back down the stairs. Alone, Douglas breathed steadily and slept on, a ship crossing the sea in the night. There was a light on in the hall at the top of the stairs. Outside, orphaned flakes of ice and snow fell now and then out of the clear, blue-black sky, like shavings from the moon.

In the church, Sarah, Richard, and Anna sat in their pew, three rows from the front on the pulpit side of the aisle. Just in front of them, all the candles in the advent wreath were lit and burning. When the choir began to sing "O Lamb of God, Who Takest Away the Sins of the World" they rose together and walked to the Communion rail. They kneeled in a row and waited.

The priest came by, pressing a wafer into each of their cupped palms. He said, "The Body of our Lord Jesus Christ, which was given for thee, preserve thy body and soul unto everlasting life. Take and eat this in remembrance that Christ died for thee, and feed on Him in thy heart by faith, with thanksgiving." He said a piece of this phrase over each of them as he passed by, in a voice just above a whisper, as though he were telling them a secret that could be comprehended only if they sat down together and compared the parts each of them had been given. He repeated the phrase again and again as he moved down the line of communicants at the rail, and his voice drifted away like a stream of southbound geese.

The MacEwans stood up and returned to their pew. Had they believed what the priest said? Had they thought about it and given their assent? Had they prepared themselves sufficiently in heart and mind to participate by right in a sacrament? No, no more than does an infant when it takes the breast. And when they sat down, they daydreamed. It took fifteen minutes or more to administer the Eucharist to the whole congregation. The choir sang "In the Bleak Midwinter," and it seemed as though they sang it again and again, like a record going round on itself.

Sarah saw herself in a carriage. She was thirteen. She wore a fur-lined bonnet and a muff to match, a russet coat and black lace-up boots. She held in her lap a carpetbag, red and brown and purple as eggplant. Her father was taking her to the station. The bells on the horse rang brightly, like shattering ice. She was going on the train to Minnesota, to stay with her cousins for Christmas. Her father sat next to her while the driver drove. He threaded his away among the cars and other carriages, through slush in the streets. Her father smelled of tobacco, of things that were dark like animals in their dens. His hair and clothes shone rich as a beaver pelt. His laugh came from deep inside him, as if from a room beamed and paneled in oak.

In the station there were bells ringing and whistles blowing and a roar of voices. He led her down through passages and tunnels into the dark and onto the platform, where the train huffed and steamed like a bull. He was holding her hand and he led her into the railroad car. The light was gold and the seats were green velvet. "This is your seat and this is your ticket." He handed her an envelope with her name, in his handsome copperplate writing, on it. He sat with her for five minutes until it was time for the train to leave. He told her how much fun she would have. He told her how pretty she was, that she was a princess the likes of which people in Minnesota had never seen.

The train bolted north and west through the fields of corn stubble and the kerosene-lit towns, bellowing, steam running off its back. She might have been Persephone, being sent away for the winter, parted from her parents, sacrificed. But she had a delightful Christmas, and for the first time she met Richard MacEwan, only a little older than she and shy and awkward as a calf, and his little brother, James, already beautiful with the cool brown eyes of a hunter. She came to this church for Christmas Eve for the very first time. And six years later she would give herself to Richard entirely, become the queen of his kingdom. She would live in his place all the year round and they would pass every Christmas Eve here, and all the Sundays thereafter until Easter, from the Christ-child's nativity until it was time for him to die. They would do that until one of them could do it no more, until their own death, and now she reached her gloved hand over Richard's hand and wondered if she could bear it if he was the first and left her here alone.

Richard was thinking about France, about Christmas in 1917. They didn't have Christmas trees. He was stationed at a dressing station in a village called Glorieux near Verdun. The chaplain of the French regiment there spoke English and they argued about the relative merits of Catholicism and Protestantism. They argued about faith and works and doctrine, and the priest would ask him, as though to clinch the debate, wasn't it enough that God became man and sacrificed himself; wasn't that enough? Surely all the Bible reading in the world couldn't add anything to the sufficiency of that act? Wasn't the sacrifice enough, for all time, for all people? Richard couldn't answer that. He was eighteen years old.

The French stood in their churches on Christmas Eve and held candles and prayed to Mary and her baby. They held their candles and their beads like children clutching sweets. Their priests spoke to God in the language of Caesar and Virgil. The priest blessed them and told them to rejoice. They went home and drank to the baby's health with brandy and hot wine. In the dressing station, there were a few new casualties, their flesh opened, incarnadine under the incandescent lamps. Some had been hit randomly, by accident, and some drew fire upon themselves. They deliberately climbed up out of the trenches and walked into no-man's land. It was called "going over the top," the suicide of the insane, the despondent, the guilt-ridden, and the naive, who imagined that if they sacrificed themselves, it might somehow bring the war to an end. But that was absurd: There would never be enough casualties, no death could ever be sufficient.

Richard thought of the frozen mud, of the denuded fields and copses of trees, of the barbed wire. Then he thought of James in Finlay, North Dakota. James had been out of sight of the others when he died. No one saw how it happened. Perhaps his death had been something less than an accident. He could have tripped the trigger by chance or by plan. There was no way of knowing. Perhaps there was something he was ashamed of. Perhaps there was something troubling him for which death was the only remedy, the only propitiation. Richard added this thought to the other such thoughts he bore everywhere with him, the unthinkable things that knew no limit, that accreted like snow in the night.

Anna sat next to her father and heard the choir singing "In the Bleak Midwinter." It was sad and it went around and around. She thought of herself skating. From the time she was twelve until she was sixteen, she had skated almost every winter day after school. She skated long after the other girls had gone home, long after the shadows were loosed into dusk and the cold settled on the rink like rising water. She skated in amorphous circles as though she were tethered to the center of the ice, and sometimes she let the rope go slack and sometimes it stretched taut and she went around, her hands locked together behind her back. Then she would look up and there would stand her father in a heavy gray coat by the edge of the ice, under the crabbed, naked elms and the moon tawny as an onion. His car purred behind him and its headlights glowed. He would tell her it was time to come home.

Then one day, a few years later, she stopped skating and started seeing Carl Farnham after school. It was as though her father had called her from her skating, and she scarcely ever went back. But Anna could remember how it felt to skate, the music in her legs and the going round, and how it felt to be called, even now, even as all women may be called as Mary was called; to bear this night He who would bear away the sins of the world. And even now Charles Norden's child slept inside Anna's body.

III

January

ON THE FIRST DAY OF THE NEW YEAR—THE FIRST DAY, IN fact, of the new decade, of the second half of the century—Anna woke before dawn. She lay in her bed on her back, her eyes raking the ceiling. Sleep was far away, out of reach. She sat up and threaded her arms into a flannel robe, and walked down the hall into the living room.

Anna sat down by the window in an oversize armchair, upholstered in a pale green fabric. She tucked her legs under her, drew a cigarette from a pack on the side table, and lit it. She blew the smoke out as though in an enormous sigh and looked out the window. The sky was black, tending to blue at the edges, the morning implicit.

The moon was low and full and round like a pearl, steely above the vapors condensing in the frozen air. She felt the moon pull at her, tugging her stomach up through her throat and into her mouth. She realized she was nauseous, and quickly tamped the cigarette out. The nausea fell away and then returned, like a boat bobbing in and out of view among the swells at sea. Dread formed in the corners of her eyes and pushed her breathing into a narrow quadrant around her heart. Then a car drove by, its headlights sweeping the living room ceiling like a lighthouse beam, and she felt quiet again. Her period was two weeks late. That was what she was working at forgetting.

Anna pressed her face into the back of the chair. She thought she could smell Jack there. Jack was her ex-husband, the father of Douglas. When they'd separated he'd moved to California. He took his clothes, his ice bucket, and his Zippo lighter with his squadron's insignia engraved in it. In a kitchen drawer among the nails and clothespins and picture wire there were some service ribbons and a roll of the mints he liked to chew. That was all that was left of Jack but this chair, where he'd sit every day at five-thirty and read his paper and sip his drink and clean his pipe when they were content together.

In high school, Anna hadn't really known Jack, although she had seen him around town. He was good-looking and unexceptional, a solid B-student and a second-stringer on several varsity teams. His family was well-to-do but not very sociable, and Jack himself was a little shy. He wasn't sad or lacking in self-confidence, but he kept himself at the edges of things. He was affable and tidy and strove to be easygoing.

Anna might have gone out with him when she was a teenager or during her first couple of college vacations, but there was always someone else and no particular reason for her to notice him or for him to notice her. Then the war came and it seemed as though all the boys in town were gone, had disappeared into the night like children kidnapped from their beds. For the duration of the war the government ordered the clocks set ahead one hour, but they might as well have been set ahead three or four years. When the men—for now they were men—came back they were not strangers, but they were not the same people. They'd learned to drink and to josh and joke about death and fan away worry with the service caps they clutched in their hands. They'd seen unspeakable things and learned not to speak of them.

When they again met up with the girls—for the girls somehow seemed to have remained girls—it was in hotel ballrooms and bars, but it could have been the senior prom. They approached each other awkwardly, as if crossing the floor to ask someone to dance for the very first time. Whatever they would have learned about love and the opposite sex during the years the war took them away was lost to them. Now they were twenty-one, twenty-two, twenty-three and -five. They were supposed to be getting married and starting families.

Anna first noticed Jack in the mirror at Trapp's Tavern on Grand Avenue. She was sitting at the bar with Alice Mercer blowing smoke out her nose and tipping her head down, secreting herself intriguingly under her bangs. Jack was standing with four other men, mostly in uniform, and Anna saw him reflected among the bottles ranged behind the bartender. She saw his hair, which shone like brass and leather. He saw her mouth and her lips, red and glossy as Chinese lacquer, and her breasts beneath her sweater. He bought her a drink, a brandy alexander, and then he asked her out. She could not remember much about their first date. She thought they saw *The Blue Dahlia* at the Orpheum. Six months later he asked her to marry him and three months after that they were husband and wife, living in this very house.

Not much more than a year after that, Douglas was born. Then they were happy and then they were not. It was as though they had turned away for a moment and when they turned back, their love had wandered away like a toddler in a train station, lost in the crowd. They searched frantically and after a while they had to admit it was gone and it was not coming back. Jack got up from his chair and left, and now it hardly seemed to matter.

How could this be? It was not so very difficult to explain, not if you are Anna, curled up before this window that stood between her and the icy dawn. Jack asked her and she said yes because it was time to say yes. She liked to touch him and to be touched by him. He had all the requisites. She must have loved him, although she could not now clearly recall how it had felt. Relief, perhaps. Like the easing of a tight shoe, the setting down of a burden, the end of what had once seemed a free and forward motion but had come to feel like a hiatus, an endless waiting. When he asked and when she said yes, life could move on again, the page could be turned to the next chapter, the one with the house, the apron, the automobile trips, the dinner parties, the children.

Now Anna was waiting again and nausea fluttered in the top of her gullet. The world slept, denying its cares. And then, in the minutes before the dawn of New Year's Day, the night ebbed away like a flood of ice water and every sound and sensation would be an ache, an intrusion on bodies already sore and parched and shamed from too much drink and liberty. Rolled morning papers would pummel porches and stoops and the day demand to be recognized. Children would throw back their covers, seize the morning like a lemon drop, and let it pucker their mouths into anticipation. They knew nothing of the time before dawn. It could have been somewhere on the other side of the moon.

Anna could not recall having ever been awake in those hours until she was seventeen or eighteen and stayed out late with Carl Farnham and some friends after a dance. They tended the night like a fire. They watched the sun boil up out of the horizon for the first time in their lives and went home to their beds, initiated, triumphant, cocky as tightrope walkers. But now, an older Anna had discovered, that time belonged to the sick and the sleepless, the fretful, the guilty, the fearful, the despairing and despondent. If you could go back to bed while it was still dark and sleep past the dawn, you could pretend your sleeplessness had been a dream. But if you were caught awake in the end of the night, if you saw the sunrise begin to color the horizon like smoke, it was as though you were marked; as though Charon had you in his boat, had pushed off into his river of bile and was rowing you to the land of the dead.

Anna thought she saw something, ring-tailed and masked like a raccoon, in the shrubs beneath the window, scuttling into the shadow of the house amid the rising of the light. Then the sun was on the snow, the compacted drifts and ice shone like gems, and she heard Douglas singing to himself in his crib, waiting for the day to take flight.

———

CHARLES SAT AT HIS DINING TABLE. THERE WAS AN ACHE, LESS A pain than a heavy shadow, behind his left ear. He drank from a glass of orange juice. It was thin, tepid, and metallic, sour enough to sate a car battery. He drank it like a penance. Last night he and Anna had had drinks and dinner, more drinks at the club, and finished up at a party in Minneapolis whose location he was still attempting to recall. Anna had been restrained in her drinking. He had not.

The letter Charles had received yesterday lay on the table half unfolded, like a crab on its back. He picked it up and read.

IN RE JOAN EVANS NORDEN, PLAINTIFF, V. CHARLES EVERETT NORDEN, DEFENDANT

Dear Chuck,

Further to our telephone conversation, I want to confirm that the judge is prepared to settle this matter on Wednesday next week and approve the final decree.

Joan has agreed to change the cause to irreconcilable differences, and acknowledges that the original cause of mental cruelty was without foundation. Alimony is to be set at $250 per month and is payable until Joan's remarriage or death.

I realize this is not everything you could have hoped for in bringing the matter to a conclusion. No doubt the law remains an ass in this particular. The important thing is that as of next week, you will be able to get on with your life.

Let me know if there's anything else I can do, and of course I'll be talking with you next week in any case.

Very sincerely yours,
Randolph Tyrell
of Wyndham, Farrell & Hart

It was not a consolation nor had Charles ever expected it to be. But he imagined there would be a clean break, a sense of the end of one thing and the commencement of another. Instead, he saw that he and Joan would go on together forever, that what they had been would shadow each of their lives until its end, like the tin cans and confetti tied to the back bumper of a honeymooner's car. The priest had the last laugh: only death, indeed, would part them. Or would it? Love, or the husk of it, might be as immortal as the soul.

Charles did not so much think these things as feel them as a kind of weight, a leaden, downward pressure merging with his hangover, a dumbwaiter slowly carrying the ashes in his mouth down to the dank pit of his stomach. He took another swallow of juice and looked out through the picture window in the living room wall. From here to the horizon there was nothing but undulations of land sheathed in snow, naked trees set apart like desert hermits, twisting shafts of smoke and vapor, light like a blade of sharp, clear glass. He had come here when he separated from Joan and he had felt like a homesteader on the high plains, exposed, thrown entirely onto his own resources, alone with his dog, and utterly free. That had seemed the important part—to be loosed from Joan and their house, its overheated rooms, its airless pessimism and despair. Yet when he and Joan had first gone there as newlyweds that house had been as imbued with possibility as this one.

Something had worked a transformation there, conjured a spell, poured a virus as invisible as radiation through the walls and infected them first with mutual lassitude, then fear, and finally contempt. One day he found himself wondering if Joan was still pretty. He came to believe she was not, and he started to look away when she spoke to him. And then he noticed she was doing the same thing, that she looked at him only obliquely, or not at all. They moved around the house in synchronized separation, never in the same room, as though tiles in one of those sliding puzzles whose pieces need to be arranged in order with only one empty space to spare. He thought it was Joan he wanted to get away from—from the burden of her, the torpor and parasitism of their relation—but after a while it seemed to be the house itself. When he moved out, he tossed his key through the mail slot like a stone into a river. Now he had a house of his own. It was lonely and perhaps it had no point, no justification—a ghost ship tacking into the wind, heading nowhere. Better that than a house haunted like the one he'd had with Joan. Beware of houses, of destinations.

Sometimes when Charles saw Anna's eyes, he could not distinguish the love in them from what he thought must be pity; or perhaps he more truly felt the pity in himself and it was with that feeling that he wanted to remain. He saw her body, imagined its rises and concavities, its gift of nothing more than the yielding of itself, and he wanted to yield himself to her. She would loosen her hair, unfasten her clothes, unfetter her breasts, part her limbs and retwine them round his, and there, bound with her in her flesh, he could lose himself. Love was taking pity and love was abandon, taking leave, taking faith in the belief that in binding was loosing and not loss. For what is there to do with love but take shelter in it and give love itself shelter, not carry it off to sea but give it a home, a house?

The notion seemed vastly preferable to his present situation. He touched his face, flyblown with a growth of beard. The sensation behind his ear had crept around the circumference of his skull to his brow and blossomed into a full-blown headache. His palate felt as though he had dined on six courses of failure. He wanted to be nursed; he wanted, it must follow, Anna. He would call her, ask her to come out with her wavy-haired boy and have lunch at his home. But then he thought again: Beware of houses.

IN JANUARY THE NOVELTY OF WINTER IS GONE. WHAT ONCE seemed a land frosted in bridal organdy turns gray as a flophouse bedsheet. The snowdrifts that were light and white and shiny— a spill of soap powder on the world's laundry room floor—are congealed and scabrous, sulfured with exhaust, road salt, dog urine. The earth awaits a new snowfall like a Saturday night bath and until then abides filth, gravity, decay, the abradings of clear wind and cold.

Richard had been waiting. He had always understood that perhaps the better part of life consists of biding time; that good times eventually follow bad, that patience is not just its own reward, but life's only true option. He was not quite sure that virtue inevitably triumphs, but he was sure that time heals all wounds, that the wheel will someday turn. This wasn't fortune or happenstance. There was an economy of exchange, a physics of action and reaction at work, and perhaps behind them, the hand of a merciful and just God. It was not a matter of luck, nor was it abstract or abstruse: Do your duty, put in your time without complaint, bear grief without self-pity and good fortune without pride and more often than not the world will smile on you. It was that simple. Richard's life was proof.

That belief had stood Richard in good stead thus far and he tried to keep it in mind at all times, like a framed photograph on his desk. But his dependence on it had grown less casual, less confident. In fact, of late—knowing the things he did, being unable to avoid thinking the things that followed from them—he clutched at it. It was his only hope: that time would prove there was no wound, or at least bind it, and feather the agony into an ache. Redemption would come slowly, like ice sheeting across a river night by night, unseen, while the whole world slept. Once Richard had believed such a thing must be a miracle, a transformation, but maybe it was nothing more than a different view of the same reality; maybe it was simply ceasing to care, the easing of pain, the shrug of oblivion.

On the first workday of the New Year, Richard went to his office. There was a man standing on a ladder in the hall changing lightbulbs. The partners had decided to replace all the fixtures with fluorescent lights, starting next month. There were ribbons of crepe paper stuffed into the wastebaskets and a wooden case of ginger ale and tonic and charged water empties by his secretary's desk. She hadn't come in yet.

In his office, Richard set his hat on top of a stack of Minnesota state code volumes on the credenza. He hung his gray wool coat on the hat rack and balled his gloves into the pockets. He sat down in his chair, picked up a stack of papers, and tapped it edgewise on the desktop glass. He was unsure who would be working today, but began to place the morning's telephone calls. He dialed and waited.

"Wyndham, Farrell & Hart," a woman's voice answered.

"Richard MacEwan for Mr. Tyrell, please."

"Just a moment." Richard looped a rubber band around his thumb and forefinger and flexed it.

After a time, a man came on the line. "Randy Tyrell, Richard. How goes it?"

"Not badly. And you?"

"Can't complain. Hard to get started after the holidays, but justice must grind on—better that than grind down, at least." Tyrell laughed throatily.

Richard wasn't sure he understood the joke but chuckled anyway and added, "Absolutely." He waited a beat. "Randy, I need the Bauer file back this week if you can manage." Franklin Bauer was a probate client of Richard's, but did his company business with Wyndham, Farrell & Hart.

"I don't see a problem. I need to get my girl to type a copy of the codicils. Send you your original and one of our carbons. That okay?"

"Excellent. I appreciate it."

"Oh, I gather one of my clients, Chuck Norden, is a friend of the family."

Richard hesitated. He'd never heard Charles referred to by that name before. "Yes, of my daughter, Anna. He's been her regular escort for some time."

"Well, as of the end of the week, he's a single man again. Decree nisi settled and all."

"Rancorous?" Richard asked cautiously.

"Not really. Wife's attorney put her up to suing on mental cruelty for leverage's sake. Nothing to it in reality. Mutual disaffection, no adultery that anyone's heard about. Alimony rather stiff, if not odious."

"How did he adjust to that?" Richard asked, a little more confident in his probing.

"Took it like a man. Do you know him at all?"

"Not really. We've seen him a few times with Anna. He's talked mostly to my wife." Richard waited for more.

"He's a brick, you know. Solid. Not one of the clubhouse types—keeps a bit to himself—but dependable, bright. Should be up for partner in the not distant future. He'll be wanting a suitable spouse, I'd wager. Anything in the cards with your Anna?"

"It's conceivable."

"I'd recommend him. Really. His marriage was just one of those things that didn't work out. He made a mistake, and that's all."

"I doubt my opinion will be solicited, but if asked I'll bear the endorsement in mind."

"It'd be a good match, I'd guess. And the law *will* out, Richard," Tyrell said, evidently pleased with himself.

Richard found the point of this last remark obscure, but sighed good humoredly, and added, "Definitely. Well, thank you, Randy. I look forward to seeing the file."

"On its way."

After he laid the telephone handset in its cradle, he paused for a moment. He was not sure of the value of Tyrell's good opinion, but it seemed to be part of a positive consensus about Charles Norden. Moreover, his legal status was no longer an issue. If Anna could be happy with him, Richard could be happy for her. And with that, Richard felt perhaps not optimism itself, but its precursor: the sense that good again might show its face in this world.

He saw how it might pass, the bargain he might be destined to participate in: A measure of his happiness—only the peace his heart had known for thirty years—yielded in exchange for Anna's, the scourge on him and Sarah recompensed through Charles and Anna. He would accept that. It was a duty rendered through loss, but it gave back something to take faith in, to believe in, to lose himself to.

ANNA HAD NOT SEEN CHARLES SINCE NEW YEAR'S EVE. HE HAD called the next day, said he would like to see her, but thought perhaps he ought to surrender to his hangover in solitude. Anna seemed to register disappointment on both her behalf and Douglas's but in truth she needed some time to think, though to what exact end she could not imagine. New Year's Day had been a Sunday and it had passed as other Sundays: coffee darkening in the percolator and the day drifting toward dusk like a leaf floating on a slough; Douglas slamming blocks together explosively and shrieking, running into the kitchen and circling Anna's legs like a planet in orbit as she stood at the sink, darting back to his toys, the incipient sounds of motors, propellers, and wheels buzzing on his lips though he could scarcely form a phrase.

She fed Douglas scrambled eggs at noon, and a half-hour later she made herself a grilled cheese sandwich. By one o'clock she wanted to call Charles, and she picked up the phone, felt the black Bakelite of the receiver against her lip—cold, the smell of old paper—and she put her finger to the dial as though trying on a ring. But what could she say and with what reason? She put the telephone down. She felt desperately lonely, and she thought she might cry. She sat on the red vinyl chair in the kitchen and smoked cigarette after cigarette, like a widow at her rosary.

At two o'clock she walked out into the living room and seized Douglas's hand and steered him toward his room. "We're going to Grandma and Grandpa's," she said. "Gramma and Grampa," he responded, half question, half affirmation, and, as the thought took hold of him, he squealed brightly. Anna drew his arms upward and he held them there while she pulled off his pajama top, and then she pressed him down on the rug on the floor and removed his bottoms and diaper, damp and heavy as bread dough. She mopped his loins with a washcloth, powdered him, and re-diapered him. "Now, Mr. Man, what shall we do with you?" He looked at her quizzically. She decided to dress him up: a white shirt with a Peter Pan collar, gray flannel shorts with navy blue suspenders, brown Stride Rites, shiny from the box with scarcely a rough spot on the soles.

They drove through the streets to her parents' house in the stark afternoon, the shadows like lances and pickets. Her mother answered the door. She seemed distracted, as though having been wakened in the middle of a dream. She scanned Anna's face and body mechanically, and then her eyes lit on Douglas and her expression melted into graciousness. "My, what a handsome young man you have as an escort today, my dear." She smelled of face powder and perfume, and Anna could hear logs snapping and sputtering in the fireplace.

"Look who's here," Sarah announced as they entered the living room. Richard stood a little stiffly and thrust out his arms, ambled toward Anna, and hugged her. He patted her back softly and whispered "Happy New Year" in her ear. Then he crouched down and took Douglas's limp hand and shook it. He cocked his head and said, "Many happy returns, sir." Douglas looked puzzled, and tentatively moved his arm from side to side. Sarah went to the kitchen and returned with a plate of Triscuits and Colby cheese. She pulled a drawer of mismatched playing cards, backgammon pieces, and dice from the desk and set it on the floor before Douglas. He sighed appreciatively. They all sat together by the fire for the next hour, quietly, speaking occasionally, as though slowly turning the leaves of a picture album and, as memory moved them to, remarking on one page or another.

"YOU CAN TELL THINGS ARE LESS THAN SWELL," ANNA TOLD Alice Mercer that Wednesday. Douglas sat on the floor with Alice's two-year-old, Linda, swiping at her Raggedy Ann. Linda's cheeks were beginning to color. "They're dab hands at all the social graces—especially Mother—and Daddy's always so sweet, but something's up."

"With your father?" Alice intercepted Linda's hand in the

middle of a swat aimed at Douglas. Linda's mouth shaped a fierce "no" that collapsed into an exasperated whine. Anna pulled Douglas toward her and his hand released the doll.

"No, with her. I'm sure. There's something she needs to tell him, something between the two of them."

"How old are they?"

"He was fifty last year. She's forty-nine, although that's top-secret."

"Do you think one of them might be, you know . . . " Alice hesitated, as though dangling a maraschino cherry over her mouth and debating whether to eat it.

"Fooling around?" Anna snorted, rather surprising herself. "Daddy wouldn't know how to *imagine* such a thing. Mother— Mother would probably like to, but she's got too much g.d. rectitude."

"Do you feel like you know them that well?"

"Everything and nothing. I mean, I haven't a clue what either of them thinks, but I always know what they'll *do*—how they'll react or behave."

"Maybe that's all anyone ever knows. When Roger and I got married, I thought I knew him as well as, well, as well as my own self. But when you're in love, you're so close that it feels like yourself and his self are all mixed up and you just mistake yourself for his self. All you really know is yourself." Alice stopped and shook her head. "Or whatever," she said, and giggled. "Anyway, I know *how* he *is*. I can depend on it."

"And would he ever—"

"Heavens no. The only thing he has eyes for other than me is his job. Up the career ladder. Like he's fighting the war all over again—beachhead by beachhead. And he loves Linda. And—" she paused conspiratorially "—just between you and me, I think there's another baby on the way." She stroked her stomach and smiled contentedly, as though she had come into money or was displaying her most attractive feature.

Anna tried to smile, to fashion a mien of delighted surprise, but she felt instead as though something had been taken from her. Her breath was in the roof of her mouth, but she managed to speak. "Are you sure?" she said with almost a gasp.

Alice appeared not to notice. "Oh, I'm weeks late. I see the doctor on Friday. But of course there's no mistaking how it feels, really, is there?"

Anna nodded and Alice continued. "But enough about me. What about you and Mr. Norden?"

"Oh, fine. His divorce came through. You should come look at the television set."

Alice was not diverted. "So if he's single, you two are free to go ahead and—"

"Oh, anything's possible. But we're not kids. There's no hurry. We could go on very nicely just as we've been." Anna reached into her purse and began to rustle her keys. She kneaded her gloves in her palm for a moment.

"Oh, we'd best be going," she said and began to gather up Douglas's things. She sat him on her lap and Alice came and kneeled before them, slipping on Douglas's boots while Anna pushed his arms into the sleeves of his jacket.

"You know," Alice said, "I really want it to work out for you this time, both Roger and I. I really do. You deserve it."

Anna smiled and rose, carrying Douglas. "You're very sweet," she said. When they reached the front door, Alice said, "Maybe this weekend, maybe you and Charles and me and Roger—"

"Oh, yes, maybe," Anna said, and opened the door, then turned back, wanting to say Alice's name and stop where she was; but she said, "We'll see," and then good-bye and walked, carrying Douglas, to her car.

SARAH LAY ON THE EXAMINING TABLE IN TED FIELDS'S OFFICE, A sheet draped over her, her legs in stirrups. Ted's head was hidden down near her feet, but his voice echoed up, deep and merry. "Any irregularities with your periods? Heavy flows? Spotting?"

"None that I've noticed," Sarah said, as though rather bored. Ted probed her again. She drew in her breath and then exhaled slowly.

"Well, I suspect you will soon, together with other assorted symptoms of the change of life. But then we can stop the internal exams, which I'm sure you won't mind."

"The cow, retired from the barn and put out to pasture."

"Cow? Never you, Sarah. At worst, a duchess retired to her country seat."

"A dowager cow, then," Sarah sighed. "And if you have finished your business down there, may I dress?"

"You may. Then we'll talk. I like a good talk with you, Sarah."

Fields pulled off his gloves and rinsed his hands in the basin. He shut the door behind him, and Sarah sat up on the examining table. The room was pale green, the floor gray-and-green linoleum. Her skin looked very white, marbled with fine blue veins, flecked with tiny moles and spots like barnacles, like rust and the brown mottling of a bird's egg. Not so long ago, she had the skin of a girl, unmarked as a fall of new snow. Now it had a grain, like planks of wood, and here and there knots and striations, whorls and splits. Her skin was fashioning itself into a coffin to hold her last remains.

She dressed, layering the garments in their proper order: the bra, the girdle, the garters and the stockings, and then the slip. A woman dresses as a knight does, donning the strata of armor, each piece an orison set against death; or as a priest robes himself before Mass, saying a prayer while he fastens buttons and cinctures, raises his arm and submits himself to surplice or chasuble, kisses the cross on the back of the stole's neck, as though bidding an infant good night. They put on robes of sacrifice, of battle and redemption.

It was like that for a woman, or so Sarah felt. She dressed as though preparing an offering that she hoped would be acceptable and sufficient. The answer to that question would only be found in the undressing, and, in that, the robing and disrobing were one thing. She put on her blouse. The cloth slid over her arms and rasped like leaves. She stepped into the skirt and buttoned on her jacket. She bent her legs and pushed on her shoes, fetched her hat and adjusted it in the mirror. She slipped on her gloves and clasped her purse to her side like a breviary. She was done.

She and Ted Fields smoked and laughed in his office. They were connoisseurs of irony, failure, and frailty in a city of the earnest. They knew that the flesh decays, the mind slips, the spirit flags, and that accident and coincidence are numberless. They were not cynics: This was how they loved the world, and through it they felt compassion for their fellows. They knew that love and death make fools of the strong and the rich and philosophers of the weak and the poor; that loss is as daily as bread; that happiness alights where it will; and that for all this, life is good.

Fields leaned back in his chair. His voice was deep, bemused, thick as caramel. He listened to Sarah's account of her mother's addled behavior, her incapacity to remember anything, how her apartment was a maelstrom of flying and weightless misplaced objects, words, and thoughts.

"After lunch, she can't remember if she's eaten. She calls a fork 'the thing you hoist the food with.' She can't find her glasses, her shoes, her *Reader's Digest*," Sarah said. "At the rate she's going, this year she'll be able to hide her own Easter eggs."

Fields laughed, and exhaled a jet of smoke. "But isn't it a blessing to be oblivious to it all, to see everything new like a child? I mean, suppose she could genuinely contemplate her life, her health, her future?"

"It's not a blessing to be around, and you should try spending an entire weekend with her. It's like supervising a decrepit toddler."

"No, it's no picnic, I'm sure."

"Mind you, I only see her two or three times a year—last fall, sometime later this spring, and so forth. We talk on the telephone once a week. It's always the same conversation. I imagine I could read or balance the checkbook while she drones on."

"And what of the rest of the family? I imagine I'll be seeing husband and daughter for checkups shortly, but your version of things is so much more . . . piquant."

"Morbid, you mean, Ted—perfect for the pathologist in you. Anna is seeing a lawyer named Charles Norden. A nice young man, recently divorced, not terribly forthcoming, but with good prospects."

"Remarriage among them?"

"To Anna? Could be. But Anna doesn't confide in me. We saw her Sunday at the house. Pleasant, but blank. I don't think she's much for self-examination or considering people's motives. Her favorite food as a child was tapioca. That suits her—she's grateful for hope, for a little reassurance."

"But Richard tells you everything?"

"Richard doesn't need to. He has no secrets, no guile. He is what he seems. That's what I always loved about him, right from the start."

"And now? Surely he's changed a little over the years."

"Ted, you don't believe anyone really changes, do you? They weather a little, corrode, maybe, but not change. And Richard scarcely at all. He loses his brother, his daughter divorces, and it's like he's come out of the office and found a parking ticket on his windshield. He shrugs his shoulders, pays up, and goes on."

"And you—how do you manage?"

"I avoid surprises."

"James had to be a surprise. Were you close?"

"We're rather the psychoanalyst today, aren't we, Ted?"

"Just asking," Ted said.

Sarah gathered her thoughts. "James was hard *not* to like, don't you think? An intriguing man, really."

"And hardly a bit like his brother. Talk about polar opposites."

"I wouldn't be so sure about that," Sarah said. "Maybe just different ways of handling the same dilemmas, same problems. Same world, different views."

"But they weren't close—"

"Not as friends, no. More like father and son. I almost want to say mother and child. Richard worried over James. But I don't think James ever worried back."

"But Richard is fine now," Fields concluded.

"Just fine, just like always," Sarah said. This was not strictly true, but it was not, to Sarah's mind, a deception to keep some of the secrets of her heart from her friend or her physician. And she could not in this instance say exactly what was the truth. Richard was not, so far as she could tell, troubled or concealing anything. But things were not as they had been between them, and perhaps the change was as much in her as in him. It was as though she could not see him as clearly, could not focus on him as sharply, as effortlessly as she once could. Sometimes the image of him wavered and bent, like a heat mirage. Maybe her sight was failing, her sense of him growing blunter, but he was just the same as always. Perhaps through no fault of their own, through blindness, deafness, and the unraveling of memory, they would not be as close. She would no longer be able to smell him, nor to recall the scent, save perhaps for an instant, like a rustle or a draft from the past in the flood of the present. But after a time she would not care. Time and death would take each of them separately, and before that could be accomplished, she supposed they must be sundered from each other.

Sarah was looking at Ted Fields, or, rather, beyond him, and she found herself feeling as if she were sitting alone in a small wooden chair in a cavernous room so dark that she could not guess how large the room might be or where she was in it. And then she saw Ted again, and she ran the back of her hand up against the corner of her eye, as if to straighten her hair. The plane of her hand, her wrist, came away moist and warm, as though steam had condensed on it.

Sarah was scarcely aware of rising, of bidding Fields good-bye with a peck on the cheek, of passing into the hallway, where the odor of alcohol and disinfectant caught her sinuses and pulled her back down into the advancing day.

CHARLES CAME TO ANNA'S HOUSE FRIDAY NIGHT LIKE ONE OF the magi bearing gifts. He brought flowers for Anna and an ice cream roll for Douglas and a bottle of Johnnie Walker Black.

They sat in front of the television set like boreal hunters rubbing their hands together before the fire. When he'd arrived, Charles had the sense of coming to make amends, although for what he could not say. Anna felt the same thing; that she had in an unnameable way broken faith with Charles and was now repentant. So she tended him, touched him as if he were bruised. He looked at her eyes, and thought they were as raw and swollen as the moon, and he held her hand. When Douglas was asleep and laid in his crib, they went to Anna's room and undressed each other as though they were peeling bandages from burns, softly, warily. They lay down and rocked together and reached their climax in whispers and exhalations.

They were still for a long time, and then they began to touch each other again. Charles brushed his fingers across Anna's breasts. They seemed fuller and tauter than before, and he thought that it must be on his account, that it was for him. He wanted to weep and he thought he might burst with desire. He pressed his face to them and lapped Anna's nipples, gathered up their dark, stippled aureoles in his lips. He pulled himself up to Anna's face, and drew himself into her loins, pulling harder and harder like an oarsman before a swell, and called her name, again and again. Then she called his name back, like a cry across a gulf, and they shuddered together for a long time and were still again at last.

Anna slid on a robe. Charles thought it sounded like silk or paper shriveling in a fire. She went out and returned with a candle in a silver stick, a lighter, and a pack of Chesterfields, and put all three on his chest as though she were setting a table.

Charles looked up at her sheepishly. "You use my body, and then treat me like a butler's tray, like a beast of—"

"Shhh," Anna said boldly. "I'm just getting us settled." She transferred the candlestick to the nightstand and took the lighter and snapped it open. The room bloomed with orange light, and steadied into yellow as she lit the candlewick. She then took two cigarettes from the pack, put them both between her lips, lit them, and passed one to Charles.

"I think I'm the one that's supposed to do that," he said.

"Be still," Anna said, and put an ashtray in the middle of his chest. The bottom read "Hotel Biltmore, New York" in blue enamel.

Charles fingered the ashtray. "Ever stay there?"

"Once or twice, on the way to college. But mostly I met people there. Under the clock in the lobby. So much nicer than the station. It's sort of a tradition."

"Like filching ashtrays from hotel lobbies?"

"They want you to take them. It's free advertising."

"So they say. So who did you meet there?"

Anna blew smoke at him. "Boys, mostly. Soldiers, sailors, marines." She waited for him to react, and reached out to finger his hair. "But none sweet as you."

"I met Joan there once—to catch a train. She was late. Scarcely made the train. We fumed at each other all the way to Albany."

"It's still a nice tradition. Daddy used to meet Mother there. I suppose my children will too. Douglas, I mean."

"You're not too old to have another," Charles said, not knowing what possessed him to say so. He quickly added, "But the clock—you and I could meet there someday, I hope." Charles thought that with one more draw of his cigarette, one more stroke down the plain of Anna's body, he would surely find himself proposing to her. He could feel the impulse welling up like tears in his eyes.

Anna said, "I'd like to go everywhere with you." And with that Charles thought he must say the words. He pulled himself up, and his elbow felt raw against the sheet. Then he thought it couldn't hurt to wait. He had hardly been divorced a day.

Anna stood up and took the candle around to the other side of the bed, to the other nightstand, where a clock stood. The robe hung off her like a veil as she bent to the clockface. She said, "It's late. It's a cold winter's night. Time for bed."

Charles started to shift. Anna touched his shoulder. "No. Stay. Sleep with me." She sat down at the edge of the bed and looked at him, as though a little fearful.

"What about Douglas?" Charles asked.

"Douglas would think it was fine. And he's too little to tell anyone, too little to even remember."

"And the neighbors? In the morning, when I come creeping out the door in my business suit?"

"Only busybodies would be looking or care in the first place. Besides, who do you know out here, in this neighborhood?"

"Not a soul," Charles confessed. But every instinct told him this was not wise; that offers of partnerships collapsed over smaller indiscretions than what she proposed. But he wanted to say yes to her, to never disappoint her. And in his body and in his heart he wanted to stay with her. "Blow out the candle," he said, and then he took her in his arms and held her against the cold, against the frost that was settling on the roof and glazing it in ice.

WHEN ANNA AWOKE, CHARLES WAS GONE. IT TOOK HER SOME time to realize that he should have been there, so accustomed was she to an empty bed. There was a note on the nightstand, tucked under the ashtray.

Darling Anna,
   I slipped out early while you were sleeping. Thought I'd better go and catch up on some work at the office. I'll call you this afternoon. Thanks for a wonderful, wonderful evening.

Love,
Chas

She clutched it in her hand as she shuffled to the toilet and then to the kitchen. She put it on the counter while she rinsed out the percolator, and then she read it again. She put water on to boil for Douglas's cereal and inserted a slice of bread into the toaster for herself. She read it again. It was nothing, but it filled her. She began to weep, as though someone had saved her from a very close call.

She opened the door to Douglas's room. "Good morning, my sweet little man," she whispered, and went to the window and lifted the shade. Douglas squeaked softly, mewled, and tipped himself into sitting position in his crib, rubbing his eyes with his fists like a cat at its bath. "Mumma," he murmured. She went to him, lay him down, pulled his pajamas off. She undid his diaper, sodden and laden with turds small as quail eggs. She cleaned his bottom, his thighs, his penis—a bud of fluorescent pink. He smelled of saliva, and of things like coffee and grass.

After she dressed him, Anna thought she would try letting him sit by himself in front of the television set, assuming there was something being broadcast. There was: a man dressed like a cowboy with a fringed leather coat talking to a marionette with bulbous features and pompadour hair. The squeals and laughter of children poured from the loudspeaker like the drone of bees. Douglas's eyes grew large, and he leaned forward onto his palms, his mouth agape.

Anna went back to the kitchen, to her coffee and the bright prattling of the radio. Sunlight was beginning to puddle the floor. She sat at the table and cupped her chin in her hand. She could smell herself and Charles on her fingers, sharp, sour, and deep as humus. She thought she might call Alice. She had avoided talking to her yesterday, although she knew she ought, as a friend, to have asked her about her doctor's appointment, about her test. Anna had pretended to herself all Friday afternoon that she was forgetting to call, when in fact it had been weighing on her. Today she found she could bear it; she could even be happy for Alice.

She dialed the phone. Alice answered.

"It's Anna. Well?"

"Oh, you mean about what I told you about?"

"Well, yes, about the doctor, about being pregnant."

"Oh, no doubt about it. I'm maybe eight weeks along," Alice whispered.

"Is this still a secret? Did you tell Roger?"

"I'm waiting. Maybe tonight at dinner." Alice's voice dropped again. "It wasn't really planned, you know—not for exactly this time."

"Oh, he'll be thrilled."

"I'm sure. But you know how they can be—their moods and the way they are about things that weren't their idea. But no, he'll love it. I'll make him pot roast."

"Charles was here last night. Brought me flowers and ice cream for the baby."

"It's time for you two to get serious," Alice said, a little mockingly.

"Oh, we are."

"I mean officially."

"Soon, I hope. I think."

"I hope so too. But always be careful."

"You know, you mentioned the four of us getting together. I suppose tomorrow would work."

"Let me see how tonight goes, and I'll call you in the morning if we're free."

"Okay. I love you, Alice. And congratulations."

"Love you too.' Bye."

Anna spent the rest of the morning cleaning the house. At noon, Charles appeared at the door, coatless, shuffling his feet and hunching his shoulders in the cold. "Oohh, let me in there," he said and held Anna tight in the foyer.

"Where's your coat, sweetie?" Anna asked.

"In the car. I left it running. Grab Douglas and come and have lunch with me. Then I've got to go back to the office. Big stuff that can't wait."

"But you'll come back tonight?"

"Of course. But I've been thinking. I wonder if it would be okay if I go home afterward. Between work and everything, it's just simpler right now. But soon, I promise, things will change."

Anna felt a little wounded, but it was nothing beside her underlying happiness, her sense of the good things that lay ahead, all in a row, almost touchable before her. "Oh, that's all right, darling. Just as long as I get to see you as much as I can, as much as you can manage. Let me get Douglas."

Douglas was still in front of the television. A huge man with hangdog features that looked like cast molten rubber sat in a big easy chair talking in a high, rasping voice. A creature appeared in a puff of smoke and greeted the audience maniacally. Anna pulled Douglas's arms into his coat as he stared raptly at the screen. When she lifted him up and turned the dial of the set off, he began to howl and she carried him out the door with his arms flailing, his face a squall of distemper. Charles walked to the car at a little distance from them.

They ate at the big drugstore four blocks away. Anna sawed a hamburger into little pieces for Douglas and then she fed him spoonfuls of Charles's chocolate malt. Anna ate a tuna salad sandwich and drank a Coke. After Charles dropped them at home, Anna helped Douglas scribble on paper at the kitchen table. He made strokes and sharp-edged squiggles like barbed wire and lightning bolts. Anna laid down a fresh sheet of paper and took his hand and guided it. She pushed it stiffly across the bottom of the paper and lifted it twice to make two vertical lines.

"Here's our house. The floor and two walls. And now the roof and the chimney." Douglas eased his grip on the pencil a little and Anna bit her lip in concentration. "Make me some smoke for the chimney," she said, and steered Douglas's hand up. He drew a jagged curl. "Good. Now, here's the door. And the big window. And we'll put some shrubs around the front." She beamed. "Oh, we need a sun. I'll make the circle and you make the beams." Anna drew a disk at the top of the page, and she freed Douglas's hand. "Draw lines all around it, sweetie." He drew long beams downward right through the house, like waves of heat, like arrows of grace.

Then Anna put her son down for his nap. He snuffled twice and fell straight asleep. She tidied the living room and hummed with the radio. After she was done straightening, she went back to her bedroom and stroked and smoothed the bedding and plumped the pillows. She picked up the ashtray, their cigarette ends of the night before bent and stiff as old bones, and carried it out to the kitchen.

SOMETIMES THE WORLD INSISTS ON BEING HEARD, DESPITE OUR ignorance, our protestations, our denials. It opens itself up beneath a person's feet and demands she look down into its depths. That Sunday morning, for example, Anna had been wanting another day like the one before—expectant, ebullient, sated with good things. But she awoke nauseated, and she staggered to the bathroom and hung her head over the toilet, dizzy, her eyes floating loose in her skull. Her hands clutched the rim, cool and damp like fogged glass, and she waited, holding her blanched and sweaty face over the pit of the bowl. Then her head cleared and she sat down on the bathroom floor, shaking. She felt flecks of grit cutting into her hands and feet and saw dust bunnies coiled in the corners behind the hamper. As of today, her period was four weeks late. She was going to have to think about this.

At church that same morning, Richard sat with Sarah, whose face was screened behind the veil of her hat. These days, Richard used such times to empty his mind, to lose himself in the hum of the service, the zombified cycles of standing, sitting, and kneeling. It was like sitting on a curbstone while traffic went by, hooves and spokes, tires and tank treads. But while the priest read the Gospel, the words crept into his mind: how after King Herod had ordered the slaughter of the innocents, and Mary and the baby and Joseph had gone into Egypt, Joseph had a dream and an angel told him, "Arise, and take the young child and his mother, and go into the land of Israel; for they are dead which sought the young child's life." This had something to do with wives and children, with fathers and daughters. It had the quality of a message, and Richard would have to think about it again sometime.

JOHN ALCOCK'S OFFICE WAS AS LARGE AS CHARLES'S LIVING room, Charles realized as he sat down. Alcock was a senior partner at Byrne, Alcock, and Wood, the law firm where Charles worked. Charles had been at his desk on Monday morning when Alcock stuck his head in the door and said, "Norden, come on down to my office and let's have a little visit." Alcock bobbed his chin toward the end of the hall as though to show the way. Charles followed him. Alcock wore a suit of fine gray wool and a striped tie of yellow and blue silk. There was an Oriental prayer rug on the floor by his desk.

"Sit. Relax," said Alcock. "Coffee?"

"Oh, no, that's all right."

"Good, good," Alcock said. "This is just an informal talk, although I certainly speak for the other partners. The long and the short of it is that we're very pleased with your work."

"Well," Charles paused, "that's very gratifying to hear. I find the work fulfilling. And congenial, too."

"We'd like to think you'll be here with us for the long haul. In fact, I believe I can safely say that on present indications that perhaps by the end of the year, we would be prepared to offer you a partnership."

"Well, well," Charles's voice rose and he smiled, more boyishly than he would have liked. He recovered his equilibrium. "I'd be honored and thrilled. But whatever the case, you can count on me to keep my nose to the grindstone, so to speak."

"Oh, you don't have to worry about that. Your hours on our behalf are . . . prodigious. If anything, you might ease up a little. I don't mean slack off, but shift your attention to other areas that can be rewarding. I don't have to tell you how much business is done outside the office—in social situations, on the golf course, at the club, at parties, even at church."

"Absolutely," Charles agreed.

"In fact, it's not so much that one cultivates prospective clients. It's that the firm makes its presence felt in the community, that when people require counsel, they think of us, as they would their doctor or pastor. We're a conservative firm. We don't hawk our wares. Our reputation—which is to say the individual reputations of our partners and associates—is everything."

"It's implicit," Charles nodded, feeling he was now showing some sophistication.

"And explicit. This isn't a criticism, but you ought to think about putting yourself out a bit, into the community, I mean. Join a church—a good church—if you haven't got one. Do a little work for Community Chest. Winter Carnival is coming up. Great fun. Good cause. Back off the billable hours a little, and represent us in something there. You've got our blessing."

"I'll get right on it."

"I know you will. Where were you in the service?"

"The navy. Lieutenant j.g. Never west of Honolulu, I'm afraid."

"It shows. Not the combat experience part, I mean. Hell, I missed out on the First War entirely. But the bearing, the sense of duty—it shows."

"Thank you," Charles said.

"You're seeing Richard MacEwan's little girl, I hear. Richard's good, steady. Anything in the offing there? Bachelorhood doesn't suit a man, I don't think."

"I think there very well may be, perhaps soon."

"Well, let me congratulate you. Unfortunate about her divorce. But it's modern times. And you're divorced yourself—we don't hold that against you, Norden—and so that kind of evens things out. And I'm sure from this day on, it'll be clear sailing with you."

"You can count on it."

"Good, good. Well, that was all I really had to say. It's been a nice little visit, don't you think? We're very happy with you, and we want you to be part of the family."

Charles pumped Alcock's hand vigorously, and had to restrain himself from bounding down the hall on the way back to his office. He would call Randy Tyrell about the Winter Carnival. And he would call Anna. He had things to discuss with her.

AS HE WAITED FOR HIS ELEVATOR IN THE LOBBY OF THE FIRST National Bank building, Richard felt a tug on his sleeve and heard a whisper like a mosquito burrowing in his ear canal.

"Dicky, goddamnit. Like ships in the night, you and me," said Henry Finch. "Gotta minute?"

"Oh, surely," Richard said. Deeper acquaintance with Finch seemed to be James's sole bequest to him, and he accepted it resignedly.

"Come on over here," Henry said, pointing to the shoe-shine stand on the other side of the lobby. "Sit down. Have a shine on me."

"That's kind of you, Henry." Finch clambered onto a chair, set his feet on the stirrups, and patted the seat next to him. "Give him your damnedest, Isaac," Finch said to the old negro in the white waiter's jacket. He looked to be at least seventy years old.

The old man began to daub black polish on Richard's wing tips. "Isaac gives the best shine in the Twin Cities, Richard. He's from Mississippi. Aren't you, Isaac? His parents were slaves."

"Yes, sir." Isaac sighed and muttered, "Under pharaoh's yoke, out of Egypt," or so Richard thought he heard the words. The old man began to buff.

"You know, I remembered something the other day, Dicky," Finch continued. "You know you asked me if I knew anyone Jimmy might have been dating before—before last fall. Well, I remembered. There was this girl, not Jimmy's usual type, a graduate student at the university, war widow, I think. Serious gal. Anyway, I remembered having a drink with the two of them, maybe in August or even September."

The old man finished with Richard's shoes, and moved over and sat beneath Henry's feet. Richard asked, "Did you get the sense they were serious?"

"Oh, no doubt in my mind. She was curled up next to him like a cat rubbing on a radiator. And he was putting out the juice, the Jimmy MacEwan charm."

"I don't suppose you remember her name?"

"Oh, that's the odd thing. I do. It was Susan. You see, I dated someone named Susan once, and she wasn't anything like her, so in a funny way it made me think of her." Finch's voice trailed off and he resumed. "In fact, I even remember her last name: Nash, like the car. I was shopping cars then, so it stuck."

"You have a wonderful mind, Henry," Richard said, and stood up. The old man gave a final flick of his rag to Henry's shoe, and rose slowly, bent in back and neck like the blade of a scythe. Henry handed him two quarters. "Thank you, Isaac," he said.

"And thank you, Henry," Richard said and started to move toward the elevators. Finch came up alongside him. "Well, I hope that helps, with your curiosity or whatever."

"Oh, it's of no consequence now," Richard said. "But good to talk with you."

"And you—" Henry Finch began, as the elevator door closed in front of him and Richard ascended to his office. He collected his mail off the secretary's desk. He thought of asking her to track down James's woman friend, but thought he might better do so himself.

Richard swept his files and mail to one side of his desktop and pulled the Minneapolis telephone book from the credenza. He found the registrar's number at the university and put his finger to the telephone. The dial sang and wound back to its resting place seven times. A woman's voice answered. Richard said, "I'm calling from Miles, MacEwan, and Booth law offices in St. Paul. We're trying to locate a graduate student there, Susan Nash, with reference to an estate we're settling."

"Oh, she's coming into money?" the woman queried. "They all need that, graduate students."

"Yes, no doubt."

"Well, I can look it up. Your name, sir?"

Richard hesitated. "I'm just a clerk here in the office, no one really." He hesitated again. "The name's Finch."

"Very well, Mr. Finch. I'll be right back with you."

The line was silent for perhaps a minute, and the woman came back on. "Only one, luckily. Susan Nash, master's candidate in anthropology, lives in St. Paul. Nineteen-sixty-two Marshall Avenue. Telephone is Midway 5-4932. That's all I have for you."

"Well, you've been very helpful."

"My pleasure, Mr. Finch."

CHARLES HAD TELEPHONED ANNA, AND ANNA HAD TELEHONED Mrs. Clay to come over and mind Douglas, and now Charles and Anna were sitting down to eat at the Madison. Charles told the waiter to bring them two Scotches on the rocks. Anna looked at him expectantly, perhaps even nervously. He might have noted this had he been less preoccupied with his own good fortune.

"Just wait until the drinks come. We have something to toast, I believe."

"All right." Anna smiled unsurely, her hands folded on the table.

The waiter returned and set the drinks down. Charles told Anna about his meeting with Alcock, and Anna punctuated his account of it with grins and exclamations. "So," he concluded, "my future, as they say, is assured. I'm set, if I keep my nose clean, for the rest of my mortal days."

"Charles," Anna said, "that's wonderful," and rested her palm on his fist. Charles placed his other hand over hers. "And, although this is nothing formal, I think we have a future together too. I was thinking I might go into Bockstruck's during my lunch hour someday this week and look at jewelry. And you might want to consider what your response might be if I came back with a ring."

Anna cried "Charles" in a choked voice, as if the wind had been knocked out of her, and her hand clenched in an involuntary spasm. The corners of her mouth quivered and her eyes were damp and fearful.

Charles pressed down on her hand. "Steady, girl. Nothing you have to decide about tonight."

Anna broke in. "You know what I'd—"

Charles went on calmly. "But we ought to have a nice dinner together this weekend. There's a place in Minneapolis with strolling violinists and French champagne. And we can talk then."

"Oh, Charles," Anna said, and shook her head, not in wonder at Charles's good fortune or even her own but at the love, at the pity, at their miraculous, fateful turnings.

THE NEXT MORNING WAS A TUESDAY, AND THE SUN SEEMED never to come up. At eight-thirty, the streetlights glowed like illuminated clouds amid the gray, and by nine the snow began to fall, first gently and then in billows, eddying and curling like tendrils on the wind. Anna let Douglas sleep and she moved through the house with the lights out, without the radio, as though it were empty of people, the furnishings coped in sheets and dust. She sat queasily at the kitchen table and the percolator burbled like a beating heart. She drank coffee until her stomach settled and then she lit a Chesterfield and dialed Alice Mercer's telephone number.

"Alice?"

"Oh, Anna. We're really sorry about Sunday. The day just got away from us. Roger was thrilled. He says maybe we'll buy a bigger house, move to Mendota or something."

"That's wonderful. I'm so pleased for you. But Alice, I really need to talk to someone. I wondered if I could—"

"Come right over. Be careful. It's blizzarding out there. Promise me."

"Okay. I've got to get Douglas up and fed, so I'll be maybe half an hour."

"See you then, dear."

Anna woke Douglas and dressed him quickly, even a little roughly. She sat him in his high chair and spooned cereal into his still sleep-befuddled mouth. She filled a bottle with milk from the refrigerator, twisted the nipple home, pulled Douglas into his snowsuit and boots, and carried him to the car. The snow whipped and threaded around her ankles.

At Alice's, she pounded on the storm door as the flakes spun like moths around the porch light. Alice let her in without a word, putting her arm around Anna's waist and steering her to the living room. Anna felt the snow begin to melt in her hair, the clots of ice melting in her shoes. She sat down and pulled off Douglas's boots. Douglas ambled tentatively toward the fireplace, where Alice's Linda sat looking away, her pout waxen with studied indifference.

"So . . . " Alice began.

"Charles wants to marry me—I mean, he hasn't proposed yet, but he's going to, this weekend probably."

"But that's wonderful!" Alice said. "That's everything you want, everything you *could* want."

"There's a problem." Anna looked up at Alice glumly, and tried to smile.

"Which is . . . ?"

"My period. I'm a month late. I wake up feeling sick. I feel puffy."

"Are you sure? I mean, have you and Charles been—"

"Since November. Usually with a diaphragm. But sometimes not." Anna felt worldly, clinical, weary. She didn't feel cheap. She thought she might have. She thought perhaps she should.

Alice was talking rapidly. "But maybe it's something else. Maybe you could talk to your doctor. . . ."

Anna was looking at her feet. They looked big. There was a little worm of ice melting on the carpet by her shoe. "Dr. Fields? Who is Daddy's doctor and Mother's doctor, and my doctor since I was twelve. I don't think so. And I don't think there's any mistake. My breasts are swollen too." Alice didn't say anything. Then Anna added, "Even last weekend, I thought maybe there could be nothing to it. That it would go away."

"I'm really sorry, Anna," Alice said at last.

"So what do I do? He's getting a ring. He's going to ask me."

"Maybe he wouldn't care—"

"Goddamnit, Alice!" Anna spat, and caught herself. "Oh God, I'm sorry, I'm so, so sorry. It wasn't anything but nerves. Forgive me?"

Alice sat helplessly, wounded, her hands knit together, her ankles splayed. "I just wanted to say something, be of some use," she muttered, and then she straightened herself and swallowed audibly. "And there's nothing to forgive. You're entitled."

Anna began to sob. "I love you, Alice," she whimpered. "Tell me what to do."

Alice got up and sat down next to her and took her hands. "I'm sure there's something. But I don't know. I mean, I knew about this happening in high school and college. To girls who knew someone that I knew, never directly. And they went away and when they came back, there was no baby. You know, they went to a home and sat it out, or they found something to—to do about it . . . "

"I can't do that, Alice."

"I think you have to tell him. I think if he really loves you—"

"But he wants to marry me. So I tell him about this, and does he still want to then? He'll think I'm cheap."

"It's *his* baby. How can that make *you* cheap?"

"It doesn't work that way, you know it doesn't."

"It's his problem too. He's the father."

"I'm the girl Mother told me I'd become. She'd love this, she'd relish this . . . "

"That's beside the point, Anna. It hasn't got anything to do with her. It's for you and Charles to—"

"It feels like it's got everything to do with her, that and breaking Daddy's heart." Anna's voice lowered. A blast of snow and wind buffeted the windows. "I'd like to die."

Alice waited a long while before speaking, as though to let the last remark be forgotten. "You have to tell Charles, and then it's a problem the two of you solve. That's all I can say." Alice hugged Anna and held her for a while. Alice looked out the window and said, "You'd better go home while you can. It's piling up out there."

At the door, Alice held Anna again. "It's going to be okay. He's a good man. You'll see," Alice said.

"Thank you, thank you, Alice."

"Call me whenever you want, dear. Day or night, okay?"

"Okay," Anna said, and carried Douglas out into the blizzard, bending against the wind, the snow like wind-driven salt. She drove with her lights on, with the wipers scurrying back and forth across the windshield. The streets were dark and empty. There was no sound, no echo; the world was muffled, dormant, still as stone, save for Anna's tires, which spun and whirred through the snow.

SUSAN NASH WAS MAKING A LIAR OUT OF RICHARD; OR RATHER, Richard had yet to tell her a single truth other than his name and relation to James. Richard was not a liar by nature. If anything, he had a tendency to blurt, to reveal more of the facts of a situation than was strictly necessary. A legal education and nearly twenty-five years at the bar had taught him to moderate this impulse, at least in professional circumstances. He had even learned to excise the verb "lie" from his vocabulary, substituting "dissemble," "misstate," or "fail to recollect" with reasonable ease. But the lawyer in him remained discomfited by how genuinely shocked he could still be by calculated falsehood and deception: Surely he ought by now to be unsurprised by this and all other aspects of human conduct. Happily, there was comparatively little lying in the estates and trusts business.

On the telephone, Richard had told Susan Nash that he understood she had been a friend of his late brother, James. She had told him that, yes, she had known James. Richard explained that he was attempting to tidy up James's affairs and estate, and that there were unanswered questions she might be able to help him clarify. Susan doubted she could be of any help, but agreed—with wariness, Richard imagined—to see him.

She lived in a wood-framed duplex in a middle-class neighborhood halfway between downtown and the university. The snowstorm had been succeeded by brilliant sun and the day was brittle and cold. Richard rang the bell and shivered, shuffling his feet on the icicle-festooned front porch. Susan Nash answered the door in a sweater and pants. She was between thirty-five and forty, Richard guessed, with some gray in her hair and the corners of her eyes scored with tiny fractures. She wore little makeup and was pretty in an unadorned, rather austere way. She smiled and bid him enter with a flex of her wrist. They climbed the dark stair together, exchanging pleasantries about the weather, about the blizzard and its aftermath.

She settled herself on a sofa. The walls were painted gray. The furniture was new and modern in style, stark in its lines, fabricated of light wood. The floor was bare but for a bright throw rug. "Well," Susan said as though snapping a book shut, "how can I help?"

Richard explained that there were some bills that James's estate needed to settle, and that Susan might be able to shed some light on where and how they were incurred. Susan looked at him guardedly, or so Richard thought. "There's nothing untoward involved," he added hastily. "But with an estate, the court demands that we account for every penny, however silly and trivial it may seem."

"Well," Susan began, "I don't know what I could possibly tell you. James and I went out together for a few months last year. I read about him dying in the paper. I was hardly privy to his financial affairs, whatever they were." This was true enough, Richard realized, and he was now unsure in which direction to move the conversation. He had not really thought about what he would say after he had sat down with her and announced his pretext for coming. He feared she was already a little exasperated with the pointlessness of his coming to her at all, perhaps even suspicious. He decided to be direct. He found himself speaking in the first person plural he used with clients at the office. It made him feel more legitimate in his queries, less a solitary voice.

"In particular, we need to account for out-of-town trips he made where an invoice for a hotel exists, but we have no record of him going. We wondered if he might have said anything to you about travel plans or, indeed, if perhaps the two of you might have gone anywhere together." The words were scarcely out of his mouth before he realized that their effect would not be what he intended.

Susan looked at him first with faint irritation, and then smiled bemusedly, as if to register sympathy for his ineptitude. "Really, Mr. MacEwan," she said, arching her eyebrows. "Naughty secret weekends together? In a country hideaway, a discreet, anonymous hotel, or whatever?"

"Oh, no," Richard said emphatically. "No such thing was implied. I'm terribly sorry. That wasn't at all what I meant." Susan continued to smile, and he suspected she was about to say, "Poor thing, you're really not very good at this, are you?"—rather as Sarah might under such a circumstance.

But instead, Susan said, "No, we never went away together," and exhaled faintly, as though ending a fairy story. Then she added, "I wish we had." Richard sensed no offense had been taken, but he continued to look down at his knees for a while, at the floor. Neither spoke. They might have been sharing a happy recollection together.

Then Richard looked up and, against his better judgment, bore on. "It was a trip to Chicago we were wondering about. In late September last year. To the Drake Hotel, actually."

Richard saw that Susan had been looking away too, through the window, past the curtain, at the sky, bright as a flare. "James and I weren't even seeing each other anymore by September."

"I see," Richard said and started to gather his gloves and coat and hat. He felt disappointed, thwarted but relieved. Now he could stop being a liar. But Susan said, "Wait. Have some coffee. I'll tell you what I can about James and me, I mean. You've come all this way."

Richard sat back down. He felt an ugly situation was being salvaged, as though he and Susan had been having a domestic quarrel and he had been on the verge of walking out in despair or disgust. "All right. Yes. That would be very kind."

Susan went into the kitchen and returned with two cups of coffee. She handed him one. "I'd just put it on before you came. Honest." She sat. Richard said, "So how did you meet?"

"Actually, I had an investment account with his firm. My husband was killed in the war. There was a pension and some other money. Tony Greenwood in James's office was handling it for me. Tony introduced us. We went out. It was like falling off a log. James made it easy to say yes to him."

"Just like that," Richard said, almost talking to himself. Then he said, more loudly, "Yes, he did, didn't he. And when was this?"

"Oh, April of last year. I don't think I'd been out with anyone I really found interesting since Tom—that was my husband's name—died. In forty-five. In Germany."

"At the very end."

"Yes, and after eight years in the service. He was a captain. He was going to be a career officer. He wasn't at all like James."

"So—"

"I liked him because he was different. You have to understand about the life of a soldier's wife. It's all waiting—everything's suspended. He's either home or he's not. He's either alive or he's not. So you wait instead of living, wait to find out if you're going to have a life at all. Does that make sense?"

"Like attending someone gravely ill. Sitting by their bed."

"Yes, like that, but when you're a soldier's wife, it's your profession. I found out being a widow is the same thing. People leave you alone. They think that's what you want. Or that it's infectious. So you wait. Graduate school is the same, come to think of it. It feels like more waiting, like serving time. That's why I decided to register at the university. I had a little money. I was interested in anthropology and folklore. I'd learned to like to read all those years while Tom was away. So I thought I'd do something useful, get a degree—while I was waiting." She laughed.

"Like Odysseus's wife."

"Yes, like Penelope. Good for you. You know about that kind of thing. So did James, in his way. Or he understood it instinctively. Do you know how they think those poems—*The Iliad* and so on—were made, were composed before they had writing, when it was all memorization, thousands and thousands of lines?"

"No," Richard said. "Tell me."

"The bards learned repeated formulas of words—'the wine dark sea' or whatever—and put them together while they sang the stories, like stringing beads together. That's how they did it, that and memory, and a knack for sensing how things need to be in order to please people. That's what your brother had. He didn't just know to bring flowers. He knew exactly what *kind* of flowers to bring. He didn't just know that a woman likes to be complimented. He knew when you needed to be complimented and what you needed to hear, what words would sound like they were just for you. Actually, he had the memory too—he'd remember your mother's name, the way you liked your drink, how you'd worn your hair the last time you saw him—and he'd lay these little things before you when you'd least expect it, casually, like charms."

"But really rather calculated."

"No, not calculated, not like deception. Unless you think Homer and Michelangelo were calculating. No, just the artifice behind the art. Part of the gift, the grace, the knack for beauty."

"But it didn't last—he and you."

"We had a good few months," Susan said. She pulled her legs up under her and lifted her arms in a stretch. "But I wanted more—marriage, maybe even children. I'm not too old. He didn't want that. He just wanted to go on like we were, indefinitely. So for me, that was just more of waiting for a life to happen to me. But for him, you see, that wasn't waiting: That *was* life for him. He was like an artist in that, although perhaps he never saw it that way."

"So you broke it off?"

"No, he did. In August. He knew I wasn't happy with the situation. He knew when it was time for him to go. That's part of the gift, I suppose."

"So it was amicable, at least."

"Heavens no. I hated him for it. For taking himself away, for taking all his charms away."

"Even though you knew you really wanted something else entirely?"

"Oh, of course. Perfectly consistent. I mean, I loved Tom, but I hated him for dying. For leaving me here. To go on waiting for him forever. Or so it sometimes seems." She laughed quietly, as if to herself. "It's just me now—me and Tom's father. I look in on him every day or so. We eat grilled cheese sandwiches. He's a retired doctor."

"What's his name?" Richard asked.

"Albert Nash."

"Don't know him."

"No reason you should. He's a pathologist. People tend to make his acquaintance rather late in life, so to speak." They laughed together.

"Rather like myself," Richard added. "I'm in estates, you see."

They sat silently for a moment, and looked at each other, and Susan tilted her head, as though to put a question to him. Richard saw how handsome she was, how radiantly clear and spare and direct. He made himself look away. Then he began to gather his things quickly, almost fumbling with his hat and gloves. "I'd better go," he said apologetically. She nodded.

On the way downstairs, she became more formal, striving to find a way to bring a satisfactory close, a tangible ending to the time they'd spent together. "I'm sorry I couldn't help you more," she said.

"That's all right. The coffee was delicious and I enjoyed talking with you about James. Sometimes I think I'm just learning to get to know him now, after he's gone."

"Perhaps that's really why you came."

"Oh, perhaps I did," Richard said, as though conceding the philosophical truth of the matter without acknowledging that it was also the practical fact of it. At the door, he shook her hand tentatively, limply clutching her fingertips. He wanted to find a way of saying that he wanted to come back, in words that were not a lie. But he thanked her again for the coffee and said good-bye.

ANNA HAD INVITED CHARLES TO COME FOR DINNER AT HER house Friday night. She couldn't bear to wait to see him until their big evening out on Saturday, she had explained. She arranged for

Mrs. Clay to take Douglas home with her for the night, something she had done before on occasion. Then she set the table with her wedding silver and linen and her monogrammed napkin rings. She cooked pot roast.

Charles arrived at six-thirty, red-faced from the cold but cheerful. Anna took his coat and sat him in the big chair by the window. She brought him a drink. He looked around the room and saw the candles burning on the dining table. "Where's Douglas?" he said.

"He's spending the night with Mrs. Clay. She's like an extra granny to him, and he loves it. And of course I thought it might be nice for us to have an adult evening together."

"Nothing wrong with that." He looked around again through the dim lights, as though surveying the evening ahead. "Well, they'll be hard pressed to top this at the Flame Room tomorrow. It's all very elegant."

"You're sweet to say so," Anna said, and kissed him on the cheek. "But I'm needed in the kitchen."

She checked the pot roast and replaced the lid of the Dutch oven. She picked up her drink from the counter and sipped quickly, like a bird pecking at seed. By the time she'd finished the gravy, she was halfway through another. Charles sat in the chair, his legs sprawled, humming contentedly.

Anna called Charles to dinner. He pulled out her chair for her and kissed her neck as he slid her to the table. They shook out their napkins. Charles toasted the two of them. The shards of melted ice in Anna's drink bobbed like gulls on sea swells. Charles ate enthusiastically.

"You really can cook, you know," he said, spearing a carrot. "Did your mother teach you?"

"Mother couldn't open a can of cat food without help," Anna said. "I taught myself."

"Well, it's another reason to love you," he said. They ate and then they drank some more, Charles in ebullience, Anna in burgeoning numbness, steeling herself against what must be done. When they were finished, Charles leaned over and kissed her softly on her mouth and brushed his fingers against her thigh. He said, "Why don't we go to bed? Right now? I'm *so* tired after all that delicious food." He grinned at her.

Anna tried to sound game. "That's a fabulous idea," she said, and kissed him back. "But let's just have one more little drink." Charles was agreeable, and she went into the kitchen to get more ice and Scotch. They moved to the sofa, and Anna set their drinks on the coffee table. She felt impelled to make conversation but was aware that that only put her at a farther remove from the subject she needed to broach. Charles sat happily, expectantly, as though he too thought Anna had something to say. She felt stuck. She realized she was not adept at unprompted, declarative statements. She felt as though she were trying to frame a complicated sentence in a foreign language.

Charles said, "About tomorrow night. I can't wait—" and Anna leapt, as though she were falling head over hands into a chasm. "There's something I need to tell you. My period—I'm late, very late."

Charles looked at her unsurely, as though he was not clear what was being discussed. He tried to tease the sense of what she was saying out of the silence. "Could you . . . ?" He trailed off, even as he began to understand what she had said.

Anna sat quietly for a while. Then she began again, faintly. "There really isn't any doubt. It must have been back in November, one of the first times we were together."

Charles said nothing for a moment. He was not sure he was breathing. His body seemed a long way off, and although Anna was sitting right next to him, it was as though she too were across the room from him, speaking softly, or that his ears were muffled in cotton. Panic started to gather in his face like a weight, like air pressure, the way he had imagined it would be if his ship went down, if he had drowned in the war. Then he began to feel angry.

"You're sure?" he said, half gasping. He tried to compose himself, to organize his questions, to elicit the information he needed to reason effectively. But the questions bent themselves back in one direction like a runaway team of horses and refused to be curbed. "How long have you known? Why didn't you tell me?"

"I told you when I was sure—when I knew it wasn't going to go away." Anna could scarcely answer one question before another was upon her. She felt besieged.

"But how could this happen, Anna, how, goddamnit? I mean, weren't you using something?"

"Sometimes we got carried away. You were there. You wanted me. You didn't want to wait. Neither did I."

He snapped at her, "And it's supposed to be up to you to show some restraint. It's up to you to be minding these things. How am I supposed to know?"

Anna spoke softly, defeated. "It was a mistake. I'm not perfect. I don't think of everything. We wanted each other. It was us, our wanting each other and just forgetting."

Charles was not satisfied. He drove toward the precipice. "A lot of good that does us," he hissed. "How do I even know that I'm really the . . ."

He did not finish the sentence, but its meaning struck Anna like a hail of shot, and she threw her face on the arm of the sofa and wept. But Charles felt he had gained some control over himself in being able to stop himself from saying even that one final word; the word that, as much as he might wish to hurt her, he could not for his own sake bring himself to say. He realized he had to go on being good to her, that it was the only way to save himself.

Charles stood and then he let himself down on his heels next to Anna. "I'm sorry. I'm so, so sorry. I had no business saying that or even thinking it. I was just very upset. I mean, it's quite a surprise," he said, and found he might almost have chuckled. Anna looked up at him, her expression drawn, scarlet and damp, like a breathless face surfacing from the sea. She stared at him a while, as though trying to comprehend him. Then she turned away and said in a whisper, "It's ours. It's yours."

"I know," Charles said. She kept her face averted from him, and he found her hand and took it in his. It seemed tiny and swollen, shiny and taut as a child's. He laid his head down behind her neck, his eyes in her hair, his cheek on her sweater, and he felt her back rising and falling. He could feel her breath, like steam from a cavern deep inside her. He whispered, "It will be all right. You'll see."

After a while he stood and cleared his throat. "I need to think about this. I need to go home. Just to figure things out and clear my head. Then we'll know what to do. Trust me, please. Trust me."

Her back was still turned to him. He got his coat and scarf and gloves, and when he had put them on, he bent down to her head again. He took it in his hands and she looked at him and he kissed her eyes and he let himself out.

IT BEGAN TO SNOW AGAIN SATURDAY AFTERNOON AND BY Sunday morning there was nearly another foot on the ground. At church Richard daydreamed and heard snatches of the Gospel: how the boy Jesus slipped away from his parents, who then searched for him for three days and at last found him in the temple. Mary said to him, "Son, why hast thou thus dealt with us? Behold, thy father and I have sought thee sorrowing." Jesus answered her coldly, indifferently. Or that was how Richard heard it.

That afternoon, after lunch, Richard thought he ought to feed the birds. The feeders in the yard would be buried in snow, and any other forage impossible to find. He went down the basement stairs. In the corner, next to the rose dust and the lawn dressing and the rakes, he kept a burlap bag of seed. He filled a galvanized bucket from it and started to go outside through the basement door. But he stopped and turned to face James's desk, glowing faintly from the light of the window above the laundry tub, glazed with a coating of dust.

Richard took off his gloves and bent to the middle right-hand drawer. He slid it open slowly, as though it contained something very fragile. The envelope of photos he had found in this drawer in November was gone, and he wondered where it might be. Then he fingered the envelopes one after another until he found the blue envelope with Sarah's handwriting on it, postmarked September 26, 1949. Perhaps it was an invitation to a party they'd had that he had forgotten or perhaps it was a newspaper clipping or a snapshot Sarah thought James would find amusing. Richard had imagined all these things, and many more. But when he slid the paper out he saw it was a letter written in Sarah's loping, backhand script.

Jimmy dear—

You probably wondered whatever became of me in Chicago Friday night. I could tell you that Mother got difficult and that I couldn't get away or that her companion had to leave suddenly or that I suddenly felt ill. But that wouldn't be the truth, and we have always been honest with each other, haven't we? I know you'd planned for us to have a lovely evening together—finally, after all these years and false starts—and I am sorry if you were hurt or disappointed that I didn't come.

I love the Drake, don't you? Daddy took me there when it was just open and I had just turned twenty-one. It was a few weeks before Prohibition was to take effect and Daddy told me he wanted me to have a real cocktail in a proper setting before what he called "the time of trial" began. I had a martini. We sat and looked at the lake and someone liveried brought the drinks. I think it might have been where the Cape Cod Room is now. Much as I adore you, maybe I just wanted to go on remembering the Drake that way and not for anything else.

The truth is, I suppose, that it's so awfully hard to do the right thing in this world—it's so rarely fun or interesting, at any rate—and this was a chance to do it with comparative ease. I've done so many foolish things, but I've never hurt Richard deliberately. I know he would have never known, and it might have been rather thrilling—rather like secret agents—but I also know that if he had found out, he could never have believed that we would do such a thing. And also, that he would feel that he had no choice but to forgive us. Even after I'd rationalized everything else, that was more than I could bear.

I'm sorry, dear, but I think you must understand. We are the last of the grown-ups in an ever more childish world, aren't we?

Fondly,
Sarah

Richard's hands were shaking, and it took him a while to get the letter back in the envelope. He stood with it in his hand for a long time, trying to decide what to do with it. He saw the flames lapping through the slits in the furnace door, and for a moment he thought he might burn it; that by doing so it would make an end of the whole business and put it behind him. But he could not bring himself to part with it, and in fact the idea frightened him, as though he would be unmooring himself forever from something that he had come to need, to rely upon. On the beam above the furnace there was a large card tacked up where the coal man used to record his deliveries. Richard slid the letter behind it, where it would be secure and unseen.

Then he took the bucket of seed and carried it outside. The sky was darkening and the air was still and moist. His breath seemed to billow around his head and he began to scatter the seed in arcs around the yard. He swung his arm aimlessly and he found himself thinking of Susan Nash, of her sandy hair that was like a boy's in high summer, but for the flecks of gray. He felt very small himself, chastened, as though he had been sent out into the winter yard at dusk as a punishment. He threw out more seed, and then out of the silence, he heard a rush of cheeping and the birds gathered around him.

When he was done, he went back into the basement and up the stairs. He hadn't seen Sarah from the top of the stairs, and nearly bumped into her in the hall. He looked away from her, as though he'd been found out. She didn't appear to notice. She smiled as though at peace with the world.

"I saw you outside, from the window. You're awfully sweet to think of feeding the birds. I wish I'd had the Brownie to take a picture of it. You looked just like Saint Francis of Assisi."

CHARLES AND ANNA HAD SLEPT WITHOUT REST THAT FRIDAY night, each in their separate beds, their bodies rolling fitfully, unable to remain in any one position as though they feared that the ceiling might collapse just then over that very spot. Anna imagined getting up and chain-smoking and drinking alone until the dawn came, like an alcoholic. She didn't care what rules she broke, what virtues, decencies, and conventions she abjured. She wasn't among other people anymore. She was helpless and beyond the pale, and she found herself wishing she were dead.

Charles got up at five-thirty and went and sat on his couch. His dog came over and rested his muzzle on Charles's knee and rolled his yellow eyes up to lock on Charles's face. Charles rubbed the dog's head absentmindedly with the base of his palm. He thought he knew what needed to be done, although he wasn't going to rush himself. He didn't want to think about it in a precise way yet.

He called Anna at nine. He didn't want to add to her pain, he told her, but he thought maybe they should skip the Flame Room that night. She said that would be a relief, that she didn't feel like going anywhere. Charles found himself talking to her as though she were a child, softly but emphatically, taking time to explain, to assure himself that she understood what he meant, that she was not afraid. Anna spoke back to him only when he put a question to her, in flat affirmations that she had heard, that she had understood. She felt like she were being led somewhere, that she was being lined up to march in a parade.

They talked in this way for the next several days. They did not see each other, but Charles called every morning and said the same things: that he was thinking about it all the time and that everything would be all right. Anna could not imagine how anything could be made all right under the circumstances, but she had nothing else to believe, and she shut out everything and everyone that might raise any doubt of it. Alice Mercer called her every day, and Anna kept telling her that she and Charles were deciding what to do and that it would be fine. Alice sounded worried even as she tried to be encouraging. Anna kept their conversations short. She changed the subject suddenly, inquiring about Roger's job, about Linda's rash. Sometimes Alice thought she sounded a little bit nuts.

The following Saturday night, after Douglas was asleep and his cup and Anna's plate and fork lay dripping on the kitchen drainboard, Charles finally came over again. They sat on the floor, by the fireplace, and Anna could smell the dead ash and the blackened hulks of logs. Charles spoke as though he were enumerating points one by one on his fingers. But he was stammering. He was trying to sound thoughtful and kind, measured and wise, but to Anna he was like God, sending Isaac and his father up the mountain, insisting on blood and sacrifice while saying how much it pained him.

"If we're going to have a life together, we can't begin it like this, you know—an elopement, a baby months too early, everyone talking about us. Your family would be ashamed of us. I'd probably be asked to leave the firm, never mind becoming a partner. It wouldn't really be a life at all, would it?"

Anna wanted to ask why it wouldn't be, why there wasn't some other place and some other people to live among, where they could take this baby and live simply with it and with each other. But she knew there was no other life, none at all.

"We'll have a baby, darling, but not this baby, not this way."

Anna said nothing. Her silence mounted up like snow and stood softly as apparent assent to everything Charles said. Charles felt he was being good. He felt a little heroic and very frightened at the same time. He put his arm around Anna and kneaded her shoulder. Anna turned her head and looked at him as if she was going to disagree. But she said, "Just tell me what to do, Charles."

"Don't worry. I'll take care of everything."

Anna began to weep softly, and then she stopped and stood and took his hand and pulled him up. "Come. Please."

In her bedroom, she undressed. Her breasts were full and ruddy, and he thought there was a faint swell in her belly. He sat down on the edge of the bed, motionless. She crawled across the bed and put her arms around him from behind. "Please," she said, her voice dry and faint. He reached down and began to unlace his shoes.

After he had taken off the rest of his clothes, he lay down next to her. He touched her breasts restlessly, as though tousling a child's hair. She touched him back, but his entire body was flaccid, resolutely lifeless. His eyes combed the freckles on Anna's arms, the translucent hairs around her nipples, the cracks in the ceiling. He might have been waiting for a train to arrive, for a flock of ducks to light on the pond in his backyard.

Anna slid down his side and took his penis, limp and somnolent as an empty glove, and put it in her mouth. She had never done this before. It was warm, soft, inert. Then it began to stir like something feathered, and its length stretched to fill her mouth. She ran her tongue along the bottom, where it felt like a tiny thread ran. She heard Charles sigh and she felt his hand on her head, pulling her up to him. "No, not that," he said sadly. "Just lie here with me. I'm sorry. Sometimes you just can't make things happen." He sounded a little angry. He rolled over. "Let's just lie here, okay?" he said. "We can just do that, can't we?" Anna nodded and pressed herself against his back. She wondered if he had ever gotten a ring for her. She wanted to ask him if he still loved her, but she said nothing.

IV

February

IT WAS NOT, CHARLES THOUGHT, WHAT ALCOCK PROBABLY had in mind when he proposed that Charles involve himself in the community on the firm's behalf. He was standing in his shirt-sleeves with Randy Tyrell in the men's room at the Lowry Hotel. The costume was red with a cape, made of rayon, and there was a cloth helmet with horns. There was also a tube of black grease-paint, another of purple, and some kind of red lipstick. "Put the makeup on first," Randy told him. "Don't want to mess up your headgear. But use lots of the black. When you kiss them, the idea is to leave a big mark."

"How do the victims get selected?"

"Just watch and follow my lead. Mostly old ladies and young dames."

"And they don't mind—being grabbed and kissed on the side-walk by a man in a devil's suit?"

"They love it. It's one of the great Winter Carnival traditions. Many are called, few are chosen. But we're not devils. We're Vulcans."

"Whatever we are, it's damned silly," Charles said.

"It's an essential part of the great allegorical drama of the car-nival. There's Boreas and his court, the god of cold, of winter, of repression. But we represent the archetypal principle of fire, heat, passion, the life force—the triumph of spring over winter."

"And we get to mash girls in the process."

"In a worthy cause. Remember to give them big sloppy kisses so you leave a nice smear on their faces. It's a badge of honor for them, to be kissed by a Vulcan," said Randy, coloring his lips in the mirror. Charles finished blacking his face, rinsed his hands under the tap, and shook the water from them. "I feel ridiculous," he said, as he pulled on the red trousers and tunic.

"Don't," said Randy, adjusting his cowl. "It's fun. It's a chance to act like a fraternity boy again—all in the guise of being a good citizen."

"I never belonged to a fraternity. How's this?" Charles said, turning his face to Tyrell for inspection.

"Your lipstick's a mess, but otherwise you'll do. Now relax. Don't be such a goddamned grind." He held open the door. "Come on—let's go do our duty."

They padded down the hall like outsized cats through the lobby and out onto Wabasha Street. The cold struck Charles heavy as a slap. "Christ," he said, "these outfits aren't exactly warm."

"The conscientious Vulcan wears long johns. Anyway, just keep moving. It'll keep you warm and get you into the spirit. We're supposed to be a bit frenetic."

They walked north toward Fifth Street, where a group of thirtyish women stood at the corner waiting for the light to change. One of them saw Charles and Randy and pointed toward them, alerting her companions. They erupted in giggles and scurried hurriedly across the street. Randy called after them, "Ladies! Ladies! You can run, but you can't hide." The women ran down the slope toward Cedar Street.

Randy and Charles continued north on Wabasha. It was the first weekend in February, and still dark at five-thirty in the afternoon. Two women in their twenties emerged from a jewelry store just in front of them. Randy glanced at Charles, nodded, and grasped the woman closest to him by the shoulders. "Happy Winter Carnival, my dear," he growled, and nuzzled her hard with his black face. The woman shrieked and then laughed. Randy looked over at Charles and hissed, "Norden!"

Charles thrust his face toward the other woman and kissed her softly. Her cheek was downy, the warmth blushing out of it in the cold. She smelled of Ivory soap and baby shampoo, he thought, and her hair brushed his face as he pulled away. He felt curiously intimate with her, as though he had broken into her house and rifled her bedroom drawers. She, too, laughed, but as if she had been a little inconvenienced. She looked at her girlfriend, grabbed her hand, and dashed away, pulling her friend after her. "Top of the carnival to you, ladies!" Randy shouted after them. The one he had kissed looked back grinning, and called back merrily, "Horny devils!"

"Oh, we get that all the time," Randy shouted back, as her friend yanked her down the street. He turned to Charles. "Now that wasn't so bad, was it? Let's go up to Schuneman's. The women come pouring in and out of there."

For the next twenty minutes they scoured the entrances of the department store between Sixth and Seventh streets, catching women as they came out the revolving doors. Charles pecked them dutifully while Randy embraced each one and laughed flirtatiously deep into her ear. The women tittered and shrieked as though reciting a pledge they'd put to memory long ago, darting away like robins in the snow, cupping their hands to their mouths in whispered commentary. From time to time Charles lost sight of Randy, and felt himself a little turned around, as though he had not walked this block a hundred times. Perhaps he was disoriented by the costume, the aimless prowling of the task they had set themselves. Then Randy found him and led him back down to the corner of Sixth and Wabasha, and they stationed themselves there for a while. A little boy tugged at Charles's trouser leg while he kissed the boy's mother, and when two elderly women appeared from the revolving door, he bravely lifted the veil from the head of one and kissed her, dusting his lips with face powder, with the dry crepe of her flesh. Charles was largely silent; Tyrell chortled, naughty but avuncular, the very Santa Claus of eros.

By six o'clock, Charles was cold and confessed to Randy he had had enough. His makeup was smeared, rubbed away in places like condensation from a window. "Let's go have a drink at the Hotel Saint Paul," Randy proposed, and they turned down Sixth toward St. Peter Street. Two policeman walking their beat doffed their caps to them. Randy called out, "Just keeping the ladies in line, much as you do, officers," and wagged his horns at them with his fingers.

In the lobby of the hotel, Randy headed toward the bar while Charles ducked into the men's room. He loosened the waistband of the red trousers and found his fly, and stood a long time urinating. The ice cubes in the urinal crackled and shifted as he emptied himself and pulled up his zipper and readjusted the ridiculous red pants. An old black man rose from his chair and handed Charles a towel, and Charles snaked his hand back into his trousers and found a dime for him. Then he went to the mirror and the basin and pulled off the cowl and rubbed the last of the greasepaint from his face. Some of it had smeared onto his shirt collar and he decided to leave on the rest of the costume.

When Charles found Randy at the bar, he was sitting with a slightly portly man in a bow tie, red-cheeked and perhaps fifteen years older than Charles. Randy spun on his stool. "Chuck, do you know Henry Finch? He's a friend of the MacEwan family. I've been telling him about your good fortune with Anna."

Charles inhaled sharply. He did not want anyone speaking to anyone about Anna and him. He himself had not said Anna's name out loud to anyone save Anna herself in days. He telephoned her each day, reassured her, and then tried to put her out of his mind so he could work, so he could live as he once had—even as the task of finding someone to do something about her pregnancy hung over him like a tax, like the payment of an overdue bill.

Finch began to speak before Charles could acknowledge him. "I don't think we've met, but I'm sure I saw you at Jimmy Mac-Ewan's funeral. And of course I've heard about you—I'm very close to Richard and Sarah. I was Jimmy's best friend." Finch extended a pink, fleshy hand to Charles. His fingers were thick and there were depressions where his knuckles should have been, like a toddler's. "Pleased to finally make your acquaintance," Charles said, and shook Finch's hand, holding the red cowl limply in the other. He flagged the bartender. "Double Scotch rocks." He suddenly felt weary.

Charles, Randy, and Finch talked for the next half-hour, or rather, it seemed to Charles, he and Randy listened to Finch, who paused only to feed himself nuts and potato chips from the bar. Charles had another double and then a single while Henry told them about the city of twenty-five years ago, when he and James MacEwan drank with Scott and Zelda Fitzgerald and there were Chicago gangsters and bootleggers holed up on Lexington Avenue. "This town was wide open as Paris, France. Now it's goddamned Kankakee with parking meters," Henry said, and unthreaded his bow tie.

Randy got up from the bar, saying he had to get home, and Charles thought to join him, but sat back down. He was not enamored of Finch's conversation, but believed he would like another drink. He told Randy he would find his own way home, and Randy slapped him on the shoulder. "You did fine tonight, Norden. We'll make you head Vulcan next year at this rate. Full-time job during the carnival." Charles groaned, and Finch reached over and slapped him on the back.

After Tyrell had gone, Finch proposed they drive up to the Admiralty Hotel and have another drink. "It has a certain savoir faire this place lacks—scene of many epic nights in the past with Jimmy and the gang."

Charles agreed. "But I think I better run back to the Lowry and get my jacket and coat from my car, get rid of this getup."

"Oh, hell, don't worry about it. They've seen stranger things up there. I'll drive you back down when we're done. Seize the day—that's what I say—or at least grab a drink: a snort in time saves nine, eh?"

Charles nodded, and he and Finch rose. Finch's car was parked across the street, a black DeSoto rounded as a tortoise. Charles had to clamber over a snowbank to get to the passenger door and nearly lost his footing. He realized he was feeling his liquor.

Finch pulled out into the street, and whistled softly while he drove, steering with one large white hand, tuning the radio with the other. "Crap, nothing but crap," he said disgustedly, and turned the radio off. The car reached the top of the hill, and Finch pointed down the street, past a skating rink on the corner. There was a white house, its windows dark, tall but half-hidden behind heaps of plowed-up snow. "That's where they lived, all of them—Jimmy, Dicky, and the parents. Now it's a goddamn Catholic retreat house or something."

Charles nodded, and Finch accelerated the car across the intersection and down the street. The house disappeared among the hulks of bare trees and dim streetlights. "What were the parents—Anna's grandparents—like?" Charles asked absentmindedly.

"Oh, antediluvian. I mean, they were the last of the nineteenth century, weren't they? I mean, they remembered the Civil War, Abraham Lincoln—all that. Grim as a grave digger's shovel, I'd say. He went to work and made money. She ordered the maids around and prayed. I'm not sure I ever saw them display the slightest affection to each other." Henry stopped the car in front of the Admiralty Hotel, stopped the motor, and withdrew his key.

"What about the sons?"

"Oh, I don't know—not so you'd notice. But that's the way it was. My parents too. My mother was sweet to me, but my father either treated me like a puppy he was trying to house-train—stern without being angry, like a goddamned butler—or it was as though he was a little afraid of me, as though if he looked me in the eye too closely I'd say boo and frighten him to death. But they loved me. It was the same as believing in God back then—it was inconceivable that they didn't."

Henry reached into the glove compartment and took a cigarette. "Want one?" Charles shook his head. Henry spun the wheel on his lighter. The flame lapped his face. "I suppose it was the same thing with Jimmy and Dicky. But it was obvious they liked Jimmy more—I mean, everyone liked Jimmy. They favored him.

Meanwhile, Dicky's doing exactly as he's told, never putting a foot wrong, while Jimmy's doing exactly as he pleases, not giving a shit. And it doesn't make any difference: Jimmy's still the favorite." Henry swung open his car door and stopped and looked at Charles. "Crazy things, families, eh?"

"Absolutely."

Charles felt acutely self-conscious as he crossed the street to the hotel and the headlights of cars scanned his red trousers and top. The Admiralty bar was empty, pulsing with only the faintest suggestion of life, like a sleeping bear. Last December's Christmas decorations hung behind the bar and a caterpillar of ash dangled precipitously from the bartender's cigarette as he dried glasses.

Henry and Charles settled into a booth. The bartender appeared not to notice them. Henry shrugged his shoulders. "This place used to have so much class." He rose, went over to the man at the bar, and ordered a couple of Scotches. The bartender nodded mutely, and a minute later shuffled over, laid down two thin cocktail napkins, and set down their drinks.

Finch surveyed the room again. "This was the place, this very booth—with Jimmy and me, I mean. Let me tell you about Jimmy."

Charles thought maybe he should call Anna, but then wondered why. He said to Finch, "All right."

"He was the best man I ever knew. It's that simple. A gentleman. A sportsman. A philosopher. A magician."

"A magician?"

"You bet. He could change people. He could enter a room and everything would change. Tell me that's not magic." Henry didn't wait for Charles to tell him. "He just pulled you into his . . . his realm, I guess, and you forgot whatever it was you'd been doing or thinking. It really was like magic. Hell, it was fun. You and I could be sitting here, sad sacks, griping about work or what have you, and Jimmy could walk in, sit down, order a martini, and just by the by, suggest that we all drive down to Chicago, just for the hell of it, right then. And you would do it, just up and do it, unquestioningly."

Finch thrust his big index finger into his cigarette pack and

116

rooted around in it for one of the last remaining cigarettes. He found one and then another. "Want one?" he asked Charles. "Sure I do," Charles said. Finch lit their cigarettes and went on.

"Christ, what a man he was," Finch exhaled, and waved his arm at the bartender, and when he had gotten his attention, wagged two fingers at him. "It's like what Ernest Hemingway says. You know, 'grace under pressure.' That was Jimmy. Not like in the stories, but in the bullfighting stuff." The bartender set two more drinks on the table as though dumping a load of coal and shambled away. Henry sucked the top quarter-inch of Scotch off his, and went on. "You know, it's called *The Sun Also Rises*. Great book. Guys down in Spain, watching bullfights, being real buddies. And there's this beautiful, sexy Englishwoman."

Charles had finished his drink and was a third of the way through the one the bartender had just brought. He was feeling a little distracted. He looked around this room where he had never been before. He wondered if they had a pay phone. Then Finch was talking again.

"Jimmy would've gotten that girl, no problem."

Charles looked at him. "What girl?"

"The English one—Lady Felicity Sparkplug-Jones or whatever. Hell, I don't know. The point is, with women, Jimmy was a charmer, like a snake charmer with the cobra in the basket." Finch's eyes looked huge and moist, although there was nothing sad about him.

Charles asked, "Was he ever married?"

"Once. For a little way. Pretty girl from high society. I don't think it even lasted a year. Everybody forgot about it, as though it had never happened. More of Jimmy's magic."

"So there were no children?"

"That we know about." Henry laughed. "He might have been a good father, at least to a son."

"But lots of women."

"Oh, lots. Not that he was a seducer—they wanted him, you see. Couldn't keep away from him, and damn the consequences. There were never any hard feelings."

Charles was feeling daring, and, he realized, quite drunk. "So there could be unacknowledged heirs, so to speak."

"You mean bastards of Jimmy's? I doubt it. It just wouldn't happen, not with Jimmy's luck. Or if it did, he'd just magic them away."

"You mean getting rid of a pregnancy?"

"Easily enough done, especially a few years back. It's tougher now, I suppose."

"How easy?"

"Easy as going to the doctor. Pay your two hundred dollars, and the problem's gone. I told you, this was a wide-open town."

Charles wanted to talk loudly, ebulliently, but he calmed himself. "But it's illegal. I mean, how did people locate the people who did this stuff?"

"Oh, everybody just knew. Or you could ask someone who would know."

"Like who?"

"Oh, a bartender, a bellman, a cab driver, a cop. Hell, maybe a priest."

"A cop? A priest?"

"Well, maybe not a priest. But a cop—sure. How do you think they'd be allowed to practice in peace if the cops weren't in on it? I mean, the cops know who they're choosing to ignore. It's just two sides of the same coin. You want to find a whore, a crap table, a bookie, an abortionist, a bar where fairies meet each other. Ask a cop. Who would know better? Just make sure he likes you first."

"And you think it's like that now?" Charles said.

"No, not so much. Maybe there's two teams competing in the world, and one's called good and the other's called evil, and sometimes they fight it out and sometimes they have a truce. When Jimmy and I were your age was one of those truce times. Everybody got along. Now it's different, I think. You know, we won the war, and now we have to defeat whatever seems like Hitler here at home—crime and vice and so forth. So good and evil are going at it again. Even though they're just two sides of the same coin. Even though they really kind of need each other. Jimmy would have put it that way—that they needed each other."

"But it's still all out there—I mean, when girls get in trouble, they still find—"

"Oh, sure, although I haven't really had to deal with those kind of problems in a while. It's just quieter, more secret, sort of underground." Finch drained the melted ice from his glass and looked at his watch. "Eight-thirty. Guess I'd better be going—get you back downtown."

Charles thought for a second. "No, that's okay. You go ahead. I'll get a cab."

Finch stood. "You sure? Well, at least let me get the drinks."

"Fair enough. I've enjoyed talking to you."

Finch reached around to his back pocket and extracted his wallet and moved to the bar. "It's been a pleasure for me too," he said, and lay two dollars on the bar. The bartender picked them up without comment, punched the register open, threw in the bills, and slammed the cash drawer home with a clatter and the dull clang of the register's bell. Finch waved his hand to Charles and began to walk out. "Be nice to Dicky's little girl, okay?"

"Absolutely," said Charles. When Finch had left, he moved over to the bar and said, "I wonder if you could call me a cab?" The bartender nodded and went over to the counter behind him and dialed the phone, waited, and then muttered some words into the receiver. He turned to Charles and said, "Be about five minutes." Charles said, "Good. Thank you." He sat down at the bar. He knew he was drunk already and didn't want to order another drink. He wondered if he should try to engage the bartender in conversation, wondered if he even might be able to ask him if he knew of someone who could help Anna. The bartender was leaning against the back counter of the bar perpendicular to him, holding a crossword puzzle magazine. Charles could see his sallow, bony handwriting in the magazine, hear his pencil scrawling. Charles couldn't bring himself to open his mouth. It was like approaching a girl he didn't know at a dance, like buying a packet of prophylactics. He decided to wait in the lobby. "Good night," he called to the bartender, who nodded.

The cab pulled up by the hotel awning a few minutes later, and

Charles walked out to meet it. He was suddenly conscious of the cold and of the costume, as though someone had shone a bright light onto him. The cab throbbed and hummed like a shaggy animal, breathing deeply and black as coal. He got in, and saw the driver's eyes in the rearview mirror. "Lowry Hotel, please."

"Very well, sir." The cab pushed off from the curb and into the street. Charles could still see the eyes in the mirror, the amber glow of the light in the meter window, the needles and dials on the dashboard. "A beautiful evening," the driver said. It was indeed, clear and cold and the stars discernible above the rooftops. "Yes. Very," said Charles, and then he found himself talking, wanting to talk. "I was having a drink with a friend. I'd been downtown, dressed up like this, being a Vulcan. Rather silly, I guess."

"Oh, not at all, sir. Good clean fun. Kiss the girls and make them smile, eh, sir?"

"I suppose," said Charles, "but I think next year I'll pass. The costume's not very warm."

"But really rather handsome, I think, sir. Anyhow, I love the carnival. Every morning I work on the clues in the paper for the treasure hunt, not that I suppose I'll ever find it." Charles was aware the cab driver had turned right at the bottom of Western Avenue, that he was apparently going downtown by a route unknown to Charles. But Charles found he didn't care. He wanted to talk and he was quite drunk. He talked about his work, about his car, about his time in the navy, such as it was. The driver nodded and said, "Isn't that the truth, sir," or "Exactly."

The window next to Charles was fogging up, but he could see that the cab had turned, that they were descending a hill. There were huge red letters flashing in the distance. "I'm not sure I know this route," Charles said. "Oh, it's a shortcut," the driver said. "It's really for the best, sir." It was clear outside, but sometimes Charles could swear a flurry of snow had risen up from the street, blinding and pelting the car in shrouds of white; that a squall of icy wind was battering the doors. He went on talking, and then he found himself saying, "This is rather awkward." He laughed lightly and the driver said, "Yes, sir?"

Charles went on. "I have a woman friend, and she's gotten herself into a tight squeeze, into a bit of trouble, you understand."

"I see, sir."

"Anyway, I know nothing about this sort of thing, but I'm told that sometimes people such as yourself know where a woman might be able to find help with a situation like that."

Charles waited, and then he saw the eyes in the mirror, and the driver said, "I was raised a good Catholic boy, sir. I'm sure I wouldn't know anything about such things."

Charles felt mortified. He tripped over his words. "Oh, I'm so sorry. I really am. I intended no offense. It was just that people had told me that—"

The driver's voice was soft, like smoke and the smell of breakfast cooking. "Oh, it's all right, sir. I understand. Why don't you tell me all about it?" And so Charles did.

Charles told the driver about Anna and how she didn't deserve this, that she was a good person, a fine person; that she had beautiful, deep, sad eyes and lustrous hair and a little boy she was devoting her whole life to. He said he wanted to marry her, and then he realized that this would alert the driver to his complicity in her situation, but he didn't care.

It seemed they had been driving a very long time, that they must have gotten lost or at least had driven through places Charles had never seen before, but then he saw they were at the curb at the Lowry Hotel. The overhead light went on and the inside of the cab was bald and bright as an egg. The driver turned to him, and Charles saw his face for the first time. He had black hair, immaculately Brylcreemed back, a broad, easy mouth, and finely cut nails, white and convex as moons. Charles paid him what was on the meter and tipped him half as much again. The driver said, "Well, thank you very much, sir," and Charles slid toward the door.

"Wait, sir," the driver said, and handed him a little pad of cheap, yellowish newsprint paper. "Write down your telephone number here. I think I know someone who can help your lady friend. I'll call you, or someone else will."

Charles scanned the back of the seat and the dash. There was no registration or taxi license. "What's your name? I mean, how will I know you?" Charles wrote down his number at home and handed it to the driver.

"Oh, that's not important, sir. You'll know me. I'm just your friend, sir."

Charles grabbed the driver's hand. It was dry and cool. He shook it vigorously. "Thank you. Thank you so much," he said, and bolted from the cab.

Inside the Lowry Hotel, Charles pulled off his costume in the men's room and stood at the pay telephone in his shirtsleeves, in his collar tainted with black and red stains. He dialed Anna's number. She answered, weary, removed, as though she were off in Nevada or California.

"Darling, it's me. I think I've found someone who can help you—can help us. Someone trustworthy, someone good."

"Where? How?" Anna asked.

"That's not important. I was downtown, doing Vulcan duty with Randy. We were drinking at the Saint Paul, and we ran into Henry Finch—you know him, I guess—"

"Henry Finch," Anna groaned as though she might begin to cry. "I don't want anything to do with Henry Finch. I don't want him or anyone knowing—"

"He doesn't know anything. That's just by the by. Nobody knows anything. Anyway, later I met someone, someone anonymous, and he thinks he can help. He's going to call me."

Anna said nothing for a while, and then her voice was suddenly quite firm. "Are you sure about this? I'm ten or eleven weeks along. To wait for something that's not going to come through—"

"It will. I'm sure. I mean, I'm paid to be a good judge of character, to think things through. Trust me."

"I do. But this just can't go on. It's killing me. It's killing everything."

"I know. I know. But it's going to be all right." Charles stopped, and then he said, "I really want to see you. You know that, don't you?"

"I know that."

"All right, then. I'll call you tomorrow. I love you," he said.

Anna heard the words, and she said, "I love you too. Good night."

Charles found his car only after walking around the block twice. Once inside, he pulled on his jacket and coat and revved the engine and let the heater roar until the car was warm before he drove off. Now his head was clear and he crossed the river and drove through the night, the etched shadow of his car gliding over the roadway, sharp as an ache. He was home in fifteen minutes, although he could not say by what way he had come.

IT WAS THAT VERY NEXT SUNDAY—THE FOURTH SUNDAY AFTER the Epiphany—that Richard ceased to believe. He had never asked himself if he did believe any more than he asked himself if he was a citizen of the United States of America or the son of his father or the husband of his wife. And it was because of this that he could sit in the pew at St. Botolph's every Sunday—three rows from the front, pulpit side—and daydream like a sleeping dog before the fire, yet still giving assent to his faith, standing, sitting, and kneeling like involuntary motions in his empty-minded rest. But this Sunday he was anxious for the service to end, which is to say he was bored, and that caused him to listen.

The priest prayed: "O God, who knowest us to be set in the midst of so many and great dangers, that by reason of the frailty of our nature we cannot always stand upright; Grant to us such strength and protection, as may support us in all dangers, and carry us through all temptations; through Jesus Christ our Lord . . . "

A while later the priest read the Gospel: how Jesus cured the leper, and then, at Capernaum, how he promised the centurion that when he returned home he would find that his sick servant had been healed.

Richard wondered if any such healings really happened; if, given the cast of this world, whether it was more likely that when the centurion came home he would find his house ransacked, his family and his slaves with their throats cut? And as for the prayer, he doubted whether God afforded any such protection from temptation to anyone, though they might spin their prayers like spiders at their webs. Richard had reined in his own temptations by dutiful willpower and sheer ignorance. Now, he thought, he might regard them more deliberately, hold them up to the light as does a jeweler a gem or a pawnbroker a pocket watch, and consider what it was he forsook or sacrificed. God, such as he was, could keep his nose out of it.

Richard ruminated in this fashion through the ponderous sermon. When Sarah rose to join the line of communicants waiting to kneel at the rail, he shook his head and stood to let her get past him. He did not always receive the Eucharist, and so this would not strike her as anything unusual. He sat and watched the herd of communicants shuffle forward. They were like squads of infantry marching away from him, leaving him to himself.

Afterward, at home, as he laid the fire in the fireplace, he said nothing about his thoughts to Sarah, nor was there any reason he should, about this matter or the other: that she had wanted to do the wrong thing but had done the right thing, not from nobility or virtue but out of pity. He did not want to reflect too much on that pity, or to what extent it was the same thing as love. The ground of their relationship was the fact that they had once adored one another, and that adoration had solidified into companionship. It was not about talking—about speaking and being heard—but about regard; about looking and being seen, about sensing the presence, the gravity of the other, and taking assurance from it that there was beauty and permanence and good in the world; that spring would follow winter, and that in the melting and budding and the glory and horror of it, they too would persist. So it was not about talking: Talking was the least of it. Its precise virtue was that so very little needed to be asked, said, or answered.

Perhaps it was about routine, the rituals that enacted their relation as the Eucharist enacted redemption. Despite the urgings of *McCall's* and *Ladies Home Journal* to revivify one's marriage much as one might refurbish the home or spice up one's cooking, it was not surprise but immutability that anchored them: that Richard would hunch his shoulders in exactly the same sly and impish fashion when he made a pun; that Sarah would stand in the hall, her jaw set, hands on hips, her legs planted like a commodore on the wheeldeck, and survey her parlor, its flowers and decorations, as though she were God on the seventh day; that Richard would lay the fire on Sunday as he was doing now and Sarah would make them toast and soup. That they should do these things in their peculiarity and eccentricity and that they should notice each other doing them and know that each was dependable in these endearing duties and follies—that was a wonder, an absurdity that made them keep faith with each other.

Richard put a match to the fire, kindled with last week's Sunday paper, and prepared to sit down and read this week's. Sarah had put a can of tomato soup on the stove to simmer and came into the living room. "What a lovely service today," she said.

"Oh, yes," said Richard, "Very," and opened the middle of the business section with a sound like the fluttering of wings. Sarah took up the women's section and the travel section and sat down across from him. She snapped through the pages until she found something that interested her. She read and then sighed with annoyance. "More nonsense about hats and gloves—how the fashionable will be giving them up. Good Lord. A woman isn't dressed without gloves." She looked up and spoke to Richard, who was nodding his head from side to side. "It's not a question of custom or fashion. Silly idiots. The point is, it's a filthy world, it's getting filthier, and you don't want to get it on you—not on your hands, or anywhere else."

Richard seconded her with a mumble. Sarah stood and went to the kitchen to make the toast. A few minutes later she returned with a tray. There were four slices of buttered toast, two slightly charred, and two bowls of soup, one with a nebula of pepper ground across it, as Richard liked. He looked up. "Thank you, dear," he said, and put the paper aside. Richard instinctively took the two burned slices of toast for himself and they sat together wordlessly, their spoons ticking and ringing against the bowls in their laps, the fire gasping and sighing. After five minutes, Richard rose and thanked Sarah again, and as was his custom, he put the bowls back on the tray and carried them to the kitchen to wash them together with the empty saucepan. He stood over the sink, scrubbing with a frayed brush and a red checkered washrag, and when he was done he put everything on the drainboard and shut off the light.

Sarah was already seated at her desk in the hall, filling her pen with blue ink. She would spend the next two hours writing letters to addresses on the north shores of Chicago and Boston, the main line of Philadelphia, and sundry towns in southwestern Connecticut—friends, relations, schoolmates from forty years before. Sarah looked up and saw Richard putting on his coat and she smiled. "Going out?" she said.

"To the yard, to check the bird feeders." Sarah tipped her head, as though to motion him to her, and Richard took three steps toward her. He put his gloved hand lightly on her shoulder, and she looked at him and said, "Sweet, dear man," and then, "Don't be long. Don't catch a chill." He nodded pleasantly. Afterward, he knew, around four o'clock, they would take their walk. Then he would make them drinks and they would eat a sandwich and listen to the radio together. Sunday was the hollowest evening, the most eventless and purposeless of the week. There was nothing in it but the radio and the incipience of what needed to be done tomorrow. And lately, the radio had been urging them to buy a television set, as though the radio would soon absent itself from them.

Richard went down the basement stairs. He felt the coalman's delivery card on the beam. The letter was still behind it, soft and springy like gauze beneath a dressing. There was not much seed left in the bag and he picked it up and carried it out the door to the yard. When he was in the house, he never thought about the letter. When he was in the yard he thought about nothing else, and to stop himself from thinking about it, he thought about Susan Nash. And because he could displace the thought of the other thing with the thought of her, he imagined that she—her company, her voice, and maybe the touch of her—could put aside and perhaps heal the pain of his situation, which was not so much now pain as a bottomless confusion. He thought that if he could be with her, he would not be here, and if he would not have the answer to his confusion and his broken faith, at least he would know some other thing there that was solid and real.

There was ice in his big bird feeder, covering what seed was left. He worked it free and tossed it against the arbor of Sarah's rose garden and it shattered like a potsherd. He scooped more seed into the big feeder with his palm and went to the smaller feeder, which was suspended from the branch of a tree near the back of the yard. Snow, settled, partially melted and refrozen, had formed a bench along the rear fence and was tall enough that he could reach the feeder by standing on it. He put a few handfuls of seed into the feeder. When he finished, he looked down around his feet and noticed there were holes in the snow, tunnels dug by squirrels and God knew what else in search of whatever acorns and organic matter might still rest on the ground beneath the snow. Richard could look down into some of the holes, and it was like looking down into a well where the black earth was the water. He decided to scatter the seed he had left on the ground, for whatever it was that dwelled here.

Richard put the empty sack in an ash can that sat by the basement door and went inside and climbed up to the hall. Sarah turned to him from her desk. "All squared away?" she asked. "Fine," he said. "I'll just go finish the paper." Sarah said, "I'll only be a little while, dear."

He sat down on the sofa. The fire had ebbed to coals, glowing tangerine and oxblood on the grate. He could feel the heat drop over him like a gown of dull, heavy felt and then he was asleep. When he awoke, Sarah's hand was on his shoulder. "You dozed off for an hour or so." She had on her fur coat and her gloves. The coat hung to her calves in chevrons and stockades of fox pelts. "I got to write just about everyone. And now I'm ready, if you are." Richard still had on his coat. He rose a little unsteadily.

They shut the front door behind them. The sky was deepening.

Drips fell from the eaves of the porch intermittently and hit the snow with the sound of fat dropped on a hot grill. Sarah and Richard locked arms like intertwined teacup handles and descended the steps. They would walk down to the bluff above the river and then back on the street that ran behind their house.

Sarah pressed her arm against his and nuzzled him with a tiny shiver. "I didn't think it was this cold," she said.

"It wasn't earlier, when I was out back. But the sun's going down. And it's still the middle of winter," Richard said.

"Yes. And March still to come. And what passes for April. I could never get used to what passes for spring here: May and a week at either end."

"I've never known anything else," Richard said.

"And you make the best of it. I remember the first time I came up here. You and Jimmy had this elaborate snow castle or whatever, with doors and tunnels."

"It was a fort."

"A fort, then. Anyway, the two of you forced me to crawl around in this thing and there'd been a thaw, and it was like the trenches—"

"It was scarcely like the trenches," Richard broke in.

"Well, wet and muddy as hell. And I ruined a pair of shoes and a white muff, too. My favorite, prettiest one. It looked like a drowned rat."

"It was your initiation. And I never put you up to anything you didn't want to do. It was James who insisted—" Richard stumbled on a frost-heaved paving stone and recovered his balance.

"Are you all right, dear?" Sarah said, tightening her grip on his arm.

"—who insisted on things like that." Richard stopped. "Yes, I'm fine." His ankle hurt and he felt unsettled, as though lost or dizzy, and now he was irritated. "So you can't blame me for that. That was Jimmy. Anyhow, you were overdressed."

Sarah tried to humor him. "Oh, I hope so. I pray never to go native in that department."

Richard's anger subsided, and he felt tender, not perhaps toward

Sarah, but toward himself or the past they had inhabited together. "You were lovely," he said softly. He felt he could weep. Sarah pulled his arm tight.

"You know it's your birthday next Saturday, and I took the liberty of organizing a little something. Just a few people—at the club, so there's no messing up the house or worry."

"I don't really want anything. Fifty-one—it's rather a minor occasion. You did so much last year. Let's just give it a rest for one year."

"It's nothing, darling. Just drinks and canapés handed around. It isn't costing a thing."

"That's not the point." Richard noticed the sensation of gentle regret that had touched him a moment before had passed. But there was no anger in its place. "I just really don't want all that, dear," he said wearily. "I'm being frank."

"I'm sorry you feel that way. I'm afraid it's arranged. People are already invited. Will you just go through it for me, and I promise you that you never have to do it again, if that's what you want?"

"No—I mean, yes. That's fine, dear. I'll do it for you." They had reached the bluff. The sun was low on the horizon, glowing like a dirty incandescent bulb in the gray sky. Sarah pressed up against him and pecked him on the cheek. "You're very kind, very understanding. And you know, it's going to be fun. You'll see. You need cheering up, anyway. You don't seem very happy lately, you know. It's the season, I suppose."

"Oh, yes," Richard said, and clasped her arm a little more tightly. "It does that to you. Even if you've been through it all your life." Across the river and up the boulevard, the streetlights began to come on, a block at a time. Somewhere downtown, Richard supposed, there was a man deep in a basement in city hall throwing switches, bright copper shanks with black Bakelite handles, and when he was done, he would go sit by the boiler and listen to the radio. Richard gripped Sarah a little tighter and then released the pressure, as though telegraphing her. "Shall we go?" he said.

———

ALICE MERCER TURNED UP ON ANNA'S DOORSTEP ON MONDAY morning, uninvited and unexpected. Anna opened the door with an expression of befuddlement that she hastily rearranged into one of welcome. Alice's Linda saw Douglas standing next to his mother and made a face of frozen disgust. Douglas turned and buried his head in Anna's skirt.

"I was just driving by, and I thought, What the heck?" Alice said, although the truth was rather different. She had been concerned for some time about Anna's demeanor, or rather the lack of it; the sense that there was a little less of her each day, that her color and character were slowly bleaching away, that her soul was afflicted with a wasting disease. She scarcely called anymore, and she brushed aside Alice's questions, not evasively, but as though she were too tired to frame the answers.

Anna motioned Alice into the living room. "It's . . . it's kind of a mess. But sit, please." Alice smiled and said, "No, you sit. Relax. I'll make us coffee. I know where things are." She lunged toward the kitchen before Anna could object or launch into another apology.

The shade in the kitchen window was half pulled down, and the chair sat akimbo to the table, an ashtray and a pack of Chesterfields placed on it like a desk set. Alice took the percolator to the sink and filled it. The sink and the drainboard were empty, save for a baby's cup, spoon, and bowl, and a saucer gilded with toast crumbs. She carried the percolator over to the counter, set it down, and opened the cupboard. Next to a jar of toothpicks, a box of birthday cake candle holders, and a vial of red and green cookie sprinkles was a three-pound can of Butternut coffee. Alice scooped two measures into the percolator basket, and decided to double it. She plugged in the percolator and called out to Anna, "All set. It'll be just a minute."

There was no reply, and Alice went to the doorway and looked out to the living room. Anna was crouched by the fireplace, stacking blocks in front of Douglas, who sat on the rug. Linda stood a few feet away, watching, her arms folded. "I'll have some coffee for us in a minute," Alice repeated. Anna looked up, her eyes cloudy as pearls, and said, "Good." Alice glanced at Linda, who looked back at her disconsolately. Douglas was pushing a block around on the floor, making thrumming noises. "Linda, why don't you sit down and play with the blocks, sweetie? Why don't you make a house? You're a big girl, you can do that."

Alice went back into the kitchen, opened another cupboard, and found two cups and saucers glazed in a dull, dead grass green. She turned around and leaned with the small of her back against the counter, and she thought she could feel the weight of the child in her pelvis. The coffee burped in the percolator and showed chestnut in the glass knob on top. She poured two cups and went back to the living room. Then she sat down on the sofa and called Anna over to her, stroking the cushion next to her with her hand. "Come over here and talk to me, sweetie."

Anna walked over and slumped on the sofa, her back like a slide of earth on a roadside. She was clearly unamenable to small talk, and Alice decided not to make any. "Drink your coffee, and tell me about you and Charles and everything."

Anna sipped her coffee once and then again. "Do you make it this strong for Roger?"

"No, he'd blow a fuse. This is for girlfriends only." Alice put her hands on her knees. "And what sort of coffee do you make for Charles these days?"

"I scarcely see him." Anna took a cigarette from a pack on the coffee table and lit it with an ornate silver lighter that must have been a wedding gift left over from her and Jack. She sat silently for a moment with the cigarette hanging from her lip. "He's found someone."

"Someone?"

"To take care of the problem. To get rid of it."

"Where? How?"

"I don't know. He says I shouldn't know."

"But who is it? Is it a doctor?"

"I don't know. Charles said to trust him. He says they'll call him and everything will be arranged."

"When?"

"I don't know that either. Soon, I suppose."

"You don't know much, do you? It *is* your health at stake, your life."

"Beggars can't be choosers." Anna laughed. The coffee seemed to have brightened her. There was a sharp, sudden noise and she sat up straight. Douglas had clacked two blocks together with enormous force. Linda yelped and looked plaintively at her mother. Anna sipped her coffee again, and continued. "You know, I used to sort of like not knowing things—just doing what I was told. I used to like knowing what the rules were, what was expected, how it was I was supposed to be. It seemed like men *knew*, women only guessed. But now I think that even if you don't think you're breaking the rules or just misunderstand them, you can get shut out, shut away without knowing how or why. Because it seems like only men know what the rules are—the real way the world works."

"Or at least they pretend to. Maybe they make it up as they go along."

"I don't know. I thought I liked it that way—that it helped make me pretty and good and demure. And now I feel like I'm going off to this foreign country to do this awful, shameful thing that's illegal, and it's the same place they send the criminals and the lunatics—"

"Don't talk like that, Anna. This is something women have to do all the time."

"It's not something *I* have to do all the time."

"But it doesn't change who you are. And it's Charles's problem too. He's helping you, isn't he? He hasn't changed toward you."

"He hardly comes over and we hardly talk. He just says not to worry, that everything's under control. He comes over and we stare at each other and I think he can barely wait to leave."

"What about the engagement? Has he said anything?"

"No, and I won't ask him. I'd be afraid of the answer—or that just by mentioning it I'd put him off, if he isn't already put off."

"He must still love you. He's just panicky. I mean, it's an awful situation for him too."

"He doesn't look at me. I don't think he wants to touch me."

"Not at all?"

"Oh, we tried once or twice, but something always spoils it. It's like making love in a shoebox of broken china or something. It's as though he can't bring himself to be near me, that there's something foul about my body or something that's going to hurt him."

"Maybe he blames himself. Maybe he can't face what he's done, not what you've done." Alice stopped. She felt very confused and very wise. "So maybe he's afraid of you, afraid of your body."

THE WEEKEND HAD COME AND GONE, AND NOW SO HAD Monday. Charles had sat in his house every night, waiting for the phone to ring, afraid to call anyone for fear that the man from the cab would get a busy signal and never call back. He had phoned his father back east very early on Sunday, before he thought anyone in St. Paul would even be awake. His father was a doctor. He had hands that could tie tiny sutures and a voice that was mellow like an old oak barrel, like a father ought to have. They talked for a few minutes, and then his father had asked him why he had called, as though there was something in Charles's voice that indicated that he needed to ask him a question. Charles said there was no special reason. It was just that they hadn't talked in so long. So what was there to do in Minnesota in the winter, his father asked, satisfied. Had he tried ice fishing, he asked, and then laughed. Charles said no, that the weather meant you could just work that much more. You were always a worker, his father told him. Charles said that it was because he had taught him to be, and now he wanted to say, Teach me more. Tell me what to do, tell me how to walk this path, tell me what is right and how to do it. Father, save me. Do it for me. But he hadn't.

In his office on Tuesday morning, Charles went and found an associate in the office whom he knew had dealings with city commissions and boards and the like. He leaned in his office door, as though to remark on the weather or a sports score, and said, "You know, I noticed the oddest thing the other night. I was taking a cab and I was tipping the driver and I wanted to call him by his name. Normally, there's a license or an ID or something of the driver on the dash or the seat back. But there wasn't anything. I mean, aren't these people licensed?"

"Oh, they're licensed. It's a chauffeur's license and I suppose they carry it in their wallet. But this isn't New York or Chicago, where they have the thing like a wanted poster on display. A St. Paul cabdriver isn't going to do anything that anyone would need to take notice of, is he? Or at least that's the theory."

"I was just curious. One of these local customs, I guess," Charles said. He started to pull away from the doorway, but leaned back in. "So I suppose there's no way of finding out who a specific driver is?"

"You could call the cab company, I suppose. Or better still, know the license number of the cab. But who would want to? I mean, cabdrivers—the soul of anonymity."

"Yes, I suppose that's right. One of the few private places left in the world, like the confessional."

"I hadn't thought of that. Cabdrivers—like priests. Hangmen. Judges, I suppose." He laughed and Charles joined him and then tipped his hand to his brow in a gesture like a salute and slipped away.

RICHARD EXCUSED HIMSELF FROM HIS OFFICE EARLY AND DROVE up the hill and past the cathedral. He pretended to be lost, to have no destination, and when he reached Susan Nash's neighborhood he drove in an aimless but deliberate pattern, always keeping a block away from her house, skirting it in a misshapen circle around all four compass points. He did this for ten minutes and then grew impatient with his own foolishness, the delay in doing what he already knew he would do. He turned down her street and glided past her house, scarcely able to catch his breath, and took in her door and her windows with a furtive, sidelong glance. Then he drove three blocks east and turned south and went down the street parallel to hers for seven blocks and turned north again and at the corner of her street he stopped again. He was trying to calm himself. He felt like a child doing something that was prohibited to children but not to adults. And he told himself that he was an adult; that he had every right to drive where he wanted, and if by chance he happened to drive by the home of someone he knew, it was not unreasonable that he might drop in, just on the off chance they were home. It was a trifle, a casual thing of no consequence. It took him ten minutes to convince himself of this as the car smoked and melted the street ice beneath his tailpipe.

He drove slowly the last half-block to the curb in front of her house, as though he were steering an ocean liner into its berth. Then he tugged the bottoms of his gloves down, got out, and ambled to the door, hands in his pockets, all but whistling and scanning the sky for songbirds. He climbed the steps and stood sidelong to the door and then he pounded on the glass in a slow cadence. He looked down at the mat, at the porch floorboards, splintered along their joints and flaking scabrous red paint. He heard nothing and knocked again. He walked to the far edge of the porch and looked down the side of the house. There was a dead Christmas tree, brown and scuttled in a snowbank, and a bicycle leaning under a marquee of icicles, buried in snow to the spokes, its handles pimpled with rust. Still he heard nothing.

Richard went back to the door and pounded one last time, slowly, heavily, like a man driving stakes with a sledge. He waited and pressed his face against the glass and scanned the baseboard that climbed her stairs, the green runner, the rail and its fitments of blackened brass. At last, he turned his back and ambled down the steps and the walk as slowly as he had come, looking back every few steps, sure that perhaps she would come now, that she had not heard him at first, that the door would open and a voice would call. But there was nothing, and when he got into his car and sat for a while, still looking at the door, begging it to open, he thought he might die of desolation. The world was an abandoned city and he had been left, alone, to perish in it. Then he pressed his shoulders against the car seat and drove away, his heart thrusting against his breastbone like a bird throwing itself against a sheet of glass.

SARAH SAT AT HER DESK WITH A STENOGRAPHER'S PAD OPEN IN front of her. She dialed the caterer at the club and introduced herself. "I've got the library booked on Saturday night for a reception for my husband's birthday. Maybe fifty people, and we'll need cocktails and hors d'oeuvres."

"That will be no problem, I'm sure, Mrs. MacEwan," the woman said. Sarah could hear the metallic, ringing, echoing racket of a kitchen in the background. "And you'll want a cake?"

Sarah nearly said yes, and then stopped herself. "No, I don't think so. It's a minor feast, so to speak. One of those birthdays one might wish would just go away."

The woman laughed. "Yes, ma'am. Anything special for the bar, then?"

"No, just the usual gin, Scotch, bourbon, and rye. And mixes. None of these silly South Pacific concoctions, please."

"Cigarettes and cigars?"

"Oh, yes, of course."

"And now the hors d'oeuvres. We're doing some new things that are very popular in New York."

Sarah was not convinced. "Such as?"

"Well, there's little cornets—rolled up cold cuts with cream cheese inside, or deviled ham."

"That sounds rather good. Give us some of those."

"And little meatballs in gravy, kept warm in the chafing dish."

"Yes, we've done those before. The men like them. But I want things that can be passed around too—and you have got people to do that?"

"There'll be a bartender and three servers."

"Fine. Now let's have some melon balls and cheese and an assortment of crackers. But something else with a toothpick, maybe . . . "

"We're doing something that's quite popular with chicken livers rolled up in bacon—"

"Rather vulgar, that one, I think. We'll pass on it. Let's have some of those very thin buttered bread sandwiches done on dark rye, and leave it at that."

"So that's everything, ma'am?"

"I believe so. And the bill goes on our account?"

"Yes, ma'am."

Sarah thanked the woman and hung up the phone. She looked at her list on the stenographer's pad. She had forgotten flowers, and thought she'd better call the club back. And she thought that Richard wouldn't care about flowers, and she was trying to do this his way. And that was the genius of their relationship: His way was her way, and, for the most part, it seemed as though the reverse was true.

Anna's generation made a great show of their big double conjugal beds. She and Richard slept in twin beds as they always had, as everyone who married when they had did. He came to her in the night, like a man with an offering or a supplicant, and touched her as though he were patiently polishing silver. And then he held her for a while and his pajama buttons pressed into her back as he breathed. Then he would kiss her forehead, almost as her father used to do, the covers would rustle and settle back on her body, and he was gone. In the whole time she scarcely saw him.

Now he came to her once a week or so, and she was not conscious of much change in what passed between them. They were quieter than they had once been, they moved more slowly, but he still cupped her head in his palm as he pressed into her and still said her name. But when the lamps were on, when they sat reading, each with a bed tethered to a nightstand, each with a stack of books, a box of tissues, two clocks set perhaps only a minute apart, who were they; or rather, where had the lovers gone?

She thought they were the same, just as until now she thought she knew Richard and what he wanted, but now he didn't want a cake, a celebration on his birthday; and that was how she had known him, by knowing what he wanted without even having to think about it. Now she saw him apart from that, the shadow that lapped the bedclothes and the curtains when he moved away from her bed in the dark, and then as a rower in a scull on a river, his back turned, pulling himself into the haze.

THE CALL CAME WEDNESDAY NIGHT. "IS THIS THE GENTLEMAN who was riding in my cab the other evening?" a voice said.

"Yes, yes, it is," Charles said.

"I've been able to arrange something for your friend."

"Yes?"

"I'm afraid it can't be for ten days or so. The doctor's a busy man."

"It is a doctor, then?"

"Oh, yes, sir—a very fine one."

"So where do we go? When?"

"A week from Saturday. Six o'clock. Why don't we say in front of the Lowry, just where I dropped you?"

"That's it? I mean, you'll take us there?"

"Yes, sir. You'll need to bring three hundred dollars."

"Is that the—"

"Oh, that's the going rate, yes, sir. I suppose you could ask around, if you were inclined."

"No, no. I'm sure that's fair. And how do I reach you, if something changes, if there's a problem?"

"I doubt that would be necessary. Unless your friend's problem went away of its own accord, in which case, so much the better, eh?"

"Yes, I suppose that's true," Charles said. "But I've got to call you something. You have a name, don't you?"

"I suppose you could call me Joseph. Like Mary and Joseph. If you like."

"Yes, Joseph. Or would you prefer Joe?"

"That's of no concern to me, sir."

"So, Joseph—"

"A week from Saturday, six o'clock, the Lowry, three hundred dollars. Good night, sir."

"Good night."

Charles hung up the phone and stood stock-still for a moment. The dog's nails clattered across the kitchen floor, and he heard its tongue paddling in the water bowl on the floor. He went to the refrigerator and opened the door. The cool seemed to bathe him, to illuminate him, and he got an ice tray from the freezer compartment. He put three cubes in a glass and napped them with Scotch and then he stood and drank. He called Anna.

"Anna?"

"Yes?"

"He called me back, the man who knows a doctor."

"Yes?"

"It's all arranged for a week from Saturday."

"Do we have to wait so long? I don't want—"

"The doctor's very busy. It won't make any difference, not really."

"To me it will."

"It's because he's a real doctor—that he's in demand, I suppose—that we have to wait."

"And what do you know about him?"

"Well, nothing beyond that. He can't exactly advertise his credentials."

"Then what about the one who set it up?"

"His name's Joseph. I trust him. He's reliable, steady—I can tell. He wants to help us."

"And how much is it going to cost?"

"Don't worry about that. It's taken care of. You don't have to worry."

"It's hard to stop. It seems like my whole life."

"I know, I know. But it's going to be over. Soon." Charles paused. He tried to sound merry. "So what else is up? With you, with the handsome son?"

"Winter. Cabin fever. Oh, Alice came by. We talked."

"Does she know about this?"

"Of course she does. She's my only friend, really."

"Anna, no one should know, no one at all."

"Well, it's too late. And I trust her more than anyone. I trust her as much as you."

"I'd hope you'd trust me more."

"It's different with girlfriends, Charles. Don't be difficult about it."

"I'm sorry," Charles said, and he did indeed feel a little penitent. "Well, anything else?"

"Oh, yes. I'm afraid Mother's having a cocktail party for Daddy's birthday Saturday night at the club."

"Oh, Anna, I'd really just as soon—"

"Charles, I have to do it. It's my father's birthday. And what does it say to people if you're not there too? And wouldn't you want to—for me?"

"Of course. It's just not what I had in mind at a time like this."

Charles could hear Anna sigh against the mouthpiece. "It isn't what I'd necessarily like to be doing either. But don't you want to be with me anyway? We never see each other."

"I've been very busy at work. And worried sick about you. And trying to fix this predicament. There's a lot of pressure on me. Please don't add to it. Just try to understand."

"Work. Pressure. That's always the excuse, this rabbit you pull out of the hat. Work."

"You should try it sometime," Charles said, and regretted it. "I'm sorry. But can't you see how hard this all is, not just on you, but on me?"

"I never denied that. But I want to be together. I want to see you."

"Do you really? Sometimes I get the feeling that when I come by, you hardly know I'm there," Charles said.

"Sometimes I get the feeling you're just waiting until you can go, until you've done your duty."

They were both silent for a moment. Anna said, "I don't want to lose you in all this, not along with everything else. I feel like I'm in solitary confinement here, that I'm a prisoner."

"Nothing's stopping you from going out, from doing whatever you did before."

"It doesn't seem that way. It seems like the door's locked, or that if I went out people would point and stare, or the police would come and haul me away."

"That's silly, Anna. No one knows anything, no one ever will, and in ten days this will all be over."

"It doesn't seem that way. It seems like this is my whole life now, my future. Even my past, as though I was never anyone else any different from this."

"It's just the way you feel. It's not reality. You'll see. Trust me, Anna."

Anna said nothing for a long time, and then she said in a thin, high voice, "Come and pick me up Saturday night. Take me to Daddy's party. Do that for me. That's all I want from you now. That's everything—enough. It would be enough." It did not seem like so very much to ask as far as Anna was concerned. She felt quite reasonable. But Charles heard it as a scratching at his door, steady and imploring and ascendant like a prayer, buttressed by incense and beads clenched in plangent hands, impelling him to choose among contradictory goods, among awful, pitiless sacrifices.

"All right," he said. "I'll pick you up at six."

THERE WAS A MESSAGE ON RICHARD'S DESK ON WEDNESDAY morning. He'd had a call Tuesday afternoon from a Mrs. Nash at Midway 5-4932. Please call back, it said. Richard had the sensation he'd been caught out in a great mischief he had believed was well secreted, and now there would be hell to pay—not just the penalty itself, but the humiliation of discovery. He tried to distract himself with the other papers on his desk, with the fretting of the pigeons on the ledge outside his window. But nothing kept his mind from the message, and he worked instead at calming himself, at viewing it rationally. He did not succeed, but his fear was replaced by desire, the compulsion to hear her voice, even if it was to accuse him, to scourge him.

He shut his office door, sat down and straightened his back, and dialed the number. She answered, "Hello?" and he thought he might have to pull his breath down from the top of his throat to speak; that he would rasp and squeal like a newly adolescent boy. "Mrs. Nash?" he managed. "It's Richard MacEwan at Miles, MacEwan, and Booth. The law office. Downtown. I have a message that—"

Susan broke in. "Yes, yes, I called. I saw you drive away from my house yesterday. I was just coming up the block back from campus. I phoned to say I was sorry I missed you."

"You saw me?"

"I thought I did, and then I recognized the car. From the other day."

"Oh, I see. Well, you're very kind to call."

"Anyway, was there something else about James? That you needed to ask me?"

Richard swallowed. "Not really. You see, I happened to be in the neighborhood, and I thought—really, just on an impulse—that I'd just drop by. To say hello."

"That would have been lovely. I'm sorry I missed you. It was only by half a minute."

Ease fell over Richard. He felt it tingle in his shoulders and unknit his back. "I enjoyed our talk," he said, still half question, half declaration.

"So did I," Susan said. "Will you come again, some other time?"

"Of course. I'd love to." He wanted to come now, right now. Or tomorrow, before she could change her mind or take umbrage that he had failed to come right away or be put off by his forwardness—or simply by some happenstance cease to care. He began to weave together scenarios that would be decorous but not indifferent, keen and attentive but not overeager.

"Well, I'm home every day but Tuesday and Thursday," Susan said. "Drop by any time. It's just me and my books."

Richard felt he had some latitude, and although he could not bear to wait, he thought he ought to. "What about next Monday afternoon? I have an appointment in Minneapolis in the morning. I could drop by on my way back." This was not true.

"That would be lovely. I'll look forward to it."

"All right. So will I. And thank you, Mrs. Nash."

"Please—Susan would be much nicer."

"Of course," Richard laughed. "Susan it is. On Monday. Good-bye."

"Good-bye," she said and her voice hung in Richard's ear, resonant and sweet as cricket song. He was elated and his elation lasted for hours. He scarcely remembered what he did or who he spoke to. He seemed to fly over the world at a great height, and everything was pastoral, its hedgerows and meadows and copses green and sunlit. And then, late in the day, he wondered what she thought; what she imagined he was coming for; what it was they were going to do, and whether, even now, she was thinking what he was thinking; that she might want what he wanted.

SARAH STOOD BY THE DOOR OF THE CLUB LIBRARY, GREETING HER guests, and Richard stood next to her, genially shaking hands, accepting congratulations, and steering people to the bar. At about six-thirty, when it appeared no one else would arrive, she and Richard moved over to the window and looked out at the city together. A red neon "1st" glinted from the top of an office building downtown. Sarah took his hand. "Now, is this really so awful?" she said.

"No, not at all. As usual, my dear, you were right. Virtually painless." Richard's mood had detectably brightened in the last few days, Sarah felt, and for that she was glad. But there was a breeziness to it, almost a recklessness—if that word could ever be applied to Richard—as though he were caroming off the edges of the world, his good cheer unrooted in any circumstance or person. Sarah was not sure how to feel about this.

She looked back into the room and surveyed the guests, pleased with herself. Then her eyes lit on the buffet next to the bar.

"How did Henry Finch get here?" she said to Richard. "I know he can smell other people's liquor at one hundred yards, but *I* didn't call him."

"I saw him downstairs and told him to come up. There's no harm in it. He really hasn't got a friend in the world, now that James is gone."

"Indeed," Sarah muttered. "Jimmy's foundling son." She watched Finch spear a half-dozen meatballs in quick succession, swallow them down, and slide to the bar and make an expansive pouring gesture to the server. "Have you seen Anna and Charles?" she asked Richard. Henry Finch turned from the bar, saw the two of them, and waved his pinky. Richard waved back while Sarah smiled coolly.

"She came up with Charles and gave me a big kiss earlier," Richard said.

"She's put on weight, don't you think? She's always needed to watch that."

"Not that I noticed. You have a very acute eye."

"She looks a bit frowsy, too. As if she's not sleeping, or she's drinking too much."

"She's fine. Why shouldn't she be? She's got a nice fellow and maybe a fiancé in the bargain."

"I spoke to him when they came in. He was distracted, a little cowed, not as sharp as usual. Something could be wrong between them. I suppose given the way they rushed headlong into things, that wouldn't be terribly surprising."

"I don't think there's anything to worry about. Really. And if there was, there's nothing you could do about it."

"That may be so. But I don't imagine these things, darling. I'm not given to fancies. Don't be surprised if everything's not right with her." Sarah looked at Richard. He was staring down, his lips slightly pursed, stirring his drink with a swizzle stick. The ice was spinning, forming a little amber whirlpool.

At the other end of the room, Anna stood with Charles, who was listening to a partner from her father's firm. Charles nodded from time to time, whether genuinely interested or feigning assent and captivation, Anna could not tell. Having greeted her father, she was prepared to leave, and from time to time she squeezed Charles's hand to indicate this, but he gave no sign of moving. In the interim, she had a drink and then another. She was hidden between Charles and the wall, a position that suited her. She had worn a long-sleeved black dress with a high neck, and even then felt cold and exposed.

The man from her father's firm slapped Charles gently on the back and moved away. Charles nodded toward the door and Anna nodded back. Then Charles said, "Shouldn't we say good night to your parents?"

"No, I'm sure it's all right. This is just a sort of drop-by-for-drinks kind of thing," Anna said, and just then Henry Finch appeared.

"Anna and Mr. Norden, I presume," he said, smiling. "Anna, I met your charming friend downtown the other evening and we hoisted a few together. He's a gentleman, and a Vulcan too." Henry turned to Charles and added, "It's quite a racket. Did it myself one year. Kissing girls with impunity. And you, you, old man, get to escort the lovely Anna to boot! There's no justice."

Charles laughed appreciatively and Anna made a tiny, thin smile, as though she were terribly shy. "Absolutely," Charles said. "Unfortunately, we're on our way to another engagement, or we'd love to talk—really we would." Anna nodded. "Another time, though."

"Yes, indeed," Finch said and waved enthusiastically.

In the car, Anna sat next to the door and fingered the welting on the seat. She wondered why she and Charles weren't sitting close, and slid over. She put her hand on his knee and patted it. "Thank you for coming with me, for bringing me. I know it meant something to Daddy."

"It wasn't any bother. Actually, I enjoyed myself, all things considered."

"Maybe we could go out together by ourselves, like we used to. After this is over."

"I don't see why not."

Anna looked straight ahead out the windshield, and it seemed like the night was a tunnel they were driving through, the walls frescoed here and there with boreal trees and light staffs and little windows glowing hazy butterscotch. She said, "Maybe we could have that date at the Flame Room."

"Maybe."

"I don't suppose you ever got to the jewelry store."

"No. What with everything that's happened, it got past me." It was not a statement that invited or would bear close examination.

"But maybe when this is done—"

"When this is done, everything will be different. And then we'll see what we want to do."

"What do you want to do?"

"I want to get through this. That's all I want for now. I love you, Anna, but don't let's get ahead of ourselves."

"I thought it was where we'd already been," she said.

"I know. Just don't press me—don't press us—beyond where we can go right now. Okay?" He had pulled up in front of her house. "I'm really tired, sweetie. I think maybe I should just go home and turn in. Okay?"

"Okay. Good night." She brushed his lips with hers and pulled herself from the car.

"Good night," Charles said. "Thanks for bringing me to your dad's party. Honest."

Anna shut the door and Charles drove away. She turned toward the house and she saw Mrs. Clay standing inside holding Douglas, looking out at her, like a candle in the window.

RICHARD WAS AT SUSAN NASH'S DOOR AT ONE O'CLOCK ON Monday afternoon. He had checked his hair in the rearview mirror of the car. He wondered at his own eyes, how gray they had come to seem, how much like the hair in his sideburns. In the last few years, he had scarcely ever looked at himself in a mirror except to straighten his tie.

At Susan's doorstep, he began to feel a reprise of the nervousness he had felt the previous week. What, after all, had he come here to do? He wasn't sure he knew. He wasn't sure he could say he had been drawn here or driven here or led here. It was more that he had been lost and this was where he had turned up. He knocked briskly on the door and thought he heard a hinge squeak at the top of the stair and then Susan came down, descending into his view. She wore a sweater and a skirt. The sweater was rather snug, though not so tight as the ones his daughter and her friends wore. The skirt was plaid, with a pin in it. She wore a touch of lipstick, a dark red.

"So at last we meet again," Susan said as she pulled open the door, and Richard suddenly felt as though he hadn't the slightest idea what they could say to each other next. She smiled and he began: "Yes . . . It's good——." She interrupted, not rudely, but as though taking his arm to help him make his next step: "Come up. I have coffee and I made a little cake for us."

"That's very kind, but hardly necessary on my account."

Susan looked over her shoulder at him as they mounted the stairs. "You don't *like* cake?" She smiled as though she knew him well and had caught him in an unconvincing lie.

"I love cake," he said and chuckled. "I just didn't want to be any trouble."

"Your brother didn't mind being trouble. Rather liked it, in fact," Susan said as they entered her living room. "Of course, he scarcely seemed to eat. Lived on cigarettes and drinks and bar snacks, or that's the way it looked to me." She went on talking as she walked into the kitchen and returned with a tray. "Maybe that was revealing. They say the way to a man's heart is through his stomach." She put the tray down and surveyed it. "Ah, coffee. Just a minute," she said and returned to the kitchen. Her voice echoed out through the door, rising and falling in amplitude as she moved around. "So maybe it's also the way to his mind, his soul, who he is. That would be interesting." She reemerged with a glass coffeepot and a sugar bowl. "The man who requires no nourishment——

what would that seem to mean?" She sat down opposite Richard. "But we're not going to talk about him again, are we? Unless you want to?"

"Not particularly. I'd rather like to hear more about you," Richard said, and he found that he meant this very much.

"It seems to me I gabbed about myself endlessly last time—the woes of the war widow and all."

"Not one bit."

"Well, in any case, I'd like to hear about you."

"Very well," Richard said and swallowed.

"Don't seem so grave. This won't be a cross-examination." She sliced the corner from a small, square chocolate cake and put it on a plate. "Here. Eat."

Richard took a bite. The chocolate was rich; the sugar frosting sang in his teeth. "It's delicious," Richard said, and took a sip of his coffee. "So what did you want to know?"

"Whatever you'd care to tell. How about school, career, that sort of thing for starters?"

"Oh, I went to the academy here in town and then a year of boarding school in Connecticut and then Princeton. Left for a year driving ambulances in France in nineteen seventeen and eighteen. Then I finished up back at Princeton and went to law school. Came home, went to work at my father's firm, and been there ever since." Richard put his palms up in the air. "Not much of a story, really, is it?"

"It's as much a one as anyone's got. And I suspect you oversimplify." She grinned at him knowingly. "Let's try the non–*Reader's Digest* version. Where did you go to law school? Harvard or Yale?"

"Neither, actually. Chicago. It's a good school."

"Undoubtedly, but why there in particular?"

Richard did not like where this was going, but he went into it anyway. He would do what she asked. "It was my wife's home. We'd gotten married when I graduated Princeton. It seemed like the thing to do—close to her family, not that far from mine."

"And how did you meet?"

Richard liked this even less. He felt as though he and Susan were sneaking around in a closed museum after hours, and that Susan's voice, her loud, heedless footfalls would alert the guards. "As children. Our families knew each other." He was not inclined to say more.

"How charming. Childhood sweethearts. And so she knew both you and James when you were kids."

"I must have been fourteen or so."

"Which made James . . . ?"

"Nine or ten."

"So your wife—"

"Sarah," Richard said. He did not want to manifest Sarah's presence in this room by saying her name but still less did he want to go on repeating the word "wife."

"Sarah," Susan said slowly, as though trying on a shoe. "So she was—"

"Twelve or thirteen, I'd guess. When we met."

"And did you know right away—"

"Know what?"

"That you were drawn to one another."

"Oh, it wasn't like that at all." Richard laughed, and he thought of himself bare-legged in a sailor suit and Sarah standing with her fingers primly entwined and an enormous bow in her hair, watching him. "I hadn't a clue. I was supposed to entertain her, keep her and James occupied." He prodded his cake with the fork and cut off another bite. "I suppose when I was seventeen or so I began to notice her in that way. She was smart. Knew everything, been everywhere—or so it seemed to me. And she was pretty." Richard was not sure this was a good thing to say.

"And her?"

"Her?"

"How did she come to feel that way about you?"

"I couldn't possibly say. It was more a case of my asking and her saying yes."

"But what prompted all that?"

"Oh, just knowing she was the right person. That she was who I wanted, and not daring to hope I could have her, and asking anyway, and her saying yes. Like a great stroke of luck, like inheriting from a relative you didn't know you even had. I can't imagine what prompted her to say yes."

"I can."

Richard felt embarrassed and awkward, not only by the implicit compliment but by the acknowledgment of overt desire it contained; the alien notion that Sarah did not merely consent to be his wife but actively desired to become this, that she chose him—sought him—as much as he chose her, and that another woman might do the same. "You're very kind," he said at last. "But I was lucky, really—exceptionately fortunate."

"And you're too modest. I'd imagine you and James were considered the biggest catches in town. Particularly you, in fact. Much better husband material than him, I'd guess."

"Oh, I don't know. He married rather well, although it didn't last."

"He never told me that. Although I assumed something like that must have been the case." She stopped. "But there we are—back talking about him again."

"He always was a dominant presence."

"In death as in life, apparently."

"And the interesting part was, he did it without trying. I can still remember how we'd always end up doing what he wanted to do; wanting it for ourselves."

"His magic again." She looked at him. "But you got Sarah, didn't you. You got what you wanted, not him."

Richard felt she was looking very deeply at him and that it would be a kind of cowardice to look away or evade what she was raising. "Oh, I don't think he had any interest in her. Not then—"

"I mean happiness. Satisfaction. You got that. He didn't. You don't think he was happy, do you? Not really?"

Richard picked up his coffee, and the cup rattled lightly in the saucer. "I suppose I thought he was very happy. In the sense of happy-go-lucky, in the sense of good fortune, of having lots of blessings, of things coming easily to him . . . "

"I'm not sure it was really like that. More that he was good at giving that impression—that he was happy, or that he simply didn't care." She looked down, away from Richard's face. "I thought he might be a little hollow inside."

Richard looked at her, at the fall of her hair over her ears and her hand rising to cup her chin, how her face bent to receive the hand and the fingers cradled her cheek. He had assumed she and James had slept together, but he had never pictured it and now he did. He could see that her body was fuller than Sarah's, less lean and elegant; that it would be very soft and that her skin under her clothes must be very white and her nipples dark as chocolate. He pictured her and James together that way and he felt a deep spasm of regret that was almost like the feeling he had when he grieved for James's death.

Then Richard said, "I'm not so sure I'm so happy. Maybe I just don't ever think about it. Maybe it's just something I believe, that I'd rather not examine too carefully." Susan's hand reached toward him and hovered over the tray. He wanted to take it. She picked up the coffee. "More?" she said, her voice scarcely a whisper.

"No," he sighed back. She looked at him as though he were not finished with what he was saying, and he found that he in fact was not. "I'll tell you something I haven't told anyone." He paused and she nodded. "Lately, I've felt I don't really believe in God, or at least religion, anymore. And at first I felt as though I had betrayed God, that I'd let him down by not believing in him, and that I'd betrayed my parents and my family and everyone else too in the process. And then came the worst part, which was thinking that if I stopped believing—that if there weren't any God—I'd be totally alone. Or that people anyway are totally alone on the earth, just scurrying around futilely. And that's a terrible thought. Too awful to think, really. And so maybe that's how it is with happiness: You don't ask, because the wrong answer would be too terrible."

Susan nodded. "But you said you thought you'd betrayed God. You can't betray someone who doesn't exist. So maybe you still believe. Maybe you're just mad at God, so mad you wish he were dead. Doesn't mean he is." She laughed. "Sorry. Tough luck."

Richard chuckled and nodded. "And you?"

"Oh, I feel exactly the same way. Either there is no God or he's got a very twisted sense of humor. But against that, I'd have to admit that in an odd way I'm content. Not happy, mind you. But content."

"I know I'm not content, not now." Richard laughed. "Maybe that's it. I'm happy, but I'm not content. I don't like the kind of happiness I've been dealt." He looked at his watch. He had nowhere he had to go, but he felt he ought to leave. Some kind of natural break in their conversation had occurred, and ought to be heeded, if only because he was not sure he wanted to see what lay beyond it. "I'm afraid I should be going." He stood and then Susan stood and began to load up her tray with their cups and plates.

"Let me help you with that," Richard said.

"Okay," she said. He picked up the coffeepot and followed her out to the kitchen. There was a table with a checked cloth over it and a porcelain sink and drainboard. Susan went over to it and set the tray down. "Here," she said, and Richard came up behind her and reached his arm around close to her right side and set down the coffeepot. He saw her neck bent and the white half-curtains in the window and he thought he could hear himself and Susan breathing and the curtains shimmering. She turned around and her face was less than a foot from his face. He felt very afraid, his breath short and his skin alight with prickles. He made himself back away and he moved up to the doorway and the head of the stairs like he was coming up for air.

Richard stood at the top of the stairs and Susan came toward him and stopped, not quite so close this time. "I can let myself out." She nodded. He saw himself raising his arm up slowly and stretching it toward her and then he knew it would touch her neck and her hair and draw her to him and everything that would have to follow. He saw that would happen if he raised his arm, knew it with a terrible clarity, and so he kept his arm still at his side. He did not touch her at all. He turned and began to descend the stairs and he told her good-bye and thanked her so much. She said,

"Please come again," and he turned, said he would. Then she said, "I mean it," and for the first time in his life Richard understood what a woman could mean, what she could want.

TWO DAYS LATER, IN THE LATE MORNING, SARAH TELEPHONED her mother. She waited for the operator to complete the call, listening to the clicks and purrs of the lines being knitted together, and the muffled tolling as her mother's phone at last rang in Chicago. The nurse-companion answered. She told Sarah not to expect much: Her mother wasn't sleeping too well these days, and she tended to get confused, and at times was frightened or teary or spiteful.

Sarah heard voices and footsteps down the line, echoing, she imagined, off her mother's oak floors and steamed-up windows in the overheated rooms with all the lamps blazing in the middle of the day. Then her mother came on, her voice half apprehensive, half affronted. "Hello?"

"Mother, it's Sarah."

"Sarah. Yes. Sarah," her mother said in the polite tones of someone trying to recollect exactly where or when they have met their interlocutor without revealing their lapse of memory.

There was silence for what seemed a long while to Sarah, and she added, "Sarah. In St. Paul."

"Oh, yes. Sarah," her mother said with more conviction and then, in wonderment, "*My* Sarah."

"And how are you, Mother? Mrs. Laski says you aren't sleeping well."

"No, I suppose I'm not. Sometimes I don't know if it's day or night." She chuckled, as though she were laughing about the folly of some other person. "I suppose I should know—I could just look outside, couldn't I? I could just lift up—I could just lift up, you know, the thing on the window, the papery thing. With the tassel."

"The shade."

"Yes, the shade. I could just lift it up and *see*, couldn't I?"

"Yes, you could."

"But I do get so confused. And I must confess that sometimes I'm very afraid. Sometimes I'll think that I'm going to forget everything—that I won't even know where I am, and I'll be all alone."

"Mrs. Laski is always there with you."

"But I could forget she was here. And then it would be like she wasn't here at all."

"It might seem that way, Mother. But she'd still be there."

"It might seem that way to *you*. But to me, it would be like she wasn't here at all. And then I'd be so afraid—like a little girl in an empty house. And you know, I get fearful just thinking about feeling it—imagining how I'd feel."

"So really, you have nothing to fear but fear itself."

"Well, there you are. It was that Woodrow Wilson who said that, and he was wrong about everything, wasn't he?"

Sarah did not see the point in correcting her. "I suppose so. But you mustn't worry so much, Mother."

"It doesn't seem like worry. It's just what I do when I think—when I try to plan, to imagine how things will be." There was a long silence and her mother began again. "Oh, this is very embarrassing. I know who you are, dear, but I think I've misplaced your name."

"Sarah."

"Yes, Sarah. Of course. You see, I was remembering how you were. And of course, you wouldn't worry. That wouldn't be like you. You were your father's girl—a little cocksure, a little wise beyond your years. Never imagining you couldn't have whatever your heart desired. I was never like that, not really. But you and your father—so much alike and so entranced with each other, like conspirators. Like you two knew something that the rest of us didn't." There was a pause. "Sometimes I wish he were here—not even to look after me, but just to sit with me. That would be such a comfort, such a thing to picture. But then I think to myself that perhaps I've forgotten what he looks like, and so of course if he were here, that would be terribly awkward."

Sarah said nothing and for a moment neither did her mother.

Then she said, "Well, dear, I think I better go. I feel very tired. But you'll telephone me soon, won't you? And come see me? Come sit with me?"

"Of course, Mother. I'll come in April like I always do."

"Oh, yes. You always come in the spring, don't you? And then you're here in the fall too, and I don't see you all winter, but you come back in the spring. So I'll see you soon, won't I?"

"Yes, you will. In a little while. In no time at all."

ON SATURDAY AFTERNOON, ANNA TOOK DOUGLAS TO MRS. Clay's. She told him she would see him tomorrow and to be good for Mrs. Clay, to do as he was told. Then she kissed him and he said "Mumma" and she squeezed him hard. It seemed like she was going away for a very long time.

When she got home she took a bath, a long hot bath with salts in the water, and when she got out she powdered herself. She wondered what she ought to wear. She was not sure. She was going downtown and then she was going some other place she knew nothing about. Finally she put on a gray wool skirt and a white blouse and a yellow cardigan. She made her face up and then she waited for Charles to come. She sat by the window, smoking, watching.

At five-thirty Charles drove up. He kissed her lightly and held the door of the car for her. They drove downtown in silence, and then he drove up Wabasha Street once, circled back, and parked. He came around to her side of the car and opened the door. "We're early. Maybe we could have a drink," he said. She shook her head. They walked around the corner to the Lowry Hotel and went in the lobby. They sat together for a few minutes, and then Charles said, "It's getting close. I better wait outside for when he comes."

Anna watched Charles through the lobby window. He paced up and down, hunching his shoulders and clutching the top of his hat. The wind must have been rising. She could see flecks of ice and snow blowing under the streetlights. Then a taxi pulled up.

Charles looked in the window and went around and got in the front seat. He stayed inside for a minute, and when he got out he was gesticulating and then he put his hands in his pockets and came back into the lobby.

"He says you have to go alone. I can't come with you. He'll wait for you while you see the doctor, and then he'll bring you back here."

Anna nodded. Then she thought about what was being proposed to her and she said, "No, Charles. That's not the way it was supposed to be. I don't even know this person. I don't know where he's taking me. It's crazy."

"It's not far. He said you'd be maybe an hour and a half. And I know him. His name is Joseph. He's waiting. He's all we've got. Do I send him away?"

Anna said nothing for a time and then she said, "All right. Let's go."

Charles gave her a hug. "It'll be fine. You'll see." He handed her an envelope. "You give this to the doctor."

"That's the money?"

"Yes. We better go."

Charles pushed the lobby door open for her and they went out onto the sidewalk. It was very cold, and the wind seemed to run up her sleeves and insinuate itself around her chest. Charles went to the cab and held the back door open for her. She slid in. He bent to kiss her cheek and he said, "It'll be all right, Anna. I'll see you in a little bit." Then he bent closer and whispered in her ear, "I love you," and the sound was like a low gust of wind on dry snow, like satin ribbon against satin ribbon. She bit her lip in order not to cry, and then he shut the door.

The cab drove away and for a long time the driver said nothing. Then he drew up to a stoplight and looked back at Anna and said, "It's only about ten minutes away." He looked at her a moment longer and then seemed to nod and he faced forward again and started to drive. Anna scarcely registered his face, but it seemed long and hollow-cheeked, his skin blanched and his hair long and pressed down with a coating of grease. She could see his hand on the steering wheel, the knuckles knobbly and enlarged, like the wounds where a tree has lost a limb.

He drove and after a while he said, "There's a blizzard coming, they say. I've no doubt of that—the wind, the weight of the air. I've got the night off tomorrow, and I'm glad of it—fit for neither man nor beast, I'd bet."

Anna nodded, and then said, "Yes, I'd imagine so."

After a few minutes more the taxi drew up to the curb and stopped. The street was wide and fronted with two- and three-story buildings, businesses dark and closed for the weekend. Anna guessed they were on University Avenue. The driver turned around. "It's right there, with the light on upstairs." Anna looked out. They were in front of a building made of dark red brick. The brick was textured with striations, rough enough to catch the wool from your sweater or abrade your skin if you rubbed against it. The driver spoke again. "It's the right-hand door at the top of the stairs. I'll be waiting here." Anna started to get out and he said, "Good luck, okay?"

Anna said "Yes, of course," and then she shut the door. There were some black and gold placards on the building by the windows, a dentist and two chiropractors. It was very dark and she didn't try to read them. She opened the door and went in. There was a sconce illuminating the stair and a worn, brownish-purple carpet. She climbed, clutching the rail as though the weight of her body was dragging behind her reluctantly and she might fall backward. At the top, on the right, there was a door of frosted glass with a nimbus of light glowing behind it. She was breathless and afraid.

She knocked, and a moment later the door opened. There was a man, stocky and gray-haired, not much taller than she, in his shirtsleeves with a brown striped tie. He must have been about sixty-five years old. He looked puffy and distracted, as if she had woken him up. He said, "You came in the cab?"

"Yes. With—I think his name's Joseph . . ."

"Joseph?" He chuckled very softly. "Whatever. Well, come in."

There was a room with a sofa and an end table and two chairs on a green tile floor with black swirls in it. "Sit down," the man said. He motioned her to the sofa and took the chair opposite it. He put his arms on his knees and leaned toward her, as though he were going to tell her something very important, as though she were a child and he was going to tell her about the birds and the bees. "Now," he began, "you have a problem. Is that right?" He looked at her gently, as if to assure her she could think about it for as long as she liked.

"Yes. I'm, I've missed two periods."

"Did you have a test?"

"No, but I've had a baby. I know what it feels like."

"Well, we'll find out soon enough. And when was your last period?"

"The middle of November."

He put his fingers under his chin and wiggled them slightly. "So that makes you twelve or thirteen weeks, about." He stopped and began again. "That's a little later than I'd imagined. That's not so good." Dread welled in Anna's throat. He looked at her again and said, "You should have gotten some help sooner."

Anna thought she might cry. "But I—I didn't . . . "

The man broke in quickly. "Oh, we'll manage. Don't worry. It just makes it a little more complicated, a little more work."

"Do you need more money?"

"No, it doesn't matter now. But if you want to go ahead, you need to give it to me now."

She took the envelope from her coat pocket and handed it to him. His hand was large and soft. He lifted the flap and put his fingers in as if he were going to lift out a small animal. He combed the bills inside and put the envelope in his shirt pocket. "That's fine," he said and stood. "Why don't you come in the back now?"

He opened another frosted-glass door and beckoned her in. The room was perhaps a dozen feet on either side with a venetian blind hanging limply in the window and a radiator painted silver beneath it. In the middle there was a doctor's examination table, upholstered in black vinyl, and a desk, a table with wheels, and a cupboard with a glass front. The man opened the cupboard and took out a sheet and laid it over the examination table. He took out another and handed it to Anna. "After you get ready— take off everything but your brassiere—you can cover up with this," he said apologetically. "I'll come back in a couple of minutes, so that you can be alone, so you can get comfortable." He turned and went out and Anna could see he was slightly bent, that his back was stooped and rounded. He shut the door.

There was a hook next to the door and Anna hung her coat on it and then she unbuttoned her cardigan and draped it over the coat. She thought she heard a match strike somewhere. Then she took off her shoes and put them under her coat. The floor was cold as a slab, and she held her feet an inch above it as she wound down her stockings. She took off her skirt and her blouse, and folded them and decided to put them on the radiator so they would be warm when she put them back on. She stepped out of her panties and folded them in quarters and put them on top of the other things. She scooted herself up onto the table and pulled the sheet over herself. It was heavily starched and frayed at the edges. She was cold but very clean, like her first time with Jack in the cabins at the motor lodge near the St. Croix. She looked around the room again. There were rows of chromium instruments in the glass cupboard, glinting in the light that fell from a white glass globe on the ceiling. It was the kind you see in public buildings and institutions, an inverted mushroom or a shallow bell shape with a little knob in the center. She thought it was like sitting naked in a schoolroom.

She heard a cough and then the door opened and the man came in. He smelled of smoke, and Anna realized she wanted a cigarette very badly. "Why don't you lie back? I can put the end where your head goes up a little, if you want."

"That's okay," Anna said. She lay back, and then lifted her head for an instant and lay back down. She could see the red polish on her toenails and the man standing at the sink. She heard water and then the sound of rubber stretching and snapping and the doors of the cabinets swinging open. "I just have to get some things," the man said, as though humming to himself, and she heard metal ringing against metal and the hollow sounds of trays or bowls or pans. She could see him sit down on a stool from the corner of her eye, and heard the sound of wheels squeaking toward her. The man's face appeared near her shoulder. He was still in his shirt but his sleeves were rolled up and he was wearing gloves, a tawny brown like the glass of a bleach bottle.

"Now, you've had internal examinations before, I'm sure." Anna nodded. "This is more or less like that. I wish I had something to give you to make you a little more comfortable, but it's just not possible. I wish I had someone to help me too, but we'll be fine. You just lie still and it won't be very long." He rolled away from her and then he stood and she heard metal dropping into metal like billiard balls into pockets. He lifted one ankle and then the other into the stirrups. They felt the way snow felt that had snaked into her socks when she was a girl. He pulled the sheet back and folded it just beneath her navel, and then dragged something across the floor and a switch clicked and bright light poured up her body from near her feet. He sat down again and she heard him moving and rocking on the stool, the wheels skittering and chirping like tiny mice.

"I'm going to go ahead now." He said nothing more. She felt cold steel ring her groin and tighten, and then more metal clacking against that metal, and a long, piercing pain sliding up deep inside her, as though an enormous blunt needle had been inserted between her legs and was pressing up to her heart. Then it withdrew, leaving a raw ache behind, like a burn inside her.

She heard metal against a tray, like a busboy dropping silverware as he clears up a table. "Well, you're certainly pregnant," the man said. "Now we get to work. This is going to hurt a little, but you just have to hang on through it. I'll tell you what. You can hang on to this handle here and when it gets real bad, you squeeze it as hard as you like, okay? I might need you to hand it to me though. That way you'll sort of be helping out. Maybe that will keep your mind off things." A piece of round metal, perhaps a

160

quarter-inch in diameter and embossed with some kind of pattern, slid into her hand. She clutched it tightly.

She saw the man's hand, or perhaps it was the shadow of it darting across the ceiling, and she thought it held something like a metal straw. Then she felt more metal against metal in her groin, as though a dentist were tapping on the teeth in her mouth, and another piercing sensation, not so deep, but spreading outward. Then there would be an instant of nothing, and then it would begin again. After a time, she stopped hearing the rattle of the metal or the breathing of the man, and instead she was looking at a white circle, like a midsummer sun. She was looking into it, although she knew she wasn't supposed to look at the sun. But she kept staring at it and it got bigger and whiter and suddenly she felt it. It was like someone had flipped on a radio with the volume already turned up to high, and it slapped her eardrums like a palm laid fast and hot on her cheek. And now the sun was inside her and she felt it, burning and widening and spinning itself apart.

She didn't say anything. She didn't make a noise. She just kept looking. She figured it would be better than screaming or crying. After a while, it settled down to something softer and steadier. She imagined it would feel like this if someone dipped a washcloth in lye and laid it across her forehead, a sting like lapping flames, steady and bright. She realized she could hear the man down between her legs, breathing shallowly and straining as if he had dropped a penny down a grate and was trying to get it back out but his fingers were just too big. Then she looked up and she could see the shadow of his head and shoulders on the ceiling, spread out and tipping from side to side, like he was a big bird of prey and was carrying her away in his claws.

Anna heard him say, "There. I think we got it all," and then three or four instruments fell on the tray and she felt the strain on her groin ease and only the burning and the ache—where someone might have been beating her sore again and again with belts and hammers—from her navel to her thighs.

The man said, "Well, we're done. I'm sorry if it hurt very much."

Anna started to sit up, and he said, "Wait. Let me clean you up a little." She lay back down and heard water running in the sink. Then she felt a warm cloth dabbing her loins, softly mopping and swabbing like kisses, like the way she cleaned up Douglas. She lifted her hand to her face and saw she was still holding the metal object that the man had given her to squeeze. It was long, with a sort of hoop in the end. She held it up for the man to take from her, although she felt that it was fused to her hand and that her fingers couldn't possibly release it. "Oh, the six millimeter," he said, and slid it from her grip. "I *wondered* what I'd done with that."

He handed her a sanitary pad and said, "You'll need these—probably for a day or two. Now, why don't you get dressed and I'll come back and then you can be on your way." The man left and Anna stood up slowly, lowering her feet to the icy floor, clasping the edge of the table to steady herself. She felt as if her feet and her legs had gone to sleep, that her knees had locked and were stiff and unsteady as rusted bedsprings. She unfolded her panties, pulled them on, and stuffed the pad inside, and then she put on her blouse and stockings and skirt, which was soft and warm as a kitten's belly. She crossed the room, steadying herself with one hand and then another, and took down her cardigan. She slipped it on and buttoned each button, right up to the very top of her neck.

Anna opened the door a crack and called out, "I'm done." The man came in, smoking a cigarette and looking very weary. Anna was standing by the door, and she said, "I wonder if I could sit down for a minute. I feel kind of weak." She started to move back to the examining table and she saw that the sheet on it was stained with spots and whorls of blood. She reached for a corner of it, to ball it up and put it away somewhere. The man said, "Oh, leave that." He pulled the sheet off and stuffed it in a receptacle next to the cupboard. Anna pulled herself up onto the table and sat dangling her feet like she was on the end of a dock, swinging her legs and scraping up sprays of water with her toes.

"Let's have a drink," the man said and slid open the file drawer of the desk. "All right," Anna said shyly. He took out a bottle and two small glasses and began to pour. "This is real Kentucky sipping whisky—the good stuff." He handed Anna a glass. He didn't proffer a toast and Anna, unsure what to say, glanced around the room. Her eyes lit on the table next to her. There was a tray of bloody instruments and a porcelain enameled bowl. She didn't look in it. The man saw her and said, "Christ. I'm sorry," and flung a cloth over the table and everything on it.

He raised his glass. "Drink up," he said. He drained half his glass, and Anna sipped quickly from hers. The liquor was warm and sweet and syrupy. "You know, I think you might be my very bravest girl ever. You didn't even peep or move a muscle. That was a long one, a hard one, because you were so far along." He finished his drink and repeated, "Yes, my very bravest girl. You should be proud of yourself."

He reached into the cupboard. "I want to give you something." It was a little box, orange with green print on it. It looked old and the print said, "Sulfanilamide U.S.P.," and beneath that, "U.S. Department of War." "If you get feverish, you take those—two before meals, three times a day. Not that you will. Although you should expect you'll hurt and feel tender for a while."

Anna said, "And if I needed anything else, if something wasn't right, I could call you?"

"No. It can't be that way." He moved toward the door and took Anna's coat off the hook and held it open for her. She got up and went to him and turned her back and slid into her coat. "You don't know me, okay?" she heard him say. "It's like we never met, like I don't exist."

Anna turned back. "Okay." She nodded, and he steered her through the front room. "But you're going to be fine. I promise you—and such a brave girl."

"Thank you," Anna said. "Thank you very much." His hand had been resting on the door frame, and she saw that he had been leaning on it and that his hand was spotted and sallow. "You're welcome," he said. "Good-bye."

She pulled herself down the stair rail like she was paying out rope, and at the door, she stopped to catch her breath. She thought she might be shaking; the ache in her groin and the bottom of her abdomen was a pot on a steady simmer and now and then it boiled up. The cab was outside, the tailpipe smoking. She let herself out and crossed the pavement to the driver's window and tapped on it. He had been sleeping, and he awoke with a start. When he saw it was her, he jumped out and held her door open while she lowered herself gently to the seat.

He got back in and drove away. "So," he said, "everything's done, taken care of?"

"Yes."

"And you're fine too?"

"Yes. I think so."

"Well, he's a good doctor. Everyone says so." He drove on without speaking for a while, and Anna looked out and realized she knew where she had been, that she might have walked or driven by the place two dozen times and never glanced at it. Now she had traded the fear of earlier that evening for this pain, but in the pain she could see clearly again.

The cabdriver spoke as he slowed and stopped for a traffic light. "You know, I don't have a daughter, but if I did, I bet she'd be about your age. I'd have loved to have had a daughter. We had a son, but we lost him in the Pacific in forty-five."

Anna said, "I have a son, a little boy."

"I bet you love him very much. I bet you're a wonderful mother."

"I don't know about that. But I do love him."

"You'd have to be a good mother, pretty as you are. Is your father alive?"

"Very much."

"I bet he's very proud of you. I bet he loves you very much. I would have liked a daughter. I really would have. There's something special, I think, between a father and a daughter, a dad and his girl."

Anna said nothing, and then, as though she had never been away, they were at the Lowry Hotel. She saw Charles behind the glass like a fish in an aquarium, and he ran out and opened her door and clasped her shoulder. He probed in his pocket with his other hand for his wallet and took it out. "How much for the taxi?"

"Oh, nothing, sir," the driver said. "It's part of the arrangement."

"Well, thank you, Joseph," Charles said. "Thank you very much," and he helped Anna from the car and held her around her waist. The driver said, "Good night, sir. And good night, ma'am," and drove away.

Charles looked at Anna as though he were searching her face for marks. "Are you all right? Can you walk?"

Anna said, "Oh, yes, I'll be fine. Let's just go." They walked around the corner and Charles held her arm as she got into the car. The car was very cold, as though it had been parked there for days. "Brrr," Charles said, "let's have some heat." He started the car and revved the motor and let the heater blow, and then they drove away. "So tell me about it. Was it all okay?"

"It was like going to the doctor." Anna sighed. The pain was shaping itself into cramps, spaced like a line of geese in flight, steady and regular, and they overlay the hot ache. "For a female examination. Except it hurt a lot more."

"How much more?"

"A lot. I guess it will stay that way for a day or two. I think I've got some pills at home."

"Or I could go to the drugstore and get you something."

"I'll be fine, I think." Anna shuddered as another cramp mounted and broke.

"So the doctor. How was he?"

"Like a doctor, I guess. Without the white coat. Kind of a shabby office. He looked kind of tired. He was almost elderly."

"But he was nice? He seemed to know what he was doing?"

"Oh, nicer than I thought he'd be. He gave me some pills if there was any fever and he told me I was brave."

"I bet you were."

"Maybe. I just want to go home. I want to have a drink and go to sleep and wake up tomorrow with everything the way it was last Christmas."

"I think that can be arranged," Charles said.

Charles held her arm when they got to her house. She fumbled with her key and he took it from her and undid the bolt and they went inside. Charles went around turning on lights and the house looked very empty and still, as though they had been away on a long vacation. She went down the hall to the bathroom to change the sanitary pad. It was sodden and crimson to the very edges. She found a belt and put on another, and then she sat on the toilet lid for a moment to gather her strength. She looked at the tub and she saw the bath salts open on the ledge and a few stray suds and hairs from her bath of a few hours ago around the drain. She thought she would like another bath now, but she was too tired and she was afraid that she would begin to bleed in the tub and would never stop.

She went back out into the hall and turned into the bedroom. She started to undress and laid her clothes on a chair. When she was naked save for the sanitary belt and pad, she pulled a night-gown over her head, not the negligee she usually wore, but a flannel one she had scarcely put on since college.

Charles came in and said, "You look very cozy," and added, "I'm making you a cup of tea. It'll just be a minute."

"That's very sweet of you, but I don't think I want anything but to sleep."

"That's fine. Let me just turn the kettle off. Then I'll come sit with you, keep an eye on you."

Anna nodded and climbed into bed. Charles returned and he sat down next to her and she laid her head against his chest and he encircled her with his arms. He felt her breath against his hand and the flannel dampening under it, and then he reached up and turned out the lamp. Her breathing grew slower and deeper and he could smell her: the soap in her hair, but also the perspiration dried on her forehead and far below it, but as though coming from every pore, a deep smell a little like what he smelled on himself after they'd made love; more intense than that, but similar, like the scent of her sex mingled with blood and sweat and

166

old earth, the sweet moldering of death and life, torn and bent back on itself.

IN THE DAWN THEY WERE ALL SLEEPING, AND SNOW WAS FALLiNG outside. Douglas lay in an old brown crib with flaking decals of lambs at his head, and as he breathed the snow fell like feathers, as though he were breathing it out and swaddling the world. His hand clutched his blanket rhythmically. It was lost in this crib; it wanted something soft to touch, something sweet to taste, something new to see; a breast, stars, passageways hidden in the earth, home.

Sarah lay on her back in her bed. She turned her body slightly and the sheets rustled. Even in sleep Sarah rustled—like silk and feathers and leaves and dry skin—as she did when she spoke, when her eyes skimmed the town, appraising it. Now she felt her husband was missing. He was lost to her and she discovered, against all likelihood, that she was lost without him.

Richard was lying two yards from her, sprawled on his stomach, his arm stretched out over the edge of the bed. He was reaching out to Susan Nash; his mouth was forming a question he wanted to put to his brother, but that he was afraid to ask; he was looking for his god in a city where all the streetlamps were out.

Anna was moaning in her sleep. Her mind and her eyes were empty. Her gut ached and throbbed, like coal turbines deep in the bilge of a black ocean liner. White corpuscles were massing in her veins, high summer clouds congealing, fluorescing into storms. She was burning up. She had already lost everything a woman can lose that night.

Charles dreamed his father had died and he had gone back east for the funeral and he went to the church but it was the wrong one and when he came out he didn't know what town he was in. Then he woke up. He pulled himself up and looked around. He hadn't remembered that he had fallen asleep here in Anna's bed with all his clothes on. It took him a long while to gather his wits, sitting with his feet still on the floor like a pair of empty shoes.

He went into the kitchen and made coffee and turned the radio on, the volume low so the voices were hisses and soft rumbles, like an argument overheard from the house next door. He went back down the hall and stood in the bedroom door and watched Anna sleep. Her forehead was moist, and she turned her wrists back and forth on top of the bedclothes. Then her eyes flickered open and she moaned. Charles went over to the bed and sat down next to her and took her hand.

"How are you feeling?" he said.

"Awful. Awful cramps. And like I've got the flu."

"Is there something you can take?"

"There's . . . some codeine in the medicine cabinet. Bring it. And some water."

Charles got up and found the pills in a little brown glass bottle next to a spool of adhesive tape and a crumbling styptic pencil. He filled the bathroom glass and brought it and the medicine back to Anna. She said, "Thanks," and unscrewed the cap. "I'm going to have two."

"I made coffee."

"That's nice. But I just want to sleep. I need to call Mrs. Clay, though." Anna pulled herself up in the bed, and Charles turned on the lamp. There was no light outside yet. "She's supposed to bring back Douglas at noon, but I think I'll ask her to keep him until tomorrow morning. I just need to sleep."

"I could call her."

"Would you? The number's on the wall by the phone."

"I'll have to do it later. It's too early."

"What time is it?" Anna asked.

"Maybe six, six-fifteen."

"Oh, God."

"Go back to sleep. I'm going to sit for a while, and then I'll call Mrs. Clay. Then I'm going to go home for a while and I'll come back tonight. Is that okay?"

"That's fine. I'll be asleep, dead to the world."

"Okay." He kissed her cheek. She was very warm. "Sleep tight."

"Love you, Charles," she sighed, her voice dry and drawn. He turned the lamp off.

Charles went out again and into the kitchen. He did a few dishes, crossing and recrossing the linoleum in his stocking feet. After he was finished, he turned off the light and the radio and went and sat down in the living room. The drapes had never been pulled the night before and the black was leaching out of the sky. He lay his head on the arm of the sofa and he thought he could see the dawn coming, reflected in the face of the television screen, black ebbing to green. He fell asleep for a little while, and when he woke up it was nine o'clock and snowflakes were floating and quivering outside the window like a swarm of bees. He got up and went to the toilet and urinated for a long time. He rubbed his hand over his cheek. It was rough and shaggy as moss. He decided to go straight home.

He looked in on Anna. She was lying with her back to the door. Her breathing was deep and hollow. The bedspread was wound around itself like a new skein of wool and hung halfway on the floor. He shut the door. After he put on his coat and scarf, he found a broom and went outside. There was a shovel by the door and he put the broom aside and pushed the shovel down the walk to make a little footpath in the snow. The blade of the shovel scrapped roughly—singing like a plane, rasping like sandpaper—on the cement and caught in the joints between the slabs. Then he took the broom and went to his car. He knocked the snow from the windows and fenders. It was falling fast, and by the time he had finished there was already a thick, fresh dusting on the windshield.

He went back inside and put the broom back, and then he remembered to call Mrs. Clay. He found the number and dialed. A black woman's voice answered, a soft drawling meld of galvanized metal and syrup.

"Mrs. Clay? This is Charles Norden, Miss MacEwan's friend."

"Miss *Anna* MacEwan?"

"Right, the daughter."

"Yes? Everything okay?"

"Fine, but Miss MacEwan's a little under the weather. The flu or something."

"That's Miss Anna you're talking about?"

"Yes. Anyway, she's not feeling well and she wondered if you could keep Douglas with you until tomorrow."

"That's okay with me. I come to clean tomorrow anyhow."

"Good," Charles said. "Good. Anyway, bring him then."

"Okay. He's a happy little boy, a good little boy."

"I'm sure he is. Anyway, thank you."

"That's no problem, sir."

After he hung up the phone, he locked the front door behind him and got in his car. He let the car idle a while and smoked a cigarette, and the wipers whipped back and forth, scarcely keeping up with the snow. Then he pulled away and rolled down the street, his tire tracks the only marks in the snowfall. He could see only fifteen or twenty feet in front of him and he drove slowly, leaning over the wheel, his face almost pressed against the windshield. At times the wind would gust, and he was completely blind. He worried that an animal, a child, or an old man might wander out into the street at just that moment and that with the wind and the wheels spinning and the leaden, muffled air, he would not even hear the car hit them.

It took him over half an hour to get close to his house, and it was as if he was at the helm of a ship, cutting a tiny slit through the seamless wind, climbing swells and hurtling down them, blinded, skidding, falling through the storm. He only saw his driveway at the last instant and he cut the wheel hard, too hard, to turn into it. The back of the car slid sideways into the mailbox, and the left rear wheel finished up fecklessly spinning in the snowbank at the side of the road.

Charles spent some minutes trying to extricate the car, and then gave up. He was tired and his shoes were wet through to his toes, probably ruined. He got out of the car and looked up his driveway, which was perhaps one hundred-fifty yards long. He couldn't see his house or a light in any direction. The snow spun and dove

170

at him like flocks of birds. He could just see the fence paralleling the driveway and he decided he could follow it to his house. He left the headlights of the car on in case he needed to get back to it. He figured the wrecker was going to have to come to pull him out and they could just as easily put jumpers on his battery too.

He went into the snow and then he couldn't see his car anymore. His gloves were soaked through and as he slid his hand along the fence wire he thought he could feel the sting of the metal, like something electric and cold. He kept walking, touching the wire, and he was enveloped in a sphere of white that swelled as he went into it and that, once inside it, was almost silent, like a hole in the world through which everything was pouring and emptying out.

V

M a r c h

IT WAS ON THAT NIGHT THAT CHARLES BETRAYED HER, although he thought he had only fallen asleep. He had followed the fence wire to the crest of his driveway and then he saw his porch light glowing like a lump of melting butter. The snow sloped against the back door and blew around his head, harrying the hem of his coat and blasting and shaking the storm door. He pulled the sodden glove off his right hand and delved in his pocket for his keys. But no sooner had he extracted them than they fell, disappearing into the snow like a gopher down a hole. He thrust his hand after them, and pulled it out quickly, as though stung. His hand glistened, encrusted with beads and scales of ice, his fingers crimson, his palm white as a fish's belly. He pulled on his glove, and began to feel around his feet again. His hat toppled off his head and he swiped at it angrily, and then he found the keys, nestled against his foot.

Charles opened the door. The house was dark and cool and hollow. He heard the dog's nails ticking toward him across the floor, and its breath beating against his knees, imploring. He kneaded the dog's neck and it sidled against his leg. He turned on the light, and the room shone starkly as though caught unawares, dishevelled and naked. It was nearly noon, but the sky outside the windows was dark as blue suiting, and the house shuddered against the wind like a luffing sail. He opened a can of food for the dog, shoveled it into a bowl, and set it down by the baseboard. It was horse meat and smelled sweet and unctuous. The dog began to lap it eagerly and then bolted the food, working its jaws crossways against the mushy flesh.

Charles took off his shoes and set them over a heat register. His trousers were soaked through up to the knees, and as he pulled them off they clung to his calves and his feet. He draped them over a chair and set his coat and his jacket over another chair. He took off his socks, balled them up, and cast them in the direction of his shoes, and then he crossed the room again, almost on tiptoe, dressed only in his shirt and his pale blue shorts. He turned off the light switch. There was daylight enough to build a fire, and he gathered newspaper and kindling and laid them on the hearth and set them alight with a blue-tip match from a box on the mantle. The sky was beginning to lighten, but Charles did not see it. He watched the flames spread and rise like a rose unfolding, and then he laid logs over them one at a time until the fire began to sing and pop. He took a blanket off the arm of the sofa and lay down and drew it over him, catching his toes in the crack between the cushion and the side of the sofa, nestling his head in the pillow like a ship in its berth. The dog shuffled over to him and pressed its head down on the cushion next to him, nosing his chest. Its breath broke against his face, fetid and meaty, and Charles stroked its skull. Then Charles fell asleep and the dog lay down on the floor before the fire, which lapped and consumed the logs much as the dog might nurse a bone.

WHEN CHARLES AWOKE IT WAS SEVEN O'CLOCK IN THE EVENING. The coals in the fireplace glowed dully. He had slept deeply, and when he sat up and put his feet on the floor it was as though he were a sailor stepping ashore after a long voyage. He felt unsteady and he sat for a while with his palms pressed flat against the cushions before he pushed himself up. He walked to the window. The storm clouds were beginning to drift apart and the moon glowed dimly, like a lamp behind a net curtain. Charles was hungry, ravenously hungry. He opened the refrigerator door to see what food was in the house, but the light didn't go on and it was too dark to see inside. The bulb must have burned out, he thought, and he swung his arm toward the light switch on the wall and flicked it up. Nothing happened. He twisted the knob on the radio on the kitchen counter, but the dial didn't glow; there was no hum, as when the tubes gathered their charge. He walked across the room and tried another light. Nothing. He felt annoyed and then a little afraid. He realized the furnace was silent and went to the thermostat and twirled it, but nothing clicked on. Then he began to feel, or to imagine that he felt—for he could no longer make the distinction between the two things—the cold pooling around his feet.

Charles's apprehension was swelling into panic, and he felt chilled and out of breath. He went to the telephone. It was black, scented like something medicinal and synthetic, cold in his hand. He held the handset to his ear and it was silent. He thought that now, for the first time in his life, he was utterly alone and that when death comes—when you see without mistake that it has come for you—it must feel this way. He thought he heard water dripping somewhere in the house.

He staggered to the sofa and sat down, pulling the blanket over him and knitting his hands together, the fingertips restlessly tapping together and darting apart as though repelled by magnetic force. He felt defeated, stupid and helpless in the face of his predicament. Then he saw the coals in the fire and, in the shadow of the hearth, his woodpile. It numbered perhaps two dozen logs and he recalled that there must be half again as many in the basement.

Charles found a flashlight in the kitchen drawer and he took it and went back to his bedroom and sat it upright on his chest of drawers, where it circumscribed a ring of light on the ceiling. He found a pair of wool socks and a plaid flannel shirt and a pair of tan worsted trousers and put them on and tugged his bedroom slippers onto his feet. Then he took the flashlight and went back out to the fire and laid four logs across the bed of coals, and watched them begin to hiss and then to snap and at last to catch fire. The flames blazed up and he felt them lay pickets of heat across his face, his arms, his legs. The room filled with orange light and he felt a little safer, almost at peace in his solitude; so much so that after a time his hunger came back to him.

He got up and moved back toward the kitchen, into the cold and the shadows. There were matches on the back of the stove and he struck one and lit one burner and then another. The flames glowed blue, tipped with gold and pure white, giving little light but much heat. He felt pleased, and, as he thought about it, even happy; perhaps as happy as he had been in a month or more. He had a fire burning on his hearth and propane to cook with, and, he realized, canned soup and stew and corned beef hash in the cupboard. There was even a bottle of Scotch in the bar cabinet. Charles thought of all this and he felt almost rich, handsomely provisioned and set free on a ship to sail wherever he wanted. Outside, the moon poured light across the snow toward him, and where it fell it illuminated the snow, cresting and troughing across the fields like water.

Charles found a cast iron pan under the stove and scooped out a can of hash into it and set it on the burner. Then he decided to make himself a drink, as big a drink as he wanted. He opened the freezer door and felt for an ice tray and withdrew one. Its cells were filled with tepid water. It was like that line in the seafaring poem, he thought: Ice, ice everywhere, but not a cube for my drink. He did not care. He was rich in every other way. He walked to the bar and filled a tumbler with liquor and came back to the stove and idly pushed the hash around the pan with a spatula until it was done. Then he went back to the fire and sat and ate, and the dog rested its head on his foot.

After he finished the hash he was still hungry so he heated a can of stew and drank another drink and ate the stew. He stretched out on the floor in front of the fire with his feet up on the hearth and his hands in his pockets, his back and shoulders slumped, his mind empty with ease and contentment. By ten o'clock, he felt tired; not tiredness borne of labor and exhaustion, but of languor and desire, a yearning to pull sleep up around his shoulders like a comforter.

Charles thought he ought to stoke the fire before he slept again. He stood up and laid the remainder of the wood from the pile on the hearth, and put on his slippers and took the flashlight to go downstairs for more. At the head of the basement stairs, he flicked the light switch out of habit and then remembered that the power was still off. He looked down the stairs into the darkness and the cold, and the scent of cold and damp and laundry powder came up to his nostrils, as though from a grotto on the edge of the sea. He shined the light down and began to descend. The flashlight seemed only to make a tiny rondel of light amid the darkness, and as he went deeper he felt afraid again. It was a child's fear, and he told himself it was silly to be afraid of a dark basement—that it wasn't real, it was an imaginary fear—and forced his feet one at a time to the bottom of the stairs, as though easing into a black pond. But the fear felt real, as real as the conviction of well-being he'd felt upstairs. As he tried to move his feet closer to the woodpile, his breath congealing before him in a cloud, down the windowless corridor along which the furnace spread its silent metal ducts, it felt more real, seeping up from his bones, as though the happiness he had felt upstairs had been nothing more than an illusory buzzing in his skull.

Charles was feeling these things even as he tried to talk himself out of believing in them. He spoke to himself impatiently, and, when that failed, as a reasonable and learned counselor, but his own voice was muffled amid the visions and smells and sensations his heart and imagination fashioned: the creatures that would assault his fingertips when he reached into the woodpile, that would insinuate themselves up his sleeves, scratch the tender flesh at the base of his neck and scamper through his hair with their cartilaginous feet; the shadows that loomed in the doorways and corners, watching him with yellow eyes; the furnace that hulked blackly at the end of the passage, waiting for him like an executioner.

He was scarcely breathing and he stood in the center of the corridor, his knees bent and locked and ready to spring away. He shone the flashlight onto the woodpile and as he did he thought he felt a cold breath against his neck. The logs were nested against one another like bottles in a wine cellar, bark brown and furrowed, smooth and silver-gray as pewter, white and pocked with spots and fissures. His hands shaking, he reached out and seized two pieces of birch and clutched them against his chest and then he grabbed three more and turned and fled up the stairs. At the top, the logs spilled from his arms and rolled across the floor. He slammed the door shut behind him, brushed the bark and threads of dried moss and lichen from his clothes, and gathered up the wood. He laid the fuel that was already on the hearth onto the flames and set the birch on the floor in reserve. The fire flared up, almost seeming to overwhelm the fireplace, and Charles sat down on the edge of the sofa and let his breathing slow, let his heart settle until he was calm again.

He set about forgetting how he had just felt—the naked fear and cowardice, and then the blushing shame that succeeded them—and he felt relief in realizing that no one had seen him then or now; that no one could ever know. Once he had dispensed with that, he began to convince himself that the entire incident was anomalous, inexplicable, and unconnected with the rest of his life—that it had come from without; that it had nothing to do with him or who he truly was. By the time he had made himself a drink and sat before the fire finishing it, he had nearly come to believe this. But just then he thought of Anna, and realized he had not talked to her all day and that it was now late in the evening and his phone was dead. And with that, all the shame came back and the hollow sensation in his gut, hard and transparent as a globe of ice, that he had been caught out in an act of supreme cowardice, not mere dereliction of duty, but of desertion. And the only remedy for it was to go out into the night, into the ebb of the storm, and walk a half mile through the snow to the nearest neighbor, wake them, hope their telephone was in order, call Anna, call the wrecker, start the car, and drive through the bottom of the night to her bed—all merely to see her, to assure himself about her condition, which was surely perfectly fine.

Charles would not do it and could not do it. Perhaps his exhaustion had made him a coward just as he had been a coward to his fear in the basement. But he could not bring himself to go out into the cold and the snow, any more than he could compel himself to descend the stair and go down into the things that were so awful and real to him, the things that once acknowledged and confessed came so easily to life.

BY SEVEN THE NEXT MORNING, CHARLES WAS WALKING DOWN the road, the snow crunching and singing beneath his feet, the air black and brittle as mica, as though the world were so cold it might shatter. He waved down a truck, which drove him to the filling station, where the owner drove him back to his car in the wrecker. They fastened a hook to the bumper of Charles's car and when the wrecker began to pull, the car lurched and staggered out of the snowdrift like a heavy man climbing a steep riverbank.

They opened the hood and put the jumper cables on the battery. Charles got in the car and sat at the wheel with the door hanging open and began to crank the ignition. The engine moaned and churned, and then with a series of pops and belches, it caught. Charles and the man from the filling station sat for a while to let the engine warm and they drank coffee from a beige thermos with red stripes that the man had in the cab of the wrecker. Then they disconnected the cables, shut the hood, and Charles drove down the road behind the wrecker. The sun was all the way up and the sky was clear and deep as glycerine.

Charles planned to drive straight to Anna's house, but he thought he would call her first from the filling station. He found a nickel and it clanked in the innards of the pay phone. Anna's line began to ring. After it rang five times, he imagined she was in the bathroom or maybe Mrs. Clay had already brought Douglas, and she was in the middle of changing or feeding him. Maybe she had gone out to buy groceries or to the drugstore to get some feminine thing she needed. By then he had lost count of the rings—they were like water over a spillway, going on and on—and their incessant, unbroken regularity began to nauseate him, to make his breath short and hot. He hung up and ran to his car and began to drive very fast.

He was at Anna's house in twenty minutes and it was nearly nine o'clock. The sidewalk was unshoveled but crowded with tracks, as if a great many people had been up and down it. He went up to the door and looked under the mailbox, where Anna had told him she kept a key. He found it and opened the door and called Anna's name, softly, timidly. There was no response, and he walked back through the living room to the hall, leaving the front door open. He looked in the bathroom and then in the bedroom. The light on the nightstand was on and the bed was empty. The linen was tangled and then he saw the sheet, circumscribed with a broad, ragged stain, crimson and ruddy. He pulled it toward him and gathered it in his arms while he thought what to do. The box of pills Anna had got from the abortionist lay open on the nightstand, the cardboard flap frayed. The sheet smelled like Anna and like something fetid and tropical, like something from the South Pacific. He held it to his face.

There was a black person in the doorframe, and Charles gasped and then saw it was Mrs. Clay, and standing at her hem, Douglas, who raised his arm and pointed at him like a mariner spying land. "Uncle Charles," he said. Mrs. Clay looked at Charles blankly.

"Where is she?" Charles said. The black woman moved toward him and took the sheet from him, balling it up and holding it loosely in her worn and battered hands. Her hair was pulled tight around her head, steely black and gray like tarnished silver. She didn't say anything for a time.

"I came with the boy at seven-thirty. She was sleeping. I couldn't rouse her and I felt her head and it was like she was on fire. I called Mr. MacEwan and he came about an hour ago and bundled her up and carried her out—"

"Where?"

"To the hospital, he said. To St. Margaret's."

"Has he called here? Do they know what's wrong?"

"I haven't heard nothing. I've been minding the boy."

Charles looked down helplessly. His hands were facing up, as though they might cradle something or swing idly before him. He looked at the woman's shoes, at the bagged and twisted stockings on her legs. He said, "Do you think she's all right?" and then he looked up into her eyes and their sienna irises, the whites yellowed like old ivory.

"I couldn't say. It's a woman thing, I'd guess. A bad one," she said and thrust the sheet toward him and nodded. "I've seen it before. With colored girls, at least."

Charles felt her eyes lay heavy on him, as though they both knew that all this was his doing. He began to stammer a little. "When I left her yesterday—you know, when I called you, she was fine. She was sleeping in, since it was Sunday, I guess. I wanted to get home before the snow closed the roads. And then my telephone was dead and my car was stuck. But I came as soon as I could this morning."

Mrs. Clay kept looking at him silently, as if he were speaking in a foreign tongue or as if she were patiently hearing out the transparent casuistries of a cornered adolescent. And then he wondered why he was defending himself to this wizened old negress and he simply said, "I'll go down to the hospital now. You'll tend to Douglas?"

She nodded. "Good," Charles said. "I'll call you as soon as we know anything."

Charles went back out into the living room and felt the cold moving across the room from the open door like a bank of fog. He turned and faced Mrs. Clay, who was standing in the hall, and said, "I left the door open. By mistake. I'll close it on my way out." She nodded.

Charles drove east toward the hospital. There were children sledding in the park and on the slopes of the golf course. As he got closer to downtown, buses purred at their stops, coloring the drifts amber, then lurching away, their wheels milling the snow beneath them to a porridge of grains and clots of ice. He drove without thought or impulse, like a fish on a line, once a pursuer, now a captive, drawn speedily and tautly through the world by an unseen force.

At the hospital there was a saint's portrait carved over the door, her eyes patiently cast down, awaiting a blow or a reproach. The floor was black terrazzo, and nurses and nuns and orderlies clomped across it in their heavy shoes like dray horses. At the desk, a woman told him where Anna was without surprise or alarm, as though it was entirely natural that Charles should find her here. He climbed a flight of stairs and then another and the terrazzo gave way to black and green linoleum. His hand was clammy on the rail, and then at the landing he looked down the hallway of the third floor and saw Richard MacEwan.

Charles tried to walk toward Richard in a manner that conveyed mature and reasonable concern, but he felt himself cringing, wanting to approach Richard warily, sidelong, as he would a headmaster, a policeman, or a bully. But Richard looked up, and his eyes brightened, as though he were relieved to see Charles. "Oh, you've come," he said. "Good, good." Richard reached out and squeezed Charles's shoulder, and Charles began to breathe again. "How is she?" he asked.

"She has a one-hundred-and-four-degree fever. She's delirious. I couldn't get her to talk when Mrs. Clay got me over to the house—she just muttered and moaned. Nobody's told me anything else. But Ted Fields—he's our family doctor—is in with her now. He said he'd come out and talk to me as soon as he knows anything."

"He's with her now? Examining her?"

"I guess. And talking to the hospital doctor."

Charles wondered if he'd seen the sheet, or if Mrs. Clay had said anything to him. He wondered if he could avoid discussing the matter, or if he could somehow excuse himself before Dr. Fields came out and gave his opinion, and perhaps began to ask questions.

Richard was looking away and then he spun his head directly toward Charles. "But what about you? When you last saw her, was she well? Did she have any symptoms of anything? She called me Saturday afternoon. Sounded fine. Said you two would be seeing each other that night." Richard paused and shook his head. "I don't understand this at all."

Charles tried to think quickly, and realized he must choose among a set of falsehoods, all with multiple consequences, none of them good. He could claim ignorance and simply lie to Richard as Anna's father, as the man who might very well have been his own father-in-law. Or he could lie to Richard as a senior partner of a distinguished law firm and as an officer of the court, charged with serving the law. And of course, he would utter these lies— or confess to procuring and abetting a criminal act—as an officer of the court himself and as a promising member of the bar, of whom great things were expected by his firm.

Charles began to speak, a word or a phrase at a time, as though laying a bridge across a bog plank by plank, seeing with each board where the next one might go and what load it could sustain. "Ah, yes, we saw each other Saturday night. We were at her house. And I'm sure she was fine then. Although I suppose something could have been wrong, but I didn't really notice anything. . . . " At that point, Charles saw that he was openly circling the matter rather than progressing toward a conclusion that would satisfy Richard. But just then a door opened and a man strode toward them in a long white coat and took Richard's arm in his hand and held it.

"Richard, why don't we go back in the lounge here and talk?" he said, and then he noticed Charles, and Richard saw this and said, "Oh, Ted, this is Charles Norden. He's . . . "

Charles said nothing and the man regarded him coolly, Charles thought, and then said, "Oh, yes, I know about you. You're Anna's—"

"Anna's friend," Charles said quickly.

"Well, then, I suppose we should all talk. I'm Ted Fields. I attempt to practice medicine on the MacEwan clan from time to time, but normally they're too damn healthy to give me the chance," the man said with what Charles took to be dry good humor. He smiled but didn't offer Charles his hand, instead motioning Richard and Charles down the hall and directing them inside a doorway. There were some chairs and a vinyl-covered couch and a window looking down on the cold-storage warehouses along the river. Charles was not sure if he should sit down, and he stood alone at one end of the couch, fingering the cool plastic welting.

Fields sat down in a chair and leaned forward, his elbows resting on his knees and his hands extended forlornly before him. "Anna's a very sick girl," he said. "I suppose you know that. She has a very high fever, and I suppose that's also self-evident. In itself, that's not necessarily so alarming, but it has all the signs of septic fever about it—of septic shock, in fact."

"Like with an infected battle wound?" Richard said.

"More or less. If the infection persists or spreads, you get cardiovascular failure, renal failure, and then there isn't much we can do. The body just sort of burns itself out."

Charles had remained standing all this time, but now slid soundlessly onto one end of the couch. Richard sat with his face in his hands at the other end, then looked up, and Charles saw his eyes were moist and that he was becoming more animated than Charles had ever seen him.

"But what—" Richard stopped to compose himself. "What is this thing? What can you do about it?"

"Oh, plenty. I don't mean to sound as if we're helpless. It seems to be a pelvic infection of some kind—you know, of the female organs. Rather like peritonitis, like you have with a ruptured appendix."

"But from what?" Richard asked. "She was perfectly healthy two days ago."

"Oh, it could be bacterial. There could be some infection of one of the organs. Or perhaps some insult to the uterus or whatever."

"Insult?" Richard said.

"A wound."

Charles looked at Richard again. He seemed skeptical, irritated. "A wound? From what?"

"No way of knowing. And it's not very important right now. Regardless of what it is, we need to remove the source of infection as quickly as possible—surgically, probably by dilation and curettage, where we'd clean out the uterus. But it's rather a paradoxical thing: In order for her to stand up to the surgery, we have to get her fever down and her other signs stable. But in order to get them down, we really need to remove the source of infection, which of course entails the surgery. Rather a rum thing."

"Christ, Ted," Richard said. "This is not helpful. This is just confusing, going around and—"

"Dicky, we handle this all the time. We have antibiotics to tame the infection, and we get her fluids and signs a little more balanced, and we choose our moment. I'm hopeful. I'm confident. You're all strong as horses."

Charles had been picking at his nails, tugging at his shirt cuffs, and he looked up and saw Richard look deeply, almost coldly, at Fields. "So you're saying she's not going to die?"

Fields's hands dropped nearly to his ankles and he seemed a little exasperated. "I'm not just going to come out and tell you that. I'd like to, but I won't. I respect you. I love your family, if I can be so bold. This is grave. This is where the science leaves off and you look into the stars or pray or whatever. But I'm confident, I'm hopeful. I won't be the one to do the surgery, to make the decision. That's Abrams, the gynecological fellow. But he's very good. He's dealt with exactly this situation before. Many times. Successfully. Exactly this situation."

Richard looked somewhat more reassured, but still testy, still aimlessly petulant. "What situation is that? It doesn't seem very exact to me. Just a lot of not knowing, a lot of whistling past the graveyard, a lot of cocky ignorance. I'm not much for taking things on faith these days, for believing everything will come out all right in the end. But then I'm not very high on luck or fate either. I guess I don't have a lot of alternatives."

Fields didn't look at him, and then he slowly rose and stood for a moment with his hands in his coat pockets. "Dicky, why don't you call Sarah and tell her what we know? She needs to know.

You tell her I said it's going to be all right. There's a phone over there. We'll let you talk in private." Fields looked at Charles and Charles followed him out into the hall. They walked down the hall toward a window that looked west up onto the bluff. Fields dug in his pocket and took out a pack of cigarettes and pulled one out. He shook the pack and produced another and offered it to Charles.

"No thanks," Charles said. "I don't smoke. At least not very often." They stopped at the window at the end of the hall, and Fields leaned there and lit his cigarette. There were a few icicles hanging above the window and water ran down them and dripped onto the sill. The city shone glassy and wet in the sun. "It's warming up, I'd say," Fields said and then looked away from the window and blew out a cloud of smoke. "You don't have any children yet, do you, Mr. Norden?" he asked.

"No. And you can call me Charles. Or Chuck. Whatever you like."

"Okay, Charles. No, I didn't think so. Or at least you don't have any yet." Charles had the sensation that Fields was pressing him up against the window frame, although neither of them had moved. Charles rolled his shoulders as though squirming. "No, not yet."

"Well, I don't want to lecture you or belabor the obvious. But there's nothing like having a child and there's nothing worse than losing one. I haven't been through it myself, but I've seen it enough times to feel I know something about it—infants in incubators on up. Imagine losing the woman you love more than anyone you've ever loved in your life, and then imagine that times ten, and you might have it." Fields exhaled noisily. "I don't know why it should affect people so much. Maybe with an adult, a sweetheart, a sibling, or whatever you still have something left—yourself, other people, the rest of the world. But when you lose a child, it seems like it takes everything away with it. I see these parents, and it's more than grief—it's devastation, utter defeat, like on a battlefield where there's nothing left. Just mud and cinders."

Fields tossed his cigarette on the floor and ground it out with his foot. "The orderlies are going to string me up," he said grimly and then sighed. "Anyway, Charles, I say all this because I want you to know what Dicky's facing with Anna. I think you're wise enough to sense that and I don't want to take anything away from your own worry, which I know must be overwhelming. But frankly, I want to look out first and foremost for Dicky and Sarah and, of course, Anna. That's because I know you can look out for yourself. I sense that about you."

"Thank you. I appreciate that. And of course, anything I can do to make all this easier on the family . . . "

"Good, good," Fields said, and took out his cigarettes again. "You sure you won't have one?" Charles shook his head. "Well, I'm glad we understand each other—that we can confide." He spun the wheel of his lighter and pulled deeply on his cigarette. "Because," he continued, "there are some things I need to ask you— to work up Anna's history so Abrams and I can give her the best possible treatment."

Charles was aware that he had scarcely spoken a word; that Fields had been the total master of their conversation, seamlessly speaking all the lines for both of them without giving any impression of dominating it. Ordinarily, Charles admired such men—their knack for disguising total control for genial cooperation. But now he felt too much in Fields's power.

Fields began again. "This part is a little complicated. But trust me. I have to be a bit blunt, but nothing bad will come of it, okay?"

"Okay," said Charles.

"We're pretty sure Anna underwent a gynecological surgical procedure, maybe in the last forty-eight hours. And since I'm her doctor, I'd have a pretty good idea if such a procedure was indicated, wouldn't I?"

"Yes, I suppose—"

"That's okay. You just listen. Don't say anything. Specifically, I'd wager that the procedure was what we call a therapeutic abortion. Now don't say anything here either, because this is the tricky part. As a physician, if I learn—say, from you or Anna or somebody else for whom it's not just hearsay—that such an illegal procedure has been performed, I'm obliged to inform the police. I suppose as an attorney you're probably in a similar position. You can answer that one."

Charles swallowed. "It's a little more vague, but yes, more or less."

"I thought so. Fortunately, nobody's told me that such a thing's taken place. You haven't told me anything, have you? Although I suppose I could take your silence as assent that I'm on the right track. But you haven't told me that anything illegal's taken place, have you?"

"No—nothing," Charles said.

"Good. Ignorance is strength. I read that somewhere. Anyway, now that we've disposed of that matter, I can put some hypothetical questions to you. Or at least questions that, if they weren't hypothetical, wouldn't strictly be germane to anything illegal having taken place. *Germane*—that's a nice word. We have lots of nice words in medicine. Mostly Latin. And Greek, just like theology. Take *homoousia*—sounds like a disease, but it's theological. Doctors must be close to God, I guess. With law, it's mostly Latin and French, right? French—so romantic."

Charles felt Fields might be teasing him. But he nodded amiably. "Yes. I hadn't thought of that."

"Oh, yes, the language of love. Anyway. If such a procedure had been performed on Anna—which no one has said is the case—we'd want to know a little about the circumstances. For example, if she had been pregnant, how many weeks pregnant might she have been when she obtained such a procedure? You could answer hypothetically. Trust me. You're the lawyer. You'd know if anyone was trying to outsmart you."

Charles thought for a moment, and then he said. "Well, if such a thing had happened, she might have been about twelve weeks. She might have said that."

"Good. That's a good hypothesis. And just along the same lines, it would be helpful to know how the procedure might have been performed—who might have done it, under what circumstances."

Charles knew they were getting onto dangerous ground, but he felt safe with Fields. In a curious way, he was enjoying himself. "Well, in this case, it might be that no one was present except the patient and the doctor. So an account would be thirdhand—would be hearsay."

"So much the better," said Fields. "And one could be reasonably confident it was a doctor?"

"That's how it was presented. Anna thought—Anna might have thought—that he seemed like a real doctor. That he had professional instruments and pills and so forth."

"And where might such a doctor have been practicing?"

"Maybe in a chiropractor's office, maybe out on University Avenue, near Snelling."

"Oh, you know, I can almost imagine who that might be. Which is beside the point. But I wonder if he—whoever he was—might have used any liquid or maybe inserted something to cause the uterus to empty itself out later on, at home? Whoever was there with her certainly would have seen her pass something—tissue and so forth."

Charles tried to think back and then to cast what he remembered into the terms they were employing. "If anyone had seen anything, they didn't see anything like that. Maybe they just saw a little blood."

"Okay, it seems as though this hypothetical doctor would have tried to evacuate the uterus right there in the office with dilation and curettage. That would take some skill, some luck at that stage in a pregnancy. I would guess that he wouldn't be very lucky this time—not in this instance."

"Probably not. Evidently not."

"Careful, counselor," Fields said, and put his finger to his lips. "Well, this has been a helpful discussion, however hypothetical, and I appreciate your willingness to have it. Because of course I couldn't—actually can't, under the circumstances—ask Anna. And I want to protect her father and mother from any kind of stress."

"So they wouldn't necessarily be told the cause of her condition?"

"Well, I wouldn't have any need to say anything. But these things have a way of coming out. Dicky's a smart man, and Sarah's sharp as a tack. But none of that matters right now." Fields looked at his watch. "We should go back and check on Dicky. This is killing him, you know. It doesn't look that way. But I can see it."

"And is Anna going to be all right? Really?" Charles and Fields began to walk.

"I can't say. This kind of thing happens all the time, and the woman gets very sick and we do the D & C, and she's fine. So normally, I'd say yes. But here—with the high temperature and the vital signs all screwed up—it's different. She's more or less in shock, and with that you're into imponderables. That's what Dicky was railing about—the things you can't know, wrapped up in the life of your child, dangling over them."

Richard came out the door just then, and he looked like a man descending from the gallows, from a sacrifice. "Sarah's coming down," he said, looking at Fields. Charles was standing behind and at an angle to Fields, at a long tangential remove from Anna's father and doctor, yet connected to them, like the star at the end of the handle of the Big Dipper.

Richard spoke to Fields. "Can I—" and then he saw Charles. "Can we see her?"

"Oh, of course. Let me just check to see that the nurses aren't in the middle of something." Fields led them down the hall in the opposite direction from the window where he and Charles had talked. He tapped on a door painted in cream-colored enamel with a metal grate in the bottom, said, "Just give me a second," and slipped in. Charles and Richard looked past each other, and then Richard glanced over at Charles, moving his head very slowly, as though scanning the horizon, until he fixed on Charles's eyes. "She doesn't deserve this, you know. She's had a hard couple of years. And life is just hard for her anyway. It just is—even when it seems good."

"I know," Charles said.

"I'm glad you understand that," Richard said and smiled. "She would have wanted you here." And then Fields opened the door and beckoned them in. Anna lay dwarfed in a big metal bed and light poured down on her face from a porcelain shaded wall lamp. Her face was florid and sweaty, and someone had pushed the hair back from her forehead. Her left arm lay straight at her side with a needle fixed onto it into which two tubes fed by two bottles drained. Her right arm was bent, the hand half open and resting on her stomach, as though clutching a piece of fruit.

Fields spoke. "You can stay as long as you like. There's chairs and the nurse can bring you coffee." He picked up the clipboard hanging on the end of the bed and shielded it against his chest. "It's just the waiting now. The fever drops a little bit and then Abrams can go ahead and she's out of the woods." From the bed there was a sound of sheets rustling and of a long exhalation and then a breathy muttering. "She's not in a coma, you know. Not even necessarily asleep—just too sick to really be awake. She can probably hear us." Fields looked at Charles and grinned. "Be careful what you say, Chuck. Nothing ungentlemanly. She'll be back with us soon." Then he left.

And surely she was among them, suspended over them, the shadows of her limbs, her fingers, and the strands of her hair cast on their faces, shaping their features, inscribing their thoughts. They each pulled a chair close to the bed and watched her breathe, and though they did not know it, within a few minutes they were all breathing in one rhythm, so slowly that Richard and Charles might have joined her in sleep. Her face was tipped a little to one side, her mouth agape, her lips pale as milk, and to Charles she looked like she did after they had made love—disheveled, damp, entangled in her nakedness. Richard could not see her face so clearly, but he saw the folds and embayments of her ear and the wisps of hair stuck to her temples and throat, the rocking of her lungs beneath her breasts, perhaps even the tick of the pulse in her neck.

Anna did not see them, but she must have heard them. A chair rasped and barked across the floor, and she heard a steel door swinging open and she was in a boiler room, stewing in the heat, but then it was the indoor swimming pool at the club, and she got in and swam and felt cool for a minute. She swam back to the shallow end and stood for a while waist deep in the water and Alice Mercer swam up in a white swimsuit with ruching like smocking all down the front. They talked for a while, and then Alice asked her, did she know she was naked? And Anna looked down at herself, and saw that she was not only naked but pregnant, her stomach full and round as an egg. She ran up the steps out of the pool, covering her nipples with her arms, shielding her pubis with her hands.

She pulled a towel from a stack by a deck chair and then she saw the pool was not indoors but outside—there were tables with umbrellas and cabanas and close-cropped grass leading down to a beach—and she realized she was very cold. She lay down on her back on the grass and pulled the towel over her but she couldn't get warm and she didn't know where her clothes were and the fetus in her belly began to kick and she thought she heard Douglas calling from down near where the waves were breaking. His voice was rising and falling and then it sounded terrified but she couldn't turn her head to see him and when she tried to get up, she found she couldn't move, that something was sitting on her chest, pinning her down, and not only couldn't she cry out but she realized she couldn't breathe. Then she heard her mother's voice, and she kept trying to rise, and she thought maybe this was a dream and she should wake herself, so she did, or at least she went to sleep in a way where nothing was happening to her.

Charles found he had nearly dozed off, but then the door opened and he heard the click of a woman's heels and Sarah's voice saying "Anna? Anna?" with a plaintiveness he had previously imagined her incapable of. Richard stood up and looked at her and then at Anna, very still on the bed and scarcely seeming to breathe, and he said, "She's asleep."

Sarah nodded, and moved past Charles, glancing at him as though checking traffic on a lightly traveled street, and moved to the bed. She regarded Anna a long time, from her feet to her head, the red and white dappling of her complexion, the verdigris and yellow coloring around the place where the intravenous needle went into her arm, the catheter emerging from beneath the bedding and snaking into an enameled beaker. Then Sarah touched Anna's forehead and wrapped her hand around Anna's fingers, holding them, her gloves still on, loosely, like stalks of lilies.

"I don't know if you should touch her," Richard said.

"There can't be any harm in it," Sarah said, as though commenting on a matter whose outcome was already decided. "Do they know anything more?"

"Nothing but what I told you on the telephone."

"It's very odd," Sarah said, and looked at Charles. "You saw her Saturday night and she was fine." It was not a question. "So this was just out of the blue." Sarah shook her head. "Hmm." She sighed quizzically.

The door opened, and Fields entered and put the clipboard he had carried away on a table. He crossed the room and stood next to Sarah and gave her a little squeeze around the waist. He said, "If she's anything like her mother, she'll be up and around in a day." Sarah said nothing, and then turned to Fields and said, "So what is this, Ted? Tell me."

"That's frankly irrelevant at this point. A pelvic infection. The treatment's the same regardless—stabilize her and remove the source of the infection."

"And how, Ted, does one remove the source of the infection if one doesn't know what the source of the infection is?"

"One seeks. And then one finds. And if one is a member of the patient's family, one trusts one's physician."

"That goes without saying. But you can see how we'd feel—wanting to know everything that you know . . . "

"Which isn't very much. Or very important," Fields said. The door swung open quickly and a nurse came in. "Dr. Fields, you're needed on the telephone at the nurses' station," she said. Fields began to follow her out, turning to say, "I'll be right back."

Richard moved toward Sarah and said, "Why don't you take this chair, dear?" Sarah nodded, biting her lip, and she sat down, hooking her heels under the seat. She took off her gloves, folded them together, and pressed her handbag into her lap tightly, as though it might fly away.

Richard began to walk the perimeter of the room, his hands locked behind his back. From the bed there was a murmuring like one word being repeated again and again. Richard looked at Sarah, at her eyes a little stunned and frightened, and said, "It's nothing. It's just what she does. Like talking in her sleep." Sarah looked back down at her handbag, at the gloves draped over the clasp like pelts hung on a fence.

Richard was moving along the wall to the door and when he came to the table he stopped and looked at the clipboard. He saw Anna's name at the top of it, and he spun it around on the table-top and began to read it, idly, to pass the time. It said, "Treatment and Medication Orders," and beneath that was a list in backhand script, in dull blue ink:

1. Diagnosis: Septic probable incomplete D/C with en-dotoxic shock (?)
2. Vital signs hourly
3. Record intake/output
4. Observe for bleeding and passage of tissue
5. IV fluids
   a) 1000ml 5% dextrose/water w/ aqueous penicillin 20 million units
   b) 1000ml 5% dextrose/saline w/ aqueous penicillin 20 million units
6. Streptomycin 0.5 IM stat and Q 12 hours
7. Tetanus toxoid 1.0 IM stat

Ronald Abrams, M.D.

Richard read this once and then he read it again. It was like an English crossword puzzle, half perfectly comprehensible but half infuriatingly ambiguous. It called up the lawyer in him from out of his grief, from out of his stupefied helplessness. Fields came back in and saw him beginning to read it a third time and frowned.

"It's just Abrams's technical stuff. Nothing to worry about," Fields said and seized the clipboard a little too quickly. Richard's mouth formed an O, but then he closed it. The nurse came in pushing a cart. "Time to check her signs," she said. Sarah and Charles stood to leave, but Fields waved them back into their chairs and handed the nurse the clipboard. "It's all right. You can stay. Just taking her temperature. In fact, why don't I come back after the nurse is done and we can talk about the results—if there's anything to report."

Fields turned and left and for a moment Richard stood still beside the table. But then he stepped around it and followed Fields out into the hallway. "Ted, I was curious about something," he said. "I had a question."

Fields stopped, turned, and backed away from Richard a few feet. "Sure. Fire away."

"On the paper with Dr. Abrams's signature. It seems to say Anna is supposed to get a tetanus shot. Is that right?"

Fields sucked in on his lips. "Yes." He nodded.

"Well, why would she need one? Isn't that for cuts with rusty knives and bites and lockjaw and so forth?"

"It's just a precaution. Routine thing. Something we like to do before someone has surgery anyway. I'd guess that's what Abrams had in mind."

"And then at the top of the sheet, Ted—it says 'probable incomplete D-slash-C.' Is that the D & C you mentioned before?"

"Well, I don't know what kind of shorthand Abrams—"

"Because if it were, I'm confused. Because I thought that was what Anna was going to have after she was stable. But here it's as though she's already had it—"

"Dicky, I don't have it here in front of me, and I didn't write it. Maybe it's what Abrams is noting is indicated—what he wants to do."

"It said 'diagnosis,' Ted. And why 'incomplete'? That's an odd thing to *want* to do, isn't it?"

Fields looked up at the ceiling with a look of disgust and resignation, and then he looked down again at Richard. "All right," he said. "I'm not going to do this. You better come talk to me in the lounge. It's nothing to worry about, honest." He cocked his head toward the hall, and walked to the nurses' station. "Let's get some coffee," Fields added, and wearily asked a nun there to fetch them two cups. Then they went into the room with the vinyl couch and sat down with the door open just a crack. The nun shuffled in with two cups of coffee, and after she had left, Fields took a sip from his cup and set it down on the floor by his foot.

"This isn't going to help anything, Dicky. It hasn't got anything to do with Anna getting better one way or the other. But I'm not going to mislead you. If you have to know—if you want to open the whole mess—I'll tell you. But it's going to be awkward. Personally and professionally. Frankly, it's just going to make you more miserable. But I'll go ahead, if that's what you want."

"I think I know anyway." Richard heard himself confess this and was surprised. Until then he had not known what he had known, nor had he believed he had formed any conclusions. "So it's too late. I think I know what happened to her—that she got into trouble."

"And she went to get it taken care of, and the procedure wasn't done properly. There was material left in the uterus, and now it's infected. So really, we're right back where I said we were before you knew anything about it. So you see, it really doesn't change anything, does it?"

Richard thought for a moment, but beneath his thinking he felt his heart falling into his gut like a meteor into a cold and depthless well. "No, not the material facts," he said. He was trying to mirror Fields's demeanor. "But the perspective one brings to them—that changes, I suppose. It colors things. Irredeemably."

"If you let it. But the point is to get Anna well."

"How did you find this out, Ted?"

"I'm not going to say. There's a seal of confidentiality in medicine, just like in other professions," Fields said a little testily. "In any case, it was obvious when she was examined, when you brought her in."

Richard felt slightly dizzy; he swayed imperceptibly, and flattened his hand parallel to the floor as though to steady himself.

He saw, or perhaps only felt, Anna dropping away from him, tiny and spinning end over end, like the cradle that falls when the bough breaks. He breathed in deeply. "Do you have to report it? I think the statute says you do."

"Not under these circumstances. At least that's my opinion. Or at least that's how I'm going to proceed. I don't have any direct knowledge of any criminal activity."

"From what you've said, that's rather a disingenuous statement, Ted."

"I really don't care. Maybe I should. You're an officer of the court. Do you want to worry about it? I only want to worry about Anna right now."

Richard said nothing and looked away, blanched and trembling. Fields saw him, and said, "I'm sorry. I didn't mean that to sound— to shame you. But suppose we just have a hiatus about this whole subject, at least until she's better. I think that would be in everyone's interest."

"I do too," Richard said. Fields grasped his shoulder and said, "Why don't we go see how she is?" and Richard nodded. As they reached the door he said, "Does anyone else know?"

"Only Abrams and the nurses—no one who would ever say anything."

"What about Charles, Charles Norden?"

"What do you think, Dicky? What do you think?" Fields said wearily. "Please—just leave it alone for now, okay?"

"Yes. Okay. I will."

At the door to Anna's room, the nurse handed Fields the clipboard, and he went to the window and stood in the light, leafing through the pages. Charles rose when Richard entered, a moment after Fields, but Richard didn't seem to see him. Charles went and stood against the wall at the far end of the room, pressing his back against it, waiting for someone to speak. Sarah had pulled her chair close to the bed. The bed was high and Sarah's shoulders were at the same level as Anna's chest. Sarah had threaded her fingers into Anna's hair and she could feel her daughter's hot, damp breath cresting and ebbing through her parted lips, the sensual, unguarded sleep of a child.

Fields looked up from the clipboard and his eyes met Sarah's, ten feet away, and then he looked at Charles and then at Richard. "There's really no change to speak of, and we really wouldn't expect one so soon."

"She's exactly the same?" Sarah said.

"Not exactly. Her fever's half a degree higher. It's not good, but it's not that significant in itself. Her other signs are the same. I'm going to go talk to Dr. Abrams and see what else we might do—maybe give her a touch more antibiotics. Otherwise, we just have to wait." Fields crossed the room and stood in the door and turned back. "You're welcome to stay with her here, of course, but maybe you should all consider getting out for a while—going about your normal business. Come back this afternoon or this evening. I promise that we'll notify each of you if there's any change."

Richard nodded and began to gather his hat and his coat. He looked at Sarah and said, "Why don't you come, dear, and get something to eat?"

Sarah shook her head without looking up. "No, I'll stay. I'll get something in the hospital cafeteria."

"Then I'll come back at four. Can I bring you anything?"

"No, nothing." She paused. "Well, actually, maybe a pack of cigarettes. I'm out. Or will be soon."

"Of course," Richard said. Then they said their several good-byes—Sarah, Richard, Fields, and, quietly, Charles—that passed over Anna's supine body like small, darting birds going their different ways. Fields went to find Dr. Abrams, to confess his frustration and his fear, to propose they had nothing to lose by doubling up Anna's streptomycin. Charles saw Richard waiting at the elevator and forced himself to go and wait with him. Richard didn't appear to notice him at first and Charles exhaled softly and said, "I can only imagine what this is doing to you and Sarah, but I want you to know that if there's anything, anything at all . . ." and his throat dried up. Richard was about to say something automatic, something like the things he had said at James's funeral, but instead he found himself framing several replies, all of them cruel or sarcastic, and he fretted his hands beneath his coat. But, as the elevator arrived, and the two of them stepped forward into it, he only said, "You care for her very much." And Charles said, "Yes," although he was unclear if a reply was called for or even welcome. He watched the operator push a button and rock the control arm clockwise and rest his hands there. They were shiny and weathered and lined, like an old pair of dark brown shoes.

At the ground floor, Charles excused himself to exit through the back of the hospital. Outside, he had to circle back to reach his car, and when he reached it he found a parking ticket flapping on the windshield, pinned under the wiper blade. Richard had come out through the lobby, passing among the nuns and the relatives of the sick and past the statues in their niches; the Madonna and her self-possessed child, one tiny fist raised in benediction, the other clutching a plaster fold of his mother's blue gown. Opposite them, the same child, now bearded and grown, was suspended limp, downcast, and pathetic on a cross, now the God of pity and affliction, the maker and judge of the world made plaintive, hapless flesh. Richard was still puzzling, still perhaps shaking his head, when he stepped outside and saw Charles half a block down the street standing next to his car, reading a slip of paper and stuffing it into his pocket.

SOMETIMES SARAH THOUGHT THE SWEAT ON ANNA'S FOREHEAD could be condensation—vapor beading on the icy white vessel of her skull—and then she would see that her daughter was hot, almost on fire. Sarah daubed her face with a cloth and then she rose and smoked a cigarette. Then she would sit next to Anna for a while, and the nurse would come and lift the sheets and the blanket and take Anna's vital signs and slip away in a rustle of white starch, in dull, hollow beats of rubber soles on the linoleum. The sky colored and deepened like a stain and the night rose up as Sarah looked out the window. It had been that way in Chicago last September. She had stood at the window of her mother's apartment while her mother hummed and did petit point in her big wing chair. Sarah could see the lights arcing down the shore of the lake to Oak Street, where the Drake Hotel glowed in the night like a cake bristling with candles and the beacon on the Palmolive Building behind it spun around, guiding her, pulling her toward it like a ship to port. She knew James was waiting there for her, and she just stood at the window, watching the lights as though they were a distant fire. She had thought of Richard and she said, almost out loud, "I'm doing this for you. I am forsaking this for you, for your sake." And she had wondered if that was how it always was for Richard; whether everything he did was for someone else's sake and what that must be like. And then she thought, with some contentment, "It must merely be like this."

She turned away from the window and back to Anna in her bed and she wondered for whose sake she was standing here now, or if indeed there was any point to it at all. Because it seemed to her to be no more than watching, attending the rise and fall of Anna's breathing, the leaching of heat and moisture from her mouth and brow. And she had to wonder to what end and for whose sake Anna was suffering at all—if it was at the behest of some microbe or God Himself or merely a man. Then she remembered the time, twenty or twenty-five years before, when she herself had laid abed, feigning some obscure influenza, but in fact clenching her jaw against the pain as her womb bore down on itself, again and again, buffered only by some tablets Ted had passed her as she had slipped out of his office. That had been for Richard's sake too, she supposed, although he had never known—just as he hadn't known about her and James. These were her sacrifices, unheralded, unspoken, dependent on silence for their virtue. They were like wreckage, the ribs of sunken ships resting in deep water, whose location only she knew.

Sarah turned away from Anna and looked out. She could see the bluff and the hill, flocked with skeletal elms and overhung by the cold, bone-white moon. Then she found herself thinking of James, of his being truly gone, and of his beauty and of how she had wanted him that September night. But she had given him up, never imagining he would be altogether lost to her; that she would have nothing of him but the memory of their unassayed desire, an Advent candle never lit, a ticket for a voyage never taken. That was all that was left of him—what had never been. She cupped her hands over her eyes as if shielding them, and then she was weeping. The tears rolled over her face powder and her rouge like beads of quicksilver, and then like rivulets coursing over a parched and dusty yard.

A WHILE LATER RICHARD RETURNED WITH A LITTLE PAPER BAG with cigarettes and a roll of mints in it. Five minutes after that Charles came in. Charles never sat down. He stood uneasily, never looking directly at Sarah or Richard. Sometimes he would come and stand at Anna's bed, never on the same side as Sarah and Richard, but opposite them, her body a croupier's baize they faced one another across.

Anna dreamed weakly, formlessly, in images she would scarcely be able to recall. There was water and steam and ice and sometimes she floated and sometimes she waded and trudged through a marsh among loons and cattails. Sometimes her body felt very small and dense like it did when she was little, and sometimes it seemed vaporous, like it was coming apart, like a rag of tattered, diaphanous silk. But no matter what she dreamed, with each step she moved a little more slowly and she could see only a little ways in front of her, her hands stretched out to part curtain after curtain of sodden gauze.

At six o'clock, Fields was talking to Dr. Abrams in the doctors' lounge. They had gone through Anna's chart, and Abrams had taken off his glasses and was putting on his coat, preparing to go home. "You'd better say something to the family. This isn't going well." He piled some magazines in a stack and put them in his briefcase.

"I don't want it to be out of the blue for them," Fields said, nodding.

200

"I have rounds at seven tomorrow. We can talk afterward."

"She could go before then."

"I don't see it—not that soon."

"I suppose so."

"If she'd just plateau out a little, I'd do the D & C. Really I would. Nothing to lose."

"I appreciate it, Ron."

"Good night."

"Good night," Fields said, and he steered himself out the door and down the corridor. The orderlies were pushing carts of dishes from out of the wards, and the crockery and glasses were rattling and shaking. When he got to Anna's room, he saw Sarah by the window, smoking, and her eyes drifted up to gaze at him and her mouth was a flat line. He began to talk and he talked quickly, hoping to get it done, to say it all, and turn and leave again. But after he started, he leaned on the arm of a chair and when he was done he just sat and no one said anything. Her fever was up to one hundred and five, and her pulse and blood pressure had fallen. She wasn't passing much urine. She wasn't an awful lot worse, but she had crossed a line where he could no longer say she was likely to recover. She still could, but it wasn't an even chance at this point. They ought to maintain their hope, but they also ought to know that.

Fields thought that then they would all talk: that Sarah would press him closely over some fine point, as though she could find a hole in his argument that would mean that Anna was really just fine; that Richard would pull on his lip and then he would ask if there was anything else that could be done, and once he knew what it was, he would somehow find a way to do it; that Norden would nod and nod and drift back into a corner like a timid ghost. But no one said anything, and Sarah lit another cigarette, and then Richard said, "How soon? Until it's clear, one way or another?"

"Not tonight, I'm pretty sure. Tomorrow, perhaps, maybe this time tomorrow. But don't forget she could turn around. She truly could. I just don't want you to be under any illusions. But there is nothing yet that precludes her recovery. Keep that in mind. And go home. Stay if you want to, but I'd say go home and come back in the morning."

They said they would, and then Fields touched them: He wrapped his hand around Sarah's wrist and kissed her cheek, and laid his hand on Richard's neck and patted his ear, and shook Charles's hand and exhaled through his lips in a gesture of weary commiseration and squeezed Charles's hand again very tightly. And then Fields said, "Good night," and walked back down the hall, tightening his necktie around his neck and centering the knot.

Charles sat down after Fields left, hoping to indicate that he planned to stay for a while. He was hoping that Anna's parents would leave and that after all this time he could be alone with her. He wanted everyone gone and the door shut and then he would go to the bed and take her hand and tell her he was sorry and that he loved her and that he was sorry again. He saw himself doing those things and he knew he would weep and then he realized he was on the verge of weeping merely thinking of them. He wanted Anna's parents gone and he hated them for not being gone, for the weight their presence laid on every motion of his body; that made him feel that he must monitor every word he said and every expression that crossed his face. He felt he couldn't even think without wondering how his seeming to think might appear to the MacEwans. And he needed to think and to be alone: to touch Anna and say—very low, so no one could hear—that he loved her, and then he would know if he still did love her, or if it was only pity and regret.

Suddenly Sarah said to Richard, "We really need to go, dear. I'm just a wreck. I'll leave the car and ride with you."

Richard said, "Fine," and then he said to Charles, "I suppose we'll see you in the morning," and Charles said, "Yes. Absolutely." Sarah looked at him quizzically and said, "Are you coming?" Charles shook his head. "No. Not just now. In a minute."

After he heard their footsteps pass away, he shut the door, as though he were going to do something furtive and shameful. He went to the bed and watched Anna for a long while, holding the rail, and her breaths came a long time apart, attenuated, like lights flashing from an island far away. He took her hand. It was hot and dry and he leaned over her face and her breath came up to him like a vent of steam, milky and sour, not sharp, but blunt and fetid, the way he imagined menstrual blood to be. He tried to say the words he had planned, but all he could do was whisper, "Baby, darling baby," and sob. He was afraid he would never speak to her again, and he wished he had given her the ring and gone off with her somewhere. Then he knew that all this was his doing and his to bear; all this and—he had never thought of this before, not even the previous Saturday night while he waited at the Lowry Hotel— the baby, a tiny remnant of which rotted in Anna's womb and was spinning death into her blood like a pinwheel. It was killing him too, fashioning its justice, or at least it was killing a part of him. And once he had thought all these things and taken them all on—the sacrifices he had ordained through his cowardice, which had now become debts that must require his own sacrifice—his heart was empty, even of love for Anna.

He wanted to go home now, and he loosed his fingers from Anna's and pulled his hand away. He thought of the dog and the fire he would build and the light glowing yellow on the end table next to the couch. And then he thought of his bed and the hall that led to it. Now that and soon all the spaces of the house seemed to him like the passage in the basement, waiting, implacable and inescapable, and he found himself dreading going home. He took Anna's hand again and wept until a nurse came in. He tipped his head agreeably to her, as though he had been working closely at a puzzle, and said he was just leaving and slipped out.

WHEN RICHARD AND SARAH CAME HOME, SARAH COLLECTED the mail and, as she thumbed through it, she walked through the first floor of the house switching on all the lights. She heard the icebox door slam in the kitchen and then cupboards opening and a minute later Richard came out into the hall carrying two drinks.

He handed one of them to her and said, "A long, long day." Sarah nodded and they moved to the living room and sat down. She lit a cigarette and the smoke rose toward the ceiling and hung beneath it like scarves floating on the air. She began to open the mail, nibbling on the inside of her lower lip as she read.

"There's a letter from Mrs. Laski—mother's nurse," Sarah said. "She wants us to know that mother's addled most of the time now and that we should begin to think about a nursing home."

Richard looked up from the newspaper. He had been reading stock prices, running his thumb down the columns, using it like a gunsight to focus on the listings he owned. "Is it urgent, do you think?"

"I don't think so—not from the sound of this," Sarah folded the letter and pitched it onto the coffee table. It fluttered down, landed, and skidded on the polished wood, spinning. "I'll call and talk to Mother and see for myself. She has a way of slipping in and out of lucidity—always has done, as far as I've been concerned. This could just be a spell."

"You'll go see her in April?"

"As always," Sarah said and resumed studying the mail: a bill from the milkman and another from the grocery. A Princeton alumni magazine. An invitation to the wedding of the youngest daughter of one of Sarah's old school friends with an RSVP card with a lavender bow. A card inviting them to a cocktail party at the Middletons' next week. Next week scarcely seemed real. Here, nestled in her lap, inscribed and gummed and stamped and folded like flocks of paper wings, was what she thought was her life. Now it seemed pathetic, a child's forgotten trove of cheap souvenirs; rocks and feathers, jacks and abraded rubber balls housed in a biscuit tin.

Richard stood up. "I think I'll turn in. We'll want to be down there early, I suppose." Sarah nodded. It was the only allusion they would make to Anna, the only time they would speak of her, and then not as a person, as their child, but as a destination: "down there." Sarah rose now too, and together they climbed the stairs, and as she hung her clothes and put pins in her hair and ran water in the sink, she wondered who she and Richard would be if Anna were dead. Would she still be a mother? She was not inclined to think she ever had been. A daughter? Her mother had ceased to be her parent years ago; now she was a dotty acquaintance. Soon, as senility bleached memory from gray fissures of her brain, she would be a stranger. She and Richard would still be husband and wife, but would they still be lovers? Would they want to be? But maybe the outcome had been destined already, regardless of Anna's or anyone else's fate. She suspected they would be together in their old age, although perhaps only as companions, like partners in a bankrupt shop whose stores and furniture has long ago been hauled away. She saw then why it would become necessary for her to believe again that the things that came in the mail, that she had just dismissed, were important after all—because they would be everything she had.

Richard had put on his pajamas and now he was brushing his teeth furiously. He spat into the sink and saw a thread of blood coiled in the pink spume of the toothpaste. He was not imagining how his life would be if Anna died. He was imagining who he would kill. He had never killed anyone, never wanted to, or even comprehended the impulse in anybody else. But now he imagined the abortionist and Norden and the smug and ineffectual Fields and their respective fates, their respective justices. Jail or worse for the abortionist. Shame and a shattered reputation for Norden. Mere guilt for Fields, haunting him, tied to his life like an anchor, pulling him down.

For now, though, he would keep his agreement with Fields. He would not ask him anything more about what he or anyone else knew. But then Richard wondered what Norden knew, what the exact nature of his complicity was. He knew that Norden was involved. But did Norden know that he knew? Richard thought it was unlikely that Fields would have told him so, assuming he and Fields had talked at all. He was thinking about this when he got into bed and told Sarah good night and pulled the blanket up around his shoulders, and he was thinking about it when sleep overtook him, weary and loose-limbed as an exhausted athlete. He wandered through it all night, a labyrinth, a catacomb.

ANNA HAD BEEN LYING ON HER BACK IN THE BOTTOM OF A BOAT, down in the bilge where it was damp and there was an inch or two of icy saltwater slithering against her skin. It was dark and hot and sometimes she could hear footsteps above her on what she supposed was the deck. She thought she might be able to see if she could push the hair out of her eyes, but her hand was ten feet away and she couldn't seem to retrieve it, not in the dark, with the water and the rocking.

She didn't know how long she had been there, maybe for days. Maybe she was being taken somewhere across the ocean, down in the hold of a slave ship; maybe she was going to be forced into prostitution. She felt like she was drugged. Maybe they had given her opium. Then she felt hands on her, four or five or six, she thought. They pulled her whole body sideways and she heard voices and saw slats of light going by, gaps in the boards of the deck, she supposed. Then it was quiet again. Something was moving up her arm from the crotch of her elbow, inside her arm, an ache.

She knew she was asleep, that she was dreaming, because what she was dreaming about was the abortion, and she had already been through that. When she realized that was what she was dreaming about—that she was hearing the clatter of the instruments and feeling the pushing that came before the splitting and the opening out into the agony—she thought she would start screaming. But she didn't, not even when she realized that there was more than one abortionist now, more than one voice, and none of them was the voice of the old man in the chiropractor's office. She didn't because she knew this was a dream, and in her real life she was going somewhere where they couldn't hurt her anymore. So she just lay there and listened to them talk and felt them touch her.

After that, someone was patting her face and she heard a woman's voice calling her name. For a moment she thought that she was awake or that she was having a dream inside the dream she was having about the abortion; that she was lying in a bright room and she wondered where she was and she felt as if she was going to throw up. She decided to sleep for a while and there were no dreams at all. Hours later, or maybe it was days later, she opened her eyes again, and she saw hands on a rail and let her eyes follow the wrists up to the blue sleeves and beyond to the face, and she saw it was her father's face. She tried to say "Daddy," but her lips were swollen and dumb as if they were full of Novocain and gummy with what must be the bilgewater of the ship. So she tried something else. She tried to say "Papa." It came out slurred and soft, like "Obba," but it must have been loud enough, because she heard her father call back "Anna" like a deep-voiced bell ringing out over the water.

ANNA DIDN'T SPEAK AGAIN UNTIL THE NEXT DAY, AND THEN SHE mostly nodded. There were faces around her bed—her mother and father and Charles and Dr. Fields and two or three different nurses—and mostly they smiled and plumped her pillow and said how she was going to be fine. She remembered a book she liked to read to Douglas in which a little girl gets her appendix taken out and all her friends at her convent school come visit her, all lined up by her bed in two rows. Then the little girl stands up in her bed and lifts her pajama top and shows off her scar and all her friends are very impressed. But so far, everyone who came to see Anna was still being very polite and nervous, as though she were a bomb that might go off, as though they were afraid of her.

No one had even asked her a question, except for inquiring how she was feeling this morning or this evening or this afternoon, and nodding before she even answered. Then Alice Mercer came to see her, a few days after she had woken up, the morning the nurse told her her temperature was only a degree or so above normal. Alice was nothing but questions, and Anna realized she didn't have any answers; that she had to think each one through. Alice asked her, "So what happened to you? What do you think happened?"

Anna thought for a long while and said very quietly and deliberately, "I think I must have died."

"They say you nearly did—that last Tuesday they didn't think you'd survive the night. And then, since there was no hope anyway, they decided to operate on you, even though it could kill you—which I guess it nearly did. But you know all that."

"I don't know any of that. No one's really told me anything. Just that I was very, very sick and they were worried. It's like I'm a little girl."

"Well, you were about as sick as you can get and still be alive. So I guess you could almost say you *did* die."

"Not *almost*," said Anna. "I think I really did, really must have. I can remember what it was like. It was like I was in the water and I was coming apart, splitting into parts. You know when you tune the radio, and you haven't quite got it in tune? You can hear part of the music clearly, but some of it is indistinct, like it's behind something else—another show or static."

"Sort of."

"Wait—this is better. On the television set Charles brought us, sometime you have to tune it to make the picture clear. There's one picture and then another picture on top of it, but not lined up with it, just floating on top of it. If you tune it, you can get them lined up and there's only one picture, but if you don't, they just float away from each other, sometime three or four images, like ghosts."

"I've seen that happen."

"Well, that's how it felt. There were these images, these images of myself. They were all me—I could see them all—all floating apart. I was in this boat and I could feel myself coming apart like that, and I think I knew I was dead."

Alice looked down and shook her head. "I can't say that didn't happen, Anna. I don't know anything about these things. Did you talk to anyone else? What about Charles?" Alice looked around the room to assure herself that no one had come in. "Did he have to tell anyone . . . what happened?"

"I don't know. He's never here alone. Mother and Daddy are always here and he sort of lurks behind them and grins and stares at the ceiling."

"They say he was here through the whole thing, night and day."

"Hanging like a bat on a curtain rod," Anna said nasally. "I shouldn't talk that way, I know I shouldn't. But, Alice, I look at him and I think, 'I know where I was. Where were *you?*' "

"He was right here, Anna. And think of his position. Sitting here with your parents, knowing what he knew. Not being able to say anything."

"Maybe he did. I don't know."

"How could he possibly want to? I mean, you had to do it, but it was against the law. If he said anything, it would only be because the doctors had to know—to save your life. I mean, it must have been . . . what caused all this."

"I suppose. I was sick the minute I got home—cramps, blood, fever."

"So do you hate . . . the person who did it?"

"He was kind of nice. So, no," Anna said and paused. "How could I hate anyone? I died and then I came back. It's sort of a miracle, isn't it?"

"I suppose it is," Alice said, and the door opened. The nurse strode into the room, carrying her blood pressure cuff. "I'll only bother you gals for a minute," she said. The nurse put the cuff on Anna and she felt it tighten on her arm like the grip of a scolding schoolmarm. The nurse hummed merrily to herself while she held Anna's wrist and scanned her watch, and then she said, "Still ticking very nicely," and got up and left.

Alice said, "Is there anything I can bring you?" She stood up, and for the first time Anna noticed Alice's belly, that she was showing, although she wasn't wearing maternity clothes yet. After a moment, Alice repeated herself: "Anything you'd like?"

"A hair wash. To see my son."

"I can't do anything about the hair. Your cleaning lady's minding Douglas, I suppose."

"That's what Mother says. But you can't bring children that age in here."

"So there's not much I can do, except come back."

"I'd like that. Really I would. It's very lonely here, you know, when you get right down to it."

"I bet it must be. So I'll come back tomorrow." Alice leaned over and patted Anna's cheek, and Anna thought that Alice looked like she might cry. Then Alice said, in a whisper in Anna's ear that was like the whistle in a seashell, "You know I'd never tell anyone anything."

"I know you wouldn't. But don't you see—that doesn't matter anymore, that I was dead and now I'm not? That everything must be all new, all different?"

"I see, Anna. I don't understand. But I see," Alice said, and she saw Anna turn away, at first sleepily, and then as though gazing into the distance, as though looking for a ship.

"SHE COULD BE HOME IN A WEEK," FIELDS TOLD RICHARD. "SHE'D need looking after, but maybe just by whoever's tending the boy."

"Our cleaning lady, Mrs. Clay."

"That's who found her, right?"

"She called me. I went over, and then I called you."

"And now it's almost done—three weeks of bed rest and it's behind all of you."

"I don't know if it's that easy," Richard said, and then he sat down on the sofa in the hospital lounge and crossed his legs and looked up at Fields. "Ted, I did what I told you I'd do. I didn't ask you any more questions about how all this happened. But now it's done. I have the right to know. She's my daughter."

Fields didn't say anything, and then he sat down, right next to Richard. "And she has a right to her privacy, her life. She's an adult. Strictly speaking, I don't have to tell you anything, and I probably shouldn't."

"But you will."

"Maybe. Even probably. But I think I'd be doing you more of a favor if I just refused to talk about it, refused to help you dwell on it."

"Ted, someone nearly murdered my daughter. Some butcher."

"It's not that simple. I think you know it's not that simple."

"I suppose you could vouch for this person's good character, then?"

"I have a pretty good idea who it was, and it's not that simple."

"You know who it is, and you're content to let them continue on their merry way?"

"Do you like the alternative, Dicky? Arresting him? Having your daughter and her boyfriend testifying in court? Maybe me and you, too? Sarah can just sit with the reporters and listen. She probably isn't culpable." Fields stood up. "God, Dicky, you're a good man. But sometimes you're just a total ass." He paused again and said, "Sometimes I think the good are just insufferable."

Richard said nothing for a long time. He was stung, hurt, and he felt some obvious injustice had been done to him but couldn't put it into words. He wanted to tell Fields, yes, he was right, but he didn't believe Fields was right. Finally, he said, "I'm sorry you feel that way, Ted."

"I'm sorry I said it. But can't you see that that's all this business produces? Rancor and bad feeling with no place to go? There's no remedy for it, Dicky—none that any of us wants to pursue. It'll just eat you up, if you indulge yourself, if you don't put it behind you."

"I suppose you're right. But before I can let it rest, I have to know a little more. Just to feel like there's an end to the story—that there *is* a story, even if it's a sad one."

"I don't think it will give you any peace. You don't heal wounds by reopening them, by rooting around in them."

"Funny thing, Ted. Isn't that more or less what Abrams did with Anna? Reopen the wound?"

"To clean it, not to irritate it. And remember how dangerous it was. It was a last resort."

"This isn't going anywhere, Ted. Just talk to me, just for tonight, and we'll never talk about it again. Just placate me."

"If you insist. But not here. Let's take a walk."

Richard nodded, and Fields gathered up his coat and hat. They went by Anna's room. Sarah was sitting next to the bed, and she and Anna were listening to the radio. Sarah was crocheting. Richard didn't even know she knew how.

"What's that?" he asked her.

"I thought I'd make Douglas a hat for next winter. If I start now, it might even be done by then. Keeps the hands busy. I learned when I was little."

"I didn't know."

"There's lots you don't know about her," Fields jumped in. "She also weaves webs, spins the threads on which men's fates hang."

"Go away, Doctor," Sarah said. "We've seen quite enough of you lately."

"Very well. I'm taking Dicky out for a walk. We'll be back in a while."

"Good riddance to you. But bring *him* back."

"Yes, ma'am," Fields said, and Richard took his hat and coat off the radiator and the two of them left.

Outside the sun was down, but the sidewalks were still wet with water melted out of the snowbanks during the afternoon. Sand and salt ground sharply beneath their soles, so loud it seemed that only the roar of a passing car or bus could mask it. It was cold but not so cold that they needed gloves. Richard kept his hands in his pockets, his shoulders hunched. Fields shook out a cigarette, and cupped a match in his palm, and the flame dappled his face as the wind snaked around his fingers.

"So," Fields mumbled through the cigarette clamped in his lips, "what"—and then he took the cigarette out—"do you want to know?"

"About the one who did it."

"God, the stork, Mr. Norden?"

"Don't mock me, Ted. And Norden's a separate subject. You know I mean the abortionist."

They scuffed along the sidewalk and around the corner to the street behind the hospital. "He's a doctor, an M.D. Really an old man, actually. Or ought to be. He was a pathologist, taught at the university. Quite eminent at one time. Then—I don't know, fifteen years ago, maybe longer—things started to unravel. His wife killed herself. It was hushed up, but everyone knew and talked about it rather cruelly: the ghoulish story of the pathologist's wife and so forth. He got a bit drinky after that. Lost his job at the medical school. Worked in the county coroner's office, and lost that job too. Then the war came and his son, his only son—only child, I think—was killed. Somewhere in Germany, at the very end of the war in some stupid skirmish when everyone else's sons were coming home. I think that finished him off. He's been doing abortions since then, at night in a chiropractor's office on University Avenue. I don't know why. I don't think it's for the money."

"To bide his time?" Richard said archly. "As a form of consolation?"

"You don't know it, but you could be right. It's awfully hard to give up doctoring, you know. It's not just passing the time. It's the magic of it. You see a wound. You contemplate it and touch it and there's healing."

"Some of the time."

"Some of the time. But all the time if you do it right. That's what we like to believe. Like a priest at the Eucharist. Transubstantiation."

"But this guy spent his career with corpses."

"With bodies. With organs and specimens and biopsies. With tumors and clots. And wounds. It wouldn't seem so to you, but it's the same thing."

"But he wasn't very good with the living, was he? Not with Anna, anyway."

"Frankly, I hadn't heard of any problems with him before. And you know what happened to Anna happens all the time. Not so severely, because the pregnancies aren't so advanced. But I bet at the city hospital they get a couple a week. Put them in bed, give them penicillin, send them home."

"So what happened to Anna?"

"Do you really want to know?" They had reached another corner, and Fields dug in his pocket for his cigarettes. Richard didn't say anything. "I suppose you do," Fields sighed. He pointed across the street to a small, forlorn park, its fountain boarded up for the winter. "Let's go sit." They crossed the intersection and went into the park and sat down on a bench beneath an elm, its huge bare limbs raised upright like arms in surrender.

"You see," Fields said, "it's really a very simple procedure. Normally, all you have to do is merely irritate the lining of the uterus and the uterus will expel the fetus spontaneously—like a sneeze. You can do it with chemicals, even a stream of water, or insert something through the cervix—a catheter or a wire. The risk is that some of the material won't be expelled, and that infection will set in."

"Which is what happened to Anna."

"On a larger scale. Because once the pregnancy's advanced beyond, say, ten weeks, that method doesn't work very well. The fetus is too well established. There's too much material to pass through the opening in the cervix. So the cervix has to be dilated and the uterus scraped out. It's hard to make sure you've removed everything, hard even under ideal conditions. With Anna, he didn't quite manage to get it all."

"And she nearly died," Richard said. He looked down. The moon had laid a lattice of shadows from the tree around his feet and Fields's cigarette glowed. Fields drew on it and the coal flared. "That's really all I can tell you, Dicky."

"You know an awful lot. Does this guy have a name?"

"You know I'm not going to tell you. You could find out easily enough if you wanted to—if you wanted to worry this thing to death, drive yourself and your family crazy with it."

"But why not tell me? What could be the harm? You talk about him like he's just another member of the local medical community."

"In a way, he is. He performs a service people want, that they need."

"Except he's an incompetent and a crook. And for him, there are no consequences. Because everyone looks the other way."

"I wouldn't want to live his life. Would you? And who would do what he does? Probably someone worse. Think of that, Dicky. Who would do the abortions for these women? They're not all lowlifes and strangers." Fields looked down at his hands. "Sometimes they're our children. So how would you have it, Dicky? Who would do our daughters' abortions?"

Richard felt insulted, slapped raw. He sat silently while Fields ground his cigarette out, and then he said, "So we're all complicit. And that seems to you like a reasonable state of affairs?"

"I suppose I'm complicit," Fields said. "It's a procedure most doctors don't want to perform. It's illegal and unpleasant and morally dubious. We don't want to be criminals. We don't want to feel the guilt, maybe burn in hell, for extracting these fetuses. But we know it's necessary, so we let someone else do it on our behalf. We settle for being hypocrites."

"And do you like being a hypocrite? Or do you not mind it as long as you can convince yourself that everyone else is, too?"

Fields seemed oblivious to the ferocity in Richard's voice. He went on quietly, deliberately. "I suppose I don't think about it. Which I guess makes me a hypocrite twice over. I just think of it as irony, I suppose."

"Irony. Like it's a play or something. A sophisticated novel."

"All I know is that the world is not as we would like it. We like to insist that it is, but it's not. We squelch it, blind ourselves to it with propriety and high-mindedness and good cheer; act as though there's a few bad eggs out there, but the rest of us are just fine. But there's another world—a counter-world, you could say—where life is complicated and mistakes get made and women get pregnant when they're not supposed to and people do stupid things and betray each other." Fields stopped, and then he sighed. "And we are those people. But we can't acknowledge that. Someone has to do it for us, has to clean up after it for us. You think this poor old man who did your daughter's abortion is a butcher, a bastard. But maybe he's a sort of angel, someone who mediates between the world as we believe it is and that other world, like between the land of the living and the land of the dead. Maybe to do that he must have a kind of courage. Maybe he's really a heroic figure."

"That's just bizarre, Ted. I don't know. Maybe it's insulting, and I'm too dim to see it." Richard looked up into the branches of the tree. "But it sounds like you're just defending the indefensible—doctors, lawyers, police looking the other way, pretending not to notice, everyone complicit. Frightening. Nightmarish."

"It's just a modus vivendi, a peace negotiated between who we are and who we'd like to be. Think of the alternative—insisting not just on the letter of the law, but on everything according with the ideal, everyone, all the time. You'd have everyone in jail or in exile or in the nut house. Or suing one another—because every mistake, every little affront, would be an offense to somebody and be actionable."

"A world without sin."

"Or forgiveness. And therefore without humanity or much trust: suspicion everywhere—the ice cream man's presumed to be a child molester; the Sunday school teacher's a witch. A dull, humorless, graceless world. Not a scrap of irony in it." Fields chuckled. "Lawyers would do well."

"And doctors? Doctors always do well," Richard said.

"Maybe not. It would probably be a crime to be sick." Fields looked at his watch. "We'd better get back to your wife and daughter." They stood and began to walk. On the other side of the street the hospital lay in the dark and an ambulance shrieked by. They waited for the traffic light to change.

"You know what they get once in a while at City Hospital? Some girl will get into trouble and she'll get some minced-up butcher's scraps and some blood and put this stuff inside her and show up at the emergency room claiming she's miscarrying or had a botched abortion and is passing blood and tissue. They figure they'll get a D & C that way, an abortion right under the hospital roof, totally legal."

The light changed and they began to walk again. "And the hospital's taken in by that?" Richard said.

"It's hard to see how, but sometimes, apparently, yes. I haven't seen it, but I've heard about it."

"So there are things in this wicked world you haven't seen? I'm surprised, Ted."

"So am I. But that's its endless fascination." They walked in silence to the steps of the hospital, and then Fields said, "You're never going to broach this whole business with Anna, are you?"

"No. She's suffered enough."

"I think that's wise. And Sarah? She hasn't heard anything from me."

"I don't know what I'd do if it came up. I can see her going and beating Anna over the head with it," Richard said.

"Give her some credit, Dicky. She's probably already figured it out and knows nothing good can come of pursuing it." Fields moved forward and held the door open into the foyer and its sore and afflicted bodies of plaster and marble and flesh. "We're all in the same boat with this thing. It's not a particularly good boat, but it's the one we're in."

IN THE MORNING, AS SHE SCRAPED THE KNIFE ACROSS HER TOAST and the heat bled gently from her coffee cup into her palm, Sarah thought spring might come soon. She thought she might smell the peppery scent of pine loosed by the sun and hear the trickle of meltwater sheathing the earth, creeping over the pavement in streams and sheets, eroding the dense and clotted snowbanks from beneath. The sun was falling through the windows and pooled on the carpet in columns and trapezoids. She imagined daffodils, gentians, foxgloves, and bluebells. She thought she would buy Anna a potted lily for her room.

At ten o'clock she decided to call her mother. Mrs. Laski answered. She said, "Don't expect much. Remember what I wrote you."

A moment later there was a voice on the line, slightly breath-less. "Yes," it drawled expectantly. "Hello?"

"Mother, it's Sarah."

There was a pause. "Sarah," the voice said. "Yes, Sarah." And another pause. "Do I know you from school? Who's your father?"

"My father's Franklin Woods, your husband. He died fifteen years ago."

"Oh, Frank Woods. I always adored Frank Woods. Do you re-member him?"

"He was my father, Mother. Of course I remember him."

"He was so handsome, so wry. Do you know what he did once? When he came calling? He came in an old beaver hat, like from fifty years before. A beaver hat. Can you imagine that?" The voice chuckled. "I don't suppose you remember him. You sound too young."

"I was his daughter, Mother. I have a daughter of my own— Anna, your granddaughter."

"You have a daughter? That's lovely. Does she have a beau? I always had lots of beaux. I bet she does."

Sarah gave up trying to argue with the voice, to insist on a history of events and relations with it. She just talked, as though passing the time of day; and then, as though she were confessing herself, unburdening her cares to a disinterested but pleasant-mannered stranger. "Yes, she does. I think they'll become engaged soon."

"Really. Won't that be a thrill!"

"But she's been sick. Very sick, actually."

"What a shame. Something grave?"

"Female trouble. Fever."

"The worst thing, the worst. I used to get the vapors. I'd get very faint and you could have just blown on me sideways and I'd keel right over."

"She was delirious for three days," Sarah said softly. The voice went on.

"Is she better now?"

"Oh, all better.

"Well, that's a blessing. Do they know what caused it? Was it something going around, a contagion?"

"They just say that she was infected with something."

"Wherever do these things come from? These infections and influenzas. It's as if they invent new ones each season, like hats."

"It's a mystery."

"You say it was your daughter?"

"Yes, my daughter Anna."

"That's a lovely name for a daughter. I was lucky. My daughter Sarah never got sick—fit as could be. Oh, of course she could be a trial at times. Very headstrong and willful."

"Mine's the same way," Sarah said.

"I suppose they all are," the voice said. "One can't tell, though—not really. I think my husband always knew Sarah better, understood her. She took after him, I suppose. Rather thought she had it all figured out—how the world worked. But I'm not sure she really understood about people. She always seemed to think her own wishes were like facts and everyone else's were just fancies." She paused and then sighed, as if emptied out. "Well, I'm afraid I'm feeling rather tired, so I suppose I should go."

Sarah heard herself say, "I should too. I'm going to take my daughter some flowers."

"Well, that's very thoughtful of you. Will you tell her I wish her a swift recovery?"

"Of course."

"Good. And send my best wishes to your father. And your mother too, of course." Then there was a high, bright click and the voice was gone.

Sarah put down the telephone. She was numb, as though she had just had a terrible quarrel with someone and they had agreed that they would never see each other again. But there was no color in her face, no tingling or breathlessness in her chest. The woman she had intended to telephone was gone, and someone else had answered in her place; had taken over her mother's house and possessions and voice. She was not dead, but rubbed away like a pencil entry in a journal, and something else was written in its place.

For a long time Sarah would think she could still see a haze of gray erasure marks and transparent strokes embossed in the paper, that if she held it at oblique angles or screwed up her eye and looked very closely, she could discern the text, the entries recording all those things from long ago. But soon, Sarah could see, she would say to herself, "Did I imagine all that?" and then she would cease to care, and her own erasure could begin.

CHARLES CAME TO ANNA LATE, IN THE EVENING WHEN HE thought no one would be around. He nodded to the nurses at the desk and opened the door to her room. She was sitting up in bed, her knees bent, her lap cradling a magazine. She saw him and set the magazine on the table next to the bed. They had not been alone since she had recovered.

"You look well," Charles said. "Actually, you look pretty."

"Should that be a surprise?" Anna had meant the remark to be a jest, a tease, but it fell between them like something leaden that would now take some effort to push out of the way. Although Charles had sat in this room with her for the better part of the last week, it seemed they had not seen each other in a very long time.

"No. No. Of course not. But after all you've been through—"

"I got the nurse to help me wash my hair." Anna tried to sound merry. "Of course it needs a cut and a set. Then a manicure would be nice. And a very, very long bath. And another and another. Until all this"—she gestured around the room—"is washed away."

"That shouldn't take so long. They say you can go home in five days."

"To sit in bed for three weeks. I'll do it somehow. But then I'd like to go out. I'd like some new clothes and then dinner out. I'd like beef Stroganoff and a martini with a big fat olive. Then maybe I'll go back to college or get a job."

"That's a lot." Charles was a little taken aback by her ebullience. "Maybe you should just concentrate on getting well a little longer. And on Douglas." He did not mean for it to sound censorious, but he knew it did. "I'm just glad you're well. There'll be plenty of time for all of that."

Anna went on: "I'd like to get Douglas's picture taken too. A formal one, all dressed up."

"I went by your house this morning. He was fine. He misses you very much. But Mrs. Clay keeps him entertained. She had her little nephews over there today, and Douglas was happy as can be—him and the two pickaninnies, racing around and hollering."

"I miss him. I miss my house. Sometimes I could cry, I miss them so much." Anna turned away, and Charles thought to sit down on the bed and hold her. But it did not seem right somehow. "Mrs. Clay says your mother's been by, making sure everything's in order."

"Snooping around. She scarcely ever turns up when I'm home." And she looked at Charles and he knew she was going to say it. "Does she know anything? Does Daddy?"

Charles moved a little closer to her. He wanted to make himself more comfortable—to kneel on the floor or sit on the bed—but he remained standing. He lowered his voice. "I don't think so." He didn't offer anything more.

"You don't *think* so? What do you know? Are we going to get in trouble?"

He sat down at last and took both her hands in his. They felt thick and cold and heavy. He looked around the empty room. "As far as I know, no one knows except the doctor. And he's told me it's not going to be reported—that there's absolutely no reason for that to happen."

"Did he come and ask you what happened? What we did?"

"He seemed to already know—they can tell from the symptoms. He just wanted to know how long you'd been . . . how long since you'd missed your period. And where the doctor was and what happened afterward."

"He wanted to know who it was?"

"Just so he could figure out what went wrong."

"What did go wrong? Mother says you weren't there—that Mrs. Clay found me and she got Daddy."

"It's not that simple. I was stuck—I couldn't get out of my house—"

"I remember waking up the day after. The house was empty. It was dark and snowing. I felt so sick. I got some water and took some of those pills the man gave me. And I tried to call you and there wasn't any answer."

"The telephone was out. So was the electricity. All I had was the gas from the stove. I had to build a fire—"

"Why didn't you come back?"

"The car was stuck. In a drift. And the battery was dead. It was a huge storm, Anna. I could have gotten lost. I could have frozen, nearly died—"

"I did die, almost, at least. Why did you ever leave in the first place?"

"We agreed it would be all right, that it was okay."

"Well, it wasn't okay, was it?" Anna said, as though she wished to drop the matter.

"You have to remember that we didn't know anything was wrong. You didn't feel good, but we thought that was normal. You just wanted to sleep. We agreed I'd call Mrs. Clay, tell her to keep Douglas until the next day, and then I'd go home."

"And come back."

"Christ, Anna! That was not my fault. You're really being un-fair—"

"Don't talk to me about what's unfair. If anyone suffered . . . " Anna stopped for a moment, and then, after a great exhalation of breath, went on. "This was your problem as much as mine. But I paid the price for both of us. Damn it, I died for both of us. So don't talk to me about what's unfair. Just don't."

"You *died*?" Charles said. "That's a little dramatic, Anna. I don't want to take anything from what you went through—"

"You're doing rather nicely at it."

"I don't mean to. Really I don't." He tried to take breaths, to ease the pressure that was bearing down on his forehead like a stone, to quell the heat inside his skull that was rising to meet it.

"But some of this is just the way things are, anatomy, the facts of life." Anna was facing away from him. "I mean, I can't be the one that's pregnant and that goes through this. I sat here every day for a week. I hardly went to the office. I hardly went home. I hardly ate. I hardly slept. What do you want from me? If there'd been a way that I could have taken half the pain, half the sickness, I would have done it."

Anna looked at him coolly, cat-eyed. "Half? That's very generous of you."

Charles's cheeks felt hot. He was going to cry or he was going to get very angry. Either would serve. But for a week he had been mute with fear and propriety, and now he decided to speak.

"Do you know what I think, Anna? I think you're so full of self-pity that you can't see what anyone else might have gone through. Never mind me. I mean your parents, the doctors who saved your life. And you won't even grant them that. You spout this crap about having died like it was some great achievement, like you were the phoenix, like you redeemed yourself, resurrected yourself or something. And all of it was just a bunch of delirium. The only person that died here—" The thought and then the phrase came to Charles suddenly, as a revelation, and just as suddenly he stopped himself, arrested by the dread and the cruelty of saying it.

He saw the tears overrunning Anna's cheeks, moving silently as clouds, falling like drops of blood, blotted by the sheet she held at her throat, brittle as meringue. Her voice shook. "It was yours, your child—"

"Ours."

"Ours. But you acted like it was mine, mine to deal with, mine to get rid of. Like it was some *problem* I had that you were willing to help out with. And you couldn't even be here."

"Anna, we've been through that—"

"I know. I know. And it's not what you did or didn't do. It's about how it felt, about what it said about what you believed."

"What I believed?"

"About me, about us."

"I don't know what I believed. I wasn't . . . philosophizing. I was dealing with what needed to be done. I was acting, not meditating."

"But you have to believe something, to feel something," Anna said, looking up, her eyes glistening.

"I don't even know what I believe about God," Charles said, trying to keep his voice low. "I haven't got around to figuring out what I *believe* about us." Charles felt the tables had been turned on him, that he was being scolded.

"It's not something you think about and then make a decision about. It's not a thing you *do*. It's just what you feel, what you assume, like a tree you're always standing under. You don't think about whether it's there or not. It just is."

"I don't think I understand this, Anna. I did the best I could. If that's not enough . . . " He let his voice trail off, half in despair, half as a kind of petulant threat. He looked at her. She was moist and disheveled, like something melting. He could imagine touching her, but he felt he would never touch her again, that the obstruction between them was immovable, locked like a clenched jaw, and also invisible, that it could not even be located.

Anna spoke. "I just wanted not to be alone through this."

"You weren't alone."

"I felt alone. I felt like I was being sent up one of those pyramids in the jungle to be sacrificed. Like you just handed me some money and said, 'Here. Go get rid of this thing. Come back when you've taken care of it.' "

"How else could it be, Anna? It was in your body. We wanted to get rid of it. You wanted to get rid of it."

Anna turned her face toward the window, toward the sliver of moon above the rooftops. "I don't know what I wanted. I don't know what I believed. Like you, I guess."

"It was for the best. There wasn't really any other choice."

"I don't know. You can laugh. But I did die. I suppose I had to. There had to be an exchange, an evening up. It could have been your son, you know—"

"Don't do this, Anna. It doesn't go anywhere, it's just punishing yourself—"

"Or your daughter. And every time you'd look at my face, you'd see her, and wonder about her—about what she might have been."

"Anna," Charles said, and he didn't know what else to say. He wanted to stop her. It was like a curse, a blasphemy, the lunatic rant of a witch. But, he knew, it also was true.

"She'd be like a ghost, hanging between us," Anna continued. "It would be the same for me. I'd see our son in your face. I'd think about him, about where he was, about what we'd done."

"Anna, you have to stop. We can't go on together, talking this way, imagining things that aren't real, that are just speculation."

"No, we couldn't, could we?" Anna said, and the door opened and a nurse came in, shaking a thermometer, her arm a fluttering of white.

TWO DAYS LATER, THE WEATHER TURNED COLD AGAIN AND snow flurries wound about the glowing heads of the lampposts. Sarah and Richard drove down to the hospital to take Anna home. Richard turned at the park where he and Fields had sat a week before, and rounded the side of the hospital.

"I'll leave you off in front and then go park the car," Richard said.

"Why don't we just leave it at the entrance, darling?" Sarah said. "Surely they don't mind if you're just coming to take someone home. You don't really want to walk in this wind."

"It's going to take a little while to get everything sorted out. I have to go to the accounts department and settle up."

"Why? Ted sends us a bill, and the rest is on Blue Cross, isn't it? It all goes through the insurance, I should think—an illness like this. Hardly elective, is it?"

Richard halted the car in front of the hospital steps. He responded without hesitation. "Oh, yes, I suppose so. But I still need to go through the bill with them. There's a portion we have to pay, a deductible."

Sarah opened the door. "Do you want me to meet you there? Ted's a friend, but sometimes I think the medical profession is rather . . . grasping. You need to keep an eye on them when money's involved."

"Oh, no. I'll be fine. They won't put anything over on me. You go ahead and make sure Anna's all packed and ready and I'll come up as soon as I can."

Sarah said, "All right," and shut the door. Richard drove back to the hospital parking lot and left the car there. He walked to the back entrance of the hospital, and the wind whipped at his trouser cuffs. The accounting office was down a hallway near the laundry. He went in and a receptionist told him to sit down at an empty desk and someone would be right out to help him. He webbed his fingers together and waited. There were a dozen filing cabinets, wooden boxes of index cards, and an adding machine with an impossible number of red, green, and black keys. Suddenly there was a rustle and a hand pulled away the chair opposite him. A nun sat down.

"My name is Sister Beatrice. I understand we are discharging someone and you want to settle their bill."

"My daughter. Anna MacEwan. *M-A-C*," Richard added haltingly. The nun nodded and stood up. Her habit was black, save for the wimple, and it hung stiffly on her, as though it were a ball gown. A long string of beads hung from a piece of rope fastened around her and they clattered as she went to the filing cabinet. When she returned, she sat down and peered at the papers through little steel-framed glasses. "She was with us for over two weeks." Richard waited for her to finish reading, wondering if the nun could surmise Anna's true problem from it. "It's a rather substantial sum," she said finally. "But I'll send it off to your insurance company, and they'll bill you for the difference."

"Oh, I'll just take care of it now." Richard took out his checkbook from his inside breast pocket.

"And then you'll collect from them?"

"Well, yes, I thought—"

"The normal procedure is for us to bill them directly. Are you sure you wouldn't rather do it that way?"

"Actually, we don't really have insurance. As such. In the usual sense."

"I see." The nun looked at him deeply for a moment, as though confused. "Well, however you prefer to do it." She rotated a sheet of paper toward him and pointed to a figure at the bottom. Her fingernail was unpainted, unvarnished. Richard wrote out a check quickly and tore it free from the checkbook. It was in excess of a thousand dollars.

The nun stood and Richard stood. She said, "I hope your daughter is much better," and smiled. "You know, you really should have insurance. Even if you're comfortably off. Things can happen so suddenly, so unexpectedly. Things we aren't at all prepared for. I don't want to meddle . . . "

"Oh, not at all. I'm sure you're right. In fact, I'll look into it right away. You're very kind to be concerned. Thank you."

"Thank you, Mr. MacEwan. And God bless you."

"And you, Sister." Richard walked down the corridor, his wing tips clicking brightly on the linoleum. He was thinking how adept he had become at falsehood and fabrication; how something he had once scarcely been able to imagine was now almost second nature. It was what loss and pain had taught him. He could have learned it from James, but while his brother had been alive, Richard was blind to its uses, appalled by it. So now, after James was dead, it had been bequeathed to him, and he was using it only for good, as a gift, out of love.

IT WAS IN THE MIDDLE OF MARCH, THAT AFTERNOON, THAT Anna returned to her house and her child. Her father held her arm with one hand and carried her bag with the other. He opened the door for her, and she saw Douglas sitting on the floor pushing a plush toy before him, making sputtering noises. He looked up and his eyes locked on to hers and he cried out and launched himself toward her like a rock from a catapult. He encircled her knees with his arm and his head pressed against her groin insistently.

Anna turned to her father. "I'm not supposed to lift or bend. Could you pick him up for me? So I can see him?" Richard lifted the child, and he put his arms around her neck and pressed his face against her cheek. He smelled of soap and jam.

Mrs. Clay stood outside the kitchen in an apron. "Better close that door or we all catch our death," she said with a slight smile. Anna laughed. Sarah had pressed in behind Richard and Anna, and she said, "If Douglas could ask his guests to move, that could be arranged." They all shuffled forward, and Sarah closed the door. It shut loudly, with a plosive sound, as though sucked out by the wind.

Anna looked around. Her house was the same and yet altered, as though she were seeing not the thing itself but a photograph of it, bled of color and dimension. The lights glared in the living room and the hall. The radio was playing in the kitchen, tuned to what sounded like gospel music. Anna smiled at Mrs. Clay. "You've kept it up much better than I normally do myself," she said, and then she turned to Sarah. "But I imagine your place could use some attention."

"Mrs. Clay has been sending her sister around," Sarah said. "She's very meticulous. Anyway, nothing ever really gets disrupted or even moved at our house. Someone just has to scoop up the dust periodically."

Richard spoke to Mrs. Clay. "Anna's going to need you here for a little while longer during the day. She's supposed to stay in bed and not do any lifting or bending. But you can go home at night. In fact, why don't you plan on leaving at four in the afternoon starting next week? I can come and cook dinner for these two, get them ready for bed."

"Fine with me. My Lucius is probably wondering if I'm still alive," Mrs. Clay said and disappeared into the kitchen. She came back out carrying sheets and pillowcases. "I just laundered these so you'd have fresh when you come home." She went into the hall that led to Anna's bedroom. Sarah and Anna followed her. Mrs. Clay turned on the overhead light and Anna saw her room, smaller than she remembered, the walls a light gray. The closet door was open and her bathrobe hung on it from a hook. Her slippers lay on the floor, and next to them, a black open-toed shoe with a long heel and an ankle strap, capsized on its side. Her mother was looking at the bed, and then she pulled a cigarette from her purse and lit it.

Anna, too, looked at the bed and she saw there was a stain the color of weak tea, perhaps a foot and a half in diameter, on the mattress pad. She quickly sat down on the edge of the bed, just in front of the stain, blocking it from view. Mrs. Clay regarded her impatiently. "Honey, I can't make it up if you sitting on it." Anna stood and said, "Oh, yes. Mother, why don't we go out while Mrs. Clay attends to this?"

Smoke arced slowly from Sarah's nostrils and she nodded and began to move toward the door, but then she suddenly turned back and picked up a little box from the nightstand. "Oh, I meant to ask you about these. I saw them when I was over the other day." She held up the orange box and shook it. A few pills still rustled inside. "I just thought your illness had come out of the blue—that you hadn't had time to get anything for it."

"Oh, those," Anna said hollowly. "I just took a few when I started to feel crampy, when I started to think I was getting a fever."

"You got them from Ted Fields? I didn't think he knew anything before your father called him—"

"Oh, no. Not from him. From . . . from Alice. They were Roger's, from when he was in the service."

"She brought them over for you?"

"No, no. She gave them to me a long time ago."

"Not very effective for cramps, I shouldn't think." Sarah put the box back down. "Not a very wise idea to be one's own physician, is it, dear? Those didn't do you much good, did they?" Anna followed her out. Richard was sitting on the floor with Douglas, affecting rapt concentration as Douglas pushed around a cushion and shouted, "Truck! Truck!"

Richard looked up at Anna and said, "You look a little peaked, dear. Maybe we should let you get some rest."

"I think maybe that would be a good idea. In the hospital, you think they're keeping you in bed unnecessarily—that you've really got all this vim and vigor—and you get up and feel weak as a lamb after just a little while."

"Of course, dear. We'll let you get some rest," Sarah said, bending over an ashtray on the coffee table to stub out her cigarette.

After Richard and Sarah had gone, Mrs. Clay drew Douglas into the kitchen with the promise of a peanut butter cookie and Anna went back to her room and began to undress. She opened the closet and got her robe. She heard Mrs. Clay singing in the kitchen, something rhythmic and plaintive, and then she saw her reflection in the mirror on the front of the closet door. She stood up straight and gazed at her body, naked save for underpants. It was thinner than she recalled, and whiter. Her skin seemed very soft, not slack or drawn, but yielding, like damp felt or batting. She had imagined that she was hard and, now, after everything that had passed, her skin would be like a glaze, crazed and laced with tiny cracks and hairline fractures. But it was not that way.

She got in bed and pushed two pillows behind her back, and she sat and looked across the room for a long time. She could still hear Mrs. Clay, singing and humming and sometimes stopping to say something to Douglas. She looked around and saw where she had spilled paint at the bottom of the baseboards when she'd repainted the room after Jack had moved out. And then she thought she smelled something, something hot and gamey, like the breath of a dog, or of wet, dirty fur. It was not unpleasant, and then she wasn't sure she could smell it any longer.

Douglas came in, followed by Mrs. Clay. "I'm sorry," she said. "I can't keep him away. He wants to see his mama."

"And so he should. You leave him here, and he and I will have a little chat."

"He ain't much for conversation. But he likes to laugh."

"That's good enough for me."

Mrs. Clay started to leave but Anna called after her, "By the way, have you noticed any smells in here? Something kind of gamey, like an animal?"

"Something funky? I don't think so. 'Course, all kind of things can get under the house. Dying dogs, snakes, coons. When I was a girl, we used to sweep the yard smooth every day so's to see the track of anything that might get under there. 'Course, that wouldn't do here, not with snow and the like."

"Well, I probably imagined it." Mrs. Clay nodded and left. Douglas put his palms out and began to wriggle up onto the bed on his belly. He was nearly two years old, and although he had yet to frame a sentence—his speech was still no more than an assortment of exclamations—he was strong and agile. After he pulled himself onto the bed, he rolled himself upright and sat cross-legged by her feet.

Anna reached out and touched his hair and said, "I missed you, Mister Man. I'm sorry I had to go away so long. I won't go away again, not if I can help it." She looked at him, aware that he had no real comprehension of the words she used, only of their intent. But that sufficed. She enjoyed talking to him, even about things he could not understand. It was not like adult conversation. It was like feeding him or stringing beads with him. He smiled and tangled the fringe of the bedspread with his fingers, as though weaving or splicing rope.

She went on. "It was like a trip I went on. To Africa or someplace very far away." At the word "Africa," Douglas looked up at her with what seemed to be anticipation. Perhaps he had heard it in a story and associated it with something exciting, like monkeys and lions. Or perhaps it was simply strange, a sound that stuck in his ear that he hadn't heard before.

"I hope you never go there. It was much too scary. I was asleep for days and days and all the time I thought I was on a ship or walking on a beach or in a swamp. Anyway, I could have gone on that way forever—for eternity." Douglas seemed to react to that, to look

231

puzzled. "That's the same thing as forever, going on and on. Like there isn't anything before or after. Or maybe it's all the past that ever was, and you get pulled out of what's now, and just live there forever. Anyway, I didn't want to stay there. I wanted to come back here and see you. And stay here with you, with my little boy. Forever. For eternity."

Anna stopped and reached out and tickled Douglas under his arm. He squealed, and she said, "Is your mother silly? Is she the silliest girl in the whole world?" and tickled him again. Douglas slid off the bed and ambled out of the room. Anna called out loudly for Mrs. Clay. She came, and Anna said, "I just wanted to let you know he'd wandered off. And to see if there was anything to nibble on."

"There's some cookies. And I was going to make some chipped beef for dinner, if that's okay."

"That's fine. And I'd love a cookie. You know what else? I wonder if we could bring the radio from the living room in here? You'd still have the one in the kitchen."

"Wouldn't be no problem. You want it now?"

"No. I'll just read the mail and then maybe have a little nap."

"So I'll get you a cookie and your mail," Mrs. Clay said, and went out. She came back a moment later with a cookie swaddled in a paper napkin. She handed Anna the mail. "There's not very much. Mr. MacEwan took all the bills, said he'd pay them."

"That's very sweet of him."

"Wish somebody come to our house and do that," Mrs. Clay said with a wistful chuckle and went out.

Anna looked through the mail. There was a copy of *McCall's* and a few envelopes. One of them was from Jack, probably with his check in it. She opened it while she ate the cookie. There was a note.

Anna—

I put in an extra $10 this time for Dougie's birthday next month. I figured you would know what he would enjoy in the way of a toy.

Hope you are well. Let me know how Dougie is doing when you get the chance.

Best,
Jack

She dumped the crumbs that had fallen on the note into the ashtray and folded the check and put it down next to the orange-and-green box of pills on the nightstand. She would buy Douglas a truck, a red fire truck with little ladders that came off and a tiny hose that unreeled from the back. She would put it in front of the fireplace on the morning of his birthday and let him find it there. She folded her hands and thought about that and then she fell asleep.

BY THAT THURSDAY, RICHARD WAS BEGINNING TO FEEL THAT their lives had recovered some of their former normalcy. He had gone to the office on each of the previous two days and worked steadily until five o'clock. Then he drove by Anna's house to see how she was and to play with Douglas while Mrs. Clay fixed dinner, and then he came home at a little after six. He and Sarah had drinks and a light supper, and then they listened to the radio and read and went to bed.

On Friday he left the office after lunch. He went by to see Anna early and then he came home about two o'clock. He walked into the house and all the rooms seemed to be empty—not empty of furniture, but of habitation, as though the moving van were due at any moment to move them out. In fact, everything was exactly as it always was, as it had been more or less the past twenty years. Yet he could not say if it was truly the same place, dwelled in by the same persons, or if it were a mirror image or a shadow of them; the unseen counterworld that Fields had spoken of and to which Richard now wondered if he might have been transported. He found Sarah in the kitchen arranging flowers.

"You're back early," she said.

"I thought I deserved the afternoon off."

"Spring fever? It does seem to be warming up."

"Probably temporary. We could just as easily have another blizzard."

"You have to have faith, darling." She put down her secateurs and began to crumple up the damp newspaper the flowers had lain on. "Like the daffodils?" she said, and held one up with mock earnestness. "Silly flowers, really. Come up before practically anything else, oblivious to harm. Naive. Simpleminded. Merry little yellow garb, like a little girl's frock. No finesse, no self-regard. But charming. Says, 'Here I am. Spring must be here. Just believe.' And the next morning they find themselves up to their knees in snow." She put the flower into the vase with the others. "And that's the moral of my story," she said and carried the flowers out to the dining room.

Richard followed her out. As she put the flowers on the table she said, "I called a man today about converting the furnace to oil. Like we'd talked about. He's going to come out and do an estimate next week. I thought perhaps we ought to join the twentieth century, even if it's ten years after everyone else."

"Oh, good idea," Richard said, and then he added, "I think I'll go run a few errands, prowl the hardware store and such. Then maybe take a drink at the club. Be home by six-thirty or so."

"Very well," said Sarah, standing across the dining table from him. She waved her pinky. "Have fun with the bolts and the nails and the mousetraps."

At first, Richard drove aimlessly, west to the river, north along the bluff, south again and then east. Sarah was right: The sun blazed bone-white and the world was wet and melting, dripping steadily and rhythmically like the ticking of a long-arrested, now newly wound clock.

He found himself at Susan Nash's ten minutes later. He sat in the car with the motor running for a time, twirling the knob on the radio. The voices glided past each other like curtains on rails moving in opposite directions. He put his hat on the seat. He turned the engine off and walked up to the porch. His feet echoed damply, dully, on the steps and the floorboards. He rang the bell and waited. The other times he had come here, he had felt a consuming nervousness at first. But he did not this time. He was too weary and although he would not look it in the face, he knew the reason he had come.

The door opened, and Susan said, "Well, stranger, what a surprise. I bet it's been three weeks." Her hair was pulled back and tied carelessly, and she wore a skirt and the same sweater she had worn the first time he had seen her.

"I'm sorry to have been out of touch," Richard said, and he was aware he was staring at her and caught himself and looked at his hands for a moment. "It's been . . . a very hectic time."

"Well, come in," Susan said, and reached around his waist to shut the door. He could smell her, the soap and the wool and the humid warmth of her body. She climbed the stairs, and he watched her skirt swing over her calves. "I was just thinking about you," she said when they reached the landing, and turned to face him. "In fact, I was thinking that somehow you might come today. I don't know why."

He stepped toward her and she reached out her hand, as though to take his coat. But instead she put her hand on his lapel and held it in her fingers. "I really was thinking that," she said and her other arm began to rise. A long time seemed to pass, and Richard at last said, "Whenever I think, I think I must be thinking of you," but his voice was shaking and his breath was caught in the top of his throat, and it came out in a series of spasms. He felt her arm fall to his shoulder, or perhaps he imagined it was his waist, and he fell forward and his mouth fell on hers, one hand clutching her shoulder and the other her buttock, as though clinging to a rock face. They were breathing into each other's lungs.

She began to walk backward, still holding him, their mouths locked together, and his feet shuffled forward without lifting from the floor, like a skater gliding, like a very old man, as she backed through her bedroom door. They stopped moving and she put her face on his neck, breathing damply, slowly, and he looked over her shoulder and saw that they were standing at the foot of her bed. And then she was kissing him again, their mouths swallowing each other's breath so that no one could speak or think. He was pressed up against her, his penis hard as stone, arced and insistent. He tightened his hand on her buttock and drew her even closer against him, against it, like a weight he was pressing into her, and then he lifted his hand above her waist and inside her sweater and the heel of his palm coasted across her side and her belly to find her breast.

But then she moved away from him, and he thought she was going to tell him to stop, and he didn't know if he could stop— not because he could even begin to imagine taking her by force, but because his desire was an immeasurable, incomprehensible burden, falling and unstoppable. But she didn't stop him. She looked up at the ceiling—he wasn't sure their eyes had met since they had first touched at the top of the stairs—and crossed her arms before her and pulled her sweater off her body, and then she pushed his coat off his shoulders and then his jacket and they fell, nested within each other on the floor, and she began to pull at his belt, to pull it tighter in order to loosen it.

He began to feel around the perimeter of her skirt with his thumb, and he found the button and the zipper and the skirt fell away. She had freed the waistband of his trousers and they slid down his legs and puddled around his feet, and she had reached within his shorts and was grasping his penis and he thought it might burst or shatter or split and double itself again and again like a vine driving and arcing through the world.

He fell to his knees before her, wresting off his shoes with one hand, clutching her buttock with the other, pushing his face against her underpants. He could smell a deep moisture spiced with sharpness, like earth and rust and vinegar and fresh blood, and he slid her underpants down over her buttocks, the waistband clinging against the hair of her mons as he dragged them down, and he put his face against her and let the hair abrade his face and his tongue.

Then she drew him to his feet as though lifting him from water, or perhaps he rose, and she stepped back and sat down on the bed. She had removed her bra and her breasts crested upward as she raised and held out her arms to him, and then he saw her eyes, steady, past imploring, welling with calm, as though everything that was about to happen was already passing before them like a memory. She began to ease herself farther back onto the bed, to pull herself backward, skidding on her palms, and then she lay nearly flat, holding up her chest a little, supporting herself on her elbows. Richard unbuttoned his shirt and came forward to the edge of the bed and put his knees down on it and began to clamber forward and then he stopped.

"I want to see you," he said. She smiled and their eyes met, Richard and Susan's eyes, and as he looked at her she seemed to be getting smaller or to be disappearing into a distance and he saw her body against the bedspread and somehow against the floor and the walls of the whole room, as though he were above them both, watching. He was watching, and thought with some bemusement, This isn't happening. It was like two images of himself, one floating above and adjacent to the other, like leaves in water, and he wasn't sure which was really him. They might have been ghosts. And then he saw himself, on hands and knees, crouched before this beautiful woman, the shaft of his penis slapping and bobbing against his belly as it hadn't done since he was a boy, and he saw that it was happening, and that he was seeing himself. Then he began to color from inside out—from his gullet to his loins—with an unbearable dolor and shame, the weight of which did not fall and pull him after, but which sat like a mass of lead within him, pressing nausea from his stomach up to his throat. He turned himself over slowly, as though stiff or bruised, and sat on the edge of the bed, his back to Susan.

"Richard?" she said softly, as though calling to him, as though they were lost in the dark. "Are you okay?"

"Yes. I'm sorry," Richard said, and then he sat quiet for a long time, and he felt Susan crawl forward toward him on the bed and settle just behind him. He edged away a few inches from her. "I'm sorry," he said again. "I hadn't thought this through. But I can't do it. And I wanted you so much . . . so very much." He stopped. "It was like love, but more than love. It was irresistible, like there was no choice involved, like I had to . . . assent to it."

"I know," Susan said. She covered herself with her hands and arms in a V, like Eve leaving Paradise in a painting Richard had seen somewhere, and moved to the spot on the floor where their clothes were piled. Richard turned away and she began to dress.

He looked at the chest of drawers to the left of the bed. There was a lace cloth hanging over it and some paper flowers and a framed picture of a young man in a uniform. "Are you angry?" he said.

"Maybe a little. More like disappointed. Let's not belabor it. And you can stop looking away."

He faced her, and she was dressed, looking just as she had when he knocked on the door except for her face, which was marbled with crimson. "I think I better make us a drink, okay? Scotch all right?"

Richard said, "Fine."

She left and Richard looked at the heap of clothing at his feet that lay disconsolate and tawdry, like a trapper's sack of stiff and bloodied rabbits and squirrels. He began to button his shirt and then he pulled the tangled, inverted legs of his trousers right side out, and repeated the process with his jacket and coat, which were locked together like twin flayed skins. He put everything on and bent to tie his shoes, and then he draped his coat over his arm and walked out to Susan's living room.

Susan approached with a drink and Richard hung his coat over a chair and took it. He sat down, his knees together, his feet splayed. He sipped his Scotch and it went down like smoky fog, and after another sip he began to feel composed. He looked at Susan, who was looking into her drink, and he said, "I'm sorry. I just couldn't—"

She cut him off. "Let's just agree not to talk about it—for a while, at least, a little while."

"All right. But I just wanted you to know it didn't have anything—my not wanting to—to do with you."

"Considering I was lying stark raving nude on the bed not five minutes ago, I'd say it has a little to do with me." A match snapped into flame in Susan's hand. She lit a cigarette and it seemed to Richard she was gazing away from him, up at the ceiling.

"I meant in the sense of not wanting you. It was other things that stopped me, not lack of desire, of feeling."

Susan interrupted him, her voice sharp and nasal. "Don't tell me about them—about your wife or your family or whatever it is." She looked away, glaring. "It's not very dignified."

"I'm sorry," Richard said, and Susan turned toward him. He saw there were tears running down each of her cheeks, dividing from a single stream into many, like the delta of a river. "I feel rotten," he added.

"I don't mean for you to," she said and cleared her throat, and she forced a diffident smile and her eyes fluttered up and down. "Maybe we should have a hiatus—for a little while, and we can go back to the way we were." But she said it without any conviction, without any desire. Richard nodded hollowly, like something was spoiled or altogether lost.

They sat without speaking for some time, sipping their drinks, bent forward at the waist in their chairs, their feet perfectly flat on the floor. Then Richard stood up and said, "I suppose I should go," and Susan nodded to him and also stood. He gathered his coat, and then, although he knew he had agreed not to say anything more about what had just passed between them, he felt compelled to speak, as though the desire he had felt in his body an hour before had returned to haunt his lips and animate his voice.

"I won't go into it, but it's been a harrowing couple of weeks for me. I just wanted to say that."

Susan nodded and smiled. Then she said, "Dad says God afflicts those whom he loves."

"Your father says this?"

"Not my father—my father-in-law, Tom's father. My parents are dead. Tom and Tom's mother are dead. We're the only ones left in the family. So I call him Dad."

"And he says that—about pain, about loss. That's a generous view."

"He's a generous man."

"So God afflicts the ones he loves. That's an odd way for God to show his affection."

"Maybe it's His one weakness, loving us. But apparently He can't help Himself. He created us. We're irresistible to Him."

"So affliction is a blessing."

"That, or caring for the afflicted."

Richard sighed. "What did your father-in-law do to arrive at this view?"

"He was a doctor."

"I guess that explains it. A healer of the sick, the afflicted."

"Not exactly. Actually, he was in pathology."

"Still practicing?"

"No he's retired. I told you about him. He taught at the university for a long time, and then worked for the county. Now he sits at home and reads. I go over most every day and make him lunch."

Richard swallowed, and then asked casually, "A shut-in?"

"Oh, no. He walks. And sometimes in the evening, he helps out at a medical office on University Avenue."

Richard would not ask any more. He only nodded, and he thought to reach out and touch her hair. But he only said "Well, good-bye," as if they would never see each other again. And she called after him, "Come see me again. In just a little while," trying to undo all the irrevocable things that had passed between them, that must now always accompany them, springing up whenever one thought of the other or even of this time and this place, like the ghost of a lover, a brother, a child lost in a world of shadows.

"I THOUGHT WE OUGHT TO TALK—TALK SERIOUSLY," CHARLES said, and the words jangled down hollowly like pennies in a cigar box. It was Saturday afternoon. The cleaning lady had walked Douglas down to the grocery store with her, and Charles sat in the living room with Anna. She wore a red sweater and plaid slacks and she sat with her arms crossed, rubbing the tip of her middle finger against her index fingernail, against the cuticle. She didn't look at him except to scan his face for an instant, just long enough for him to see how large, how alarmed her eyes were.

Charles had seen her twice since she'd come home, and neither of them had said anything about the abortion or about what they'd said to each other the last time at the hospital. Neither had said anything to the other about the future, and maybe that meant their future together was assumed; or maybe it meant they had no future. Neither of them wanted to raise it, for fear of finding out.

Anna finally said, "I suppose we should."

Charles began. "At the hospital, things were said—"

"I said things. You said things."

"Right." Charles halted for an instant. "Things where we might have misunderstood each other, where maybe we didn't say exactly what we meant to say," he began again, and felt that already he was making matters worse. He was trying to think of how to recover, how to retrace his steps when Anna spoke.

"I didn't want to argue with you. That wasn't what I wanted."

"And I didn't mean to say anything to make you think I wasn't concerned for you, totally concerned—

"I guess we were both in a state of shock."

"Yes. Absolutely," Charles said. Now he was on the right track, he thought, and he felt a bit more confident. "Maybe we just got sidetracked—onto a lot of things that are water under the bridge, that just lead to blame and bad feelings."

"I wasn't trying to blame you for anything."

"Neither was I," Charles said. "I mean, blame *you* for anything."

Anna was shaking a cigarette out of her pack and leaning forward to seize the lighter from the coffee table. "Could I have one of those?" Charles asked. Anna looked up at him and said, "Of course," and held out the pack. Charles put his finger in and dug around and at last withdrew a cigarette. Anna held out the flame before him and he leaned into it and drew deeply.

Charles sat back and then, as though he were speaking to someone else altogether, he said, "I did the best I could, and still, this is where we end up." He stopped. He had said everything he could say, and now he was circling the history that lay between them like a burned-out cottage in a forest clearing; he had viewed it from every angle and he could think of nothing else to say about it. He inhaled the cigarette smoke again, and he felt a little light-headed, a little nauseous. Then, with his voice quavering, almost keening like wind in rigging, he whispered, "Do you still love me?"

Charles was taken aback at having said it, and he thought Anna would be too. But she answered as if someone had asked the time or the price of eggs. She said, "I don't know. It kind of depends on you." She looked at him carefully. "Do you still love me?"

Charles cast his eyes down and shook his head back and forth, not to say no, but in bewilderment. His words fell quietly to the floor like leaves. "How can I know—after everything?"

Anna was silent and then said, "I don't see why it has to be complicated. I don't want it to be that way. You ought to just be able to look and see what's in your heart."

"My heart. That's what I know least of all. I thought it was the sum of what I did—where all the desire came from." Charles stubbed out the cigarette. "So maybe I lost it. You tell me."

"I can't do that. You have to tell me."

Charles said, "But you don't know what you feel either. Do you?"

"Oh, I think I do. But you have to tell me—for me to be sure. That's your part in it."

Charles was feeling hemmed in, goaded and irritable. "I don't understand this, Anna. It's obtuse. Why should I be telling you?"

"Because that's the way the world is made. Look at everything I had to choose, had to decide. You can do this one thing."

"I still don't know—not for both of us."

"You have to, Charles. I just can't take—." She stopped. "No, I just can't *do* any more."

Charles again shook his head, back and forth like a horse browsing tall grass. "I really don't understand this. I want to do what's right. But I don't feel like you're helping me."

"Just tell me what you want, Charles. Tell me what to do. Tell me how you see us, how you imagine it."

"I can't see anything, not for everything else that's happened, the things that were done and said and can't be undone and unsaid; the things that were set loose, that can't be called back—irrevocable things. I don't think they'll ever be gone."

"So that's what you see?" Anna said.

"It's not what I want to see. It's what I'm afraid of."

"But it's how you imagine us?"

"Don't blame me for this, Anna."

"I'm not blaming you. I was just hoping you might picture something different."

"I'm being honest. I'm doing what you've told me to do. Don't make out like I'm the one that's doing this, that wants to break us up."

Anna paused, then said, "Is that what it is?"

"I suppose practically speaking, it amounts to that."

Anna nodded. "I see. That's reasonable."

Charles felt as though he were looking down into his own chest and found that the floor of his heart had been cut away and beneath it he could see an infinitely deep sky with little round clouds floating in it, going on and on, down and down, dizzyingly. After a time he spoke. "Maybe we just need more time to think, to be apart, to adjust." Anna shook her head, and he thought she meant to confirm the futility of his suggestion. Charles watched her, and he wanted to shout at her, to accuse her; to tell her she had never really loved him at all, not ever. And then he thought that indeed she might be thinking the same thing of him, so he said nothing. He only stood and she stood and he put on his coat, and she nodded toward the door like it was the inexorable next step in their lives. He stopped there and put his arms around her and he could feel her shoulder blades through the fuzz of the sweater, and then her hands, limply poised on his arms for a moment, and then they drew apart. He went out and he turned back and he thought he saw her nod again, or maybe it was a smile, and then the door closed.

Charles went to his car and sat still in it for a while. He laid his forehead against the steering wheel and after a time he realized he was weeping, as though he had woken up from a cat nap and saw that the sun had gone down in the moment that he had been sleeping. He pulled out the choke and turned the key and the engine caught. He let it idle a little while and he saw the boy and the negro woman coming down the sidewalk toward him and then they stopped. The woman stood looking back toward the boy, her arms akimbo, her head uncovered in the cold of the afternoon, and the boy was prodding the clotted remnant of the snowbank with a twig.

VI

A p r i l

FIFTY YEARS AFTER THAT SPRING OF 1950, ANNA'S MIND WAS going the way of her grandmother's. When at last there was nothing but memory, when the past closed over her like water over a sinking ship, she could see it all very clearly—even the things she hadn't known about then.

Charles had come to visit one day that far ago April, some weeks after she'd gotten home from the hospital. He sat on the edge of her bed and they passed the time of day for ten minutes. Then he said, offhandedly, "I'm selling the house."

She looked at him blankly and tried to smile. "Oh. What for?"

"Well," Charles said. "It's very exciting, actually. A friend of mine from law school, George Shepherd, just made partner at a firm in New York, Phillips & Gass, very old, very Wall Street. Anyway, through his good graces I've been offered an associate's job. And George said that's really just a formality—that I could be a partner within a year. On Wall Street. At Phillips & Gass. How about that?"

Anna tried to make sense of this announcement and to convey enthusiasm at Charles's good fortune, only latterly considering what its implications might be for her. She said, "That sounds like wonderful news," and waited for Charles to tell her more, to fill in the gaps in the plan, the details that opened up like crevasses in its smooth and perfect surface.

"Yes, it is, isn't it?" Charles said, and added, "A real coup. Absolutely."

"When would all this happen?" Anna asked.

"Oh, as soon as I can come. I've already talked to Alcock. Says they're disappointed to lose me, but that he's not surprised, that I'm a real talent. Can you imagine that?"

"I've always thought so," Anna said, and then she felt despair gathering inside her like a damp, gray cloud she'd swallowed. She was waiting for him to ask her to come with him, to turn like a father to his daughter at the bottom of a path they were climbing and say, "Come along now," as though there were no other possibility. But he didn't say that or anything like that. He was talking aimlessly, ebulliently, about his future, about what prospects investment banking might hold over the next ten or twenty years. And Anna felt she was pacing the platform at the station, trying to keep warm, waiting for a very late train. And she saw that she was completely alone and cold and that that train was never going to come.

Charles wasn't saying anything now. Maybe he was aware of what was going unsaid. In any case, Anna felt her face must be reddening, as though it had been slapped very hard, and the hurt had condensed into humiliation, like beads of blood glistening on her skin, and was there for anyone to see. She hadn't even asked herself if going with him was something she really wanted, and perhaps after everything that had befallen them, it was not. But that was beside the point: The injury lay not in the thwarting of her desires, but in the barrenness of his, in what he had forgotten to want.

They had spent hours naked together, charting each other's bodies and the rest of their lives, and they conceived and then sacrificed a child together. Now Charles sat on the edge of her bed like a swimmer preparing to slide from a dock into the water and Anna pressed her back deep into her pillows, staring away, blooming anger and grief like poppies. They sat together awkwardly and gravely, like fallen-out neighbors returning tools they'd once borrowed from each other.

It wasn't until much later—years later, when she was as old as her mother had been—that Anna imagined what Charles was thinking, the words he contemplated saying but did not speak; how he wanted to say, "Is this what you really want, for us, after all this?" He was daring her to tell him to stop, to wait for her. But he, too, knew what she would never say. He believed he had understood her and what she had said to him that night in her hospital bed. He knew what she believed about him, about his faithlessness, and how she could not love such a man.

TO SARAH, RICHARD LOOKED LIKE A MAN NEARLY STRUCK BY A streetcar, shaken and befuddled, haunted by a glimpse of the land of the dead. There was an expression of recollected horror on his face, or perhaps of shock, as though he had come home to find his house in ashes, a lank skeleton of charred beams. That had been at the end of March, and now, in the first week of April, Sarah meant to speak to him, to find out what was consuming him so, and see how she might help. He was working long hours, speaking little, and sleeping fitfully. When he did sleep, he lay in the bed opposite hers like a comatose, scarcely animate heap, a pile of laundry with a cat resting on it. The truth was, she was scared: She had feared his absence, his death, but this was worse, as though she were sharing their home not with Richard, but Richard's shell or some spectral impersonator of his voice, his body, his mannerisms.

She thought she might do it that Thursday, a few days before Easter. In the late morning, the furnace man came to make an estimate on converting their heating from coal to oil. He wore a gray boiler suit and what looked like a bus driver's hat with a shiny black bill. He said his name was Wayne Jorgensen. Sarah said, "Come in, Mr. Jorgensen," and the man said, "Oh, please call me Wayne, ma'am. Everybody does." She said nothing to this advice, but inwardly determined that she would do no such thing. She thought the new fashion for calling people one had business dealings with by their first names—as her mother had called her drivers and cooks—was pretentious and silly. If he pressed her, Sarah decided she would call him "Mr. Wayne," like a hairdresser. That would fix him.

They went down the stairs to the basement. Jorgensen regarded the furnace, swaddled in cloth tape and asbestos like a burn victim. "Here's the old war horse. She served you well?"

"I imagine so."

"The last of the Mohicans, these ones. Brass and copper fittings, like the boiler of the *Titanic*. But it's time to retire her, I'd say." He plucked the coal man's ledger card from the post next to the furnace, saying, "You won't need this anymore." An envelope fell from beneath it and sailed to the floor, and Jorgensen picked it up and handed it to Sarah. "A billet-doux from your coal man, I guess." Sarah did not like this Mr. Jorgensen. She told him she would be upstairs while he finished his inspection and to call her when he was done. He said, "You bet, ma'am."

Sarah sat at the dining room table and looked at the envelope. Her fingers seemed to quake and she looked at them and thought she needed a manicure. She knew by the postmark and the address what it was, but slipped the letter out to inspect it. She was afraid. Usually Sarah's fear was alloyed with embarrassment, with a sense of incipient shame, but on this occasion it was mixed with a kind of wonder: How had this letter, which she had imagined she would never see again, found its way back to her, into the bowels of her house? She wondered how many times it had been folded and unfolded, read and reread. Then she read it herself, and beneath her dread, she felt a kind of wistfulness for her and James, a fondness, and, deeper still, an ember of longing. He had never written back, never said anything about it. In fact, she had seen him only once after that, at a cocktail party. She had expected that there would be a look, the suggestion of a smile—if no words—to acknowledge that all was well, that he had understood. But he never looked at her. It was as if she were invisible.

She couldn't imagine he was angry or hurt. She wasn't hurt, and to be hurt was, if anything, more contrary to his nature than hers. Then he had gone hunting and never returned. She held the paper loosely and thought of his hands, his large, graceful hands.

Sarah put the letter back in the envelope and laid it on the table before her as though to interrogate it, to puzzle out how it had ended up hidden by the furnace. The daffodils she had arranged a week before and forgotten to replace drooped over it, their cups brown and singed at the edges. She laid her arms on the table and a little pollen showered down on the envelope, yellow against the blue, and then she saw the basement and saw the envelope's progress through it, from James's old desk to the place behind the coal man's card, borne by Richard's hand, read perhaps a half dozen times by his eyes.

A voice came from the basement door. "Ma'am? Wayne here." He strode forward into the hall and she rose to meet him. "I'll go back to the office now and make some calculations and put our offer in the mail to you. And of course the work can be done anytime this summer."

"That would be fine."

Jorgensen pulled the bill of his cap down slightly. "Well, it's been a pleasure, ma'am," and he looked over his shoulder. "Oh, I left that basement light on."

"That's all right," Sarah said. "I'll get it."

"Well, okeydoke, then," he said and moved to the front door. "Bye now, ma'am."

"And good-bye to you," Sarah said. She took the letter from the table and went back down the stairs into the basement with it and stood in front of the furnace. After a moment, she opened the door. The coal glowed inside and the furnace gave a throaty roar, as though it were digesting something. She started to throw the letter into the furnace, to flip it into the very back of the fire box, and then she stopped herself. She realized she would not be hiding anything by destroying the letter, still less undoing what had taken place between her and James. Richard knew about that, and if he were to look for the letter in the place he had hidden it, he would know that she knew. And that would only serve to complicate matters further. As it stood, she was checkmated by him—he knew what she had done, but he had chosen to do nothing himself. Then she wondered how long ago he might have discovered the letter, and she thought about the way he had been behaving for the last week, and she knew with perfect clarity what it was that had set him off.

If Richard had only found the letter a week ago, perhaps he wasn't sure what he was going to do. Perhaps he would come down here and read the letter again, to flail himself with it. Perhaps that was what he had been doing when he wandered through the house at night during the last week. And maybe he was going to decide to confront her. But over what, exactly? What she had desired and not done, out of love for him? She would see. She bent to pick up the coal man's card from the floor and pinned it back on the post with the rusty thumbtacks and slid the letter beneath it. It could stay here, perhaps forever, like a secret memorial, a seal of what they had not said and had not done. It was another thing that bound them together.

THAT SUNDAY, ANNA AND DOUGLAS AND ANNA'S PARENTS WENT to church. It was Easter Sunday and Douglas stood on the pew so he could see the choristers march by in their red cassocks and white surplices. They sang "Welcome Happy Morning" and there were a hundred candles burning. There were lilies all over the sanctuary, waxen white feathering into butter yellow, and the white altar cloth with the gold lettering shone like snow and hanks of blond hair.

Richard sang and his singing was like his own breathing in the background of his thoughts. He was scarcely aware of it. He was thinking about the dream he had had two nights ago, on Friday. He was still a little shaken by it. He had been running in a cornfield, between the rows, and the corn was so tall he couldn't see more than a few yards in front of him. It was cold and even though the cornstalks were brown and shriveled they were still standing tall in their rows, blocking him. The ground was frozen, the furrows and clods of earth hard and sharp as broken pottery.

He could hear James's voice out in front of him somewhere, and it was James's voice as it had been as a child, laughing and teasing, heedless. He was running toward something dangerous, and Richard was trying to catch him, calling after him, begging him to stop. But James went on running and laughing, just out of Richard's sight, and Richard couldn't catch him. The brittle, desiccated cornstalks blocked him, and he tripped on the frozen earth and fell on his bare hands, the flesh stinging, at once burning and numb. He ran on and on, calling James's name, begging him to stop, but he could hear James's shoes clopping over the ground and then the sound was more muffled, duller, deeper. He must be coming to the shoreline of the lake, where the tall grass and the cattails grew; or maybe it was the edge of the meadow, where the fence was, with the gun leaning against it, waiting for him.

Richard had woken up gasping, shaking, terribly frightened. He wondered how he would tell his parents what had happened, how he had failed, and then he remembered that his parents were dead, that he was sitting up in his bed in his room with his wife, and that whatever had happened must have been long ago or, he finally realized, had never happened at all.

Richard did not sleep for the rest of the night. By dawn he was convinced of two things: that it had been a dream and yet that in some inutterably real way, he had let James down, that he had failed his brother, his parents, his wife and daughter; all the persons and things in the world he was charged with protecting. He was not only no wiser or better than James, but scarcely different from him; when he had followed James down his trail, he had found it was identical to the track of his own desires, leading to and through the same woman, taking Richard to Susan Nash even as it had led James to Sarah. He could not have saved James; he could not save himself. There was, he sensed, two days later standing in his pew, nothing for it but to bend himself to the song he was even now singing; the same song that in a different guise he had forsaken a season ago when he had believed he had been abandoned but was in truth only lost in his bewilderment.

Anna had sat while her parents stood singing, her mother's voice a steady nasal drone, her father's fading windily in and out of the hymn's lower register. She still felt weak, but she was pleased to be out. She had wondered what it would be like to be in so public a place—whether she would imagine herself the object of whispered gossip, of furtively tapped shoulders and nods and fingers wagging beneath coats and hats. But she did not feel that way at all. The singing had stopped and she was hearing the prayers and then the readings, not continuously, but intermittently, like children playing in a distant room, like wind beating on sailcloth. But she knew the story anyway. Over a score of Easters, it had sunk into her flesh and bones like groundwater until it had impregnated her very heart and that was how she knew it.

Mary Magdalene had gone alone to the garden, to the tomb, in the hour before dawn on Sunday. Mary had been a fast, loose woman. She knew how to make herself alluring, how to make her auburn hair hang like a glossy pelt. She had been in trouble. She had known shame and gossip. Then she had crept under a table in a house where Jesus was a guest, and she had washed his feet and dried them with her hair. He took away all her sin and all her shame and she had followed him ever since.

Now Jesus was dead and Mary Magdalene was going with spices and a pot of ointment to anoint his body and bind it in fresh cloth. But when she got to the tomb, she saw that the stone had been pushed aside and that the tomb was empty. She was afraid. She didn't know what to do, so she went to Peter and the others and told them what she'd seen. They didn't believe her. The men went to the tomb and saw for themselves, but they didn't know what to make of it. They left Mary Magdalene standing in the garden weeping as the dawn wicked up out of the earth. There was cold dew on her feet, and she cried as one who comprehends that she has nothing in the world. Then she heard a voice and she saw a man and he asked her why she was crying. She asked him if he knew where Jesus had been taken. She thought the man was the gardener, but then he called her name and she answered, knowing at last who it was.

Mary wanted to go to him, to hold him, but he stopped her, and it stung her like a hail of salt. He said, "Don't touch me—you must not desire that anymore," as though his body was dead to her even as he spoke to her; that that was all behind them now, lost and gone. Then Jesus told her to tell Peter and the others that she had seen him, but who can say whether they believed her? After that, Mary went on a long voyage in a ship, all the way to what is now southern France. She found a cave and she lived in it for the rest of her life, grieving, love-scourged, and doing penance, naked but for her long russet hair.

That was how Anna remembered Mary Magdalene's story, how she saw it amid the smell of the damp, sweet lilies and the candle flames lapping the air and the shuffling and coughing of shoes and silk and rayon and wool as the congregation waited to take Communion. She remembered Mary's waiting—waiting for her life to end—and then her own waiting: through the not knowing and then the not telling and then waiting for Charles to tell her what to do, where to go, when to go, whom to go to. And she remembered waiting for Charles's ring. She had imagined she was being looked after, then and for all her life, but she had really been alone all the while, especially as she was dying and coming back. Anna could see it was that way necessarily, and with that she could begin to forgive Charles a little; to begin to teach herself not to want to touch him.

RICHARD HAD BEEN COMING TO TEND ANNA AND DOUGLAS every day at four that last week. He had been oddly quiet, making no attempt to cheer or entertain her. She heard him in the kitchen down the hall, the pots clattering, the gas hissing, the occasional sputtering expletive, and then more silence. He heated soup and stew and hash from cans, accompanied by toast and milk, and he brought it to her on a tray and then he fed Douglas in the kitchen. Afterward she talked and he listened and held Douglas in his lap and then he would get Douglas ready for bed, and leave the two of them together and drive home. He was outwardly calm and sometimes even cheerful, but Anna looked at his eyes and thought that he might very well have been crying.

The Monday after Easter, Anna was reading in her bed and she felt rather cheerful, animated by the festivities of the day before and by the sense of incipient spring. The drip of water was steady off the roof and the windowsills and the light seemed to flare around the window, as though the sun had at last come out from behind the veil of winter. She could sense the warmth moving into the house from outside and the dull stony smell of melting ice and the gamey scent from beneath the house.

She was reading books Mrs. Clay had culled randomly from around the house: old things of Jack's and books she had meant to read in college. She could not concentrate as well as she would have liked and some passages would stick in her mind while she skimmed over others, and sometimes she would find her eyes resting at the bottom of a page and realized she had no idea what had transpired in the paragraphs above it. That had happened just now, and she read the last sentence again:

> She wanted—what some people want throughout life—a grief that should deeply touch her, and thus humanize her and make her capable of sympathy.

Anna smiled. It sounded like her mother, or perhaps what her mother avoided so assiduously. On the other hand, it was something her father had no need of. And as for her, Anna: Was this—if she were honest with herself—how she had spent the last dozen years of her life, hurling her heart against men and the world? The thought was forming and then she heard noise in the front of the house and the thought was gone, jerked down and away in a snap, like a rolled-up window shade.

Richard came in, carrying Douglas and bouncing him on his forearm. Douglas's arms had been looped around Richard's neck like a life ring, but now he released them, thrust them into the air, and let himself fall backward with a whoop, letting his grandfather catch him. Richard put Douglas down and the boy skittered away out the door. "So how are we today?" Richard said with a trace of a smile.

"Not bad. Of course, not much happens with us shut-ins."

"But you're feeling fine?"

"Just fine. And you?"

Richard looked down at the floor and sighed faintly. "Oh, perfectly well, I suppose."

"You suppose? I've been a little worried about you. You seem a little low."

"It's nothing. Just the season. Spring fever's supposed to make you perky, but the Germans say it brings on what they call 'the circulation collapse,' or some darn thing. Lays you out, supposedly. At least in Germany." He smiled. "But don't worry about me, precious. What about you?" Richard sat down next to her.

Anna said nothing for a moment and then she drew in her breath. "Well . . . ," she said and stopped for an instant, "Charles and I are . . . going our separate ways. I didn't want to say anything this weekend—not in front of mother."

Richard said, "I see," and then added, "Whose idea was that?"

"I can't really say. He's moving to New York. He's got a new job. With a firm called Phillips & Gass, I guess."

"Very spiffy outfit, that one. Did he ask you to come?"

"No. But then, I didn't ask him."

"That's hardly the girl's job in these situations. And he seems like a young man who knows what he wants."

Anna sighed. "I don't know if that's true. I don't know what I wanted. I would have liked to have been asked. Even just so I could say no."

"I'd like to tell you what a rat he is, but maybe it was for the best—maybe you two were going to split up, and this was the excuse."

"But not like this, Daddy—without saying anything about it, just drifting away from me like we'd never been together. We were going to be engaged, you know."

"Then it's good it didn't get to that stage, precious."

Anna pressed her lips together and her eyes began to well. "But why shouldn't it have gotten to that stage? Why does it never get to that stage, time after time after time?"

"I don't know why. No one does. With love, there aren't any promises. People make them, but they're really only . . . declarations of intent. Sometimes things just wear out. Or things happen that can't be sustained, that can't be survived." Richard looped his fingers together. He hoped he was helping. He felt the things he was saying sounded wise, banal but wise.

"I suppose something like that might have happened to us . . . "

"Well, with everything you two had to go through—." Richard caught himself. "I mean, with you being so sick. Maybe he just realized that in a crisis . . . he just wasn't the one for you."

Richard looked at Anna and he saw that her cheeks were sheathed in tears. She said quietly, "There was more than that." And before Richard could stop himself, he whispered, "I know there was," and he reached out and took her hand.

"How did you find out?" Anna said after a time.

"The doctors knew. It was obvious to them. And I found out by accident—no one volunteered anything—and Ted Fields confirmed it. No one else knew."

"Mother?"

"No, not that I know. I would never tell her, precious."

"And you talked to Charles about it?"

"Heavens no. It wasn't my business."

"And you didn't think we were wrong?" Anna pressed her hand across her eyes, and then uncovered them, dark and red and huge, looking directly at Richard. "You didn't think I was dirty?"

Richard took her other hand and then he pulled her close. "Oh, no, no, no," he said. "No one cared about that. We just wanted you to live. That was something that was done and over, that wasn't your fault." He pulled back and held her by the shoulders. "We just wanted you to live. You were almost dead and you lived. You came back to us."

"And you forgive me?"

"You didn't do anything that needs forgiving."

"So there's no shame, no anger?"

"Not for you. Oh, I was angry with Charles for getting you into the predicament. And I would have liked to have killed the . . . the one who caused you to get so ill."

"But not now?"

"No, not now. I guess I see how so much of what you think is evil is just happenstance that people fall into, that chooses them and that they follow. Especially with love. It's very insistent. It doesn't brook refusal. If you go against it, there's hell to pay."

"There's hell to pay if you go *with* it," Anna said wryly, sounding like her mother, Richard thought.

"No, you can't win, can you? That's what strikes me as odd about the law. Maybe two-thirds of what we do—criminal and civil—is trying to bridle or punish what people do out of love: adultery, theft, divorce, embezzlement, assault, murder, you name it. All the crimes of passion, and most of the crimes of calculation. We think we can legislate and litigate and make laws against love. It's crazy. It's completely out of our control, and maybe there's nothing to do with any of this stuff but forgive."

"I don't think I could be that noble, not very often, not if I'd really been hurt."

"I don't think it has to do with nobility. Maybe it's just expedient—to maintain some capacity for forgiveness, like a well or a woodpile. Because you never know when you'll require it for yourself. You never know when you might hurt someone—or whom you might betray—and need them to forgive you."

"But what about being good—being decent and law-abiding and upright?"

Richard sat up and swung his feet off the bed. "Oh, I'm going to be good. You'll see," he said and cupped her damp cheek in his

257

hand. "I'm going to make you and Douglas hash. I'm going to make you toast." And he got up and then she heard noise and clattering and water running in the kitchen and the radio switched on and her father whistling above it, like there was life where there had been none before, like it was a tomb and someone had rolled away the stone.

THAT EVENING WHEN HE GOT HOME, RICHARD FELT NEARLY content for the first time in two weeks. Sarah smiled at him, told him to go in the living room and relax with his Scotch and read his *Dispatch,* and she would organize dinner. She was calm and deferential, as though she were currying his favor or were seeking reconciliation. It made no sense, because it was he who, unbeknownst to her, had transgressed, who deserved her scorn and disdain. It made no sense, but it was somehow consistent with what had happened at Anna's. Perhaps it was some sort of happenstance, some kind of miracle that had followed him home from one household to another like a tiny flitting bird.

Sarah called him into the dining room. There was meat loaf and creamed corn and Parker House rolls. He ate hungrily, deeply, with a kind of abandon, and he mopped up the last of the creamed corn with a segment of roll. Then he leaned back in his chair and cradled his drink in his hands and sighed and asked Sarah about her day. She wore a high-necked blouse and she fingered the collar, and then put out her hand for his inspection. "I had my nails done. And my hair. Because Monday is the day nature has ordained for that purpose. And I went to the bakery and I came home and did the things wives do. Oh, and I read the *Reader's Digest.* That was so taxing that I bathed. And waited for you, dear. How are things at Anna's?"

Richard swallowed and wondered what he should say. He entrusted himself to the truth and to the conviviality of the situation. "Well, things are fine," he said. "She seems even stronger than she was at church." He paused. "But she told me some bad news about her and Charles. He's got a new position at a firm in New York and—"

"And Anna's presence is not required?" Sarah spoke, her mouth scarcely moving, her lips held thin and straight, as though stung with vinegar. "How charming of him." She loosed a long, exaggerated exhalation of breath.

"Sarah," Richard said, as though uttering her name would soothe her. "It's all right. She's really taking it well. Even thinks it might be for the best. Evidently they hadn't been getting along as well recently, so this was really an opportune time—"

"For him to drop her?" Sarah cut in. They were both silent for a moment, and Sarah lighted a cigarette. "You can't say I didn't warn you. Months ago—that she was rushing in and she'd get her heart broken and would end up terribly embarrassed." She drew on her cigarette and hurriedly expelled the smoke through her nose. "I feel like damned Cassandra," she said and rolled her eyes up at the ceiling. "And I'm frankly tired of it."

"You can't blame her. Things just didn't work out. Would you prefer that she marry someone she didn't love? Or that she just be alone for the rest of her life, like an old maid?"

"Don't *lawyer* me, Richard. You know perfectly well those aren't the only choices. I'd just like her to show some sense, some judgment."

"Sense wouldn't have helped. There was another person involved—with his own feelings, his own career. She can't control that. And there were circumstances—"

"Her 'female troubles'?" Sarah offered.

"Well, yes. Think of the strain her illness must have put on the relationship. The whole business must have been harrowing for them."

"Abortions generally are."

Richard sat still, and then he looked up at her. She was grinding out her cigarette. "How did you know?"

"Oh, Richard," she said and then her voice was soft. "You are such a naïf. And then you try to make me out to be a fool. Any woman would have known. When it's happened you can sense it, you can smell it in the air. Like a baby, like souring milk. And I must admit Ted was rather transparent about it—by what he didn't say. Did he tell you?"

"I read Anna's medical chart, and then I pressed him about it. He told me. He promised he wouldn't say anything to you."

"He knows he wouldn't need to."

"I wanted him to tell me, so I could go kill the one that did it."

"And did he—tell you who performed it?"

"I found out. In another way."

"So who was it?"

"An old doctor. A pathologist."

Sarah shook her head. "A pathologist. When I was Anna's age, it was the county coroner."

"How do you know so much . . . about this kind of thing?"

"It's part of the female condition. Part of the human condition, even if men don't see it—going on right under their noses. Of course some men do. Ted's been known to perform one or two himself, to lend a helping hand."

"Christ," Richard muttered.

"Do you despise him now? Think he's wicked? Think he ought to go to jail?"

"No, of course not. Do you despise Anna?"

"No. I only pity her for her stupidity."

"She wasn't stupid. She was in love. She made mistakes that couldn't be helped. She sacrificed so much—"

"For nothing. For love. She almost died. She aborted a baby. She nearly left Douglas an orphan. She broke her parents' hearts. And the law. And now, she's lost her fiancé. All for love. All for nothing."

Richard was furious. He wanted to shake her. He walked away, toward the living room, and stood silently. Sarah's eyes raked the walls, the floor, the ceiling, as though she were hollowing something out, scraping it bare with her exasperation. She took another cigarette from the pack on the table and struck the match so hard that the head broke off, flaring and sputtering for an instant, and skittered across the floor. "Damn it to hell," she said. Richard turned back to her and then he thought he felt pity at the sight of her, the cigarette and the broken matchstick each hanging forlornly from either hand. She looked up at him bleakly. He smiled. "You don't really believe all that," he said. "That love's such a waste."

"I've approached it more sensibly than most."

"And you were luckier."

"Yes, I was lucky. It's scarcely hurt me at all."

Richard wanted to say the same thing, but then he thought it might lead somewhere neither of them wished to go. So he only nodded and walked toward her. And Sarah looked up at him and whispered, "And with you, not at all."

Richard reached out his hand and squeezed her fingers, the nails glinting against the grain of her skin like the sun against a dusky prairie. Sarah said, "Do you understand? That I just don't want her to suffer for her—for whatever it is she does—for her passion? Because it can be such a blight, such an awful wound."

"But such a gift. It's easy to forget how it feels—like immortality."

"Or death." Sarah laughed softly, and it sounded like a tiny sob. "I'm sure there's some middle ground, but I can't see it. I suppose you can—," she clamped her hand around Richard's hand, "—see all the sides of it, the good in it. You have a knack for that."

"Maybe I'm just willfully blind to some things, to certain realities." Richard said it almost wistfully. He paused and then began, "There's one other thing. You won't say anything to Anna, about what you know—"

"Heavens, dear, I'm not a witch."

"I think she'd just like to forget it. I think she imagines you'd condemn her."

"I suppose she would think that. But I wouldn't. And I won't say anything." Sarah stopped and then she said, "Sometimes the better part of love is silence," and struck another match. They both pondered all the things the other might take those words to mean.

The phone had been ringing, perhaps four or five times by now.

Richard said, "I'd better get that," and pushed back his chair and went out into the hall. Sarah put her elbows on the table and folded her hands together and her bracelets clattered down her wrists like sleighbells. A minute later, Richard came back.

"Who was it?" Sarah asked.

"Henry Finch. He's corralled me into meeting him for a drink next week—something I'd been avoiding since last fall."

Sarah smiled. "Think of it as a penance for all your folly, for being such a silly, credulous man."

ALL THAT WEEK, RICHARD WENT TO ANNA'S HOUSE EACH AFTERnoon. He took to sitting next to her on her bed and reading to her, and each day the sun seemed a little higher, a little warmer. The light poured in through Anna's window and the bed was like a little boat they were floating in. Sometimes Douglas sat opposite them, like a sailor perched in the bow, and sometimes he was in the living room, gazing steadfastly at the television set.

On Friday, Richard had cream of tomato soup simmering on the stove, and he came in and read aloud to Anna. He had been enjoying himself with the book, putting on the voices of English provincials and hayseeds, and now he cleared his throat and began again: "In old days there were angels who came and took men by the hand and led them away from the city of destruction." He cleared his throat once more and continued:

We see no white-winged angels now. But yet men are led away from threatening destruction: a hand is put into theirs, which leads them forth gently toward a calm and bright land, so that they look no more backward; and the hand may be a little child's.

Richard took a breath and looked at Anna and he saw there was a tear forming in the corner of her eye. He said, "Anna, are you all right, dear?"

She looked over to him and she was biting her lips. "I was just

262

thinking. About children. And I wondered what I'd done when I got rid of the baby—what becomes of such children, what becomes of people like me." She pressed the heel of her hand against her eyes and sat still, waiting for Richard to say something.

"I just don't know, precious. I just don't. I don't think it's something you ought to dwell on."

"But do you think it's like killing someone?"

"Well, I suppose technically something dies, but I'm not sure you can say it's a separate, independent entity. It's more like a part of yourself."

"So I killed a part of myself."

"I wouldn't want to put it that strongly. Maybe you sacrificed it, gave it up."

"You know, I thought I died when I was sick. I was sure I did. But maybe it was just that part that died, the part I sacrificed."

"That might be a good way to look at it," Richard said.

Anna pulled herself up a little straighter in the bed. "Of course, that ignores the whole question of whether it was wrong, whether I should suffer for it."

"I think you suffered enough already. I think if there was a price to pay for what you did, you paid it."

"But how would I know if it was enough? Or if the suffering was just coincidental?"

"I don't suppose you could know that. You'd just have to believe."

"I'm not sure I believe in anything. Maybe everything that happens is just accidental, senseless—pointless."

Richard thought for a moment. "Then that would have to include the good things, too, wouldn't it? Not just everything that went wrong and all the suffering, but your coming back to us, your not dying."

"I don't know about that," Anna said.

Richard went on. "You know, someone told me, 'God afflicts those whom he loves.' "

"So suffering's a kind of blessing. That's a crazy idea. Who told you that?"

"Just someone I met. They were quoting a relative—no one we know."

"That seems like blind faith to me."

"But at least it's something to think about, to hang on to. It's better than nothing."

"But even if I believed that for myself, what about everything else? What about the baby, or whatever you want to call it?" Anna's voice became quieter, firmer. "I want to know what happened to it. I want to know where it went."

"I know you do," Richard said. "And I can't help you. Sometimes I wonder where your Uncle James is—whether he's somehow up where he died in North Dakota, in the fields. I never saw the exact place he died. I heard about it. And I've imagined it. I kind of see him there. But with your . . . I can't help you. I guess it went wherever the part of you that you thought died went."

"I was out on the water, in a boat," Anna said. She began to sniffle, and then stopped herself. "I always imagined it was a girl—maybe just because I already had a boy."

"A girl would be good. I loved having a girl," Richard said, and he squeezed Anna's hand.

"Do you think about him much? Uncle Jimmy? Do you miss him?"

Richard thought for a while and he said, "I think I do. But we hadn't been close in a long time, since we were little, really. Maybe that was my fault. I always saw myself as being responsible for him. And I think I didn't care for how he turned out, for the life he chose." Richard sat up and breathed out. "Maybe I was afraid of it, intimidated or something. So I kept my distance. But really, I thought I could—or ought—to be able to save him from himself, and I found out I couldn't. I found out I could hardly save myself." Richard spoke softly, as though talking to himself. "You choose one little thing, and everything that follows—maybe for the rest of your life—chooses you. So you pray for mercy, for whatever it takes to bear it gracefully. And give thanks for all the good things that come along, despite yourself, despite all the stupid, awful things you believe and say and do."

Richard bent his head toward Anna. "So don't be too hard on yourself, okay?" She nodded. Then he began to rise and said, "I think that's enough of that. Dinner needs—"

Anna raised her finger to her lips and shushed him. "Listen. Do you hear it? The scratching or whatever? I think it's the same thing as the smell. I'm not imagining it, not any more than anything else."

Richard thought he did hear something, although he wasn't sure about there being any smell. "I suppose it's under the house, in the part where the basement doesn't go through. I could look."

"Would you, Daddy? There's a flashlight in the kitchen drawer." Richard nodded. "Sure. Why not?" he said.

Anna put on her bathrobe and her slippers and went out to the living room. "Come on, Dougie. We're going out in the yard for a minute." She went into the kitchen and strode back carrying a flashlight and Douglas's jacket. "Now we're going to get to the bottom of this," she announced.

They went out the front door and turned left and back along the side of the house. The sidewalk was wet and there were still bands of snow here and there across the lawn, like tide wrack on a beach. Halfway down the length of the house, under Anna's bedroom window, there was a hatch made of tongue-and-groove boards and held in place by two propeller-shaped clips. Richard turned them and began to pry the hatch loose. It pulled free, trailing cobwebs and dried grass. Richard laid it on the sidewalk. He turned to Anna and said, "Why don't you keep Douglas back while I take a look? Just in case." She nodded and put her arm around Douglas's collarbone, holding him by the shoulder.

Richard knelt on the sidewalk to get a closer look inside the hatch. He could feel the water soaking his knees as he scanned the crawl space with the flashlight and then he smiled and said, "Okay, you two. Come meet your houseguests."

Anna and Douglas pressed up next to him and he shone the light inside. There were three pairs of yellow eyes set inside black patches, and as Anna and Douglas's eyes adjusted to the light they saw silvery fur and ringed tails and tapered snouts, which now began to mewl. "Puppies," Douglas exulted. "No, raccoons, sweetie," Anna said. "They're adorable."

Then they heard another noise, a scratching movement followed by a faint growl. Richard aimed the light slightly to the left and the body of a much larger animal moved into the beam, and then stood in front of the three kits. Its eyes darted back and forth across Richard and Anna and Douglas's faces, as though accusing them. It seemed to make a hissing noise in the back of its throat. Richard looked back at it, at the unwavering eyes, the barred face and the snout and the nose, black and glistening like a nugget of anthracite coal. He regarded the paws, the long and arcing digits, almost elegant, and he thought of Sarah, of Sarah's hands.

Richard looked at Anna, who was holding back Douglas with great effort. The hem of her robe was soaking up water from the sidewalk and her hair was blowing back and forth on the afternoon breeze. He said, "I suppose they'll have to go." Anna turned to him, her brown eyes as emphatic as those of the raccoon. "No, let them stay."

ON THE DAY AFTER HE'D DISCOVERED THE RACCOONS, RICHARD was supposed to meet Henry Finch at the bar at the Admiralty Hotel, although Richard could not for the life of him imagine why anyone would want to go there. Richard remembered it being red and shiny inside, but now the walls were sallow, lacquered with decades of smoke, and mottled like a tarnished old mirror. There was a cadaverous man behind the bar, fidgeting with a towel, and Henry Finch sat in a corner booth, already two-thirds of the way through something in a highball glass. He wore a plaid bow tie and a befuddled expression that vanished when he saw Richard. He waved over to him. "Dicky, old boy, pull up a throne. Or rather slide in, if you will." Richard sat down opposite him. "I bet it's been a little while since you've perused this joint," Finch said.

"Maybe twenty years. And I'm not sure I've ever had a legal drink in here."

"Repeal hasn't speeded up the service," Finch said, nodding at the bartender. "Don't mind him. They found him when they opened up King Tut's tomb, mixing gimlets for the inmates." The bartender ambled over and took Richard's order. Finch flicked up his finger to indicate he'd have another round.

"Last time I was in here was with your Anna's young Norden. Seemed clubable, at least in a Vulcan suit. Has he popped the question yet?"

"Actually, I'm afraid they've split up," Richard said. "It didn't work out."

"Gee, Dicky—I'm sorry. But she'll find someone else. She's a prize. Jimmy always said she looked like her mother, like Sarah, but with a kind shyness mixed in—vulnerability, I guess. That can be very attractive in a woman, eh?"

"I imagine so, Henry. Anyway, I'm not worried about her."

"Say, did you ever get a hold of that old girlfriend of Jimmy's, Candace Packard or whatever her name was?"

"Susan Nash," Richard said.

"Right, Nash. So did she know anything that was any help to you?"

"We met. We talked about Jimmy. But she didn't really have what I was looking for."

"Oh, well. I remember her with Jimmy. Very brainy, and kind of sly—like you couldn't put anything past her."

"Anyway, it doesn't matter," Richard said. "The estate's all settled."

Finch swallowed two gulps from the fresh drink the bartender had just set before him. Richard sipped. The Scotch tasted like something from a hardware store. Finch said, "You know it's been six months. Since the accident."

"Since Jimmy's death?" Richard asked. "Yes, I suppose it has been. Almost."

Finch drank again. "You know I loved him," Finch said, and Richard began to make sounds of commiseration, and Finch interrupted him. "No, *really* loved him. I can't believe it's been six months. And it's not so much because I miss him—because I see that he's gone—but that I forget that he's not here. I'm so used to having him be everywhere. I can't walk down this street out here, down to the park, under the trees, to the statue, without believing he's there. It's like the whole city is his place, and if he were gone, it just wouldn't exist anymore. So it's like he's here, and I'm just not seeing him." Finch took another sip from his drink and mopped his lips with the back of his hand. "Does that make sense? Because if it doesn't—if I had to believe it were otherwise—I feel like I wouldn't have a life at all."

"It makes sense, Henry. It makes more sense than most of what I hear."

"Good. That's good. Because I need to tell you something that I've never told anyone else. And I need you not to tell anyone. I need you to promise that."

"As long as there aren't any implications that might concern the law." Richard heard himself say the words, and he realized, however technically true they might be, how callous they sounded, how petty and mean. Someone should be kind to Henry Finch, he thought. It might as well be me. He began to apologize, saying, "That's really not relevant here. I don't know why I said it. I'm sorry. You can say anything you want. In complete confidence."

Finch appeared not to notice any of it. He just began to talk, speaking as though if he didn't get the words out right away, he would forget them. "You know how I told you that none of us saw Jimmy's accident? How we were all over in the next field?" Richard nodded, and Finch drank again and then began to drum his fingers on the table. He lowered his voice. "Well, that's not really how it was. I saw it, Dicky." He leaned across toward Richard and his voice grew soft and raspy, like there was a ragged breath behind each word.

"I was at the crest of the hill between the field where the others were and the field where Jimmy was. I was standing under a big tree, a big old cottonwood, I think, about seventy-five yards away. And I saw Jimmy standing by the fence. He'd leaned his gun against it and he lit a cigarette and he just stood there and smoked, like he was waiting for a bus or something, like he was passing

268

the time until the rest of us caught up with him. But then he looked around. He looked up the hill toward where I was, but I'm sure he couldn't see me. Because of the tree. And then he threw the cigarette down and he put his left leg through the fence, and he reached out toward the gun. It was leaning on the middle wire just in front of him. And he pulled it toward him, kind of under him. It was crazy. It seemed like he was positioning himself. And I could swear he had his thumb looped inside the trigger guard. Anyway, then the gun went off."

Finch seemed to be shaking, and Richard touched his forearm and then clasped it. "What did you do then, Henry?" he said.

Finch's fingers laced around Richard's wrist. "I don't know. I think I shouted his name, but it was all mixed up with the echo of the shot. I ran down to the fence. I know that. He had flipped over with his back on the wire, with his arms out. I remember seeing that the cigarette was still burning in the grass next to the fence. I think I must have pulled him down onto the ground, or he just fell down off the wire. Anyway he was on his back, and he wasn't moving. It was cold and I put my hand over the wound and it was steaming and the blood was starting to soak into his clothes, and it was on my hands and it was like vapor coming off him." Finch bolted the liquor that still remained in his glass. "I think I might have been blubbering and screaming, but I pulled myself together. I saw he wasn't breathing—that his eyes were open and he wasn't breathing. So I put my mouth over his. I thought I could get him breathing. But nothing happened. I kept trying, and then I realized I was tasting his blood—that he was bleeding from his mouth. The others got there then. I think they had to pull me off him. They had to shake me and tell me he was dead."

Richard swallowed and then breathed out his nose. "And did you tell them what you'd seen?"

"Just that I'd heard the shot and run down—that I hadn't seen anything. I was frightened. I thought maybe there'd be questions. About me. Or about him."

"That the gun might have gone off deliberately?"

269

"Yes. I didn't want anyone thinking that about Jimmy. Especially since I wasn't even sure myself."

"What do you think now?"

"I know what I saw, but it contradicts everything I knew about Jimmy. I mean, why would he do it? He of all people? I remember at the funeral you told me it was just a terrible accident, that it was like he died in the war. And I thought to myself later, when I was alone, No, it wasn't like that. It was something he chose."

"Sometimes in war it's something people choose. I remember that."

"But why would he do it? People envied him. He had everything. I think he was the only person I ever knew who didn't have any sadness in his life." There were tears on Finch's cheeks, and Richard handed him his handkerchief.

"Maybe he didn't have enough sadness in his life," Richard said. "Maybe he could never really find anyone to love, or maybe love never found him. I don't know."

"I loved him. He must have known that. So many people did."

"I'm sure he did know. Maybe it shamed him. Maybe he thought he didn't deserve it."

Finch looked up at Richard and his eyes were clear. "He never said so. But everything went without saying for Jimmy. Maybe that's why I can convince myself that he must still be around—because it would just go without saying. That's the way he would be."

"I think you're probably right." Finch handed the handkerchief back to Richard, and Richard balled it up and put it in his pocket. Then he said, "Someone—someone who knew Jimmy very well— said to me, 'Sometimes the better part of love is silence.' And I think that must be true."

IT WAS SIX YEARS LATER, DURING THE ELECTION, WHEN ANNA thought she saw Charles Norden again. She was in New York for a college reunion and she was passing through the lobby of the Biltmore Hotel and thinking of stopping for a cup of coffee. She was wearing a camel's hair polo coat with her new Adlai Stevenson button on it, pinned just above the one from four years earlier. She was going to stop, but then she saw the clock. It said twenty minutes after five and she walked under it and down the stairs and into the street. The side entrance to the station was just across the way and there were taxis huddled under a low arcade. Anna threaded her way among them to the door and went inside. She found herself on a sort of precipice overlooking the concourse, across which people were streaming toward the entrances to the platforms at the north end of the station. On the other side of the concourse, at the same level as Anna, there was an enormous blowup of a snapshot of a radiant couple with a blond little girl and a tousled-hair boy on the beach with a ball of red and blue and yellow.

Then something down below caught Anna's eye. It was a hatless man, caroming determinedly through the crowd toward one of the gates. Anna could see his hair, his angular nose and chin, the way he strode like a combine cutting through a field of wheat. She was sure it was Charles Norden.

The man disappeared into a gaping doorway marked "13A" in black serif letters, and Anna began to descend the steps to the concourse. They seemed very steep and she felt she might fall. At the bottom, she stopped herself, drew a breath, and began to walk at a measured pace toward the gate. There was a board that said "Greenwich," "Stamford," "Darien," and some other towns. Anna stopped at the portal and looked down the platform. There were some incandescent bulbs glowing dully, and beyond them, a red light falling away into the distance, into the black. She watched until it was gone. It must have been Charles's train.

Anna turned and walked back across the concourse toward the ramps that led up to the street and down to the subway. She found a bank of telephones and a rack of directories and she began to thumb through them. She could smell the scent of the doughnuts and hot dogs and popcorn percolating up from the subway. At last she found the listing: "Norden, Charles & Virginia, 129 Hawthorne Lane, Darien." Now she knew. There was his life.

For his part, it was indeed Charles running to his train that day. He could smell the platform as he darted for the door of the club car. It was like burning newspaper and heavy oil, but once inside the car he thought he could smell the gin—the juniper, the cold and oily citric vapors, cold as dry ice. Later on, as the years went by, he thought he could smell the gin from the concourse—even feel it swath his stomach and set his demeanor steady, like tumblers falling in a lock—and that was even after they'd stopped having club cars.

His life proceeded largely as he'd imagined it would. He had a son, Edward, and a daughter, Laura, and they'd both gone to boarding school when they were teenagers and the house seemed empty and dark without them. His career had not been everything he would have liked: His name had never moved to the center of the letterhead at Phillips & Gass, and despite cultivating all the right people no one ever proposed him for a judgeship. Then, the summer he'd graduated from Andover, Edward was riding down a highway on Cape Cod in an Oldsmobile convertible and the car rolled over three times and killed Edward and two other kids.

Not long after that, Charles decided to take early retirement. He and Ginny moved to Florida and every day they sat on the balcony of the condominium and drank gin and tonics and watched the sun set into the gulf and break apart into colored shards and smoke. Laura had moved to California with a man with a beard, and she never called them. Ginny's hair turned white, and she grew thinner and thinner until Charles could scarcely see her when he looked up to their balcony from the beach. He'd stand at the water's edge and sense that this was the last place he'd ever be; that he might as well sit down and wait for whatever it was to come and take him away.

When Anna heard that Charles Norden had died—maybe in 1982 or '83; it was his heart, he hadn't even reached sixty-five— she thought of his old house with the pond at the back, the one he'd pulled Douglas out of when the ice broke, and she wondered if she'd ever gone skating with him. She couldn't remember, but she could still recall skating when she was a girl: the glide, the floating equipoise between motion and stasis, the circling, as though waiting to be called out, away from the ice and into the world, into what was to be her life; and her eyes big with expectation, her lips framing the words, "Choose me."

ANNA'S FATHER HAD DIED IN DECEMBER 1985 AT AGE EIGHTY-SIX, and her mother had insisted that she would go on living in the house by herself, climbing the stairs, heating herself bowls of soup, sitting by the cold living room fireplace where her old Philco radio sat atop the console TV like a tabernacle on an altar. She busied herself in her usual ways, and then, after she had packed up her husband's keepsakes and put them in a box labeled "Richard's things" and stowed it in the basement, she herself died, three months after Richard.

Anna was by now in her sixties, and she had no use for anything in the house, whose furnishings had in any case taken on the shabby, yellow veneer of old people's possessions, of water-stained dentures and dull, faded chintz. She thought she would take a few things of her mother's, consolidate them with her father's keepsakes, and let the St. Vincent de Paul Society have the rest.

On an April morning, Anna went down the stairs to the basement to look for the box of her father's things her mother had put there. Light came in through a window gauzed in spiderwebs, beneath which a shelf held half-empty boxes of rose dust and lawn food and a bag of bird seed that must have been a quarter-century old. Across the room there was a furnace, its once shiny galvanized metal now a cloudy gray. Between them sat an old rolltop desk, and on top of it was the carton Anna's mother had filled with her late husband's keepsakes.

Anna had not reckoned with the desk and was inclined to ignore it, to take the box and go. But she thought she had better inspect its contents before consigning it to the rummage people. The top clattered up like a garage door opening and inside she saw there were two guns, a fly rod, and some trophies. She picked up one of the trophies, bloody orange with tarnish, and realized that these must be Uncle James's things. The drawers were full of old letters and canceled checks and souring old photos and crumbling newspaper clippings. In one drawer there was an old book, the pages spotted, the cloth cover scented with mildew, and tucked inside there was a photo, itself freckled with blossoms of white and amber.

It was a picture of two children in a boat, the elder one poised at the oars. The younger one looked like Douglas when he was little, and she realized that the older boy must be her father, and that the younger one must therefore be Uncle James. She decided to put the photograph on top of the box of her father's things, among which she felt it belonged. Then she went hurriedly through the remaining drawers of the desk, which were full of junk, matchbooks, and, in an envelope, a lump of metal. In another drawer, there was an envelope stuffed into the back, bent and curled and damp. Anna opened it and giggled: There were photographs of naked women, posed in stiff, contorted postures, their skin like white ash, like stills from a silent movie. She put them back: Let the St. Vincent de Paul Society have a little surprise, she thought. She pushed the rolltop down and it rumbled closed. Then she carried the box marked "Richard's things" up the stairs to the living room with the little photograph riding on top.

Anna set the box on the coffee table and walked upstairs to her parents' room. The shades were half pulled down and the light lapped across the bottoms of the two chenille bedspreads on the twin beds. Her father's clothes had been hauled away months ago, and she had boxed up her mother's wardrobe the day before: hats and veils and gloves and a dozen clutch purses, each with a single paper tissue wadded up inside. The only thing that remained for Anna to deal with was the drawer from her mother's dressing table where she had kept her own photographs and letters. Anna pulled it out and carried it downstairs to the living room. Then she sat down and made herself comfortable in her mother's chair, the chair that, as far as she could remember, she had never sat in before in her entire life. It was cool and soft, but as she settled she realized she could feel the frame cutting into her here and there, like bones through skin. The light green slipcover was loose and faded.

She decided to look at Daddy's box first. It was perhaps two feet square and one foot deep, and it was only two-thirds full. She thought she could get everything from her mother's drawer into it. She dug her hand around in the box, and most of what she found she had seen before: photographs and souvenirs that he had shown her more than once himself. But there were also things that she hadn't seen, things that her father must have collected or that her mother had put in the box after he died.

There was a photograph of their fiftieth anniversary. She recalled the occasion: There had probably been one hundred friends and acquaintances attending, and most of them were in this photograph. She saw herself in a pink sleeveless shift and Douglas standing next to her, stringy-haired and bearded, in a madras jacket. Next to them was Roger Mercer, still drawn and haggard from Alice's death by cancer of six months before, and next to him their son, Michael, and their daughter, Linda, her face averted to avoid Douglas's diffident but unmistakable gaze.

Besides that photo, there was an invitation to the anniversary party and a certificate of appreciation from the academy alumni association dangling from the thumb-distressed pages of a little book of daily prayers and devotions. There was a clipping from the *Twin Cities Legal Reporter* noting his retirement. Beneath it were a set of pages cut from an academic journal called *Publications of the Modern Language Association* dated December 1959. It was headed, "Some Uses of Metaphor in Bardic Poetry," and beneath that it said, "Susan Nash, Ph.D., University of California, Los Angeles." Anna had no idea where it had come from or what use her father would have for it. She shrugged, and then she noticed a blue envelope.

Anna thought nothing of it until she saw that the address was in her mother's handwriting, and then that the addressee was her Uncle James. She opened it and began to read and it didn't make any sense, and then she read again and she stopped and read the last part a third time:

> The truth is, I suppose, that it's so awfully hard to do the right thing in this world—it's so rarely fun or interesting, at any rate—and this was a chance to do it with comparative ease. I've done so many foolish things, but I've never hurt Richard deliberately. I know he would have never known, and it might have been rather thrilling—rather like secret agents—but I also know that if he had found out, he could never have believed that we would do such a thing. And also, that he would feel that he had no choice but to forgive us. Even after I'd rationalized everything else, that was more than I could bear.

After a time it became clear to Anna what the letter meant, and she wondered if her father ever saw it and why it was in the box. Presumably he had, and she wondered if her mother had known that. If she packed the box, which she did, she must have. Her mother and her father suddenly seemed incomprehensible to her, as though she hadn't really known them at all. She wondered if they had ever talked about this letter to each other, and she saw that she could not begin to hazard a guess.

Anna began to sift through the drawer from her mother's dressing table. There wasn't much in it. Her mother had not been a sentimentalist. There was a picture of Anna's grandfather, a grinning, mustached man in a tall hat whom Anna could never recall having met, and a few others of her grandmother and some people whose identities were a mystery to her.

There was also a photograph of her mother as a girl, standing between Anna's father and Uncle James. Richard and James were a few years older than they were in the photo of them in the boat. Anna's mother must have been about fifteen, but she looked much older, preternaturally poised and rather overdressed, with her hands thrust into a fur muff. They were all standing in front of a huge snowdrift.

Anna examined one other photograph she hadn't seen before. To judge by the people and their clothes, the women's bobs and the men's oiled hair, it must have been taken in the twenties. Richard and Sarah were sitting in the middle of a group of friends at a table. All of them were in evening dress, clutching highball glasses, and their eyes looked blanched and stunned, perhaps by the camera's flash. It must have been an anniversary or some other occasion, because most of the people had autographed the photo and then evidently presented it as a gift to Anna's parents. In the lower right-hand corner she saw an inscription in purplish ink: "To the happiest, healthiest couple what am! Yr. attending physician, Ted."

Anna laid the photo in the box with the others. The drawer was empty now, save for a few crumbs of tobacco from packs of cigarettes smoked long ago and, at the very back, a small brown envelope, mottled and crumbling with age, with a gummed flap at one end. She spread the end open and saw there were two or three old pills inside, and then saw there was writing on the envelope, writing at least as old and faded as the script on the photograph. She realized it was in fact the same script as on the photograph, the same handwriting, and it said, "For cramps every two hours, or as needed. If bleeding persists more than 18 hours, call me." The word "call" was underlined.

Anna put the envelope in the box and it slipped down the side and rested at the very bottom, among her father's report cards and scouting badges. She put the photograph of the boys in the boat on the top and closed the flaps. She knew she had come to understand something, but she thought that now that she had done so, it would be just as well to forget it, to let what she'd seen vanish back into invisibility.

FIFTEEN YEARS AFTER THAT, WHEN SHE IS EIGHTY AND THE century is turning toward its end, it seems to Anna that the present has blurred into the past, that there isn't a distinction between them, or perhaps the past has boiled over into the present and buried it, subsumed it. As for her parents, they are like figures in stories she had read once as a youngster, with characters who dressed in satin and velvet and lived in a manor; whose speech is not spoken, but declaimed as in a novel. She lives among those events, those people, in the past. They are her neighbors and she lives in the midst of their habitations. They move past her window like evening strollers, like squirrels on her rooftop, in the city of memory, which is now her home.

Sometimes it is February all the time. That is when Anna thinks about the child. She tries to count the months and years and calculate how old it would be, and what it might be doing now, whether its hair would be straight or wavy. She thinks about Charles too, almost always after she thinks of the child. She recalls the sting of what he said and didn't say fifty years before, and all the things she might have done, and a cold and hollow place opens up beneath her breastbone. But sometimes she sighs, "Oh, I always loved him," and that is the larger truth, the one thing that exists now, on this very day and on all the days to come. For that is the only thing that lives in eternity—the affliction and the love—and remembering is the only way to keep them alive, to tend and succor them.

Sometimes she thinks of the photograph of the boat, but the boys have been transformed: The older one is Charles and the younger one is Douglas, and in the haze above them there is a shadow that falls leaden on the lake, just ahead of them on the water. She thinks it is the shadow of the child. And now she wonders what that place must be like, now, in February. The boat is gone and she sees the rushes and cattails strangled, held fast in the ice, and the ice seamless as a rink, and where the shadow fell, there is a dark spot on the ice, a fissure, a wound.